Pegasus

ROBIN McKINLEY

G. P. Putnam's Sons
An Imprint of Penguin Group (USA) Inc.

G. P. PUTNAM'S SONS
A division of Penguin Young Readers Group.
Published by The Penguin Group.
Penguin Group (USA) Inc., 375 Hudson Street, New York, NY 10014, U.S.A.
Penguin Group (Canada), 90 Eglinton Avenue East, Suite 700, Toronto, Ontario M4P 2Y3, Canada
(a division of Pearson Penguin Canada Inc.).
Penguin Books Ltd, 80 Strand, London WC2R 0RL, England.
Penguin Ireland, 25 St. Stephen's Green, Dublin 2, Ireland (a division of Penguin Books Ltd.).
Penguin Group (Australia), 250 Camberwell Road, Camberwell, Victoria 3124, Australia
(a division of Pearson Australia Group Pty Ltd).
Penguin Books India Pvt Ltd, 11 Community Centre, Panchsheel Park, New Delhi—110 017, India.
Penguin Group (NZ), 67 Apollo Drive, Rosedale, North Shore 0632, New Zealand
(a division of Pearson New Zealand Ltd).
Penguin Books (South Africa) (Pty) Ltd, 24 Sturdee Avenue, Rosebank, Johannesburg 2196, South Africa.
Penguin Books Ltd, Registered Offices: 80 Strand, London WC2R 0RL, England.

Design by Marikka Tamura.
Text set in Adobe Jenson.
Library of Congress Cataloging-in-Publication Data
McKinley, Robin.
Pegasus / Robin McKinley. p. cm.
Summary: Because of a thousand-year-old alliance between humans and pegasi,
Princess Sylvi is ceremonially bound to Ebon, her own pegasus, on her twelfth birthday, but the closeness
of their bond becomes a threat to the status quo and possibly to the safety of their two nations.
[1. Pegasus (Greek mythology)—Fiction. 2. Human-animal communication—Fiction.
3. Princesses—Fiction. 4. Magic—Fiction. 5. Fantasy.] I. Title.
PZ7.M1988Pe 2010   [Fic]—dc22   2010002279

ISBN 978-0-399-24677-7
1 3 5 7 9 10 8 6 4 2

To the Wonder-Mods*:
Ajlr, B_twin, Black Bear, Gryphyn,
Ithilien, Jodi, Maren and Southdowner,
with love from a grateful hellgoddess

Does anyone recognise you without your capes?

CHAPTER 1

Because she was a princess she had a pegasus.

This had been a part of the treaty between the pegasi and the human invaders nearly a thousand years ago, shortly after humans had first struggled through the mountain passes beyond the wild lands and discovered a beautiful green country they knew immediately they wanted to live in.

The beautiful green country was at that time badly overrun by ladons and wyverns, taralians and norindours, which ate almost everything (including each other) but liked pegasi best. The pegasi were a peaceful people and no match, despite their greater intelligence, for the single-minded ferocity of their enemies, and over the years their numbers had declined. But they were tied to these mountains and valleys by particular qualities in the soil and the grasses that grew in the soil, which allowed their wings to grow strong enough to bear them in the air. They had ignored the situation as without remedy for some generations, but the current pegasus king knew he was looking at a very bleak future for his people when the first human soldiers straggled, gasping, through the Dravalu Pass and collapsed on the greensward under the Singing Yew, which was old even then.

They sat up quickly when seven pegasi circled the meadow above the pass and flew down to investigate. The journal of that company's second commander still exists in the palace library: a small, worn, round-cornered, hand-bound book, slightly bowed to the shape of the pocket it was carried in. He reported the historic meeting:

> We had but just come through thee final rocky gate, and had sett ourselves down in thee shade of a strange great tree, which had short soft spikes or needles all along its branches, and no leaves; when swift-moving shadows fled briefly between us and thee sunne, but against thee wind. We looked up in haste, for rocs are not unheard of, and I had raised my hand to give thee signal for thee archers to string their bows. We saw at once that these were no rocs, but still I held up my hand, for they were nothing else we knew either; and they clearly had seen us, and did approach.
>
> But these creatures are nothing like rocs except they do also possess wings; they are like nothing I have ever seen, except perhaps by some great artist's creative power. They are a little like horses, but yet far more fine than any horse, even a queen's palfrey; they are a little like deer, except that deer are rough and clumsy beside them; and their wings are huge, huger than eagles', and when thee lowering sunne struck through their primaries, for as they cantered toward us they left their wings unfurled, thee light was broken as if by prisms, and they were haloed in all thee colours of thee rainbow. Several of my folk came to their knees, as if

we were in thee presence of *gods*; and while I told them to stand and be steadfast, I did tell them gently, for I understood their awe.

The pegasi were happy to make a treaty with the humans, who were the first possibility of rescue the pegasi had had, and the humans, dazzled by the pegasi's beauty and serenity, were happy to make a treaty with them, for the right to share their mountainous land; the wide plateaus, which ran like lakes around the mountaintop islands, were lush and fertile, and many of the island crests were full of gems and ores.

The discussions as to the terms of the treaty had had to be held almost exclusively through the human magicians and the pegasi shamans, however, who were the only ones able to learn enough of the other's language to understand and make themselves understood, and that was a check to enthusiasm on both sides. "Is it not, then, a language, as we understand language?" wrote the second commander, whose name was Viktur. "Does it encompass some invisible touch unavailable to humans, as a meeting of *our* hands in greeting, or a kiss between dear friends? What can we not grasp of it, and why cannot our magicians explain this lack to us?"

Sylvi's tutor, Ahathin, had brought Sylvi to the library while they were studying this portion of the annals. Ordinary people needed a sheaf of special permissions to look at anything half so old, frail and precious as the second commander's journal; Ahathin, as the princess' tutor, had merely made the request, and when the two of them appeared at the library door, the head librarian himself bowed, saying, "Princess, Worthy Magician," and led them to the table where the journal already lay waiting for them—with an honour guard of the Queen's Own

Lightbearers standing on either side of the table. The queen was the library's governor. Sylvi looked at them thoughtfully. They were wearing their swords, but they were also wearing hai, to indicate that they could not hear anything she and Ahathin said to each other. There were two kinds of hai: the ceremonial and the invested. The ceremonial ones just hung over your ears and looked silly; invested hai had been dedicated by a magician and really stopped the wearer's hearing. You couldn't tell by looking at them which kind they were. Sylvi had often wondered how hai-wearing guards were going to protect anything if they couldn't hear anyone coming. Was there a protocol for when an honour guard wearing ceremonial hai could stop pretending they couldn't hear?

Sylvi tried to concentrate on what she was reading. She liked reading better since Ahathin had become her tutor; she would still rather be outdoors with her hawk and her pony, but it was thrilling, in a creepy, echo-of-centuries way, to be looking at Viktur's own journal. She was allowed to touch it only while wearing the gloves the librarian had given her, and there were furthermore these odd little wooden paddles for turning the pages. But she had—carefully, carefully— turned all the pages over, back to the very beginning, to look at Viktur's signature on the flyleaf: *Viktur, Gara of Stormdown, Captain of the White Fellowship, who do follow Balsin, Gara of Mereland, All Commander of His Companies.* Most of the curly handwriting was still surprisingly black and sharp against the pale brown flyleaf. A tiny faded arrow, almost invisible, had been drawn just before *Balsin,* and the word *King* written in above, and the *Gara of Mereland* following had been struck out. "Gara?" said Sylvi.

"Lord," said Ahathin. "A gara is below a prince and above a baron. It is a rank no longer much in use."

"Then Viktur was pretty important," said Sylvi. "Balsin was only a gara to begin with."

"Viktur was important. Some commentators say that Balsin would not have made king if Viktur had not supported him—that perhaps Balsin would not have been able to put a strong enough company together to come this far through the wild lands, nor to drive our foes out of it once they arrived. That perhaps our country would not have been created, were it not for Viktur."

"Stormdown and Mereland—they're *here*."

"The original Stormdown and Mereland are in Tinadin, which is Winwarren now, where Balsin and Viktur originally were from. They'd won a famous victory for their king—who now wanted to be rid of them before Balsin started having fancies about being king of Tinadin. Everyone is very clear that Balsin was very ambitious; and, of course, he had the Sword. It was apparently worth it to their king—whose name was Argen or possibly Argun—to lose half his army to be rid of Balsin. Argen married the daughter of the king Balsin defeated, so presumably he thought he could afford it."

Sylvi cautiously turned the pages back to Viktur's first sight of the pegasi, and then on to the second marker. There was something that looked like the remains of a grubby fingerprint on one corner of the page she was looking at, and what might be a bloodstain on the bottom edge of the little book. ". . . and why cannot our magicians explain this lack to us?" She stopped, startled, and reread the entire sentence, and then looked up at Ahathin. "That's not—I haven't seen that before, that last," and gingerly she touched the brittle old page. Even through the thin glove she could feel the roughness of the paper: modern paper was smooth—paper-making was one of the things the pegasi had taught their allies, and for special occasions or particularly important records, pegasus-made paper was still preferred.

Mostly she did her studying in the room off her bedroom in the main part of the palace, where she now spent several (long) hours every day with Ahathin. The copy of the First Annals she was reading was the copy several generations of royal children had read, and included several games of tic-tac-toe on the end papers, imperfectly erased, played by her next-elder and next-next-elder brothers, who were only eleven months apart in age, and a poem her father had written about an owl when he had been a few years younger than she was now. (It began: The Owl flys at night. To give the mice a fright. It soars and swoops. The mice go oops.) Her eldest brother, and heir to the throne, had never written in his school-books.

She looked up at Ahathin, who stood beside her. There was only one chair at the table. She wanted to stand up herself, or drag another chair from another table so that Ahathin could sit down, but she knew she mustn't. The single chair and the presence of the honour guard with their hai meant that this was a formal occasion. Princesses sat down. Lesser mortals did not. This included tutors—even tutors who were also magicians, and members of the Guild of Magicians. She didn't like formal occasions. They made her feel even smaller and mousier than she usually felt.

She also didn't like it that the familiar, beat-up—almost friendly, if a school-book was ever friendly—copy of the annals that she knew had a missing phrase; she didn't like it that Ahathin was making such a fuss about her reading the missing phrase. She especially didn't like it when her own binding was so near—her binding to her pegasus.

Ahathin was small and round and almost bald and wore spectacles and a harmless expression, but he was still a magician. He looked no less small, round and harmless than he ever had right now as she stared at him, but for the first time she thought: Looking harmless is his disguise.

She had known Ahathin all her life. She could remember him sitting on the floor to play with her when she was tiny—she could remember looking dubiously at her first set of speaking tiles, with human letters and words on one side and the gestures you were supposed to use with the pegasi on the other, and Ahathin patiently explaining them to her. She'd learnt to sign "hello, friend" from Ahathin.

She'd known him all her life, and suddenly she didn't know him at all. She tried to swallow the lump in her throat, but it stayed where it was.

Ahathin nodded. "It's not in any of the copies of the annals I've looked in—there are quite a few."

"Why?"

At his most harmless, he said mildly, "I don't know."

She looked back at the journal. "Does my father know? Does Danacor?"

Ahathin nodded again. "Certainly the king knows. And the heir. I asked your father if I might show this to you."

"Why?"

Ahathin said nothing. This meant he wanted her to answer her own question. But sometimes, if she said something unexpected, she got an unexpected response. "Why *can't* magicians explain what it is about the pegasi language that the rest of us can't learn it?"

Ahathin nodded as if this were an acceptable question. "It is a curious skill, speaking to pegasi, and not even all magicians can do it—do you know this?"

Fascinated, Sylvi shook her head.

"We are well into our apprenticeship before it is taught at all, and many of us will already have been sent home to be carpenters or shepherds, for we will not make magicians. And indeed there is little enough of teaching about it, to begin with. Imagine learning to swim by being thrown into a lake in perfect darkness, never having seen water before. Those who do not drown are then taught; the best of them may then go on to become Speakers. But that is the moment when as many as half of us are sent away, although by that time an apprentice has learnt enough that if he—or she—wishes he can set up as a village spell-caster somewhere."

Imagine learning to swim by being thrown into a lake in perfect darkness, never having seen water before. "But the pegasi—they—they are so *light*. They—they *fly*. Drowning in a dark sea—I—it doesn't sound like anything to do with pegasi."

"No, it doesn't," said Ahathin. "It does not at all."

Sylvi knew the rest of the official story of the making of the treaty. She was obliged to be able to parrot a brief accurate version of it as part of her training as daughter of the king. She was obliged to be able to parrot a number of historical titbits on command (although *why* this was considered a necessary attribute in a princess she had no idea, her father sprang questions at her occasionally so that she did need to was not in doubt) but this was one of the few of her history lessons that were live pictures in her head instead of dry words in her memory.

The first beginnings of the treaty had been almost insurmountably difficult; not only was there the obstacle of their spoken languages, of which neither side could learn the other's, but the pegasi did not have an alphabet as humans understood it. Instead they had a complex and demanding art form of which various kinds of marks on paper were only a part. . . . The human magicians translated its name into human sounds as *ssshasssha* and said it meant "recollection," and that it appeared to include or address all the senses—sight, hearing, touch, taste, feeling—although how this was accomplished the magicians were uncertain. There were pegasus bards and story-tellers in some manner, presumably, as there were human bards and story-tellers; there were also pegasi . . . they didn't know. This was the first time the humans heard about the Caves, and the sculptors; but none of this assisted the drawing up of a document that humans understood as legal and binding.

"Did we not both want this union very badly," wrote the second commander, "such impedimenta as there manifestly are would have stopped us utterly and our company would be homeless again; and I am grateful hourly that thee pegasi want us, for already I love this sweet green land, and would not willingly leave it."

This sweet green land was probably the most famous phrase of the second commander's journal; it was one of those phrases everyone used, like *sick as a denwirl owl* or *mad as a mudge*. One of the first songs Sylvi had ever learnt to sing herself, when she was still so small she couldn't say her *rrr*'s yet, was an old folk ballad about a wandering tinker whose refrain was: *On the road to nowhere through this sweet green land*. The second commander seemed almost to be standing at her elbow as she read the old phrase as he had put it down the first time.

Both sides at last declared themselves satisfied with the final draft of the treaty. "The pegasi ask for little," wrote the second commander.

They wish their lives—and their Caves, which appear to bee thee chief manifestation of their *recollection*. But thee Caves lie many days' journey farther into thee mountains that steeply rise from these lush and fruitful plateaus we humans desire; Gandam says he is middling sure human feet could not take us there besides, and we have not wings. Balsin laughs and says, Good: that he wants all human forces to bend themselves to thee palace he already has in his mind's eye to build upon thee greatest of these plateaus. It is his own consort, Badilla, who has begun to measure thee landscape for this building; she was trained for such work in thee old countrie,

9

although Balsin says he married her for her beauty. My own Sinsi says she wishes only to finish thee job of securing our new land from its enemies; that what she most wants is to see her belly growing too large for its battle leathers, and a safe place where our babies may play.

The first song Sylvi could ever remember hearing was about the pegasi. Her nurse used to sing it to her when she was a baby, and would then "fly" her around the room. The tradition was that Viktur's wife, Sinsi, had written it for their children, although no one knew for sure.

Oh hush your crying
Your friends come flying
In the plumes of their wings
The south wind sings

The treaty was written by human scribes and depicted or portrayed by some makers and devisers among the pegasi upon thick supple paper made by the pegasi:

Balsin would have it bee parchment, but thee pegasi demurred, that they did not use thee skins of beasts for such or any purpose, and proffered their finest made paper instead, which is very beautiful, with a gloss to it not unlike thee flank of a pegasus, and faint glints of colour from thee petals of flowers. Dorogin did not like this however, and said there was magic pressed into its fibres, but Gandam held his hands over it and said thee only magic was that of craftsmanship, and as Gandam was thee senior, Dorogin must needs give way;

and Balsin looked at Gandam and nodded, and Dorogin looked as if he had swallowed a toad.

Sylvi gave a little hiccup of laughter; the toad wasn't in the schoolroom copy of the annals either. But reading of Gandam in the beginning always made her sad, because of what happened to him after. She'd never liked Dorogin; he was one of those people who always wanted everything his way.

The signing of the treaty was interrupted by an incursion of their enemies, taralians tearing at them from the ground, ladons, wyverns and norindours soaring overhead to dive and slash from above: "It is a new sort of fighting we must learn," wrote the second commander, "for we have but rarely known aerial enemies ere now." But learn it they did; and drove off the attackers with arrows and spears, and any of the winged company who fell to the ground were dispatched with sword and brand.

"Balsin is the worthiest commander of this and perhaps any age, so I do believe," wrote Viktur. "And it is my honour to serve him. But it has seemed to me in this battle that he is something almost more than human, and that none and nothing can stand against thee Sword he carries, which he won from its dark guardian many years ago, when he was but a young man, as if for this day."

Balsin called for the treaty to be signed during a lull in the battle: "It will hearten us," he said, which was another of those phrases the citizens of the country he founded were still saying almost a thousand years later. There was a seal that had been struck by Balsin's great-grandson which the sovereign still used, which said *It will hearten us* around the edge, coiled around a heart with a sword through it, which Sylvi thought looked more *disheartening*, but it was used for things like trade agreements and mutual defence accords, so presumably it looked friendly to delegates and ambassadors.

And so a table was set up, and Balsin and Viktur and some of the most senior of the company commanders and their aides and adjutants and Gandam and Dorogin and another magician named Kond stood on one side, and the pegasus king, Fralialal, and several pegasi with him, stood on the other side, and the gleaming paper with the treaty written upon it lay between them. The pegasi had agreed to *signing*, once the concept had been explained to them; the treaty was also ratified by pegasus convention in an exchange of tokens. Viktur wrote,

Balsin had chosen thee opal he had long worne as not merely thee most valuable thing any of us carried—save perhaps thee Sword—but as thee greatest heirloom of his own family. Thee chain it did hang upon however was of a length for a human throat not that of a pegasus, and because Balsin knew of thee pegasi's aversion to leather, we had had some dismay in how to make up thee difference, for our army was much blessed with spare straps but little else of that nature. My Sinsi it was who first unbound her hair and offered thee ribbon that had held it, which was of red silk, and perhaps not too low a thing for such a purpose; and then several more of our folk did thee same, both man and woman, and Gandam did plait them together and perhaps he did say some words over them, to make them more fine and stalwart.

Sinsi said ruefully, holding her long hair in both hands as thee wind tugged at it, I do not like leather strings in my hair, but it is that or that I shall cut it off; and as I did protest she laughed and said, then it must be thee leather, alas—and she then made a noise more suitable to a common soldier than a blood and commission bearer.

But at thee ceremonie thee pegasus queen did come to her, and to those others who had given up their hair-ribbons, and offered to them instead ribbons of shining filaments in plaits so daintily coloured that our dull human eyes saw them change hue as thee light upon them did change; and Sinsi and thee others did twist them through their hair, and were happy indeed. One of these would truly have been token enough, but thee pegasus king set something else round our Balsin's neck—although when I say thee king did, in truth there were three, for while their wings are powerful beyond our imagining, thee hands of thee pegasi are but tiny claws at thee leading bend of thee wing where some birds do seem to have thumbe and first finger, and these hands have little strength nor flexibility; it is a wonder thee pegasi do with them as much as they do, for their weaving is a wonder and an astonishment.

Thee thing thee king gave was little to behold at thee first: a plain brown cord strung with large wooden beads of a paler brown. We understood by then however that thee pegasi by choice lead simple lives and I think none of us feared that thee pegasi sought to insult us, or did not honour thee treaty; perhaps thee beads were made of a wood significant to them, as Gandam wears an ear-ring that looks like rusty iron.

As Balsin had had some trouble making up thee length of chain for thee neck of a pegasus, thee pegasi had perhaps ill judged thee smallness of thee human throat, and thee necklace of beads lay more upon Balsin's stomach than his breast. He looked down at thee beads as if mildly puzzled, and I, standing near, thought only that he wondered at thee plainness of thee gift; but then he held his hand in such a way as to forbear thee sunlight which did fall upon them, and I caught my breath for then I saw thee marvel of them: these *beads* do shine with their own light, as if they were scooped out of thee margin of thee sunne—or rather of thee moon, for it is a soft and kindly light.

All of this was in Sylvi's school-book copy of the annals—as the necklace, the treaty and the Sword hung upon the wall of the Great Hall of the palace—but she read on. She couldn't remember ever not knowing the story of the treaty and the Alliance; by the time she could read about it for herself it was already familiar, as were the Sword and the tokens in her life outside the schoolroom. But books from a printing press were in anonymous black type and bound in plain fabric and board; this little leather-bound book, soft and slippery with use and age, and the extra effort needed to decipher the second commander's handwriting—and his occasionally curious spelling—made her feel as if she were reading the story for the first time.

She remembered Ahathin standing, and the guards. "I'm sorry," she said, looking up. "It's different, reading it here. I'll stop now."

"Good that it's different. Don't stop."

She went on looking at him. "Then you have to sit down."

He blinked at her, amused. "As the Lady Sylviianel wills. Er—if the Lady Sylviianel permits, I will leave her to consult with the librarian on another matter."

Sylvi looked at the guards, who were staring expressionlessly over her head. She wasn't going to get them to sit down. "You couldn't take them with you?"

"Certainly not. They remain to attend you."

Sylvi sighed. "Then the Lady Sylviianel grants the Worthy Magician's request." And she went back to the second commander's journal.

> Then was thee signing.
>
> Thee pegasus king signed first: with thee inked tips of his first three primaries, which do make a graceful, precise arc across thee bottom of thee page, like thee brushstrokes of a master painter. Afterward he raised his wing, and thee black ink had bledde farther into thee pale feathers, for he is of a creamy golden colour, and he held this up as if thee stain were itself an emblem of our Alliance, while thee gold-bound opal that was Balsin's token gleamed at his breast.

There was a mural in the Great Hall, next to the treaty itself and opposite the wall where the Sword hung, of King Fralialal holding his black-edged wing up over the paper he has just signed. The human figures, the other pegasi, the landscape and all else fade into the background: only the pale gold pegasus, the stain on his wing, and the shining whiteness of the treaty stand out—and of these it is the wing that draws the human onlooker's eye, that makes the wingless human shoulder blades itch. At night, by candle- and lamplight, it was easy to imagine that his one raised foreleg was in preparation for stepping down off the wall. When Sylvi was younger, and more all-encompassingly awed of the Great Hall, she had got so far as to hear the sound his hoofs made as he took his first steps on the floor— and the rustle of his wings.

Our leader had chosen to mark his witness second, as it is thee pegasi who welcome us to their land, and their king did offer ours—whom I must now learn to call *king*, for thee first king of our new land is he—one of his own feathers for this purpose, once he understood that we use quills to hold ink: and it was of great interest to all us humans who watched, thee elegant way thee pegasus king drew his bent wing through his teeth and plucked out a feather as gracefully as a dancer moves through a dance, or a warrior draws a sword from its sheath. We cannot refrain from looking stiff and clumsy beside thee pegasi, and I saw at last thee wisdom of our *king* in declaring that we should attend thee signing of thee treaty in our armour and with our swords at our sides, despite thee look of peril and chanciness this gives us, and all of us well aware of thee scouts posted all round us, for these appurtenances of war gave us dignity where we had no beauty.

But as our *king* bent down to sign this first and needful manifestation of his kingship, a breeze arose, and ruffled thee hair of thee humans and thee manes of thee pegasi, and blew across thee slender cut tip of thee feather penne, and thee finest spray of ink fanned over thee bright, exquisite paper, crossing thee pegasus king's signature with a maculate crescent as beautiful as we are not, as if thee local wind*gods* were blessing our compact. Our *king* laughed, and said, quietly, that only those of us standing close enough to see what had happened could hear him, *It is a pity to spoil it as we ourselves spoil thee panorama*, and then bent again and signed, neatly, where thee keystone of thee arch would be, were it of stones and not ink-spots. His is not commonly a tidy signature, and thee story has gone round that he signed against his will; but it is not that and I have countered thee tale wherever I have heard it. And indeed, loyal friend as I have ever been to Balsin from thee days when we were keeping thee king's peace in thee backmost of beyond with three soldiers and a lame dog, I never liked our *king* so well as I did at that moment, for I understood that he too understood that to save their lives, thee pegasi have invited uncouth ruffians to dine at their high table, off their finest damask, with golden goblets and plates of silver.

Sylvi, at this point in the story, who often felt like an uncouth ruffian on those occasions when she was commanded to put on her princess manners and her princess dress and sit at court or table with her parents, always felt a pang for those first humans learning to live beside the pegasi. She sighed and stretched and pushed herself away from the table and its slight, precious burden. She didn't want to read any more; after this there was too much war, and Gandam began to go mad. She very, very carefully closed the little book, and looked round for her worthy magician.

CHAPTER 2

Eight hundred years before, the pegasi marched (and flew) with their new allies to engage the forces assembled against them, but they were not much good at fighting. They are astonishingly nimble in the air and can splinter an enemy's wing with a well-aimed kick, and a blow from a pegasus wing can break a norindour's back; but they are too small and too lightweight for close work. And, as Balsin said after the first battle, while no one could doubt their courage, they aren't devious enough. It was the human swords and spears, arrows and maces, with help from human magicians' wiles, which won the war. The ladons and wyverns were killed or driven right away, and those who fled perhaps went in search of their larger and even more dangerous cousins, the dragons; if so it was a long search, for they were not seen again for generations. A few taralians and norindours fled into the wild lands beyond what Balsin declared were his kingdom's boundaries, and there they were allowed to remain, so long as they caused no trouble beyond the theft of an occasional sheep; although the striped pelt of an unusually large taralian was a highly-regarded heirloom in a number of baronial families, and the sharply-bent wings of the norindour appeared on a number of family crests, as indicating courage and ferocity in all forms of struggle and combat.

While this was not in the original treaty, the humans' superiority at warfare came slowly to be reflected in all relations between the two species, but the pegasi, mild and courteous, never gave any indication that they resented this. By Sylvi's day, the ruler of the pegasi had for many generations been expected to do ritualised homage to the ruler of the humans on feast days, and to attend the royal court, with a suitable entourage of attendant pegasi, often enough to be seen as a regular presence. Some human rulers were greater sticklers about frequency than others, just as some pegasi rulers appeared to enjoy the visits, or appeared not to, more than others. But it was quickly noted that the more often the pegasi visited the human palace, and the more of them who did so, and the longer they stayed, the more the country ruled by the human monarch appeared to thrive.

Balsin himself had predicted something of the kind. Viktur wrote,

> Balsin does strongly hold that *we* do hold our sweet green land by favour and sanction of thee pegasi, and as it is, so far as we do know, thee only land that do so hold pegasi, in some manner and disposition do thee pegasi hold thee land. Gandam agreed to this with great solemnity and declared that Balsin showed great wisdom for a warrior-king; and Balsin laughed and said that Gandam was an old worrymonger and that magicians see spears when warrior-kings see blades of grass. Gandam, who commonly did laugh at Balsin's teasing did not in this instance but said instead, king, this land

is beautiful but strange and we as yet understand it little; and forget not thee story of thee six blind men and thee Oliphant. Then did Balsin understand that Gandam spoke in all seriousness, and said, very well, I shall make it easy for those who come after us to remember that we hold our mandate from thee pegasi: and he with Badilla did create thee emblem of thee crowned pegasus which do appear upon thee banner that do goe with him on every occasion when thee king do ride out over his lands, in war or in peace, and which withal appears at thee peak of the arch into thee Great Hall where hangs thee Sword, and in divers places about thee palace.

But Balsin's coat of arms showed only the Sword and the palace and the Singing Yew.

Furthermore the human sovereign, and certain of the sovereign's extended family, were each assigned an individual pegasus, as a kind of ceremonial companion, as if such blunt discrete pairings might ease or soften the lack of communication between the two peoples. Most of these couples saw, and expected to see, each other rarely: those humans who did not live within the Wall might not see their pegasi from one year to the next. For the sovereign's immediate family it was different: those pegasi were often at the palace, and something like a relationship sometimes grew up between human and pegasus. There was genuine friendship between Sylvi's father and his pegasus, who was the king of his people, and, it was said, they could almost understand each other, even without the services of the human king's Speaker.

Some form of Speaker—of translator—had been obviously necessary from the beginning; the human magicians and pegasus shamans were the only ones who could speak across the species boundary at all. Even the sign-language, as it was developed, was unreliable and prone to misinterpretation, because of the enormous differences in anatomy between the two peoples. At first it had merely been that anyone on either side who seemed to have some talent for it learnt what they could, and the numbers of magicians and shamans were about equal. But the magicians seemed slowly to take the charge over, echoing—or perhaps going some way to causing—the tendency that in all things the humans should be superior and the pegasi should defer. The idea of the bound pairs had been Gandam's; the idea of the Speakers, magicians specially trained to enable what communication there was between human and pegasus, was Dorogin's. It had been Dorogin's idea also that the sovereign, the sovereign's consort and the sovereign's children should each have an individual Speaker as each was bound to a pegasus.

The binding was done when both human and pegasus were children; when possible the human ruler's children were assigned the pegasus ruler's children. This was supposed to promote friendship between the two races, although the children did not always cooperate.

The royal human child and its pegasus were introduced to each other for the first time on the human child's twelfth birthday. At this time several of the royal magicians would create a spell of binding between the two which was supposed to enable them some communication with each other. The spell of binding was specific, between that one human child and that one pegasus child; occasionally it worked, and there was a real connection between the two—emotional if mostly wordless—and more often it did not. Who beyond the immediate royal family was selected to be bound to a pegasus was an erratic process; the children of anyone who had grown close to or performed a significant service to the sovereign might be added to the list as the children of third or fourth cousins who never came to the palace might drop off it. It was the greatest honour of the human sovereign's court for someone's child to be nominated for binding, but it was a slightly tricky honour, because it bound the child to the sovereign and court life as well.

When a royal marriage could be predicted sufficiently in advance, the future consort might be bound to a member of the pegasus royal family, but these forecasts had a habit of going wrong. What often happened was that some adult human became a member of a royal or noble family by marriage, and thereupon was assigned a pegasus; but while the binding spell was just as punctiliously made, there were no records that these late pairings ever learnt to empathise, or to communicate beyond the few words of gesture-language common to anyone who cared to learn them. One of Sylvi's uncles, brother-in-law to the king, was famous for saying that he had more fellow feeling for his boots, which were comfortable, protected his feet and didn't make him feel like a hulking clumsy oaf.

The usual ritual and binding spell were delayed, however, till the human child's twelfth birthday because it was a strong spell and might be too great a burden for anyone younger. Very occasionally the human child nonetheless became sick or ill, or fainted, and had to be carried away, and missed the banquet afterward, although there was a folk-tale that these bindings were often the most successful. While there was no record of any pegasus being made ill by the human binding magic, pegasus children were never bound before they were better than half grown—and, crucially, capable of the long flight from the pegasus country to the human palace. The pegasi's life span was slightly longer than human, but they came to their full growth slightly sooner. It sometimes happened that there was no suitable pegasus for an eligible twelve-year-old human; usually some slightly less suitable pegasus was found in these cases, because of the likelihood that if the binding was put off more than a year or two there was no hope of its becoming a strong one. And, perhaps because of the continuing weakness of shared language, this shared empathy was greatly desired for the good of the Alliance.

It was several generations before Dorogin's idea of the individual Speakers became traditional, but for many generations now every important bound pair had had a magician assigned when they were bound, to aid their connection. The magician neither took part in the binding ceremony nor was officially presented, because the need for such a facilitator was considered shameful, a proof of continued failure of one of the pivotal aspects of the Alliance the human domain was built on. The guild of Speaker magicians was however the most revered of all the magicians' guilds—and the most inscrutable. Among the Speakers themselves the posting to a royal pair was hotly sought after.

Sylvi was the fourth child of the king and the first girl, and while her parents had been glad to see her, with three older brothers, she was not considered important to the country's welfare. She was pleased about this, as soon as she was old enough to begin to understand what it meant, because she was much more interested in horses and dogs and hawks and stealing sweetmeats when the cook's back was turned than she was in being a princess. She had a vague notion that there were lots of available horses and dogs and hawks—and sweetmeats— partly on account of her being a princess, but she believed that the connection was not all that close (her cousins, who didn't live at the palace, had lots of horses and dogs and hawks and sweetmeats too), and that being king chiefly meant that her father looked tired all the time and was always either talking to or reading something from someone who wanted something from him.

Her cousins' fathers weren't quite so always reading and talking. Her favourite uncle—the one who had more in common with his boots than his pegasus—was a farmer, and while, he said, he mostly told other people what to do, sometimes he harnessed up a pair of his own horses and ploughed one of his own fields. "So I'll remember what I'm asking," he said. He and his wife, one of the queen's sisters, had each a bound pegasus, but they usually only saw them on trips to the palace: "Can you imagine a Speakers' Guild magician living on a farm?" But both pegasi occasionally visited. "It's a funny thing, the animals like 'em," said her uncle, whose name was Rulf. "They always insist on sleeping outside—we've got a perfectly good room at the end of the house with doors that open out under that big old oak tree. But they sleep outdoors. In bad weather they may sleep in the barn. And wherever they are, the animals drift that way. The cows and the horses are all at whatever end of their pasture to be nearer the pegasi, and the outside dogs are usually curled up with them, like the house dogs sleep on our bed."

He told all that part of the story easily and often; but once, when he and his family were visiting the palace, and he and Sylvi had been riding through the park together by themselves, a flight of pegasi came over them. The palace horses were all very accustomed to this, and Sylvi's pony only raised his head and looked—longingly, Sylvi always thought, as she longingly looked as well—and the king's hounds accompanying her stopped chasing rabbit smells and sat down, and Sylvi was sure she heard a tiny whine as they too stared up. But Rulf's horse reared and bounced and neighed and it was a moment before Rulf managed to quiet him again.

"It's a mixed blessing, though, seeing 'em flying, isn't it?" he said to his niece. "First time Hon"—his eldest son—"saw ours coming in at home, the sunset was behind 'em, the sky purple and blue and red and gold, and their wings going on forever, the way they do, gold and red like the sky, and their necks arched and their legs all held up fancy as a dancer's and their manes and tails finer than the lace your dad had for his coronation robe—Hon was just on a year old, and he burst into tears, cried and cried and cried, and wouldn't stop. Never cried, Hon. Never afraid of anything. Never cried. Cried, seeing pegasi flying for the first time." Rulf's horse gave a last forlorn little whicker.

At the palace the pegasi had their own private annex in their own private grove of trees—and with their own private and exclusive latrine; pegasus dung was much prized by the royal gardeners. The annex was merely one long narrow room with three walls and a bit of framing on the fourth; trees served to screen the fact that the long fourth wall of the annex was almost entirely absent. The trees also served as a windbreak, although the annex was in the lee of the palace. Sylvi had never seen the annex—humans did not trespass there without a good reason—but she had said to her father, "Don't they get *cold?*"

Her father smiled. "Feathers are very warm. You sleep in a featherbed: imagine you could wrap it around you like giving yourself a hug."

The king rarely had time to ride out with his dogs and his hawks, and he rarely ate sweetmeats. He had told his daughter (she had asked) that he didn't much care for them, though he remembered he'd liked them when he was younger. Sylvi was glad she'd never be king and lose her taste for sweetmeats. The king admitted that he would ride out oftener with his dogs, his hawks and his daughter, if he were able to, but he was not. Here he looked at the pile of paper on his desk, and sighed; as if the sigh were a signal, a dog or three materialised from in or behind or under some piece of furniture, and laid their heads on his knees.

The queen had given Sylvi her first riding lessons, had put the first elderly and benign hawk on her fist, had consulted with Diamon, the master-at-arms, about her first practise sword and her first little bow. The queen, before she was queen, had been colonel of her own regiment of Lightbearers; she had spent several years killing taralians, plus a few norindours and the occasional rare ladon, in the west in and around Orthumber and Stormdown, and had been known as something of a firebrand. She still took charge of a practise class occasionally when the master-at-arms was short-handed. The queen's classes were always very popular because she had a habit of organising her students into a serviceable unit and taking them out to do some work: this might be anything from rescuing half a village stranded by a mudslide to hunting taralian or ornbear, and even when it was hard, dirty and boring—or hard, dirty, boring and dangerous—the students came back smiling and gratified.

Sylvi had been present one evening when Burn, one of the master-at-arms' agents, asked to speak to the queen. That day the queen had taken her class quite a distance into the countryside in response to a report from a village of several sightings of a taralian; they'd found the taralian, dispatched it, and ridden home again, although they'd been gone twelve hours and everyone but the queen was reeling in the saddle (said the horsegirl who'd been sent with the message that the queen would be late for supper) by the time they dismounted in the horseyard. The queen was in the middle of explaining that she had wanted to be sure everyone was safe and sound, including the horses, and that no bruised soles or incipient saddle sores were overlooked because the humans were too tired to focus their eyes. "Children," she said fondly. "They're a sharp group, though; it would be worth trying to keep them together, and perhaps move them on a bit, especially since it looks like—"

At that moment Burn had been announced. After asking if he might speak to the queen alone and being told that she was tired and wanted her supper and that she was sure he could say whatever it was to the king as well as herself, he hemmed and blithered, and it became plain that what he was not happy about was the queen's choice of a practical exercise. After a few minutes of failing to find a tactful way of saying what he wanted to say, he finally declared that it was perhaps *unwise* to put a group of second-years into the peril of taralian hunting, which was a more suitable activity for seasoned soldiers. . . .

The queen said, "Burn, I forgive your shocking impertinence because I appreciate that you are concerned about your youngsters, but do you really suppose that a seasoned soldier such as myself cannot see the strengths and weaknesses of the troop she leads in the first half hour of their company? Not to mention that I've crossed swords with most of them in the practise yards. Ask one of them when I announced that we were going to look for that taralian. I suggest you go and ask *right now.*"

Burn, looking rather grey, left hastily. "Fool," said the queen grimly, as soon as the door had closed behind him. "Is he the best Diamon can find? It will not do our young soldiers any favours to report to a clucking hen. How does Burn suppose seasoned soldiers *happen?* Magic?"

"My dear," said the king, "he is a good administrator, which, as you know, Diamon is not. We need administrators almost as much as we need commanders who know the strengths and weaknesses of their troop within the first half hour spent in their company."

The queen sighed. "Cory, forgive me. I just . . . we are having too many taralian sightings. And more of them farther inside the boundaries."

"And the occasional norindour. I daresay that the increased numbers of boars and ornbears are not significant beyond the dangerous nuisance they present. I don't like it either. And I don't like the paperwork that goes with it."

"Take Burn away from the army and add him to your army of private secretaries. And take a troop out chasing taralians. It'll cheer you up."

The king shook his head. "I'm an administrator myself, not a soldier. It's why I know Burn is a good one."

"You have *made* yourself an administrator," said the queen.

"I have tried to make myself what the country most needs," said the king. "But it is lucky for both the country and myself that it needs a king who is a good administrator. You are the soldier, my darling, and I have it in my mind to send you out to investigate the rumour of a roc in Contary."

"A *roc?*" said the queen. "In *Contary?*"

And then Sylvi, to her enormous shame and frustration, sneezed, and her parents noticed she was there. "Oh, gods and dev—I mean, Sylvi, my love, you do understand that this conversation is to remain strictly within these four walls?" said the queen.

"Yes," said Sylvi. "A roc? I didn't think there were any rocs any more."

"Officially there aren't," said the king. "In practise there's a sighting once or twice a decade. This is the second one in two years, which is not reassuring."

"It may not be true," said the queen. "I would go so far as to say it is in the greatest degree unlikely to be true."

"Someone can mistake a *roc?*" said Sylvi, who had studied rocs and the tactics of battle with something the size of one of Rulf's barns, and as clever—and devious—as a human. "They're—er—kind of *large.*"

"You'd be surprised," said the queen. "You're a little young to be facing up to your responsibilities as a princess, but you might as well begin to prepare yourself for being surprised at what people do. I give you even odds that this roc is a blanket, laid out to be aired before it's put away for the summer, which the wind stole. And if I'm going to Contary anyway, perhaps I could swing round past Pristin. We haven't heard from Shelden all this year, have we?"

"You could take me with you," said Sylvi, knowing the answer would be no. "My godsmother Criss lives in Pristin."

"Criss is coming to your binding," said the queen. "You can see her then. You have to get a little bigger before you start riding messenger for the king."

"You are the queen," said the king, "not the king's messenger."

"To Shelden I'm a rustic bumpkin," said the queen. "He never misses an opportunity to ask me how my family back in Orthumber are."

"Danny was riding with you when *he* was eleven," said Sylvi. Danacor was Sylvi's oldest brother, and the king's heir. "He told me so."

"I said *bigger*, not *older*," said the queen. "Your day will come."

Sylvi had mixed feelings about her binding. She looked forward to her birthday because her parents always made something exciting happen on that day, and the food was always amazing. But this birthday she was going to have to go through with the magicians' ritual, and be bound to her pegasus, and the food would be at a banquet, and maybe she'd be one of the ones who fainted. She'd never been comfortable with magicians' work. Some of the smaller charms could be comforting, and a few years ago when she'd had a very bad season of nightmares, Ahathin had made a charm for her that had finally let her sleep without waking screaming a few hours later. And everyone, herself included, knew how to make the basic ill-deflect charm, although you needed some charm string from a magician first. But quite ordinary rituals made her feel peculiar.

She thought the pegasi very beautiful, and their faces looked very wise, and being bound to one might be rather exciting—but they were also perhaps too beautiful and too wise (if you could understand them), and having one around that was supposed to be hers would not make her feel Alliance-embodying empathy, but smaller, grubbier, and more awkward. And she didn't like most magicians—except Ahathin—any better than she liked their queasy magic, and there were always too many magicians around when it was anything to do with the pegasi.

She'd been drilled and drilled in the sign-language since she had been a baby, and could still remember trying to make her fingers behave at the same time she was trying to say her first words. The language of sign and gesture that all humans who had regular contact with pegasi and pegasi who had regular contact with humans were expected to learn was complicated, and the complexity seemed only to add a greater variety of ways for communication to go wrong, beginning with the immutable fact that the pegasus execution of any sign was critically different from the human. Pegasi had mobile ears and long flexible necks and tails, but their hands were small, and had no wrists; and furthermore the number of their fingers was variable, which was the cause of another crucial difference between humans and pegasi. Viktur had described it: "Their mode of enumeration seemed to us at first most strange. Where we, having each of us ten fingers, do count most easily by tens, they cannot, for the number of their fingers on each hand does vary, being four, five or six; wherefore, having each of them four legs, they do count by fours."

All of this damped any enthusiasm you might initially have had (thought Sylvi) and perhaps that's what made concentrating on learning sign so difficult. It was worse than maths. (She was rather good at maths, but her brothers complained about it, so she thought she ought to. She could even count in fours, but no one seemed to expect her to, so she stopped trying.) It wasn't that she was bad at languages; she'd learnt enough Chaugh to be polite to the Chaugh ambassador's horrible daughter, who was both taller and older than Sylvi—although the *taller* didn't take much, thought Sylvi sadly—and who never ignored a chance to remind Sylvi of both these facts. "Oh, how *funny* that skirt looks on you," she'd said at their last meeting. "But then you're still very *young* and your legs are so *short*."

"Imagine her on the point of your sword," the queen advised her daughter. "I have got through a number of state banquets that way."

Sylvi had seen her father once, about a year ago, alone with the pegasus king, Lrrianay, signing awkwardly but determinedly and at some length, accompanied by a ragged murmur of words, punctuated by a few pegasi whuffles, *choffs* and hums, both of them utterly intent on each other and no Speaker in sight. They came to the end of whatever they were saying. Her father's hands had dropped as if they were too heavy to hold up any longer, and he was wearing a look half thoughtful and half exhausted. As she watched, he put a hand out to the back of a chair as if to steady himself—very much the way Sylvi put out a hand for a chair or a table or a tall dog's back when there was magicians' magic in the air. Lrrianay had turned his head to preen a feather or two back into place, which Sylvi had long suspected was a pegasus thinking-about-something gesture.

And the king's Speaker, Fazuur, had burst into the king's private office. Not even the king's Speaker entered the king's private office without being announced.

"Fazuur," said the king calmly, "if you would be so good as to wait a moment. Pendle will tell you." Pendle was the footman on king's-door duty that day.

Fazuur came to a shuddering halt, bowed stiffly and left the room again only very slightly slower than he'd arrived. Sylvi stood riveted, thinking about what she'd just seen—both her father and Lrrianay, and the way her father had put his hand out, and the precipitate arrival of Fazuur. He'd come through the door not like a man late for a meeting, even a man late for an important meeting, but like a man desperate to avert catastrophe.

Sylvi herself had been announced, but casually; Pendle had opened the door and said, "Your daughter, my king," and waved her through without waiting for a response—which was usual; she would not be troubling her father during his (official) working hours without cause. She had seen him and Lrrianay "speaking" before, without Fazuur present, but she thought she had never seen them speaking so *intently.*

Her father was now looking at her with mild surprise: he hadn't heard her announced. "What is it, love?" She jerked herself back to attention. "I—oh—it's just a note from the head librarian about something Ahathin wants me to read."

The king smiled. "Ahathin likes frightening the librarians, I think. Let me see. Well. You appear to be studying the beginning of the Alliance." He made a quick hand-sign at Lrrianay, who bowed his head, holding it down for a second or two in the respectful-acknowledgement gesture.

"Ahathin says every human should study the roots of the Alliance. That if it were up to him every human *would.* The head librarian says it's—it's impertinent to want to understand everything, that what is important is to understand what comes of the things that have happened." She made the Alliance gesture at Lrrianay, and drew her hand out to one side, which should mean "topic of conversation" or "studying."

"They're both right," said the king.

Sylvi sighed inaudibly. That was exactly the sort of thing her father always said.

"But you can give this to the head librarian." On the neat scrap of paper the librarian had sent he quickly drew the stylised replica of Balsin's signature on the treaty of Alliance, which had been the official mark of the reigning monarch ever since. She'd never really thought about this before; she'd seen the mark, over and over again, all her life, and she knew what it was and where it came from. But she looked at it now as if she were seeing it as an older, wiser Sylvi, a Sylvi who had studied the Alliance and who understood what had happened as a result. And she thought of Fazuur, waiting in the anteroom. . . .

She looked up and found both her father's and Lrrianay's eyes on her. She bowed to the pegasus king and he bowed back. She hesitated; she had what she had come for—she should go. But she was very curious about what she had just seen. "I thought, after the binding, aren't you supposed to start talking in your head too, the way the pegasi do, not just hands and mouth?"

She made a brave attempt to sign some of this for Lrrianay—it was considered rude to have a human conversation in front of a pegasus without making the attempt at inclusion, even if there were no Speaker present—but while she knew the signs for the binding and for the pegasi's silent-speech, she didn't know how to put them together. This could be her own ignorance, but it was also every human's experience of the muddle of sounds, words, gesture and sign that was the means by which human and pegasus attempted, and mostly failed, to communicate with each other. You could never quite say what you wanted to; your mind seemed to slip from you, like a sled on a snow-slope, and the language seemed to *writhe* away from you like a small wild animal you had inadvertently caught: let it go, or it might bite.

"The silent-speech is in the annals," said Sylvi's father. "In practise, no. Has Ahathin told you we don't know for sure how much the pegasi use silent-speech among themselves? We're guessing—our magicians are guessing. The pegasi may also be using some subtle form of sign and gesture we're too dull to pick up." Her father's hands were moving as he spoke, and he paused and murmured something, and there was a murmur—an answering murmur—from Lrrianay.

"After your binding there's a . . . a sense of someone else *there*, that you didn't have before, like knowing there's someone else in a dark room with you. Anything else . . . it's rather like weather. Every now and then you have a clear blue day and you can see a long way. Mostly it's overcast and stormy—and the rain runs in your eyes and you can't see a thing. That makes our Speakers a kind of . . . waterproof, perhaps." He smiled at her.

She took her cue, bowed to each king in turn and left. She'd never heard her father say anything sceptical about the Speakers before. . . . And the way Fazuur had bolted into the room, as if a taralian were after him . . .

But everything about the pegasi, and about dealing with them, was rather daunting. It was enough—it was more than enough—that they flew, that they were every human's secret fantasy, alive and breathing. And then they were so *beautiful*—it was impossible to get away from the fact of their astonishing beauty in any thoughts or contact with them, any more than you could forget that they could fly, and then you couldn't help feeling that they must be grand and noble and so on because they looked it.

After the binding itself there were some silly sentences you had to say to your pegasus: "Welcome, Excellent Friend, into this our Court, and the Court of our Fathers and Mothers, and welcome too into our heart this glorious day, that we may be the best of companions for many long years" and so on. "Who *wrote* this stuff?" she'd said to her father, outraged, after she'd read the script for the first time.

"No one knows," said her father. "Perhaps it—er—sounded better then, whenever then was."

"If no one knows who wrote it, and it wasn't Balsin or Gandam or Fralialal, why can't we *change* it?"

"Because, my love, you have to choose your battles, and that one isn't worth engaging."

She'd had her mouth open to ask who would *care*, but she shut it again. There would be people who cared. Great-aunt Moira would care. Senator Barnum would care. Sylvi sighed. It had been sheeting rain on her next-elder brother, Garren's, twelfth birthday, and the drumming of the rain on the roof of the Inner Great Court was so heavy and loud no one could hear him speak. She had been very little then, and didn't remember it very well, but she would be relieved if her glorious day was wet too. She was afraid she'd either laugh or forget her lines.

And besides, no pegasus was going to be her heart's best companion, even with the binding, because how could you be best companions with someone you couldn't talk to? Except through a *magician?* What was there to be a companion *about?* When pegasi came to court, or to a banquet, or some other organised human thing, you had to do things differently because they didn't sit down and they didn't eat human food. You couldn't share your lessons with them because they didn't read or write like humans. They had sigils and pictograms—they were supposed to have some record of the treaty of Alliance, besides Balsin's opal, which Lrrianay still wore on important occasions—but mostly they told stories. And they also had the Caves. Sylvi didn't understand the Caves very well, although Ahathin had tried to explain *ssshasssha* to her. The Caves sounded like a sort of large three-dimensional history in painting and sculpture. Which might be kind of interesting, but so far as she knew humans never went there.

Sylvi thought she could feel pretty bound to someone who was reading books and taking notes across a table from her, even if they were doing it in a different language (even if when they were released from their lessons they could go outdoors and *fly*), but she didn't know how she'd feel about someone reciting a long story. What humans heard of the oral pegasus language was rather *shushing* and whuffly, and she suspected that listening to a lot of it would put her to sleep, like the sound of the stream outside her window when she stayed with her Orthumber cousins. And she supposed they'd be telling it to a shaman—she wasn't sure who taught pegasi children—royal humans were usually taught by magicians as soon as they outgrew their first tutors and governesses, so perhaps royal pegasi were taught by shamans. But the pegasus shamans rarely came over the border to human Balsinland, and never stayed long.

It might be an advantage that it was a different language, if they were telling their lessons out loud (if it didn't put her to sleep); then she couldn't be distracted listening to the story. But no one ever suggested putting human and pegasus children together for their lessons, and Sylvi wasn't going to say anything that might make Senator Barnum notice her. She thought about it occasionally—it would be nice not always to be alone, or alone with grown-ups. She was the youngest of the palace children; even her parents' aides' children were older than she was. The only time she shared lessons was when she was visiting her cousins, and then they all managed to get out of most of them on the grounds that a visiting princess needed better entertainment than normal boring old lessons.

But there was no getting out of learning her lines for her binding. And so she learnt them. And she bore with being fitted for a new dress for the ceremony, which included the garment-maker having to put the hem up even shorter than he'd already put it up, because Sylvi was even shorter than he'd realised. That's what measuring sticks are for, thought Sylvi resentfully, but she didn't say it out loud; and the hem fell to her ankles instead of puddling around her feet on the day.

CHAPTER 3

On the day, her mother came to help her get dressed. Her next-elder and next-elder-after-that brothers had already been in to say "best birthday ever," which you said anyway but you said it specially emphatically if it was someone's binding day. Emphatic from Garren or Farley was a bit like being whapped by the master-at-arms with the flat of your wooden practise sword, but they didn't stay long. When they'd shown an inclination to linger to tell Sylvi stories of all the terrible things that had happened on various binding days over the centuries, the queen had suggested that they might help the housefolk carry the long tables for the banquet into the Outer Court, thus leaving more of the housefolk free to get on with things that needed tact or skill.

Their pegasi had come with them. Poih, Garren's pegasus, had given her a salute she'd never seen before, with the wings swept forward and the tips of the first few primaries interlinked, and the tiny alula-hands clasped. Even doing it discreetly took up a lot of room: pegasi wings were necessarily enormous. Sylvi was sure it was more than she deserved, and made her new long complicated binding-ritual bow back, because it was the fanciest one she knew.

Oyry, Farley's pegasus, had just barely, or not quite, brushed the back of each of her hands with a wingtip, which was a salute she knew, and knew to be a great honour: not only did it just or not quite defy the ban on physical contact between pegasus and human, it was a reference to the longing humans had for wings and pegasi for strong human hands. Then he smiled a pegasus smile at her, which involved ears going in different directions and a wrinkled nose which did not expose the teeth. She'd been startled, and startled into wondering if perhaps she'd underestimated her brothers' pegasi. It was a point of honour as a much-patronised little sister to underestimate her brothers. But it was so hard to guess anything about any pegasus, and she wondered uneasily what Oyry or Poih might know about her pegasus, who was, presumably, their little sister. And then they went after their human princes, leaving Sylvi alone with her mother and her mother's pegasus, Hirishy.

Hirishy was small even for a pegasus, and timid, without any of the usual pegasus grand manner; she was not the pegasus queen but only her half sister. Sylvi's father hadn't been expected to marry her mother; he was supposed to marry Fandora. Fandora was the eldest child of Baron Sarronay, whose family was one of the oldest, wealthiest and best-connected in Balsinland, and the Sarronays had more than a few royal consorts in their family tree already. The royal council, who determined how far the net of binding should be cast each generation, with an eye to history and the volatility of human affections, decided to bind pegasi to as many of the marriageable young female cousins as possible. But the royal pegasus family of that generation was not large enough for all the human cousins, and so two or three of the least-probable queen candidates had been given third cousins or half sisters. Eliona had been considered the least-probable candidate of all: she was known to be married to her regiment.

But there was a scandal too. Sylvi only knew because Farley told her: once King Corone IV had become engaged to Lady Eliona, Fthoom, who even then was the most powerful member of all the magicians' guilds, had suggested that the future queen be bound to another, more suitable, pegasus—"Which there wasn't one, of course, and he knew it," said Farley with relish: Fthoom was not popular with any of Sylvi's family. "And the king said no, of course not, no one has ever been re-bound, and he would not offer such an insult to our allies. And that's when"—Farley's voice sank to a near whisper—"that's when Fthoom suggested our mother shouldn't be queen!"

Sylvi listened to this with her mouth a little open. She'd been afraid of Fthoom her entire life and considered her father braver than a soldier facing a taralian with a broken stick for standing up to him. "He *said* that?"

"Oh, not in so many words—not even Fthoom would dare. But it was pretty clear what he meant. And *Dad* said that as a way of covering up the total failure of the guild of forecasters to predict who would be queen—because you know the forecasters sweated like anything over who got which pegasus—it was a pretty poor showing."

Sylvi went cold with fear and then hot with admiration. She had seen Fthoom with her father often, and Fthoom was a big man and her father a small one, but there was never any doubt who was the king, despite the fact that Fthoom invariably came to the palace wearing the magician's spiral and his grandest, most vivid magician's robes, and her father was usually dressed in something soft and dark and floppy. "Farley, how do *you* know this?"

Farley said airily, "Oh, everyone knows that story. And the only people who won't tell it are Mum and Dad. I bet even Ahathin would tell you."

Sylvi had not dared ask Ahathin, but she had asked Danacor. Her eldest brother was hopelessly solemn and dutiful and responsible, but he didn't like Fthoom any better than any of the rest of them did. "Oh, that old story," he said. "Yes, it's true enough, but—" He hesitated, and Sylvi held her breath, because Danacor, as the king's heir, knew all the best stories, and occasionally was still young enough to tell them. "The real scandal is that Hirishy was bound to Mum in the first place. When it's just sovereign-heir to sovereign-heir, like Thowara and me, it's easy. But when it's half a dozen girls, five of whom will be farmers or soldiers and the sixth will marry the king, you're supposed to try to make some attempt to match personalities. By the time Mum was twelve she already had her first war-horse, you know? And they bound her to *Hirishy?*"

Sylvi was troubled by this story. She liked Hirishy—*liked* her, not the way she liked Thowara or Lrrianay, but almost as she might like another human. She had once been trying to say something to her, something about the way families behaved and how you loved them even when you wanted to kill them—it had been a day when her brothers had been especially exasperating—which was a lot more complicated than she was used to saying in her own language, let alone to a pegasus. She had no idea why she had been trying to do something so bizarre, and so doomed to failure. But there was something about the way Hirishy seemed to *listen*. It drew Sylvi on. She'd stumbled to the end of her signing and stopped, feeling a fool ... and Hirishy had put her nose to Sylvi's temple, like a kiss from her mother, and left her.

Sylvi had slowly put her hand to the place Hirishy's nose had touched. That had been almost as strange as what had gone before: you didn't touch the pegasi, and they didn't touch you. She thought it was probably a good rule; if it weren't positively forbidden, the urge to stroke the shining glossy pegasi would probably be overwhelming.

She was sure that a pegasus flank would make the sleekest silkhound feel as rough as straw; but the pegasi were a *people*, like humans, and must be treated with respect. (And you mustn't ever, *ever* ride a pegasus, which was the first thing that every human child, royal or not, on meeting or even seeing its first pegasus, wanted to do.) Sylvi had been very young when she had realised you had to be *more* careful of the pegasi because the humans were dominant: because the pegasi came to the human king's court, and the pegasus king stood behind the human king's shoulder. But Hirishy had touched *her*.

She had in fact three times touched Hirishy. She didn't remember the first time: her mother had told her about it. She had grabbed a handful of Hirishy's forelock when Hirishy had bent a little too low over the baby lying on the queen's bed, and rubbed her face against Hirishy's velvet nose. "You were too little to understand about kissing, but kissing is still clearly what you were doing!" The queen, both laughing and horrified, rescued Hirishy—but not before Hirishy had kissed the princess back.

And it had been Hirishy who'd come to stand beside her the day that Sylvi had slipped and fallen on the Little Court steps when she was supposed to be processing with the rest of her family. It had been one of the first occasions when Sylvi had been deemed old enough—and in her case, more crucially, big enough—and sensible enough to be in the royal procession. And then she had managed to trip—by catching her foot on a bulge of hastily taken-up hem—and fall. She landed hard and painfully, but was up again so quickly that her mother only glanced at her and the ceremony wasn't quite spoilt—Sylvi hoped. She knew she was walking stiffly, because what she wanted to do was limp, but she told herself it wouldn't show under the heavy robe she was wearing. If it had been less heavy, there wouldn't have been a bulge to catch her foot.

But when they'd come to the end of the court and turned to stand in the great arched doorway, while the magicians chanted and waved their incense around and the royal family wasn't the centre of attention for a moment, Hirishy had slipped from behind the queen and stood beside Sylvi, and, after a moment, as if accidentally, as if she were merely shifting her position, put her nose in Sylvi's hand. And Sylvi had relaxed, as if her mother had put her arm around her, and as soon as she relaxed, the hurt began to ebb, so that when the ceremony had been over with and her mother *had* put her arm around her and asked her if she was all right, Sylvi said truthfully, "Yes, I'm fine now."

But Hirishy was different from the other pegasi—and not different in a way that was well-matched to a professional soldier. As Eliona, daughter of Baron Soral of Powring in Orthumber and colonel of the Lightbearers, she hadn't had her own Speaker, and neither Hirishy nor the pegasus bound to her second-in-command had ever gone out with her company as they patrolled borders, escorted ambassadors through the wild lands, chased rumours of ladons and dispatched taralians and norindours. But she'd had a Speaker assigned the moment the news of her engagement to Corone was announced—and two years later, shortly after Danacor was born, and on very dubious precedent, her Speaker was changed.

Sylvi's translation of the adult conversations she'd overheard about this was that her mother's first Speaker, having discovered that his enviable achievement was in fact career ruin, was daring enough to believe he might yet succeed elsewhere if he were given the chance. He was transferred out, on the grounds that pregnancy had altered the queen's aura in a way that another Speaker might better take advantage of, and Minial came instead. And while Hirishy was apparently even more untranslatable than most pegasi, Minial treated her with absolute respect—and patience. Sylvi liked her for that. Minial was one of the rare female magicians, but she was tall and imposing, and looked good in processions. She was also easy to have around, without that *pressingness*, Sylvi had once called it, that most magicians had, that feeling that there was no space for you when a magician was in the room.

Hirishy came wafting in after Sylvi's mother, her mane and tail already plaited, flowers woven snugly up among her primaries, and a wide blue ribbon around her creamy shoulders with wreaths of blue and yellow embroidery on it, and a little embroidered bag dangling from it like a pendant jewel. There was a word for the embroidered neck-bands the pegasi made, but Sylvi couldn't think of it. Hirishy went and stood at the window, looking out toward the long curly trails and clusters of people moving toward the Outer Great Court for the ceremony. Sylvi was trying to ignore them. Sylvi looked at Hirishy's wings and thought the flowers must itch, like a scratchy collar. Like the scratchy collar she was wearing, heavy with gold thread and heavier yet with gems. They were only lapis lazuli and storm agate, but they weighed just as much as sapphires and rubies. She sighed.

There wasn't any chance of rain. The sky was blue and clear, and the housefolk would be laying out the banquet without one hesitating glance overhead. She saw Hirishy look at the sky, and grinned to herself. There are fewer shadowy corners to hide in on a bright day.

Her mother was twisting a fine enamelled chain through Sylvi's hair, plaiting as she went, and muttering to herself. The chain hung in a loop round Sylvi's temples and over her forehead, and then the tail wound through her plait and ended with a teardrop of aquamarine. Only the reigning sovereign ever wore a crown, and Sylvi's father very rarely did so, but chains and flowers were common. The queen was wearing a garnet chain for her daughter's binding, with diamonds at her temples. "You don't have to do that," said Sylvi, trying not to laugh;

what her mother was muttering as she plaited was more suited to the practise yard than her daughter's bedroom just before her binding. "One of *them* could."

"Them" were the half-dozen beautifully-dressed ladies waiting in the corridor to escort the queen and her daughter to the Outer Great Court, only one of whom was also a soldier.

"Well, you won't believe me," said the queen, "but I would *like* to. You're the only daughter I'm going to dress for her binding; your father has had three sons to dress for theirs. And if I can plait my own hair—if I can plait a *mane*, for the gods' sake, I ought to be able to plait your hair."

"Did you find the roc?" Sylvi said suddenly.

"Roc?" said her mother, but Sylvi knew she was bluffing.

"Yes," said Sylvi. "In Contary. Father sent you to look."

The chain twitched as the queen tweaked it. "No."

She was still bluffing. "But?" said Sylvi.

The queen sighed. "You're as bad as your father. He always knows when I'm not telling him everything. My official report says 'the evidence was inconclusive.' Which is true. But I'm privately certain—which is what I told your father and Danny—that a roc had been through Contary."

"Oh." The wild lands around Balsinland were uncomfortably full of large, fierce, and often half-magical creatures, but only the taralians, who were the least magical, made a regular nuisance of themselves in Balsinland. Norindours were unusual, ladons rare, and the last wyvern sighting had been in Sylvi's great-grandfather's day.

But rocs, with their savage intelligence and relentless ferocity, were another category of hazard altogether. Rocs, it was believed, belonged to another world. No one knew why they occasionally emerged into this one; when they did, catastrophe followed.

"Yes. Oh." The queen patted Sylvi's hair. "There. Almost as good as one of the ladies could have done."

Sylvi was distracted by this, and only half noticed the sudden hush in the hall. And then her Speaker arrived.

She had been braced for this. Or rather, she hadn't been braced for it at all: she'd been trying to brace herself for it, and failing. She didn't like magicians. They gave her the creeps. The idea of having one who was assigned to *her*—who was now going to be *around* all the time, because your Speaker tended to lurk in your vicinity even when your pegasus wasn't there—was the worst thing about this whole rite of passage. Pegasi were a little scary and she knew she'd mess up what she was supposed to do with hers, if not today then tomorrow or the day after or the next ceremonial occasion or something, but this was different. She didn't like magicians—save Ahathin and Minial—and she was afraid of them—even Ahathin and Minial. She'd wasted a little time hoping that since she was only a fourth child they wouldn't bother to give her one, but she knew better. She was a princess being bound to a pegasus, and she'd have to have a Speaker.

She heard the clatter of the Speaker sticks before she turned around to see who it was—if it was anyone she'd ever seen before. The Speakers' Guild had a tendency to be secretive.

"Sylvi—" began her mother, and Sylvi turned around and bowed in all the same gesture, putting off for another few seconds meeting him, whoever he was. She heard the Speaker sticks clatter again, as he bowed too.

She straightened up slowly.

It was Ahathin. Her tutor. Little round bald Ahathin with his spectacles sliding down his nose, the way they always did slide down his nose, although she was used to seeing him trying to juggle several rolls of parchment and an armful of books while pushing up his glasses, and she'd never seen him wearing Speaker sticks. She hadn't known he *was* a Speaker. She took another look at the sticks, to make sure she wasn't imagining things, as her heart, or maybe her stomach, seemed to take a great leap of relief.

He stood up from his bow, pushed his spectacles up his nose, awkwardly shook his sticks so they'd lie flat, and said, "My lady, I am your least servant."

"Oh!" she said. "*Ahathin.*"

"Sylvi," said her mother sharply.

You met your Speaker in private, right before the binding ceremony, and you weren't supposed to know who he was until that moment (just as you weren't supposed to know anything about your pegasus). It was still an enormously formal occasion and you had more words you were supposed to have memorised to say. Sylvi had memorised them, but the shock of discovering that her Speaker was almost the only magician she'd ever met who didn't make her flesh crawl was so great she forgot them.

"Sir Magician—Worthy—sir—" But she couldn't remember any more, so instead she said what she was thinking: "I am so glad it's *you.*"

"Oh, *Sylvi,*" said her mother.

Ahathin's face twitched, but he said placidly, "Yes, your father seemed to think that might be your reaction."

The guild chose a Speaker, not the king. A king could request, and in order to have done a favour for the king, the magicians might listen to a request for a specific Speaker for an unimportant royal. But being her tutor was one thing; being her Speaker was a much closer, more demanding, and longer-lasting appointment—and tied him visibly and humblingly to a mere fourth child. The first child of one of the more important barons would be a much better placement. "Do you *mind?*" she said.

"Sylvi!" said the queen for the third time, sounding rather despairing.

Ahathin's placid expression was growing somewhat fixed. He glanced at the queen and said, "Saving your grace's presence, I would say that the king asked me a similar question before he approached the selection committee. I replied that I did not consider Lady Sylvi a lesser royal because she is the fourth child, and that I would be inexpressibly honoured if I were chosen to be her Speaker. The king indicated that he believed my lady Sylvi would not lay an undue charge upon her Speaker and indeed might be happy if he continued to spend most of his time in the library. And that he, the king, would entertain hopes in such an instance that it might possibly encourage my lady Sylvi to spend more time there."

Sylvi thought this deeply unfair, since it seemed to her that she spent a great deal of time there already. Wasn't she always bringing him authorisation slips from the head librarian? And hadn't he started asking her horrible trick questions based on what he knew she was reading? . . . Although she wasn't sure if they were horrible trick questions or not, since he was usually asking her what she *thought* about things, and if she hadn't read enough yet to have any thoughts, he said, well, let me know when you do, so then she *had* to. Sometimes he even asked her questions when there were other people around—and when she had protested (later, in private) he shook his head and said, "You're a princess. You're going to need to be able to think on your feet, later if not sooner."

Even so. She had her mouth all open to protest when it occurred to her that she was pushing her mother rather hard. She made an enormous effort and said, "Sir Magician, Worthy Sir, I thank and welcome you, and I—I—"

"Look forward to a long and fruitful dialogue," said Ahathin helpfully.

"Yes—oh, yes—yes. And we—we three—pegasus, magician and p-princess, shall be as the sun, moon and stars, and all shall look upon us and find us—uh—wonderful."

"A light upon their path," said her mother, "and a thing of wonder. I hope you've memorised the binding better." Her mother had heard her say it over just yesterday, but that had been sitting swinging her legs on a chair in the queen's office, with no one else present, and no surprises.

"I—I think so," said Sylvi, a little ashamed. "It's just that it's Ahathin. I've been so dread—" She stopped. He was still a magician, and she was being fearfully impolite. "I'm sorry," she said.

"There are tales of much worse, my queen, my lady," said Ahathin. "Razolon, who was king six hundred years ago, is said to have spoken but one word to his first Speaker: *you!* Whereupon he ran him through with his sword."

"Why?" said Sylvi, fascinated.

"He believed—with some justice—that the magicians were plotting that he should not come to the throne. He was a rather—er— precocious twelve."

"The occasion you might tell of," said the queen, "which I believe you might remember for yourself, is when my husband's second brother was bound. Do you know this story?" she said to Sylvi. Sylvi shook her head. "Well, ask your uncle some time to tell it to you. The version I heard is that there had been an episode of the throwing-up sickness, and that the youngest prince was the worst affected, but it was such a terrible omen to put off a binding they decided to go through with it. And when his Speaker arrived, your uncle bowed and—threw up all over his Speaker's shoes. But I believe the ritual of binding went perfectly."

"It did," said Ahathin. "I was one of the incense-bearers. Although the curious informality of the newly-assigned Speaker-to-the-Bound's footgear was somewhat remarked upon."

The queen laughed. "And thirty years later, Mindo is good friends with Ned, I believe, although he is rarely needed to Speak. We will therefore take the present informality as a good omen—you feel welcomed by your princess, I hope?"

"I do indeed, your grace."

"Good." The queen frowned at Sylvi. "And now we must go, or we'll be late."

CHAPTER 4

Sylvi got through the first part of the ceremony somehow, and she knew she must have remembered what to do and to say, because her father was smiling at her and Danacor (drat him) looked relieved. Thowara stood just behind Danacor's right shoulder, looking exquisite; the flowers tucked among his primaries glittered like jewels. She wanted to pinch him, just to dent his dignity a little, even though she knew it wouldn't've worked. He would have looked at her gravely and in mild surprise. Beyond Danacor and Thowara stood the rest of the family and their pegasi; the queen, Sylvi's other two brothers, two of her uncles and three of her aunts. Lrrianay was absent; he would be escorting her pegasus into the Court in a little while. What her father did have to bear him company was the Sword.

The Sword was the greatest treasure of their house, and the most important symbol of their rule, for the Sword chose the ruler. Balsin, who signed the treaty with the pegasi, had been carrying the Sword; some histories claimed that it was the Sword that Argen wanted out of his country, not Balsin. For some generations now the Sword had passed from parent to eldest child, but when Great-great-great-great-uncle Snumal had died without direct descendents, the Sword had

chosen which cousin the crown should pass to. Sylvi had never understood what happened when it passed—when the Sword had left
Grinbad and come to Great—eight greats—uncle Rudolf, how did
they know it had happened?

She'd asked her father this several times and he'd only shaken his
head, but recently she'd asked again and possibly because she was
going to have to swear fealty to him and it on her twelfth birthday, he
stopped mid head-shake, stared at nothing for a minute and finally
said, "It's rather like a bad dream. You can see it in your mind's eye, and
it's so bright you think it will blind you. You can't move, and it comes
closer and closer and . . . there is the most extraordinary sensation
when it finally touches you, somewhere between diving into icy water
and banging your elbow really hard, and even though you've seen it
nearly every day of your life—and you know you're in this fix because
it's already accepted you—you know that it's the greatest treasure of
your house and you're suddenly and shamingly afraid it will cut you
because you, after all, eldest child of the reigning monarch or not, are
not worthy of it. But it doesn't cut you, and you feel almost sick with
relief. And then you seem to wake up, only it's still there."

He stopped looking at nothing and looked at his daughter, and
smiled, but it was a rather grim smile. "And then you *really* feel sick,
because you know what that's just happened means." Her father, Sylvi
knew, had been given the Sword in a quiet ceremony of transfer on his
thirtieth birthday, when his mother retired, but the Sword had acknowledged him as heir in the great public ritual of acceptance ten
years before. "Afterward my mother said—" He stopped.

"What did Grandmother say?" Sylvi only barely remembered her
father's mother, who had died when Sylvi was four years old: a Sword-
straight and Sword-thin old lady who looked desperately forbidding
in her official retired-sovereign robes, but who somehow became be-

nign and comforting (if a little bony) as soon as she picked tiny Sylvi up and smiled at her.

The king looked at his daughter for another long minute and then said, "She said she felt twenty years younger and six inches taller."

Sylvi shivered.

"You get used to it," said the king. "You have to. And you're trained for it. Well—we've been trained for it, some generations now. I've often wondered how one of those unexpected battlefield transfers happens—how whoever the Sword has gone to copes. It's shocking and disorienting enough when it happens in the Little Court. Fortunately it doesn't happen that way very often. And you, my dear, do not need to worry: Danacor is very healthy and very responsible. And you have two more brothers to spare."

Danacor's sense of responsibility was such a family joke (as Sylvi had told her cousins, especially Faadra, who was inclined to be sweet on him) that when Sylvi asked her oldest brother what being accepted was like, she was not prepared for the king's heir to look hunted, and reply immediately, "Like the worst dressing-down you've ever had, and a little bit over, except the Sword doesn't talk, of course—it sort of *looks* at you." He fell silent and stared into space just as his father had. "You come out of it thinking that you'd be better off asking one of the magicians to turn you into a rat and get it over with, and then you look around and everyone's cheering and you can't imagine what's going on."

Sylvi had always been a little afraid of the Sword just because it was the Sword. But she wasn't the king's heir, and she'd never heard that it was especially severe to anyone but heirs and rulers, so she didn't really dread the fealty-swearing—not nearly as much as she had dreaded meeting her Speaker. But standing next to her father on her birthday, up on the little platform that was raised even higher yet from the

Outer Great Court's stage so even more people could watch what was happening, it seemed bigger than it did hanging on the wall of the Great Hall. It wasn't a large sword, for it was intended—and had, in the old days, often been used—as a single-handed battle sword. But it had presence, like a person—like an important person. Like the king. Sometimes her father was just her father, tired and kind and overworked; but when he was the king you knew it. You knew when he changed over too, even if he hadn't been the king a moment before and was now. The Sword was like that all the time.

Swearing by the Sword was the second-to-last thing in the ceremony; then Lrrianay would bring her pegasus through the Great Gate and they would meet, and the magicians would blow the binding dust over them and burn herbs and things, and speak some words that no one but other magicians understood, and then they—she and the pegasus—would pretend they understood each other, and she would say her Welcome Excellent Friend speech. Her pegasus would make some of the funny whuffling noises that pegasi did make when they were speaking aloud and which, according to the magicians, was the pegasus version of Welcome Excellent Friend.

Then the magicians would finish the spell, and blow more dust, and wave their arms around and look grand, and then the banquet would begin, when at least she could get down off the platform and have something to eat and there weren't any more words she had to remember to say. Although when there were too many people around—which there certainly were today—it was hard even to remember to say thank you: all those people were like drowning. And being polite to people like Great-aunt Moira, who always came to rituals, would be tricky, because she always told you that you'd done whatever you had done wrong, and Sylvi knew she'd have done *some-*

thing wrong, but it was going to be hard to listen to how wrong it was right after it happened.

Right after it happened. Right after she started to have a pegasus just behind her right shoulder at all important court events for the rest of her life. She was sure she'd trip over her hems even more with a pegasus standing there looking magnificent and supercilious. It had always rather suited her not to know anything about her pegasus in advance, so she didn't have to think about it, but now that the binding was *here*. . . .

She came back to herself staring at the Sword: it was as beautiful as a pegasus, in its own way. Frighteningly beautiful.

What she had to say during the swearing of fealty was easy: every time her father paused she said "I swear." She was supposed to say it with her hands on the blade of the Sword. She'd never touched it before, although her brothers all had, long before they had to swear fealty; she thought maybe it was a boy thing, *wanting* to handle swords, although she put in her time in the practise yards, like them. A sword was a sword: it was a great big knife, much too big for any purpose but killing things, and she knew the stories of it defending the realm in the hand of the ruler. Her father had never gone to battle with it, but she was glad she didn't even have to carry it on feast-days and during ceremonies.

Her father pulled it out of its scabbard and laid the blade over his palms, and she put her hands lightly on the blade between his two hands, and her father began speaking.

She heard him pause, and so she knew to say "I swear," but she hadn't heard a word he said, and her own voice seemed to come from queerly far away. She heard him start speaking again, pause again, and again she said "I swear," her voice echoing in her own ears as if she stood in a huge empty cavern. The Sword didn't scold her or scorn her but it . . . it *looked*, as Danny had said—as her other two brothers had said it didn't. "Don't worry about it, minikin," Farley had said. "It doesn't bother with us."

But it bothered with Sylvi. Its looking seemed to wrap her up all round so that she could no longer hear anything but the indeterminate murmur of her father's voice, and she could see nothing past its bright blade. She thought it looked at her with surprise and . . . and . . . What made her think it was looking at her *with* anything? Maybe it was just interested to see a girl for a change: the first daughter of a sovereign since her grandmother.

And then the swearing was over. She had missed counting—she was supposed to say five "I swear"s, and with the last one she was to take her hands off the blade, but she had been looking back at the Sword. Her father moved slightly and lowered the point of the Sword to give her a chance to recover herself and take her hands away—and the Sword *released* her—she came back into her body, her hands on its blade, with a little start—and did as she should, only a little slowly (Great-aunt Moira was sure to have noticed). He looked at her, half the king making sure the rite was going as it should and half her father, puzzled and perhaps worried, for he had noticed that something had happened. But there was no opportunity to say anything: the Great Gate was opening and her pegasus was entering.

Her pegasus.

The one thing she knew of her pegasus was that it was the fourth child of the pegasus king, as her brothers' pegasi had been the three before. But that was all she knew. Not knowing anything about your pegasus beforehand was supposed to make the binding spell grip and hold better when you finally met. Her heart was beating faster; the pegasi were strange, amazing, almost impossible, entirely unlike anything else in your human life, just by being themselves. Eight hundred years of the Alliance had not weakened the wonder of them. To have one bound to *you* . . .

For a moment all the words of the ritual that Sylvi had memorised drained away, leaving her mind a blank.

She saw a tall black shape pacing down the length of the Great Court beside the pegasus king, almost as tall as he, but still with colty legs slightly too long for its body. It would be bigger than its father when it finished growing, and Lrrianay was big for a pegasus—bigger than any of his elder three sons—as tall as a carriage pony. She tried to guess its age: her brothers' pegasi were all within a year or two of their age. She thought this one was probably near her own age too; maybe a little older.

It was having difficulty taking the slow ceremonial steps beside its father; it kept trying to prance. One of its wings kept twitching half open and then flicking shut again; she wondered if the flowers in its pinions were tickling it, and she resisted (again) the urge to pull at her jewelled collar or scratch her forehead under the slender chain.

It surged ahead at the foot of the platform, obviously restraining itself with difficulty from bounding up the steps: eagerness to meet her, to find out who she was or to have the ritual over with? Or the pleasure of being allowed to precede your royal father for once?

She stepped forward to meet it. She supposed it was rather thrilling to be standing in front of the king with everybody looking at you instead of him, but she'd rather be almost anywhere else. Her robes weighed as if they were carved out of stone, her collar was strangling her, and it was difficult to breathe.

The young black pegasus reached the top of the steps and danced forward, lowering its head to look into her eyes, the wings half-opening toward her (one ill-anchored flower fell out), the tiny alula-hands spreading—

That's not till later in the ceremony, pudding-head, she said to herself.

*I **know** that,* said a voice in her head. *Aren't you **excited**, or are you just a dull stupid human?*

They looked at each other. Sylvi's mouth dropped a little open, and the pegasus' nostrils flared.

*I **heard** that,* they said simultaneously.

You're a boy, Sylvi said suddenly. There was no reason for her to assume that the pegasus king should have had a daughter for his fourth child because the human king had done so, but she had assumed since she first understood that she would have her own pegasus that it would be a girl, like her.

Yes, and you're a girl, replied the pegasus. *I tried to tell them to have my little sister but they said no, I was next, it had to be me.*

Then you knew? said Sylvi, outraged. *You're not supposed to know anything before the ceremony of binding!*

The pegasus' skin rippled, starting with his shoulders and rustling his feathers; she thought it must be a pegasus shrug, and she was fascinated by the inclusiveness of it: it ran down his back and his forelegs like flowing silk. How little she knew of them, she thought, these creatures she had seen every day of her life—by whose leave her people lived in this country; with whom her people had an alliance that had lasted almost a thousand years. How—it seemed to her now—humiliatingly little.

That's just a human rule. I know a lot about you. You ask too many questions and you can't sit still, and you're always showing up in your father's office at the wrong time, so you know more than you should. I thought maybe it wouldn't be too bad to have a girl if she was another nosy fidget, like me. You're shorter than I was expecting though.

Sylvi felt her face grow hot. Her height was a tender subject, and here was this pegasus *looming* over her.

Pegasi didn't loom; they were too fine and delicate. Pegasus bones were hollow, like birds', and their limbs were so slender the sun almost seemed to shine through them, as when you hold your hand up to a strong light and look at the thin webs of skin between your fingers. And pegasi never just galloped, like horses; any gait faster than a jog and they had their wings spread at least a little, perhaps partly for balance but mainly to absorb some of the shock of the pounding hoofs. Pegasus legs broke easily and, because they were hollow, usually broke badly; although pegasus shamans came rarely to the human lands, there was always a pegasus healer-shaman resident at the palace.

But Lrrianay's fourth son didn't look delicate. He was broad-chested and wide-backed, and his blackness gave him an extra solidity. He gleamed as if he'd been polished all over by many small, light alula-hands, which of course he had been, for the ceremony. The flowers woven through his wings were pale blue and white; through the plaits in his mane, bright blue, white and primrose yellow, and he had a little blue bag around his neck on a golden ribbon. She wasn't going to tell him he was beautiful—even more beautiful than usual for a pegasus, she thought—which he was, because he was probably vain enough about it already. But she did think it was rather hard that she should have an extra-tall pegasus.

Their silent conversation had taken less than a minute. No one of the humans had noticed anything unusual; pegasus child and human child often stared fixedly at each other on first meeting. The magicians had come up from the rear of the dais, and now one laid his hand on Sylvi's right shoulder (she tried not to flinch), and another laid his hand on the pegasus king's son's right shoulder and turned them, gently, so that Sylvi's left and her pegasus' right, as they faced each other, were presented to the watching crowd. The two kings them-selves moved to stand behind their offsprings' left shoulders. Sylvi's eyes, for a moment, met Lrrianay's, and she wondered if he knew that his son had been talking to her, and she to him. And—even more briefly—she wondered just how much he and her father could say to each other.

Sylvi felt rather than saw the third and fourth magicians approaching, and she had a sudden clear memory of this part of the ceremony when Garren had gone through it; she had been just old enough to realise not only that what was going on was important, but that it would happen to her in a few years too. The third magician held burning herbs in a dish, and he stretched out his arm so that the fumes rose up in the faces of Sylvi and her pegasus, and the fourth magician threw a billow of light fabric over them, so light, or so enchanted, that it remained drifting a little above them, like a cloud, and the pale bars of colour woven into it striped the floor of the dais. But it touched her pegasus' glossy blackness not at all.

To her right she heard the fifth magician droning the words of binding. She had always taken the idea of binding literally, and had assumed that she would feel something happening, some tautness, some imprisoning, building between her and her pegasus. She stiffened herself for it, but nothing of the kind occurred. The magician's voice filled her ears—she wanted to shake her head to rattle the words back out again—and the smoke filled her mouth and lungs, like trying to breathe through a blanket, and eddying, drifting smoke dappled with the colours of the drifting fabric also dimmed and confused her eyes till her pegasus was nothing but a shadow behind it.

It felt all wrong. It felt as if they were being separated, not bound together. A thought came to her from somewhere: we are already bound. That was why it had to be him, and not his little sister.

Maybe that is why we can talk to each other. I don't understand—

But as she thought this, the fifth magician's voice rose to a climax, and the third magician flourished the herb-bowl, so that the unburnt herbs and the ashes and embers leaped out of the bowl and fell to the floor of the dais. The embers twinkled against the border of the rainbow fabric but left no scorch marks. Sylvi sneezed, violently, and heard her pegasus sneeze as well. It was good luck to sneeze during your binding.

The fabric was pulled away and the smoke dispersed as if it had never been. Sylvi blinked in the sunlight and watched it sparkle on the flowers laced through her pegasus' wings and mane. The magicians gathered round them—too close, Sylvi thought—and blew the spell-dust over them, and when it touched her face Sylvi involuntarily put her hand up to brush it off.

Then there was a moment's grace; housefolk discreetly gave goblets to Sylvi's father and Danacor, who in turn offered them to Sylvi and her pegasus. Sylvi found that she didn't want to swallow any of the dust and ashes that had got into her mouth; she wanted to rinse her mouth and spit it out. But she knew she couldn't. She looked up at her father; she wondered if it had been anyone but the king who held the goblet for her if she might have refused. But no. She was still a princess, and she had learnt her part of the ritual very carefully. She sipped the faintly honey-flavoured water and swallowed—with difficulty; it was like swallowing a rock. It stuck in her throat, and then lay heavily in her stomach. Her pegasus swallowed too, but she thought he drank as gingerly as she did.

Now ...

Better get on with it, said her pegasus. *You do remember your words, don't you?*

Of course I remember, Sylvi said, nettled, and began at once. "Welcome, Excellent Friend, on this glorious day ..."

The end of her dry little speech went "And so I name myself to thee, Sylviianel, princess of the line of Gohasson, daughter of the sixth of that line, Corone IV, and his queen Eliona, fourth child of them I call my parents," and as she said these words out loud she added silently, *I don't even know your name yet.*

They really don't tell you anything, do they? I've known you were Sylvi forever. My name is Ebon.

It was not surprising that Sylvi missed her last cue. Trying to give a speech and hold a conversation at the same time would be hard work for anybody under any circumstances—and under these particular circumstances it was also not surprising she could not resist having the conversation. Nor was it surprising that she forgot what the cue was. It just seemed to her—very reasonably—that it was ridiculous that she should be bound to this pegasus before she so much as knew his name.

But her father, the king, was supposed to say Ebon's name aloud, which was when she was supposed to hear it for the first time—and while she had learnt every moment of the ritual with painful precision, the ritual had not included that she should find herself able to talk to her pegasus directly. The ritual dictated that her father should say Ebon's name aloud, and then she would formally kiss (or pretend to kiss) Ebon on the forehead and repeat it. But she forgot to turn to her father. She stepped forward, kissed him (he having lowered his head so she could) and shouted his name out; the crowd below the dais cheered.

She didn't think about what she had done till much later. It was Ebon's turn now, and he stepped forward and gave the pegasus' great clarion neigh—far more like a trumpet than a horse's neigh; hollow bones are wonderful for resonance—and swept his wings forward to touch, or almost touch, his alula-hands to her temples before he gave his own speech, in the half-humming, half-whuffling syllables the peg-asi made when they spoke aloud, only she could understand what he was saying in silent-speech. The words were just as stiff and silly (she was rather relieved to discover) as the ones she'd had to say.

He stopped whuffling and added, *I was going to say hee ho, ho hee, your wings are too short, you'll never catch me, but my dad said he was going to be listening and I'd better get it right. I guess since you can hear too it's good that I did.*

Sylvi set aside for later the alarming thought that the pegasus king was perhaps listening in on them both, and said, *Do you have any idea why we can hear each other? It's supposed to take years to happen at all, and I don't think it's ever like this.*

Not a clue. I know something happens occasionally. . . . Our dads can talk, sort of. I thought it was mostly stories. Stories about what we wanted to happen instead of what does happen.

My father says he and your dad have got like a hundred words or ideas or things they can get across pretty well and then everything else has to be built up around one of them and sometimes they do and mostly they don't. He says it's like shouting in a wind—you never know what's going to get through. If you say, "To help you defend yourselves my son is sending a messenger-pigeon with news of our enemies' victory," and they hear "help-son-message-victory" they're going to be looking for the son, not the pigeon, and expecting good news.

Their eyes met, and she was sure that he hadn't liked the binding either. . . . There was a lot she was going to have to think about later. Too much. She wanted the happy, simple, delighted feeling of being able to talk to Ebon back again. . . . *My mother can't talk to her pegasus at all. Well, except for the "isn't it a pretty day" stuff that you can guess if you have to.*

Ebon made a funny noise, like a whinny with a hiccup in it. *That's because she's got Hirishy. Well, everyone thought your dad was going to marry*

63

Fandora, and everyone thought my dad was going to marry Ponoia, and they got the bindings wrong. Your big magician was really cross about it but you can't rebind. Hirishy barely talks to **us**. *My mum says she was the most awful crybaby when she was little, and all the grown-ups expected my mum to look after her because my mum was nearest her age of the cousins. Hirishy wouldn't fly over water or over any hill higher than a—than one of your houses, and she was afraid of horses. She's better now but.... My little sister isn't anywhere near as awful as Hirishy was, and it's a good thing because none of us would look after her if she was. It's too bad, because I think my mum would have liked your mum. My mum is wasted on Lorival.*

Lorival was one of the king's cousins. Both she and her husband were bound, but they lived outside the Wall, and only saw their pegasi briefly by arrangement on the rare occasions when they came to the palace.

Sylvi wanted to say something in Hirishy's defence, but the ritual was over, and they had to climb down from the platform together. She and Ebon were supposed to go first, and they went very slowly, since pegasi did have in common with horses a dislike of going down steps. The pegasi did not fly in mixed company, and there wasn't room for pegasus wings in a crowded Great Court.

And then there were too many people congratulating her, and she and Ebon were separated in the crush, and she saw him surrounded by his own people. And then her father had his arm round her shoulders—his right arm; the Sword hung on his left side, for easier drawing—and people were making way for them because he was the king. "How did you learn his name?" the king said softly to his daughter. It was the first thing he had said since the ritual.

She had been expecting something like "well done" because her father wasn't anything like his aunt Moira, and always tried to find the best in what you'd done and to recognise that you'd been trying. She realised that he was asking her if she had deliberately broken the rule that she was to know nothing about Ebon before this meeting and that he was making an effort to give her the benefit of some doubt. There should not have been any way she could have learnt Ebon's name before he told it to her. Her father sounded grim, because her answer mattered, not just because she might have done something she knew she wasn't supposed to. And she knew it must matter, or he'd have said "well done" first.

She felt suddenly cold, and again she remembered the feeling of wrongness when she and Ebon had stood under the rainbow fabric and the magicians' smoke had been so thick they couldn't see each other. And then she felt a little light-headed and queasy and she thought, No, I am *not* going to be sick. But her voice still came out squeaky when she said, "He told me, just now, on the platform. That's why I forgot to wait for you. We were talking when I was supposed to be saying all those words, and I got confused. It was—it was—" She had no idea what to say about the discovery that she and Ebon could talk to each other. She hadn't really taken it in herself yet. Maybe—maybe it wouldn't last. Maybe it was something to do with the binding ritual. This made her instantly unhappy: Ebon was already her friend. But—no. No one had said anything to her about anything like this, and someone would have. She looked up at her father. "I'm—I'm sorry. Is it very bad that I didn't ask you?" She was afraid to ask if it was very bad that she could talk to her pegasus. What if he said yes? What if there was some reason why humans and pegasi could not talk to each other that they weren't going to tell her until she was older?

She was relieved to see that the king believed her, but he still looked grim. In fact, she thought, he looked grimmer, as if he'd almost rather she'd broken the rule—broken faith. And keeping faith was the king's first rule. "You're a princess," he said to her every time she got into enough trouble that someone tattled to her father about it. "You have to know that you are no better than your people at the same time as you must behave as if you are." Hadn't she read somewhere that anyone giving the name of its future pegasus to a child who hadn't been bound yet could be charged with treason? She began to feel sick again—sick and frightened. *Was* it a bad thing that she could talk to Ebon? Wasn't the whole thing about keeping the Speakers in the background because if everything had gone the way the Alliance-makers had hoped, nobody would need Speakers?

The king said, "Have you ever spoken to a pegasus before? Spoken—I mean not just by sign?" He knew that she rarely used the sign-language if she could help it; she made the necessary courtesy greetings, occasionally said "isn't it a pretty day," and on formal occasions she was so paralysed by shyness she couldn't do the more elaborate ones fast enough to get them over with. "Lrrianay or Thowara perhaps?"

She remembered Hirishy for a fraction of a second, and then shook her head emphatically. "No. Never. Nothing. That was partly why this was so—so muddling." She thought sadly of the initial rush of delight, which now seemed a long time ago. She looked around for Ebon; the crowd was beginning to move purposefully toward the banqueting tables set round near the walls of the Court. In deference to the pegasi this was a standing-up banquet, although there were plenty of chairs for two-legs who grew tired.

Ebon was looking at her, and as their eyes met he said, *Are you catching it from your dad? I've just been getting it from mine. He seems to think it's my fault that you made a little mistake.*

Yes, I—

She was distracted by the arrival of Fthoom. Fthoom was looking at her very solemnly, and she knew at once that the solemnity was to hide the fact that he was very angry.

Fthoom was the head—the unofficial head—of the royal magicians, which meant he was the first magician of the entire country. In theory magicians didn't have a head, and any group of magicians who decided to act together—the magicians' guild and the smaller but more consequential Speakers' Guild most importantly—had to choose their actions democratically. In practise there generally was a head, and no one who spent more than five minutes or one ritual occasion at the king's court was in any doubt that Fthoom was head magician. She knew that her father wished the royal magicians would elect him chief and get it over with; he had said many times that they wasted more time and energy squabbling for a better place in the unadmitted hierarchy than they spent on court business. But no one squabbled with Fthoom.

Fthoom was chosen for all the most significant roles. He had been the fifth magician for the king's daughter's binding with her pegasus; that she was only the fourth child would be less important to him than that it would be a public spectacle involving a number of magicians with a lot of people watching. It was just like him to be the first magician to confront her with her blunder too, since she was pretty sure by the way he was glaring at her that that was his intention—once the ritual was over he could have been expected to lose interest in her.

Her father's arm tightened round her as he said, mildly, "Fthoom."

Fthoom heard the tone of the king's voice and a little ripple of self-restraint went through him. Sylvi could see him standing up straighter and squaring his unpleasantly broad shoulders: she always thought of him in terms of how much light he blocked. She understood with increasing alarm that her tiny mistake was not tiny at all. Surely there could have been some other way she could have learnt Ebon's name? But she knew there wasn't.

She didn't want any part of magicians' business. Magic was the worst of court affairs, worse even than being polite to people who were rude about your height. One of the reasons she had been able to relax her guard around Ahathin was that while he usually had a little charm-thread in a pocket, he'd never done any magic in her presence, and she'd only once or twice smelled it on him. The charm against night-mares had smelled like fresh air and spring; that had been part of why it worked. Most magicians' magic made her skin hurt.

She'd never liked Fthoom, who was a patronising bully to everyone but her parents and her eldest brother, but now, looking at him, with the reek of fresh magic coming off him like the reek of fresh blood, she was very frightened of him indeed—even with her father's arm around her. She wished she were still young enough to wrap herself up in the long skirts of her father's ceremonial robe and disappear, as she had occasionally done when she was smaller.

She glanced again at Ebon, who was still watching her. The pegasus standing next to him turned his head and looked at her too. She could guess, by the ears and nostrils, that he was saying something to Ebon, but she couldn't hear anything with either her ears or her mind; and then Ebon began walking toward her. Lrrianay had materialised at her father's other elbow, and she began to notice the number of people, both two-legged and four-, who were watching the confrontation. For confrontation was what it was.

Fthoom was apparently still trying to decide how to phrase what he wanted to say when Ebon joined them. He put his nose to Sylvi's ear and blew—very gently. It tickled, and she smiled involuntarily.

Atta girl, he said, and pawed briefly, gracefully, with one forefoot for emphasis.

This minor exchange infuriated Fthoom past restraint. "How *dare* you!" he said to Sylvi—who cringed against her father as if Fthoom had tried to strike her. "You know it is forbidden to have any contact between your pegasus and yourself before the ritual is performed!" He turned on her father and half shouted, "It is obvious these two have a long-standing—long-standing and *inappropriate*—relationship! How has this happened!"

Nobody, not even the most powerful magician in the country, publicly accuses the king of misdoing. Very, very gently Sylvi's father said, "Fthoom, you may speak tomorrow morning in court."

Fthoom started and stared at the king. He opened his mouth once or twice and then turned on his heel and strode away, across the Court, and out through the Gate. Murmurs rustled through the crowd, and those who had watched other bindings and noticed what had happened and assumed that the slight change had been deliberate now guessed it had not been, and wondered what it meant.

The king sighed and dropped his hand. "Come; let us have something to eat." He made the *come-with* sign to Ebon, who bowed his head and followed. Lrrianay bowed Sylvi ahead of him, but he often did; the stiffness with which he did it, she was sure, was not because she was a fourth child and he was a king, but because he was worried too. And he must be very worried, because pegasi were always as graceful as pouring water.

No human was allowed to begin eating at a banquet attended by the human king till the king had eaten something, so the moment Sylvi's father began to walk toward the tables several courtiers rushed up to him with bowls and plates of dainties. He chose one at random so that his people could begin. Fthoom had vanished and many of the magicians with him; those who remained were more simply dressed and could melt into the crowd. Sylvi could see a few of the Speakers:

69

Fazuur, and Danacor's Speaker, Moorcath; Minial would be sitting down somewhere, now that the ritual was over, with her knitting bag open at her feet. There was Ahathin: he didn't approach her—that would be presumptuous in public, unless she asked him to—but he made a quick gesture with one hand, smiled and turned away before she could—or had to—respond.

It took her a minute to remember what the gesture was; it wasn't one of the basic ones. When she remembered, it was with bewilderment: it was the sign for victory, and historically used mostly on the battlefield or at great state occasions. Ahathin had taught it to her after she'd read about it in some great romantic ballad, and he'd never said "don't fill your head with nonsense when you can barely remember the fundamentals." Victory? That was the last thing what had just happened was. And he would have recognised her mistake too. But it was nice of him.

People—other than Sylvi, her father and Lrrianay—began to relax and enjoy themselves. It was a beautiful day with a blue sky and a light fresh breeze. The Outer Court had been scrubbed and scrubbed for the birthday and binding of the king's child, and its pale stones gleamed almost opal in the sunlight. The old stones were already nearly as silky as a pegasus' shoulder (Sylvi guessed) from generations of scrubbing, and Sylvi always ran her hand along one whenever she was close enough to do so—sometimes her mother sent her with a message to her father, or Diamon, or vice versa, and she'd run round the perimeter of the Court so she could touch the stones, instead of straight across the centre. Today much of their surface was covered with ribbons and banners, and she had to stay in the centre of the Court and be a princess. The food was plentiful and excellent, and the king moved among his people, smiling and apparently carefree and, with the Sword at his side, very kingly indeed. The pegasi were all gracious and dignified, and those who knew a little of the sign-language spoke to them and were answered politely; occasionally a Speaker (easily identified by the Speaker's sticks worn on all formal occasions) was applied to for assistance.

Sylvi tried to pretend to be calm and self-possessed too. She knew she wasn't doing a very good job of it, but she hoped that everyone around her would assume she was tired, or shy, or unused to court events—all of which were true. And she was worried because she knew her father was worried—she tried to force the memory of Fthoom's angry face out of her mind, but she couldn't forget the sound of her father's gentlest voice saying, "You may speak tomorrow morning." She was even worried that she knew Lrrianay was worried. The stiffness with which he had bowed to her could merely be the grand manner due to a formal event, but she knew it wasn't. But why did she know? Pegasi had always been nearly as opaque as statues to her before.

Before Ebon.

CHAPTER 5

By the time she could creep off to her room and be alone, Sylvi was so tired that when she closed her eyes she still saw the crowd in the Court, moving, eating, laughing, talking—looking at her, wondering who she was and who she was growing up to be—painstakingly making conversation with the thirty or so pegasi who had come with Lrrianay and Ebon, whose shining coats sparkled more brightly than any of the jewels in the humans' dress. As she grew more tired, it had seemed to her that the sprinkling of pegasi in the crowd of humans made some kind of pattern—if she could just rearrange them a little—that dark bay pegasus should be a little closer to the Court wall, and the white one should move nearer the centre, and that clump of humans near the Gate needed to be lightened, maybe by Oyry and Poih, who were wasted where they were standing among the chairs, gravely attending to—oh, horrors—Great-aunt Moira.

No one asked Sylvi directly about the odd change in the ritual, but she could assume everyone had seen Fthoom's face afterward—many of them would have heard his outburst—and seen the king dismiss him as if he were a stableboy. Magicians used to performing in rituals tended to have deep, sonorous voices, and Fthoom's was especially so: but no one shouted at the king. If there had been any chance that her mistake would be forgotten—those not immediately concerned with pegasi by being bound to one usually had only a vague notion of the peculiarities and pitfalls of the system—Fthoom had seen to it that it would instead be a subject of intense interest. She might have hoped that the interest would fade as soon as this day was over, but her father had told Fthoom to speak to him tomorrow, which meant the morning court. . . . She heard voices rise at the ends of sentences, and saw people who had been in earshot of the question turn their heads to look at her. At her and Ebon.

Ebon had stayed near her for most of that long afternoon. He didn't mind being stared at as much as she did. *Well, they're not my people, you know,* he said. *I'd mind if you were at one of our five-seasons festivals and everyone was staring at me and you. Although I'm not looking forward to what old Gaaloo is going to say later.* Gaaloo was one of Lrrianay's cousins, bound to one of Eliona's sisters. Reesha was here for her niece's binding, although she rarely came to the palace, but Gaaloo was one of Lrrianay's courtiers and often came in his train. *Gaaloo can talk the hind legs off a unicorn.*

Are we supposed to stay together? Sylvi said anxiously.

Haven't a raindrop's idea in a hailstorm, said Ebon cheerfully. *I've never been to one of these things before. You tell me.*

Sylvi shook her head. *Children don't attend bindings unless it's someone like your brother, and I was still too little for Garren—my youngest brother's—to notice much.*

Figuratively and literally: too short to see what was going on, except when Danny let her sit on his shoulders. That was before he'd been through the acceptance of the heir, and didn't always have to be part of important rituals with their father, and had more time for his little sister. But she'd been taken away soon after the ritual—although her mother had sent one of the housefolk after her with a plate of the banquet food. She thought about it a moment. *It's funny, though, isn't it? That nobody told me what I—we—were supposed to do afterward. They've been drilling me silly in the sign-language for years of course—it's one of the first things I remember, trying to learn the sign-language. Maybe we're supposed to stand around and say things like, "Nice day, isn't it? But I believe it will rain tomorrow."* Sylvi made a creditable effort to say this in sign, and one or two *huffs.*

Ebon made the noise like a whinny with a hiccup again. *I didn't know pegasi laughed,* she said. *Well—out loud. Where humans can hear them.*

Ebon shook his head so that his already-magnificent mane (pegasus manes didn't usually come in fully till adulthood) whipped back and forth. The plaits were coming out fast, and it rained flowers. She bent to pick them up.

What a lot of old bores we are with you then, he said, but he said it with less than his usual vigour.

Maybe you don't find our jokes funny, said Sylvi sadly.

There was a pause, and he answered soberly, *I think we're all too worried about getting along. It's hard to know what to say to you. Especially since we mostly can't.*

You don't, said Sylvi. *Worry about what to say.*

Well, I'm hopeless, said Ebon, recovering his spirits. *Everybody says so. You can't have been drilled any sillier in signing than I was in signing and **manners** after they decided I had to be your pegasus. Think of the breath stoppings and the heart burstings and the dumbfoundings if they'd had any idea we'd be able to talk to each other!*

She'd laughed—she couldn't help it—and too many people turned to look at her: at her and Ebon, standing a little apart from the rest of the crowd at that moment and only making half-hearted and erratic attempts at signing to each other. And yet she'd laughed. At what?

Silence fell, and the king, as if idly, as if his feet just happened to be taking him in the direction of his daughter, joined them, and with him came Lrrianay. Shortly after this the queen, equally idly, ended her conversation with some cousins, here from the other side of the country for the princess' binding, and drifted over with Hirishy, whereupon the king wandered away again. No more silences fell, but Sylvi didn't laugh out loud again either; nor were she and Ebon left to stand by themselves again.

She lay in bed now, staring out the window. Her nurse always pulled the curtains closed, last thing before she blew out the lamp and after she made sure Sylvi was *in* bed instead of hiding somewhere with a book on hawks or a bridle she'd decided needed a different colour browband. After a few minutes, as soon as Sylvi was sure the nurse was really gone, she got up and pulled the curtains open again.

She had always felt shut in behind walls and doors; she was notorious for going for long tramps over open countryside even in the worst weather. Her father's dogs tended to jump up hopefully when they saw her, because she took them for longer rambles than her father had time to do. One of the best things that had ever happened to her was when her mother declared that she no longer always had to have a nurse or a groom or a courtier go with her—but she did have to have either a dog or a pony, and she had to tell her mother first exactly where she was going. She wondered if Ebon liked to go for long walks ... well, not very likely, was it? He had wings. Who would walk who could fly?

But that wasn't true. They did walk, he had told her. *Flying is **tiring**,* he said. *Of course we walk. We walk **more** than we fly.* He had told her too that, while their land centred on the Linwhialinwhia Caves, as Balsinland centred on the palace within its Wall, the pegasi did not live there. This made sense to Sylvi; to the extent that she understood *ssshasssha* at all, it made the Caves sound like a kind of very large library with pictures instead of books. And she preferred the outdoors herself.

The pegasi spent most of their time wandering through the high wild meadows that were their private country—as specified by the treaty—and foraging, and sleeping out of doors wherever the end of day found them; although they grew and tended certain crops for food, paper, dyes and paints, and weaving. These were planted around the *shfeeah*, which Sylvi tentatively translated as a kind of small village, where the craftspeople lived, and where other pegasi stayed for a time to help with the crops. *The story-tellers and shamans roam with the rest of us, but the sculptors stay near the Caves.*

Sylvi had some trouble with "sculptor," although she heard the word clearly enough and she knew a little about the Caves: it was one of the things you learnt about the pegasi, with the Alliance and the gesture-language. The Caves had been there when the pegasi came, so long ago that even the pegasi only had myths about their origins; but, while extensive, they had been much smaller and far less beautiful. Thousands of years of pegasus sculptors, rubbing and smoothing and chipping and carving, using such small tools as their frail feather-hands could hold, and the Caves were—*so beautiful you can't really stay there long, you want to jump out of your skin and run for it. They're **perfect**, you know, even though they're not finished—will never be finished—it's part of their perfection, that it goes on and on into the future and you'll never see it, that* *us little short-lived mortals create perfection by **not** being there long, although we keep coming, us and our sons and daughters and their sons and daughters and so on. . . . Sorry. I'm sounding like a grown-up.*

But the sculptors themselves don't stay inside long—a few weeks or months—and then they come out and join us in the fields for a while, although they mostly don't like to go far. "Remember how to not fly," is the proverb: remember how to walk. They come out and join us in the fields. And teach their beginning apprentices sculpting on the pillars of the shfeeah. The Caves knock your Courts hollow, although this one's pretty nice, he added, looking round consideringly. *But it's only barely just been built.*

Sylvi, fascinated, forbore to say that the Outer Court was one of the oldest bits of the palace, over seven hundred years old.

You can see it too clearly, Ebon went on, *where it begins and ends, your Court. It's different in the Caves. The chambers and corridors all open out of each other and weave back and forth like the king's plaits on coronation day. Very very occasionally, an old sculptor may ask for a decision to rub through a wall—the other sculptors have to agree, **and** the monarch and the decision-making shamans. It doesn't happen often. And it becomes a permanent day on our calendar, the day that someone brushes the thin-made place on a wall and suddenly there's a hole there, even if it took years to scratch open and it will be years more before the hole is big enough to climb through and see what's on the other side. I was born on Damonay—the day three hundred and twenty-six years before that they had made a hole in Damonay chamber. Ambernia chamber, which is the one they let out of darkness, is all red stone and considered one of the most beautiful in all the Caves, so being born on Damonay is lucky.*

Do humans ever go there? To your Caves?

Ebon looked at her, puzzled: head low, chin pulled in, one ear half back. *Not that I know of. Humans don't come to us. We come to you. The Caves aren't a human sort of thing.* He paused and—this was a frown,

Sylvi thought: both ears half back, head raised again but held rather stiffly to one side. *I . . . I don't know. They . . . they wouldn't fit around you, somehow. And it's in the treaty that we're supposed to come to you.*

Sylvi was human enough, and princess enough, to know what that meant in human terms. *Don't you—mind? Mind always coming to us?*

Ebon shrugged again—she was sure, now, that it was a pegasus shrug. *What's to mind? That we keep our quiet and our privacy? That we don't have to worry about providing dead flesh for you to eat? And **chairs**? I would not be your father, the human king, to have the winning of that old war carried on my back, and on the backs of all the kings and queens after me, until the end of humans and pegasi—and the winning of any other wars. We are free, we pegasi, thanks to you. We are glad to honour you in this way if it pleases you—if it means you'll go on carrying the burden for both of us.* In what Sylvi was already learning was a typical Ebon manner, he added, *Mind you, I wouldn't want to be my dad either—he still has to listen to all the bickering when someone feels left out of some decision—and he has to listen to people like Gaaloo go on and **on** because usually there's about six important words in what Gaaloo says that nobody else thinks of and since my dad's king, he'd better hear them.*

Sylvi sat up in bed. Something had moved very quickly between the window and the stars; something not only swift but large. There—there it was again, higher than the first time—no, gone again; no, not gone; it had banked and turned and—

Ebon folded his wings at the last minute, to fit through the window, and landed, therefore, rather abruptly and rather hard; his knees buckled and he rolled right over, wrapped in his wings, but making surprisingly little noise for all of that. Sylvi was out of bed and kneeling beside him before he scrambled to his feet again. *Ow,* he said. *There must be a better way. Can't you sleep somewhere with bigger windows?*

Are you all right?

He walked once around the room, lifting his legs gingerly. *Yes. Don't worry. We're taught to fall and roll like that when we're babies and first learning to fly. They taught me really emphatically because I've always been too big. There were a lot of these doomsayers when I was a baby proclaiming that I'd be too big to fly. Ha. But you don't break anything if you roll. Are you ready to go?*

Sylvi, still confused by his sudden entrance, was nonplussed. *Go where?*

Out, said Ebon mysteriously. *Can you get down to the ground without waking anybody up?*

Yes, of course, she said. She'd crept down the two stories of wall from her bedroom many times, clinging to the knobbly, weatherworn stone heads of her ancestors—with useful little ridges for her feet where their necks ended—and to the heavy vronidia vine, which seemed to grow just enough bigger every year to go on bearing her weight. There were some nights, when the wind was singing to her and the sky went on forever, she couldn't stay indoors.

Come on then. He tucked his forelegs to leap over the balustrade like a pony over a fence, but as he jumped his wings sprang out and he soared up, not down, and then turned once or twice (showing off, she thought), before he sailed gracefully down to earth—landing so lightly he made no sound at all. Because of the no-flying-in-mixed-company convention, she didn't see pegasi flying all that often, except from a distance, and had never had one land so near her. She put her leg over the balustrade, felt around with her foot for Great-great-great-great-great-grandfather Neville's nose, and began climbing.

Ebon was dancing with impatience by the time she reached the ground. *Come on,* he said, and led the way quickly through the gardens; she had to trot to keep up with him, and he was very hard to see in the dark, especially as he led her away from the more open flower-beds and into the winding, yew- and cypress-lined paths that surrounded them. In their shadow he disappeared entirely, except for the sparkle of his eye when he turned his head to check that she was still following him, and the just-discernible shimmer of motion as he passed from one shadow to the next. She noticed that he had his wings unfolded from his sides, although they were no more than a quarter spread; there wasn't space between the trees.

How did you find me?

*Spent most of the party trying to work it out. Knew about the palace—I've even been here a few times—knew you humans live inside walls all the time. And sleep in special rooms. Asked my brothers as if I was asking just because everything is so bizarre—which it is, how do you **sleep** all wrapped up like a sickly baby?—where their humans lived—slept. They told me everyone has his own separate cell. Weird. But figured all your sleep cells would be together. Saw your dad and mum standing with their arms around each other at one window, staring at the sky. Okay, that's where they are, but I wished they'd go away. Then I was lucky: I saw your nurse shut your curtains. She is your nurse, isn't she?*

Sylvi, entranced, said, *Pegasi have nurses too?*

Eah. Although the kids are all together and then there are several nurses. But I guess I know what a nurse looks like, even when she's human. And I figured your brothers are too old for nurses. So that had to be your sleep room. I was ready to be really confused and bewildered and apologetic if it wasn't. I used to wander in my sleep when I was little. I thought I might just manage to bring it off as some kind of reaction to the ritual. That . . . smoke was really peculiar, wasn't it?

Yes. It was. But don't your shamans puff smoke over you for rituals? You have rituals too, don't you?

Yes. Lots and lots. She could hear exactly her own aversion in his words, although she doubted that shyness was any part of Ebon's dis-like. *But the smoke is never like that. It never makes you feel . . .*

Frightened, she thought. Frightened and all alone.

A low laugh. "No, I don't think so," said a young male voice.

Ebon and Sylvi froze.

"Well, I'm sure I heard something," said another voice—a young female voice. "And it sounded large."

"Our rabbits are enormous," said the first voice. "Our specially bred Wall guardian rabbits are feared all over the country for their ferocity."

"Very funny," said the second voice. "I still want to go back indoors."

That was Farley, thought Sylvi. *I wonder who the girl is?*

Come on, said Ebon. *They're gone.*

The king's palace lay in the largest piece of flat ground in the country; the rest of the landscape was a patchwork of plains, hills and mountains, and abundant lakes and rivers. Banesorrow Lake lay within the Wall, and the foothills of the Kish Mountains began near its eastern gate. The shape of the palace plain was irregular, extending several leagues to the southern tip but only a league and a half to the north and barely half a league to the east. But in a perfect circle, magician-measured, at half a league all round the palace at its centre, lay a Wall. The Wall had been erected after the final battle that had given Balsin his country and his kingship, although it had taken the reigns of three kings and three queens and the best efforts of six generations of magicians to finish it. It was twenty feet high and broad enough for a pair of guards to walk on abreast, which they did, because the full circumference was patrolled, guardtower to guardtower, of which there were twelve, one on each side of the six gates.

There were many buildings, homes, offices and administrative buildings, warehouses, markets, shops and smithies that had sprung up within the Wall, although all of those people had, to be and to stay there, a royal warrant to do so. But the palace's Inner and Outer Courts were reflected in the capital city having the Inner and Outer City, on either side of the Wall, although the doors of the six gates had not been closed in defence in hundreds of years. They were closed on the nights of two holidays, that of the Signing of the Treaty—which had been followed so closely by one of the worst battles of the war that the treaty itself had been lost for a day and a half—and that of the End of the War; which also provided the opportunity to ensure that they were in full working order. Both inside and outside the Wall, the city extended in erratic clusters and doglegs, with gaps for small farms and big gardens and the occasional municipal park. Ebon was leading her to the biggest of these parks within the Wall, on the far side of which lay the lake.

She panted up to him and said crossly, being already sure that he'd led her so briskly to keep her fully occupied not blundering into anything in the dark and therefore less likely to ask awkward questions, *All right, are you ready to tell me what we are doing?*

He had stopped, and was looking up at the stars—it was a very bright night, with a half-moon brilliant as a torch—and switching his tail gently. His wings were three-quarters open but down, the tips of them trailing softly against the grass. *I thought I'd take you flying,* he said.

Sylvi was tired. It had been a long day, and while she was still too keyed up to sleep, her mind rattled and buzzed and could not focus, and her intellect veered away from trying to comprehend what Ebon had said. *Flying? I can't fly. I'm human.* And in her determination not to understand him she felt angry with him for teasing her.

I know that, he said. *Stupid. You can sit on my back. I was trying to decide how. My wings have to be free to flap, you know.*

Sylvi burst into tears. At once she felt a warm velvety muzzle against one cheek and a little feathery hand against the other. *I'm sorry,* said Ebon. *You're crying, aren't you? You're sad? I've made you sad. I'm sorry. I thought you'd want to. I've been thinking about it all day, since I saw how small you are. There's a story that all humans want to fly, that you dream about it. Like we dream about having large strong hands with wrists. But maybe it's—you can want something and not want it—I felt that way about being your pegasus. It's okay if you don't want to fly. I—I won't think you're like Hirishy.*

This made Sylvi laugh, which, in the middle of crying, made her choke, and it was a minute before she could breathe or think anything at all. *I want to fly more than anything else in the world,* she said. *But there's no point in wanting something you can't have, is there? We're taught that pegasi are not for riding before we're old enough to know what riding or flying or pegasi* **are.** *It's like—it would be like trying to steal the Sword or something.*

Grown-up rules, said Ebon. **Human** *grown-up rules. You people have too many rules. So, can you get up, or do we need to find a bench for you to stand on? You can't kick my wing on the way. If I lose any feathers I won't be able to carry the extra weight. I think maybe if you lie along my back, you can maybe hook your feet under the back edges of my wings.*

But Sylvi stood, shivering with fear and longing, and stared at him. *I—can't. It's—it's rude. It's* **horribly** *rude.*

Ebon was silent a moment. *You mean to me, I guess. I think this is another of those things like what you asked me earlier—don't we mind that we have to come to you and stand around in your Court and take places you give us in your rituals. This is a human thing, this making it matter who stands where. We think that it is mixed up in why you won the war. We do not mind standing where you want us to. If you had not won the war we would not stand anywhere at all.*

*I know humans don't ride us, but I don't know any great forbidding about it. You don't ride us because we're too small and you're too big. It's rather nice of you, I think, to make it into a big forbidding. It's—it's to do us honour, I can see that. Human honour. Thank you. But I would **like** to take you flying. My dad would tell me no—that's why I'm here in the middle of the night—not because it's rude but because it's dangerous. I bet you aren't allowed to climb down the wall from your window, are you?*

No.

Well then.

He moved around till she was facing his near shoulder. He'd flattened that wing and stretched it as far back as it would go; she put one hand on his withers and one just behind, and gave a little heave, and lay belly down over his back. She could do this without thinking on her own pony who was, in fact, a little shorter than Ebon, but who was also, of course, uncomplicated by wings. She lifted her right leg very gingerly as far as it would go and then laid it along his back—his right wing was now stretched out horizontal to prevent her rolling off the other side—wriggled her body around, laid her left leg beside her right, took hold of his mane and wriggled a little further forward. Except for his (mercifully low) withers gouging into her breastbone, she was—surprisingly—fairly comfortable.

Okay?

Okay.

He walked forward a little cautiously. She could feel him trying to adjust to the weight of her; his wings were half spread, and they vibrated as he sought his balance. He bowed his head up and down a few times, stretched his wings to their full extent—they seemed *leagues* wide to Sylvi—said, *Here we go*, and shot forward at a gallop. The powerful wings seemed to grab the air; she could feel not only the great muscular thrust down, but the kick of the released air again as the wings rose and freed it; and with each downstroke, Ebon—and Sylvi—briefly left the earth in a long bound. One . . . two . . . three . . . the sweep of wings and the boom of wind deafened her to any other sound; she could just feel the tap of Ebon's galloping feet, one-two-three, one stride for each wing-stroke, beneath her . . . four . . . five . . . six. . . .

They were airborne.

Sylvi was crying again, but it might have been the wind. She could guess at the extra effort Ebon was making to carry her; the body beneath her was taut with exertion, the muscles both as solid as stone and as live and lithe as running water. It should have been difficult, and terrifying, to stay on, but somehow it was not; the muscles of her belly and thighs seemed to know how to keep her centre of gravity so perfectly balanced over Ebon's spine that when he turned and banked she merely sank a little closer to him, almost as if she were a part of him. She knew the old horse-riding adage of striving to become one with your horse, but this was nothing like riding a horse, and she had never felt anything with her pony—whom she loved dearly and rode every day—like she now felt with Ebon, as if they were almost one creature indeed.

She'd always found the stories of centaurs a little unsatisfactory. The earthbound centaurs interested her not at all, but she often thought about the winged ones—thought of them for having human faces, voices, hands—and wings. But what would centaurs eat? If they ate hay for their horse digestion, didn't it hurt their human mouths? If they grazed like horses, didn't the human heads get dizzy? She thought, Maybe there's a very, very old story, that we aren't allowed to know about, that some magician put a spell on so we shouldn't find it, that centaurs are really humans riding pegasi.

She felt secure enough to rearrange her hands in his mane and raise her face a little so that she could glance to one side and then the other—careful not to move her head far enough or quickly enough to disturb Ebon's equilibrium.

He was gaining height, spiralling up and up in a huge gyre. Even in the dark she could see—her view came and went, like an eye's slow blinking, by the whip of Ebon's wingbeats—the great shadowy loom of the palace, spilling off in one direction with stables and barns, and in another with servants' quarters, and another with courtiers' and magicians' apartments, and another yet with the special open rooms for the pegasi. She could make out the always-lit dome of the Inner Great Court and the walls around the Outer, the whole surrounded by wide formal gardens and carriageways like the erratic spokes of a very strangely shaped wheel. She thought, This is how it *really* looks.

As all these passed under Ebon's wings she could see farther and farther, forest and parkland and a clutch of buildings like a small village at a crossroads of the inner city; and there was the Wall. Now, as Ebon turned again, the palace came once more into view, a little smaller this time. Her people were fascinated by what they called sky views; some of the most prized and valuable of the decorative artwork in the palace were paintings of hills and valleys, lakes and forests, towns and villages, as if seen from above, and there were many miniature landscapes called sky holds, made out of stone and wood and clay and, occasionally, jewels. None of them were as beautiful—or as exciting—or as shocking—as this dark-blurred, wing-nicked scene, with the wind streaking past, tangling her hair and chilling her back and her bare feet; but her hands were buried snugly in his mane, and Ebon himself was as warm as a hearth.

She thought, This is how it *really* looks. And again, wonderingly: This is how it really looks. . . .

At last he stopped climbing and flew for the Wall, and over it. It hadn't occurred to her to wonder (as presumably it had not occurred to Ebon) whether the airborne magic carefully suspended and maintained above the Wall would let a human pass; they had just proved that it would. Moving boringly at walking speed through one of the gates, there was a faint chilly press or wash against your skin rather like diving into Banesorrow Lake; she felt nothing tonight but the wind and the flick of Ebon's mane.

Sylvi briefly saw the moving figures of two of the guards walking along the Wall as they passed through one of the circles of torchlight, and guessed as well that Ebon had flown so high that they could not possibly see her. Pegasi did not commonly fly at night, but they did do so; no one would think anything of a pegasus flying so late, especially not after a day like today, when there were so many of them visiting the human king.

Once they were over the Wall he turned again, northwest, and they flew for a while over farm and field and more villages, till the mountains at the edge of the plain by some trick of the dark seemed to grow larger though they did not seem any nearer; and then, at last, although Sylvi reckoned that in actual minutes they had not been gone very long, he turned round again and headed back for the Wall, and the palace.

They had not spoken during the flight, but when Ebon was over the Wall again and losing height as they neared the park where they had started out, he said suddenly, *I should have taught you how to fall first. I'm afraid this is not going to be one of my better landings. Can you fall?*

Of course I can fall, said Sylvi with dignity. *I have fallen off my pony many times.*

She thought he laughed. *Don't tense up,* he said. *And you want to try to roll when you hit. I hope your pony-teacher taught you that. Sorry. Damn. Stupid of me. Look, I'll tip you off a few secs before I land myself, so I won't fall on you. Ready?*

Ready, said Sylvi, since she didn't have any choice.

The ground was rushing up toward them. The great wings arched and curled, and Ebon seemed to rear in the air, and stalled for the briefest fraction of a moment; then they levelled out, and now the ground was very close indeed. Ebon said, *Now,* and gave a lurch to one side, and Sylvi let herself tumble off the other side of his tail, and with a vague memory of the horse-dancers who threw themselves on and off their galloping horses to amuse people on feast days, tried to flip herself round in the air. She landed nearly on her feet, ran a few steps, knowing she was going to fall anyway, and managed to roll when she finally did so.

Ebon, who had also fallen, was already up and giving himself a vigorous shake when she staggered to her feet again. *Are you in one piece still? Are you all right?* he said, leaving off shaking and coming toward her; and a laugh burst out of her as suddenly as she had burst into tears when he had said he would take her flying. *Yes. No. But not from falling. Tonight was the most—*

Words failed her, and she went up to him and put her arms round his neck, and rested her face against his hot sweaty shoulder. She felt his nose in her hair, and then his teeth gently gripped a lock of it, and tugged, even more gently, which she would learn was a pegasus caress, like a human kiss.

CHAPTER 6

She was so sodden with sleep the next morning that her new attendant could not rouse her. It was only when her mother came and shouted in her ear, "Your father wants to see you immediately after breakfast!" that she dragged herself unwillingly to the surface. She had been dreaming about flying. She had discovered, climbing up the wall to her bedroom window the night before, that both holding on and diving off had used (or misused) more skin and muscles than she had realised at the time, and between trying to find a comfortable way to lie and an inability to stop reexperiencing the magic journey over and over in her head, it had been nearly dawn before memory slid gradually into dream, and she was a pegasus too, and it was her own wings that carried her aloft with Ebon.

Her father wanted to see her after breakfast. *Fthoom.* She was suddenly thoroughly awake, and the joy drained out of her, leaving only a leaden grey tiredness shot through with a sick-making gleam of fear.

"Where—?"

"In his private receiving room."

Not the public court then. Fewer people . . . but Fthoom would seem even bigger in a small room.

Her mother looked at her, frowning, put her hand under her chin and tipped her head up. "Did someone give you unwatered wine last night? If you were a few years older, I would say you looked hung over."

Sylvi managed to smile. "I—I had a lot of trouble falling asleep. I just kept—going on thinking about things."

The queen sat on the edge of her bed. She had stopped frowning, but she looked a little quizzical. "Yes. You're twelve years old now, and nearly a grown-up in all the wrong ways. You still can't make your own decisions—you can't even stay up late without permission—but you'll have to come to all the official banquets, although you will be allowed to leave early. As I think about it, maybe I could develop a gentle little wasting illness whose only symptom is that I have to go to bed early on official banquet nights." She smiled at her daughter, and her daughter smiled back. The queen had an old wound in one hip that made it difficult for her to sit for long periods—mysteriously, however, it did not trouble her in the saddle—but she refused to use it to get out of state events. Maybe when I'm older, she'd said when Sylvi had once asked.

"You'll now be expected to come to most council meetings," the queen went on, "at which you will have no say and no vote. But your father or Ahathin will decide on a speciality for you—farming or the guilds, or rivers and waterways, or roads—or the army: gods save you if you have anything to do with the army. It could be anything on the court schedule, and you have the misfortune to have made a very good impression on your father with your papers on village witchcraft, so he'll probably want to give you something challenging. And you'll be expected to study whatever it is carefully and have opinions about it. And they'll want you to come up with good ideas, but if you manage to do so, you'll be expected to stand up in front of everybody else on the council and possibly even the senate, and present them. Horrifying. Much worse than anything that happens in the practise yards with mere weapons."

"Mum," said Sylvi, "you've never been afraid of anything in your life."

"How wrong you are," said the queen. "I am afraid of almost everything except what I can go after with a sword. You know where you are with a taralian. When it began to dawn on me that your father was serious, I almost ran away. I probably would have run away the night before the wedding except you're expected to sleep among your attending maidens. Probably to prevent you from running away."

Sylvi laughed.

"Court etiquette," said the queen. "Court gods-save-us etiquette. I was a country baron's daughter so we had banquets once or twice a year when the queen or a bigger, more formal baron than we were came to visit. And my father held court one afternoon a week for troubles and disputes and so on, which usually degenerated into everyone complaining about the weather. I'd been to the palace for my binding and my sisters', and it was all huge and confusing beyond imagining, but we didn't have to imagine it. We had two sky views and a sky hold of the palace, which probably made it worse, being used to being able to hold the king's palace in the palms of your two hands—and the sky hold is three hundred years old, and the palace was smaller then."

Sylvi nodded. She had seen it when she visited her cousins; it was made of many different kinds of wood, cut, carved and glued with beautiful precision.

"Maiden I was, but maidenly modesty did not become a colonel of the Lightbearers; and armour and a sword did not become the king's intended. I didn't even have dress armour—useless stuff, and we couldn't afford it. The first speech I gave to your father's court, I had to brace myself against the plinth because my knees kept trying to fold up, and force my hands flat against the desk to stop them trembling."

"Was Hirishy with you?" said Sylvi.

"Yes," said the queen thoughtfully, "she was. It's funny, because she's so little, and when you look round for her she's probably hiding. But when you need—oh, when you don't know what you need!—she'll be right there. She slept with all us maidens the night before the wedding, for example. I don't know of another occasion when a pegasus slept with her human, do you? There should have been a fuss about it, I think, but there wasn't. It was just Hirishy."

Sylvi smiled.

"And now you've been bound to your pegasus," said the queen.

Sylvi heaved a great, happy sigh and felt her spirits lighten. Even the thought of Fthoom couldn't entirely spoil the thought of Ebon. "Yes. I have been bound to my pegasus. Ebon. He's . . . he's . . . um." Again she felt the thrilling, terrifying surge of the lift into the air; the wind-hammer of the huge wings.

"You two bonded yourselves, didn't you? I've never seen anything like it—nor has your father." The queen paused. "Nor has anyone. Your father told me that you can talk to each other—that that was how you knew his name."

So her mother had noticed her slip too. Maybe everyone had. Even before Fthoom. Well, they *could* talk to each other. "Yes."

"There are barely any folk-tales about such a thing. A few fool tales, I think—it's as if it's so driven into us that we can't talk to each other, we can't even make up stories about it. Maybe that your fathers can almost talk to each other is some explanation of what happened to you and Ebon, even though it didn't happen to any of your brothers."

"They tell jokes, Mum, did you know? The pegasi, I mean.

Mother"—Sylvi sat up and forward, kneeling by her mother so she was tall enough to look her directly in the face—"Mother, does it ever seem to you that we don't know the pegasi at all?"

"Yes, darling," said the queen. "I have often thought just that, and wondered what it meant, for all of us, both pegasi and humans."

Sylvi dressed carefully, taking her time about it. She had hated court clothes till her mother had said, "Court clothes are just another form of dress armour. And if it's a bad show, like the combined court and senate, you can sit there designing your breastplate, with all the curlicues you'd never have on working armour. I designed one with a roc swooping down to carry old Barnum away, the wings curling back over my shoulders and a satisfying look of fear on his face, which I think of often." May a roc fly away with Fthoom, Sylvi thought.

She might be better at sitting still today, with the dread of catching Fthoom's eye, like the hawk stooping on the rabbit (or the roc on the senator) as soon as it moves. Her black velvet trousers, she thought, with the wide red ribbons wrapped around the ankles; they made her look taller. Fthoom was both tall and big, and magicians and courtiers often wore high heels when they attended the king. She was sure Fthoom would be wearing high heels today. The custom had begun, Ahathin had told her, centuries ago, when Skagal the Giant had been king.

"They wouldn't have to do it *now*," she said.

"It is a custom," said Ahathin. Ahathin, who was even smaller than the king, never wore high heels.

"And who cares who's taller anyway?" she said.

Ahathin looked at her and permitted himself a smile.

"Don't you *mind* being short?" she blurted.

He spread his small hands and looked at them. "I am a magician, not a princess. A pony costs less to keep than a horse, which means I can buy more books." He paused. "It is not always a bad thing, to be overlooked."

As Fthoom had always overlooked her, she thought, until yesterday. She stared at herself in the mirror and sighed. In trousers rather than a skirt, she thought, it was easier to feel that you *could* run away.

It wasn't going to matter if she missed breakfast; she was now too anxious to eat. She asked one of her new attendants to bring her tea and toast on a tray. Her nurse would have brought her a proper breakfast and hovered over her till she ate it. Her nurse, in theory, was now retired—her last official act was closing Sylvi's curtains yesterday evening—but Sylvi wondered if she would stay in the pleasant little suite in the retired courtiers' wing that now belonged to her, and refrain from reappearing to scold Sylvi on the state of her underclothing. One of the new ladies brought the tea and toast and left it silently. Sylvi tore the toast into scraps to make it look as if she'd eaten something, but drank the tea; her mouth was dry.

She could have had an attendant lady or two accompany her to her father's court; it could have been her first official something-or-other, as a newly almost-grown-up person with a pegasus, who would be expected to be present at council meetings and develop a useful speciality. She thought about an attendant for all of two seconds, as she pulled her tunic straight and smoothed her hair down. In the first place an attendant would make her feel smaller and more insignificant than ever, not less; and in the second place . . . it was too much like copying Fthoom. Her father always had people around him because he was king; but they were councillors and senators and cartographers and colonels and scribes and whoever else was important to what he was doing or trying to do; he didn't have *attendants*. Fthoom had attendants.

She paused in the antechamber outside her father's private receiving room. The inner door was closed, and in the absence of a footman to open the door and bow her through it, she had a momentary reprieve. Her feet took her to one of the low shelves that ran round the room. These shelves bore some of the king's favourite sky holds. The one her feet paused in front of was a new model of the northwest gates of the palace Wall, with a long curve of Wall running away on either side. She and Ebon had flown over it the night before. It doesn't look like that, she thought, with a queer little shock, as if finding out one of her parents or some other authoritative grown-up in a lie that was not quite trifling. The curve of the Wall is more gradual, she said to herself, and the trees inside are set farther back, and the grove is more of an S shape.

She was still staring at the little landscape when the inner door opened silently; but she felt the change of air, and turned. One of the expressionless footmen—an especially tall expressionless footman— one of the footmen who had used to lift her onto her heap of seat-cushions so she could see over the edge of the dining table as recently as two years ago, stood there staring over her head. He was staring quite pointedly and directly over her head, however, so she knew he was waiting to bow her through the door. She went.

Fthoom was already there. So was her father, of course, and Lrrianay. So was Ebon.

Hey, are we in trouble? said Ebon. *How did you sleep last night? This sorry ass' great rolling eyes are making me queasy. I didn't mean to get up so early.*

Sylvi swallowed the laugh that tried to jump out of her; she felt her face wrinkle up to contain it. Ebon was right; Fthoom's eyes did rather roll around. It was all part of what she called to herself his magician act, but she was still afraid of him. She glanced at him out of the corner of her eyes, and her stomach lurched, and she no longer felt like laughing.

"My lady Sylviianel," said her father gravely.

"My lord Corone," she said, and bowed. As she straightened up again she looked at who else stood by her father: those closest were Danacor and his pegasus, Thowara, the king's Speaker, Fazuur, and Lord Cral, who was probably her father's closest friend as well as a member of both the blood and the high council, and Lord Cral's pegasus, Miaia. As she looked, someone a little beyond them moved, as if deliberately to make her notice him, and it was Ahathin.

Fthoom rustled forward. He was wearing some great stiff cape that stuck out round him as if on wires, and round his head was the magicians' spiral, this one silver and set with pale stones over his forehead and rising nearly a double hand's span in the air above him. His footsteps made a curious hollow thunder: his shoes had not only high heels but built-up soles. He looked as tall as Skagal the Giant, but he was not the king.

Sylvi looked behind him. There were half a dozen other magicians in his train, and they all looked unhappy, although they looked unhappy in different ways. Kachakon, who was about the best of them in Sylvi's opinion, looked worried and unhappy; Gornchern, who was almost as big a bully as Fthoom, looked angry and unhappy. Warily she looked again into Fthoom's face; he only looked angry. She remembered something her nurse used to say to her when she was young and sulky: what if your face froze like that? Fthoom's face looked like it had frozen yesterday morning, presumably at the moment when she had said Ebon's name. But this anger looked like the deep, powerful, strategic anger of a general about to engage his enemy. His *enemy?*

The moment stretched. She glanced at her father looking at Fthoom, and at Fthoom looking at her father. Fthoom began to turn rather purple. Majestically, her father indicated that she should sit beside him. At some other time she might have been exhilarated as well as unnerved by the honour; usually the heir sat on one side of the king and the queen on the other, but the queen's chair was empty this morning. Lucky queen, she thought, although she understood the political game being played: to have both the queen and the heir present would grant Fthoom too much power.

Very carefully, for her limbs felt strangely rigid, she settled herself in the great chair. She was accustomed to hoicking herself into chairs that were too tall for her, and had even learnt to do it (relatively) smoothly; but this one made her feel smaller than usual, for it was as wide and deep as it was tall, so she could not lean against the back of it without having her legs sticking straight out in front of her like a baby's. Her feet still hung well clear of the floor. She grasped the clawed forelegs of some vast animal that were its arms, and straightened her spine. She had chosen this tunic because she knew it would sit well across her shoulders as long as she didn't slump. Her father was the king and could stare down Fthoom; her mother was life colonel of the Lightbearers, and had twice killed a taralian single-handed, once in coming to the aid of a fallen comrade. Their daughter could sit up straight. But when one of the footmen knelt in front of her to slide a stool beneath her dangling feet, she wasn't sure but what that made it worse, not better. Silently she took a deep breath. Her father was wearing his very grandest manner; she would not let him down by being too small, too young, and too frightened. Ebon moved with her, and stood at her right shoulder; Ahathin came to stand at her left.

"My lord," said Fthoom, and knelt, somehow making the gesture pointless, almost careless, as one might raise a hand to brush a fly away, even though one was addressing a king. The stiff cape flourished out around him as he knelt and then reformed itself as he stood. When he had regained his feet, he said, looking straight past Sylvi as if she were either a criminal or an inanimate object, "My lord, I believe our country is at a crisis point."

There was a sigh from the courtiers around her father's chair. She hadn't dared count how many people—and pegasi—were present; the room was made to hold about twenty, but there were councillors, senators, barons and magicians crowded along the walls—probably nearer twice that. She saw Lord Kanf lean to whisper something in Granddame Orel's ear; Orel's look of worry deepened.

Fthoom drew himself up even taller—the tip of the spiral quivered—as the king said gently, "Because my daughter can speak to her pegasus, and he to her?"

"It is not the way, that human should speak to pegasus," said Fthoom heavily. As he said it, "the way" became "The Way," although Sylvi had never heard of it. What way?

"I know—much—much—much about the history of human and pegasus. I have read the original treaty; I have felt its aura with my own hands," and here he held them up as if there were some axiom written across his palms for all to read.

Sylvi stared at him. The treaty hung on the wall of the Great Hall next to the mural of the signing, but Sylvi could not read it. The fanciest calligraphy of eight-hundred-year-old scribes was much harder to decipher than the plain handwriting of Viktur. There was glass over it too, glass that was specially treated to prevent any interference, by magical or physical force, and this made it shimmer faintly. Sylvi had studied what it said in her schoolroom copy of the annals; when she looked at the treaty itself, she saw the pale twinkle of eight-hundred-year-old flower petals and long curling twists like vines which were the black lines of the script—and Fralialal, one foreleg raised, ready to step down from the wall, the eight-hundred-year-old ink still wet on the edge of his wing. She didn't like the idea of Fthoom standing close enough to the treaty to read its aura—leaning nearer and nearer yet till his breath misted the glass, his big hands only just clear of its surface—so close that if Fralialal chose that moment to step free of the wall, his wing might brush Fthoom's face.

"I have felt the strength of the centuries like the Wall that wraps around the palace. I have read the chronicles of the magicians who served their rulers from that day to this; I have read the diary of Gandam, who as you know put himself under intolerable duress to learn the pegasus language, that he might write the treaty, and died of the strain."

Everyone knew about Gandam. It was one of the first history lessons all human children learnt. Sylvi had always wondered who had taught Gandam, and if Gandam had tried to teach the human language as well; was there a pegasus shaman who died? She would ask Ebon.

"From that very first meeting—from the first sighting, when the soldiers knelt, for they feared they were in the presence of gods or demons—from that first contact, it is clear: it is not for humans to speak plainly to the pegasi, nor the pegasi to humans: not without the safeguard of a magician's strong magic between the two. The two races are too dissimilar: any attempt to draw them close together can only do injury—the incomprehension between our two peoples is a warning we ignore at our peril. The only other human besides Gandam who has ever become truly fluent in the pegasus language was the magician Boronax, and he too went mad. Since Boronax there have been rules laid down for us, the magicians and Speakers who serve you,

lord, and who have served and will serve all the kings and queens before and after you—rules, so that we may learn enough of the pegasus
language to make that service well and truly, and yet not so much as to
harm ourselves or you; and even so we use magic to protect ourselves
in ways we cannot use to protect you."

Maybe it's only magicians it happens to, thought Sylvi, but she was
beginning to feel a little frightened. She remembered saying to
Ahathin, when he told her of how Speaking was taught, but the pegasi
are so *light*. She thought of Fralialal, and the twinkle of eight-hundred-
year-old flower petals.

She looked away from Fthoom, toward Ebon. *What's going on?* he
said. *I can tell you're not happy, and my father doesn't like what he's hearing
from your father and Fazuur, but I can't pick up any of it.*

*Ebon, do you know about Gandam? The magician who wrote the treaty
and then went mad and died? Did a pegasus die too?*

*What? Gandam died because he was old and sick. I never heard he was
mad. D'you mean did a pegasus get knocked on the head to keep him company
on the Long Road? Ugh. Is that what old Eyeballs there is telling you?*

No. It's just—oh, I can't listen and—I'll tell you later.

Ahathin only just brushed his Speaker sticks—the faint *tock* they
made could only have been heard by Sylvi and Ebon, and possibly the
nearest expressionless footman. Sylvi said, *Oh—I'm being a featherbrain.
Ahathin can tell you.* And she made, for the first time, the gesture asking
a Speaker to translate.

Fthoom droned on: "... the sovereign families of each race are bound
to the sovereign families of the other; king to king, king's child to king's
child: here is the true strength of the treaty, as stone and brick are set
together to make a wall...."

Although not always consort to consort, thought Sylvi. And the
cousins are always a muddle. And ... Dad's dad had the same thing

happen to him; everybody thought their queen was going to marry someone else. I wonder how often that happens. I'll ask Ahathin. She could hear Ahathin murmuring to Ebon, and didn't want to interrupt. *And* what about when the sovereignship goes to another family, like when the Sword left Grinbad and went to Rudolf? And what about someone like Erisika? She grabbed the Sword when the king died because she was nearest and then there wasn't anyone to give it to so she kept it *and* she won the battle and when the king's son grew up and became King Udorin he married her even though she was a cabinet-maker's daughter because, he said, what did he want with a lady when he could have the woman who saved the realm? And she'd borne him three daughters and a son, as fast as she could, she said, because she was old for child-bearing. Sylvi told herself the story with Fthoom's voice booming in her ears, to give herself courage. Erisika would not have been frightened of Fthoom, and she, Sylvi, had Erisika's blood in her veins.

Fthoom was still going on, sentence after ostentatious sentence, about the Alliance. I don't believe any of it, thought Sylvi. It's like he's making it up and—and—

Silently and motionlessly she made an effort, as if she were stepping from under a drift of rainbow fabric and out of a fog of incense. She thought, It's as if he's looking at a tree and calling it a window. And he's trying to make us call it a window too.

"I fear for your daughter," Fthoom intoned. "I fear the damage she and her new friend may do to the body of the living Alliance between our two peoples, by the ephemerality of easy and careless speech, such as is likely between two young creatures, however well-intentioned and innocent—"

The dais and chairs that the king and his court sat on raised them up only enough that, sitting, they were a handsbreadth or two taller than the people standing on the floor before them. But Fthoom was taller than most humans, and he was wearing high-heeled shoes. He had moved closer and closer to the dais as he spoke, where the royal chairs sat so near the edge that Sylvi's footstool was precariously placed; he made as if to lay a hand on Sylvi's shoulder, looming over her, with the arched and coiling tip of his magician's headdress peering down at her like the head of a snake, and the engulfing cape flinging itself wide with the movement of his arm as if to engulf *her*. . . . She flinched and slid away from him, grateful after all for the intimidating size of her chair, ashamed of her own cowardice.

"You may not touch the princess without her leave," said her father softly.

Fthoom stopped as if he'd come to the edge of a cliff. His hand dropped to his side and he moved away, but as he had bent his obeisance to the king into nothing of the kind, he made his moving away from the princess' chair a planned stage of his performance, and not a response to reproof; and he seemed to swell even larger. "I, as Fifth Magician, felt the binding go awry yesterday. I felt the wound in the flesh of our treaty—the new bleeding wound in its side." He managed to invest *I feel* with a magician's power: no ordinary human could *feel* as he did. "I say this is a dangerous thing—as dangerous as any thing could be to our country, founded as it is on the concord between these two most dissimilar and distinct peoples, human and pegasus. And I must ask—indeed I must insist, demand—that the princess Sylviianel and"—he made the *hrrring* noise in his throat that was the human equivalent of the word that meant king or lord in the pegasus language—"*Hrrr* Ebon be kept apart, at least until a council of magicians has studied the matter and decided how, in the best interests of our countries and our peoples, to proceed."

The sigh again, running all round the room. Even the footman who had opened the door and brought her footstool, who still stood near her at the foot of the dais, was a little less expressionless: he looked dismayed. Sylvi risked turning her head and looking at her father: he was cool and regal. His gaze was bent mildly on Fthoom, as if the magician were no more than a small farmer declaring a boundary dispute with his neighbour. She looked at the magicians arrayed behind Fthoom. They looked unhappier than ever, but determined. She wanted to turn her head again, and look at Ahathin, but she did not want to be seen to do it. Ahathin was still murmuring to Ebon.

"My lord," said Fthoom, and again made his unmindful kneeling. He had never once looked at her, not even when he had tried to grasp her shoulder.

"N-no," she said. For a moment she didn't recognise her own voice, nor that she had spoken aloud; her body seemed to be scrambling—not very gracefully—out of her chair without her having directed it to move. She was shaking all over, but she realised that the words she needed to say were already in her mouth, and all she needed to do was let them out. "My lord," she said to her father, and bowed.

"Lady," he said, and inclined his head: permission to speak.

"What if Gandam was . . . was only old and sick? What if Boronax was . . . was mad anyway? When—when they needed a pegasus for Erisika, there weren't any; too many had died in the war, and the only unbound ones were children. Erisika said, What about Dlaiali? His human died trying to save the old king, and we fought side by side that long awful day. And they said no, it is wrong that a queen be bound to a pegasus who was bound before, and to a minor baron, it would *weaken* the Alliance, but she said, I am a cabinet-maker's daughter, and I count Dlaiali a friend, and Udorin spoke for her and she and Dlaiali were bound, and Udorin's reign was long and prosperous and—and happy. Ebon and I are bound. He is—he is my pegasus, and my friend."

Fthoom gave a roar like a taralian, and threw up his hands as if with a gesture he would turn her into a slime-mould or a newt; the expressionless footman, to her amazement, leaped up on the dais and thrust her behind him, knocking her footstool off the stage to crash to the floor. Gornchern and Kachakon grabbed Fthoom's arms, and Gornchern spoke fiercely in his ear; only half a stride behind the footman came Ebon, his ears flat to his head and his nostrils flared and red as a racehorse's. She found herself encircled by one powerful wing, and crushed into his ribs. She staggered—her knees were not at all steady—and a pinfeather got up her nose; she sneezed. Ebon folded the wing down far enough that she could see over it, but he did not loose her, and she could feel that he was trembling too. Ahathin, she saw, was now standing beside the footman.

Several of the courtiers were shouting; one of the magicians was making a kind of keening chant, moving his hands in the air as if creating something, perhaps a better scene than this one which he could replace it with. Danacor was also standing, saying something urgent to another footman, who turned and ran for the door. Lrrianay gave a low rustling neigh. Sylvi felt Ebon twitch; there were several other pegasi present—and they murmured back. Their wings were half roused; in pegasi this was a sign of wariness, watchfulness, alarm. She was sure they were mind-speaking to each other, but she heard no whisper of it.

The shouting died. There was her father, standing in front of Fthoom; Sylvi had not noticed him step down from his chair. She had never seen him look so angry. Even Fthoom subsided a little, and the two magicians who held him dropped their hands.

The king waited till there was perfect silence again. It came quickly, because he made the silence by his expectation of it. Then he reached out one steady hand and plucked the magician's spiral off Fthoom's head. There was a gasp, and Sylvi felt the atmosphere in the hall move and change. She leant against Ebon's side and was glad of the support, and not sorry that the tall footman was still standing near her.

The king dropped the spiral as if it were rubbish; it *tinged* against the stone floor, and the thready chime of it went on too long, as if it had a voice and was protesting its treatment. "There is no defence for raising your hand against the king's daughter; there is no defence for the raising of a hand to *anyone* met in the king's private room.

"You are hereby removed from the council of magicians which serves the king, but you are not relieved of all your duties to us. You will, as quickly and scrupulously as you can, beginning now, search all the histories in all our libraries, till you have found and documented every reference, every notation, every marginal scratch, in all the chronicles, royal, theurgical and laic, of free speech or friendship between human and pegasus; and then you will bring the list to the king—and be you sure that the citations are correct and complete to the last syllable, the last full stop—and the royal council, the magicians' council, the senate and myself shall read it, and consult over it, and decide if there is any foundation in the charge you brought before us today.

"I believe that the one thing that has come out of this—extraordinary—meeting this morning is an awareness that we have, perhaps, been careless about the critical relationship between human and pegasus, careless in our *resignation* that no better bond than what we are accustomed to can exist. The king agrees with you that his daughter and Lrrianay's son suggest a different way. But the king's view, and indeed hope, for that way is diametrically opposed to your own. Bring what the histories can tell us both, and the councils will decide whose concept of the way forward has more merit.

"The king is prepared to consider the possibility that your outburst arose from a dedication to the well-being of our country too profound for restraint; but he is only barely prepared so to consider it. You may leave us. Now."

Fthoom stood for a moment longer, swaying a little, like a tree that has felt the final stroke of the axe and will fall to earth in the next moment. And then he knelt, not carelessly this time, but heavily, and he needed Kachakon's hand under his elbow to regain his feet. Another footman had opened the door, and he turned toward it. As he turned, his eyes swept across Sylvi's face and paused there briefly; as his eyes met hers she saw how much he hated her, and she thought that if he had held her eyes even a moment longer he might have turned her into a slime-mould or a newt after all. Again she was glad for Ebon, and for the not-quite-expressionless footman—for Ahathin—and for her father. But she wished—just for a moment—that she wasn't a king's daughter, even if that meant she would not have met Ebon.

Fthoom stood now as if recalling his strength, and he walked away from them as Fthoom always walked: grandly, arrogantly, although his head looked strangely low and bare rising above the wide unyielding frame of his cloak. He disappeared through the door and was gone.

The king turned to his daughter. Ebon dropped his protecting wing and stepped back; out of the corner of her eye she saw Lrrianay cross behind her father and put his nose to Ebon's cheek, and she wondered what the pegasus king might be saying to his fourth child; but then her father put his hands on her shoulders and her attention was all on him.

"My darling," he said quietly, and sighed. "What a mess we seem to be in. But if you are ever again moved to tell a powerful magician he is a fool, to his face and in public, would you please warn me in advance?"

"Oh—I—"

"No, you did extremely well. I am proud of you—and proud of all those library slips I signed. I admit I had not considered—er—arguing with Fthoom. But—well."

He removed one hand long enough to beckon to the footman who had thrust Sylvi behind him. "I want to think it was an unnecessary gesture, but I thank you for your protection of my daughter."

The previously expressionless footman turned a deep crimson maroon and swallowed hard; footmen are not accustomed to their kings addressing them as "I" and using the familiar form of "you."

"Thank you, lord," he muttered, and Sylvi could guess he was trying to decide whether he should kneel or not. She was very interested; she had always, before today, disliked him, because she thought his expressionlessness meant that he didn't approve of her, or pitied her for being so short that she had still needed, at ten years old, a footman to lift her up and put her on a stack of cushions so she could sit at dinner with her family like a normal person. She couldn't remember having heard his voice before.

Her father could guess the footman's confusion of mind too; he laughed, and the hand he had used to beckon with he now laid on the footman's shoulder. He had to reach up to do it, for the footman was a tall man; again Sylvi was mystified at how her father lost none of his majesty by being short. "Will you fetch us wine?" said the king. The footman's face cleared, and he turned away from them with visible relief.

"Dad," said Sylvi wretchedly, "I'm sorry. I'm *so* sorry. I—of course I didn't mean to make the mistake, but I'm sorry I blurted Ebon's name out like that yesterday."

The king shook his head. "The mistake doesn't matter; it's why you made the mistake that matters—that you and Ebon can talk—really talk—to each other. Just as well, I think, that we knew from the first." He dropped his hand. "It is just you and Ebon, is it not? You hear no one else, and no one else hears you? Lrrianay and Miaia say they cannot hear you."

"Yes," she said, trying not to sound relieved: what if someone overheard them talking about *flying*? "It's just me and Ebon."

He nodded and paused momentarily, then went on more briskly: "You can be spared the rest of this scene; I am not free yet, but you and Ebon may go in a moment. Listen to me first, however, Sylviianel: listen to me carefully."

Her father only *ever* called her by her full name at formal and ritual occasions. "Oh—Dad—my lord—"

"No, child, listen. You needn't my-lord me, and you have done no wrong. But you must listen as closely as you have listened to anything in your life. If *anyone*—anyone at all—but myself, your mother or Danacor asks you what Ebon says to you about *anything*, or if you would ask Ebon a question for them—*tell me at once*. Anyone: your ladies, your practise-yard partner, a senator making conversation at court—even Farley and Garren, although I will have woken them up to the situation before the end of today, and they won't—*anyone*. Do you understand?"

"Ye-es, my lo—Father."

"We'll decide later what use we might put you and your bondmate to—if you agree so to be used. For now you have but yesterday turned twelve, and you are not only the king's child, you are under the king's protection"—for a moment the king in him was very clear indeed, strong and sharp as the blade of the Sword.

There was movement at the edge of her vision. Her father glanced that way. The room was still crowded, but almost everyone was now standing as stiff and still as statues. Kanf had his arms crossed; Orel was biting her lip; Cral was staring at the ceiling. But Danacor was speaking—Sylvi blinked—with a colonel of the Skyclears, the sovereign's heir's own regiment; it was this man's arrival who had caught her and the king's attention. He was wearing his sword and badge over his ordinary clothing, which meant he'd been pulled out of his private hours to attend to the king's heir's summons *immediately*. Sylvi did not want to think about this.

"He hates me," she said, very quietly—so quietly she was not sure her father would hear her. "Fthoom."

"Yes," said her father, as gently as he could. "I'm afraid so. You are a terrible threat to him, my darling, by being what you are—and that was before you spoke out against him in the king's receiving room in front of an audience, and that in spite of the glamour he was using. I almost threw him out for that; it's forbidden, of course, in any court or council; it is typical of the man that he thought he could get away with it."

"He's not a Speaker," she said, still half not understanding and half not wanting to understand.

"He is a member of the Speakers' Guild," said her father. "But he did not wish to be tied to the position of personal Speaker." He smiled without humour. "Fortunately he was too young when the Speaker to the queen's heir was chosen—and too established when it was Danacor's turn. But, my darling, if there were no necessary but incomprehensible pegasi, how constant and immediate to our royal lives would our magicians be? The magicians who maintain the Wall do so in secrecy."

Which would not suit Fthoom at all, thought Sylvi.

The footman returned at that moment with a tray with three goblets and three low bowls on it. He offered it first to his king, who took up one goblet; another footman materialised to lift one of the bowls and hold it for Lrrianay. The second goblet went to Danacor, who now came to stand beside his father and sister, wearing much the same worried expression the king was wearing, only it was much starker on his young face; the second bowl went to Thowara. And then the third goblet came to Sylvi—she peered into it: the water was barely pink with a spoonful of red wine—and another footman took the third bowl to Ebon.

He flattened his nose and took a brief sip for politeness: *Eeeugh*, he said. *What is this stuff?*

Watered wine, said Sylvi. *It's always watered—maybe not this much— except at really big or important parties or occasions or events or things, even for the grown-ups. I like water with loomberry juice better, but you have to make a fuss to get it.*

Ebon took a second sip. *Does not improve on acquaintance. You should drink our*—he made a pegasus noise that sounded like *"fwhfwhfwha"*— *it's much nicer.*

Upon a murmur from the human king, six more footmen had followed the first, bearing many more goblets and a few more bowls, and wine was offered to everyone in the room, human and pegasus. When the footmen came to the magicians, Kachakon and Gornchern, who were still standing next to each other, were first: Kachakon quickly picked up a goblet, Gornchern only after several seconds' delay. The king was binding them together against Fthoom; closing Fthoom out of a new alliance which included the princess and her pegasus. He would have less talking to do after they had drunk together—and one did not refuse a drink offered by the king. She could see Kachakon's hand was shaking, and that Gornchern drank his wine as if it burnt him. She thought, He would have gone with Fthoom, but he remained so that he can tell Fthoom what happened.

The king bent to kiss her forehead. "You may go," he said, speaking so that no one would hear but herself. "I do not deny you your friend, nor do I ask you not to speak to him. But I *do* ask you: try not to behave in any way that anyone looking on could mark as different from the relationship of any bound human and their pegasus—and do not answer any questions. Do you understand?"

No flying, thought Sylvi, and gulped. "Yes, Father."

CHAPTER 7

They went flying anyway, of course. They couldn't help it.

Lrrianay had given Ebon almost exactly the same orders as her father had given Sylvi. *Do you suppose they'd already discussed it?* said Ebon that morning the human king had stripped the magician's spiral from Fthoom's head. They'd just been released from attendance on their fathers; Sylvi took a deep breath as one of the footmen bowed them out of the receiving room, as if it was the first time she'd been able to breathe properly since she went in. Even Ebon was subdued as they walked soberly across the inner garden toward the more open parkland beyond the Outer Great Court. It occurred to neither of them to question that they wanted to stay together. They would be together as much as they could from the moment of their meeting.

No, said Sylvi positively. *They're just both kings. And fathers. And they've been friends for forty years, even if they don't talk much.*

Mmmh, said Ebon. *In forty years what will we be like?*

That was the first time either of them asked that question, although it became a regular one between them—less as a question than as a way of stopping a conversation that had drifted toward an undesirable topic such as the number of taralian sightings, or that the queen was now riding out with a scout troop almost as often as she would have if she weren't both the queen and officially retired. Or the rumours of Fthoom, and of the schism in the Magicians' Guild; or the way Sylvi could recognise the magicians and courtiers who did not like her relationship with Ebon by the way they avoided her. One of her attendant ladies had been replaced; she hadn't asked why, because she thought she knew the answer: Fgeela had had a tight, hard expression any time she saw Sylvi and Ebon together.

Sylvi didn't know when *In forty years what will we be like?* became code for *Can we please stop now?* But she knew it had.

That first time Ebon asked it, they had just come through the Great Arch, and the statue of Queen Amarinda was to their left, surrounded by weeping pear trees, like courtiers. Sylvi had always liked that statue; Amarinda had a hawk on her fist. On their right was the statue of Queen Sisishini, looking proud and elegant, but with her wings watchfully half raised. As she and Ebon came through the arch, Ebon was on Amarinda's side and Sylvi was on Sisishini's. As she turned her head to look at Ebon she seemed to meet Amarinda's eyes. Amarinda looked at her mildly, but Sylvi felt she was saying, *Well? And what will you do with what has been given you?*

As if on some prearranged agreement, they stopped as soon as they were on the far side of the arch, out of sight of the palace so long as they remained close to the park hedgerows. They looked at each other—Sylvi thought Ebon's eyes flicked briefly over her shoulder, perhaps to meet the gaze of Sisishini—long enough for Ebon to slash his wings out and in, and for Sylvi to pick up and put down one foot like a restless horse. But their imaginations failed them. They had still known each other less than twenty-four hours.

Race you to the cherry tree, said Ebon after the silence had begun to grow uncomfortable.

Race you? said Sylvi indignantly. *You'll win!*

I promise not to win by very much, said Ebon.

Sylvi giggled—and set off running, Ebon trotting nonchalantly at her side.

Three years later, they were still using their old idiom: *In forty years, what will we be like?* In ten, twenty, thirty-seven years what would they be like? Fifteen years old was already worlds beyond twelve; it was, in fact, harder and harder to go on not imagining adulthood. When Sylvi turned sixteen she would take her place in the council—and Ahathin would no longer be her tutor.

"And you don't need a Speaker," he said, "although for the purposes of the royal bureaucrats who need someone's name to write in the blank space, I should be honoured to retain the title."

"Oh, but I will need an adviser!" said Sylvi.

"There will be many folk clamouring to be your advisers—" began Ahathin.

"Yes, I know," Sylvi put in hastily. "I would like to appoint you my adviser on advisers."

"Very well, my lady," said Ahathin. When he said "my lady" he was serious. "Subject to your father's agreement, I accept."

Being a grown-up was something that happened to you whether you were ready or not; she and Ebon had each watched three brothers cross that threshold. Farley and Oyry were recently returned from a diplomatic visit to Peshcant, in the hopes of reminding them that if taralians, and possibly worse, were breeding in the wild lands between the two countries, then Peshcant was also at risk. Garren and Poih had been making a tour of the locations in the Kish and the Greentop Mountains that the queen had felt needed regular patrolling; there were now several semipermanent camps where soldiers could be stationed. And Danacor and Thowara had been visiting Lord Gram, who had a daughter who might become the next queen.

("She has a good head on her shoulders," said the present queen, "but she's a terrible shot, and worse with a sword. She'd make a superb quartermaster. But who are we going to marry Farley to? He's the one needs settling.")

Sylvi finally managed to talk to Danacor about how strange everything had become. Danny had less and less time to talk to anyone but messengers and ambassadors and administrators and agents, and occasional aggrieved ordinary subjects dogged enough to stay the course through the lower functionaries and insist on speaking to the king or his heir. But she thought he might understand what it was like for her—he'd been through the ritual of the sovereign's heir, which had to be even huger and scarier than having the most powerful magician in the country hate you.

She'd told Danacor about the Sword *looking* at her, and he'd said, "Unlucky for you. Neither Farley nor Garren got the full treatment. Dad says the Sword has sleepy days and wakeful days. I got a wakeful day, but the heir usually does. So did you, I guess. I don't know why, except you never know with the Sword." He grinned at her. "Maybe it was surprised to see a girl. But you know—the ritual of binding to your pegasus really counts for something. Unlike, say, the Exaltation of Water."

The Exaltation of Water was famous not only in their family but among most of the country. It was supposed to be a rite to honour the water that flowed through the kingdom and to ask that it continue to flow as it did, bright and clear and lavish—the country had many fine rivers, which provided not merely drink and washing but the running of many wheels to produce power—but in practise it had degenerated into a yearly epic water fight. A royal family with three boys in it had set the tone for so many years that by now, when all three boys were theoretically grown, the small-excited-boy version of the rite continued to prevail. Even Danacor forgot himself during the Exaltation of Water. Sylvi, as soon as she'd been old enough, joined in enthusiastically, and had no desire to see it revert to a few discreet sprinkles and some wet feet. This enthusiasm was shared by all the small, medium-sized and large boys who lived not too far from the mouth of the Anuluin, where the ritual was held, who could easily attend year after year, as well as many of their fathers—and mothers, sisters and sweethearts.

"The binding means something to everyone who goes through it. Whatever you think about the treaty and its provisions—"

Sylvi had managed to read a copy of the treaty, with Ahathin's help: the second commander's diary was mostly perfectly comprehensible if oddly spelled, but the treaty, aside from being written in a script that hadn't been used in five hundred years, was in desperately old-fashioned formal language, plus (Ahathin said) Gandam had tried to incorporate some pegasus phrasing. It could have said almost anything and she wouldn't have known.

She had thought, since her binding, that she would like another look at it, now that what it said was a real part of her life too, but she had kept putting off asking. Ahathin would be more than happy to help her, but she felt awkward around Ahathin about anything even remotely to do with Ebon. And she didn't want to read the schoolroom copy again—she wanted to try to read the true one on the wall of the Great Hall. Perhaps she could read the flower petals. But she would be seen to be doing so. And wouldn't that look silly and pretentious in a superfluous princess?

And wouldn't someone report to Fthoom what she was doing—the superfluous princess who had spoken out against him in open court? She didn't want any extra reports on her activities going to Fthoom.

Danacor continued, "You think you know about pegasi; you've grown up with them, you know Lrrianay's face almost as well as you know Dad's. You know what happens. And then it happens to you: your pegasus is a here-and-now, living-and-breathing individual. And it's not just real, it's real in ways you *didn't* know. But, Syl, *nobody's* had a binding like yours."

"Being made heir—that must have changed everything. More."

"Yes. But we knew it was coming." There was a little silence. Danacor was watching her. But she couldn't make herself say the name of her enemy out loud. "Try not to worry about Fthoom," Danacor said at last. "Dad's got him fully occupied and better than half the magicians and scribes working for him report to Dad or me. Enjoy that we don't have to listen to him bullying everyone in council any more."

Sylvi rubbed her face in a gesture she realised she'd learnt from her father. She took her hand down and looked at it as if it didn't belong to her. "But we have to listen to Soronon going on and *on*. Who cares that magician apprenticeships are down three percent this year? Or that rituals requiring magicians are up five percent in Hillshire? Can't he just submit the report and anyone who *wants* to know can read it?"

"Poor old Soronon. Farley calls him Snore-on. But it's not entirely his fault—everyone's really jumpy because of what happened with Fthoom, and Snore-on doesn't want anyone to think the magicians' guild is hiding anything."

"I know everyone's jumpy. Even the Sword is."

Danacor looked startled. "The Sword?"

"Oh, well," said Sylvi. "I mean, it flickers. It flickers blue all along its edge sometimes, so it almost looks like it's moving. Like Fralialal's wings in the mural. Especially when we're in the Great Hall and it's hanging on the wall—it almost looks like it's going to leap out of its stays. If someone's going to jump I'd rather it were Fralialal, but if the Sword would make Snore-on stop talking I'd be all for it."

But Danacor was looking at her oddly.

"What's wrong?" she said. "It does flicker—doesn't it?"

"Yes," said Danacor. "But most people don't see it. Not even the magicians. Usually only Dad and me."

Sylvi stared at him, a prickle of cold moving up her spine.

"Don't spread it around that the Sword's awake, okay?" Danacor said, trying to sound as if he were talking about something of no importance, and failing. "It's . . ." He stood up abruptly and went to look out the window as if he'd heard someone call his name. He turned back again. "It's never good news."

Sylvi attended court and council meetings, took her hours in the practise yard under the master-at-arms, bowed to people in the corridors and tried to accustom herself to the fact that there was almost always someone with her now. At first she had thought that was just a part of having turned twelve, of being bound, of being a princess with her first adult responsibilities. But the tall, expressionless footman who'd thrust her behind him when Fthoom had roared at her—and whose name, she learnt, was Glarfin—had seemingly been assigned specially to her. And there was something familiar about Lady Lucretia, who had replaced the lady who didn't like her relationship with Ebon ... which she remembered the day she saw Lucretia gleefully driving her opponent against the wall in the practise yard. When Lucretia waited on the princess, she was always wearing a dress, and had her hair beautifully done up, but Sylvi had been watching her chasing people around the practise yard for years. She'd never asked her name, although she was very aware of her. She measured her own progress against whether she was ready to ask for Lucretia as a sparring partner. Not yet.

It was the day after she'd seen Lucretia getting the better of a man half again bigger than she was that she took a long, thoughtful look at Glarfin, and said, trying not to sound accusing, "You stand like a soldier."

"I was a soldier, lady," said Glarfin.

"Sylvi," said Sylvi. "If you were a soldier, why are you a footman?"

"I was wounded," said Glarfin. "It took a long time to heal. They did not think I would make a soldier again, but I was not good at being invalided out and doing nothing. So they made me a footman."

"Wounded," said Sylvi. "But you used to lift me onto my cushions."

"You never weighed anything," said Glarfin, "and I healed better than they expected. But I had found I liked being a footman, and sleeping in my own bed every night."

"But you still stand like a soldier ... and ... and you react like a soldier," said Sylvi, remembering the day after her twelfth birthday.

"I was well trained, lady," said Glarfin.

"Sylvi," said Sylvi. "You're not an attendant—you don't follow me around to open doors and bow and make sure everyone knows there's a princess nearby—you're a *guard*."

"I'm sorry, lady," said Glarfin.

"*Sylvi*," said Sylvi.

"I cannot call you Sylvi any more than I can help reacting like a soldier," said Glarfin.

"Like Lucretia is a guard. How many of you are there? Lieutenant," added Sylvi.

"I do not use lieutenant any more," said Glarfin.

"I don't use *lady* except with strangers, or in court," said Sylvi. "How many of you? Not Celia, I think—snakes make her scream. Guridon? Alsa? Orooca? Minni? Pansa?"

Glarfin didn't answer.

"Pansa, I think," said Sylvi. "Her reflexes are really good. Maybe Guridon. Maybe Alsa. Certainly Lucretia. Well, lieutenant?"

Glarfin sighed. "Why would I know, lady?"

"Because you would," said Sylvi. "And also because there must be some kind of rota, and you'd need to know who else is on it."

"Perhaps you could take this up with the king, lady," said Glarfin.

"Perhaps I will take it up with him later, lieutenant," said Sylvi. She thought of her father, raised her chin and stared at Glarfin, trying not to think about how quickly she would develop a crick in her neck. She considered crossing her arms, but her father never crossed his arms, so she didn't.

After a moment Glarfin said, "You are very like your father, lady. Very well. It is the five of us you have named who are the core of it. Danis or Colm is usually at your bedroom door overnight."

She'd been sure she was right, but it was still worse to have it confirmed. And she hadn't known about the night guards. "Is Ebon guarded too?"

"There are extra patrols around the pegasus house, yes," said Glarfin. "But King Lrrianay did not wish Ebon to be singled out, and there are extra patrols all round the palace since the ladon was found in Riss."

Riss was a village two leagues from the Wall. It had been known since Sylvi's grandmother's day that ladons—and probably wyverns—had returned to the wild lands, but sightings of them had continued to be agreeably rare. Sylvi had been in court the morning that the report had come in, and the queen, who had just come in to the horseyards from chasing norindours and heard the news from the stableboy who was walking the messenger's horse, paused only long enough to change her saddle to a fresh horse, reorganise her squad and send a note to her husband what she was doing before she rode straight back out again. The king had sent a note back to the horseyards that the next time the queen reappeared they were to take her saddle *away* from her even if there was a sighting of forty-six rocs over Banesorrow Lake. And Sylvi knew about the extra patrols: she and Ebon had a much harder time going flying because of them.

But what she disliked most was the realisation that she was being protected not only from anyone who might want to ask her inappropriate questions about the pegasi, but from actual physical harm. She had wanted to believe that even Fthoom hadn't meant anything by his gesture that day in the king's receiving room, beyond that he was angry at not getting his own way about something. She could guess that all her guards were wearing a variety of glamour-neutralising and magic-disabling charms. She stared at Glarfin's uniform, but the charms wouldn't be anything you could see.

She wouldn't be able to browbeat Ahathin the way she had just done poor Glarfin; she wondered what Ahathin might tell her if she merely asked him what charms he kept in his pockets that he hadn't done before her twelfth birthday—what guard-magic now followed her—whether a guild spell-maker had been engaged to do the work. If so, he was a good one, because she couldn't feel it plucking at her, nipping at her heels, haunting the shadows at the corners of her eyes.

She could feel herself drooping. She wasn't really like her father.

"I'm sorry . . . Sylvi," said Glarfin with an obvious effort.

"Thanks," said Sylvi, and smiled. "You can call me lady when there's anyone else around, okay?"

She did ask her father why he hadn't told her that she had had a special guard assigned to her. Her father looked at her thoughtfully. "I knew you'd figure it out," he said. "And I hoped that by the time you figured it out, you would be sufficiently accustomed to the situation for the realisation to be less . . . dispiriting."

Sylvi was silent a moment. At last she said, "I wish you'd told me."

"Next time I will," said the king. "But you are older now: next time I would have told you anyway."

"Next time?" said Sylvi.

"There's always a next time," said the king, "unfortunately. You just don't know what it's going to be about."

And she asked Diamon if she could have Lucretia as a sparring partner—occasionally.

"She'll knock you down," said Diamon. "She's not one to pull her punches, our Lucretia."

"I know," said Sylvi. "But she could show me how she did it after, couldn't she?"

She had been assigned to the development of the river network in the Kish Mountains as her special project, and so she knew that potential locations of wheels and dams were dependent as much on their defensibility as on the geography of the rivers: because there were taralians in the Kishes—and, lately, there were also norindours. There had always been a few taralians in the Kishes, which also bordered on the wild lands, but she'd been present when one of the engineers reported to Danacor that it was the worst season for taralians he'd ever seen, and he'd been working in and around the Kishes for forty years, man and boy.

"And now a ladon," he said, and shook his head. Riss lay in the foothills of the Kishes. "Damned snaky basilisk things," he said. "They make taralians look like housecats. Nearly."

Bridges, dams and water-power was interesting work—she didn't mind being good at maths when she could use it for something—and she enjoyed trying to negotiate with water and rock. She didn't like worrying about taralians.

To everyone's surprise but her father's, Sylvi was able to make suggestions about how the village witches might be included in the planning and the defences: several of her best interviewees about village magic were from the Kishes. The engineers blinked at the idea of asking a local wart-charmer and love-potion-mixer for advice about choosing wood and stone most likely to resist interference—a ladon in a temper might well be able to pull a bridge down—but Sylvi would bet on old Marigale or young Vant's knowledge of their own neighbourhoods, perhaps even against a ladon, and said so. Firmly. The engineer, Sasko, who had said that it was the worst year for taralians he'd ever seen, smiled faintly and said, "You are very like your father, lady. I know Marigale. I will ask."

She wondered what the pegasi thought about the increasing numbers of sightings of their old enemies in the human lowlands. It seemed to her that Lrrianay never went home any more—that he was always standing by her father's chair at council now. She didn't talk to Ebon about taralians and norindours and ladons, or about the rivers of the Kish Mountains—or about the flickering Sword. And he didn't tell her what he did when they weren't together—and she didn't ask. She had discovered that talking to Ebon seemed to happen in the busy, front part of her mind. It was hard to keep anything she was excited about from him, but something she didn't want to think about was easy to keep to herself. She assumed it was the same for him—but she didn't ask that either.

She and Ebon ran away from it all as much as they could. They went flying.

It bothered them both, being deliberately disobedient: once, that first night, after their binding, was an adventure; as a habit it felt bad and wrong and sad. But it also felt bad and wrong and sad that they had been forbidden to do something both felt was bred into them, bone and blood: like forbidding a fleethound from running, or a hawk from stooping on its prey. Sylvi didn't know why it should feel urgent or imperative to Ebon—and had begun by assuming, desolately, that it didn't. But by the time she had scraped enough courage together to ask him (braced for him to say that actually it *was* rather a burden, whereupon she would have to refuse ever to go flying with him again), she knew him well enough to know that he was telling her the truth when he said flying with her was a whole other thing—a whole new thing—that he wouldn't miss it for anything.

She would have been happy to leave it there. That she didn't have to stop flying was the next best thing that had ever happened to her— the best thing after Ebon himself—even better than having gone flying in the first place.

But he was still trying to explain something. *I don't see the stuff you see. I—* He paused, whirled his ears, flattened his nose, hunched one wing, and said, *You're going to make me the greatest sculptor who ever lived—or at least the oddest. Because of the stuff you see—because of talking to you about it. No pegasus sees . . . sees the **relationships** of things the way you do. We can build an arch with a keystone—but we could never have built the palace. And that's not about strength, it's about seeing. All those walls leaning on each other, stacked on each other. . . . And those funny little landscape thin-gummies that are all over the palace—they're—they're . . . they're stranger than you are, you humans.*

Of course you don't understand them, said Sylvi. *You don't have to think about it—what things look like from overhead. You can fly. We think about it too much because—because you can fly.*

Okay. But if you flew and we didn't, we wouldn't make the thingummies.

Perhaps the difference began in the way they smiled. Ebon said it wasn't only himself among the pegasi who found that meat-eating humans choosing to bare their teeth when they smiled made you wonder what their real motives were.

I can't help it! said Sylvi. *I smile like that because that's what my mouth does!*

Sylvi had tried to feel the Alliance as she felt the binding between her and Ebon, or as she felt her love for her parents and her brothers—or the slightly anxious deferential respect she felt for Ahathin or Diamon, or even the nameless connection she felt for her land and her people: the sense of something crucially *there,* not only all around her but in her, even when it maddened or frustrated her (as her brothers often did). But she didn't. She never had. It hadn't bothered her before she met Ebon: the pegasi were part of the background of life in the palace, part of the general seethe of motion and urgency—as real, or as unreal, as the crowned pegasus on the royal banner, or the mural of Fralialal.

But the real pegasi flew. Every thought about them began and ended there: they were beautiful and strange—and intimidating—they were the symbol of Balsinland's existence—and they *flew*.

Danacor hadn't agreed with the intimidating, but Garren had. "Oh, minikin, you're so right. Lrrianay isn't so bad, but that gang that comes with him for the big state occasions—Dossaya and Gaaloo and that lot—and Fhwen—especially Fhwen. The way she *looks* at you."

Sylvi asked Ebon later, *What's Fhwen like? She's very . . . imposing.*

Ebon had laughed his snorty laugh. *You mean she looks like a pompous half-wit.*

A beautiful pompous half-wit who can fly, Sylvi amended to herself.

No, she's a sweetie really. It runs in the family: she looks just like her dad, and her daughter looks just like her. They'd all give you their last feather if you were cold.

She'd had to tell Garren. She'd almost made him promise not to mention their conversation to Poih, when she realised he couldn't. And it wasn't the sort of thing you'd ask your Speaker to say for you. Human people often looked different than you found out they were too: Lord Ranruth, for example, one of her father's councillors, whom she'd been terrified of when she was little, because he was always wearing a scowl. The scowl was short-sightedness: as soon as you got close enough, his big round face broke into an enormous smile. If people and pegasi were different from the way they appeared, mightn't their Alliance be different too?

Different how? Why was there no . . . no *feel* to it, this great important thing? Why did it seem no more than a silken representation on a banner, this thing that Balsin had called the foundation upon which their country was built? And that made magicians central to their lives? How could it hearten you when you couldn't *feel* it?

She'd asked her father shortly after the awful morning that had resulted in Fthoom's being given his charge, if Fthoom was likely to do it, well, *honestly*.

The king made a snorting, humming noise rather like a pegasus laugh. "No. But I've assigned him a huge number of helpers, which will, I hope, go some little way toward softening the blow of my stripping him from his position in my court and, at the same time, make it harder for him *not* to do what I asked him to do." The king looked bleakly into the empty air for a moment and added, "The sad thing is that I've meant for years—for most of my working life as king— to set that task. Why aren't there more stories about friendship between human and pegasus? Even your favourite, Erisika, isn't quoted much beyond that they fought together as why she considered Dlaiali a friend. But there has never seemed to be the time and the people to do it."

Sylvi had done a quick intensive study of how to avoid Fthoom. This was made easier by the fact he never went anywhere without an entourage, and by the fact that he had the sort of mind that believed that doing something the same way added to his consequence, so he *always* used the king's library's west portal, which was, of course, the grandest. The drawback was that the king's library was also the country's largest and grandest library, so he rarely went to any others, allotting any searching, fetching and carrying tasks to his staff. Before the day of her binding Sylvi had learnt to like finding books in the library—you often found other interesting ones on the way to the one you were looking for—but since the day after her binding she preferred to send messages, like her father, and have the material she wanted brought to her.

The queen one day told her that Fthoom had submitted an interim report saying that the work was going well—

"Which means he hasn't found anything," Sylvi interrupted. "He's not going to find anything because he is determined not to find anything! He doesn't want there to be any record of real communication—real friendship—between humans and pegasi!"

"No, he doesn't, but if his committee finds such a record, it will be reported," said the queen. "And don't forget Cory and Lrrianay—your and Ebon's relationship may be unprecedented, but friendship between bondmates is not."

"Dad said he's always wanted to appoint a commission to do what Fthoom is doing now, and it had never been the right time," said Sylvi.

"So there," said the queen. "We're getting some use out of Fthoom after all."

Sylvi tried to smile.

"It will be all right, love," said the queen. "Remember that the longer it takes Fthoom to find nothing—because I'm afraid I agree he probably will find nothing; if there were anything, it would be a favourite bedtime story, not to mention the basis of dozens of plays and hundreds of ballads—the longer Fthoom takes to find nothing, the more used our people will have become to seeing you and Ebon together. The more normal and ordinary it will be."

It ought to be very normal and ordinary by now, thought Sylvi a little wryly. She and Ebon were very popular guests at fairs and fêtes and festivals and, with Fthoom on everyone at the palace's minds, she and Ebon were encouraged to accept as many (carefully screened) invitations as they could bear to. Since Ebon reported that his family felt the same way, they accepted a lot of invitations. Ebon was much better about these occasions than she was. *I keep telling you—they aren't my people. It's easier for me.*

They went with an entourage—just like Fthoom, Sylvi thought

without humour. Occasionally, for a very grand one, she wore a frock and rode in a carriage, but usually she and Ahathin and at least one of her attendant guards, plus up to a dozen assorted aides and escorts all travelled on horseback, and Sylvi would pull a princessy tunic over her riding clothes when they arrived. (She also learned to bring a dog-brush on the chance that a hound or two or three would be found to have followed them and could be tidied up to join their company.)

Ebon would meet them there—with at least one pegasus attendant of his own, sometimes two or three; and they would be wearing a few flowers or a few ribbons, or especially vivid examples of the little embroidered bags around their necks that the pegasi often wore. Sylvi's pony grew very fond of Ebon and would neigh when he saw him, and Ebon would whuffle at him in a way Sylvi found very like the way she would make a conversation out of "Good dog, *what* a good dog, there's a good dog, stand still so I can get the knots out, *what* have you been rolling in?"

Pegasi looked almost more like four-legged birds, standing next to horses. Their necks were longer and their bodies shorter in comparison, their ribs tremendously widesprung for lung space and their shoulders broad for wing muscles, but tapering away behind to almost nothing; their bellies tucked up like sighthounds', although there were deep lines of muscle on their hindquarters. Their legs seemed as slender as grass stems, and the place where the head met the neck was so delicate a child's hands could ring it; they moved as if they weighed nothing at all, as if they might float away, even without spreading their wings.

And no human could ever take their eyes off a pegasus' wings.

Sylvi and Ebon's entourage stayed watchfully nearby, but the two of them were the centre of attention. All the little children wanted to pet Ebon—Ebon put up with this with unimpaired good humour, while

Sylvi tried not to let it show that she felt it was an impertinence, which she did. Not from the children, but from their parents—didn't they know you weren't supposed to touch the pegasi? No one ever offered to stroke any pegasus who had come with Ebon—but Ebon was not only the one out in front with the princess Sylviianel, he was also a terrible flirt. He would put his head down till he was eye to eye with a toddler who was smiling and waving at him, and then tap its cheek or its nose with one of his feather-hands. If one too small to walk on its own screamed in excitement and bounced up and down in its parent's arms he would very likely stamp a foot (gently) and go *"eeeeeeeee"* back at it. He even gave pony rides to the littlest. The first few times this happened, all the human eyes within range nearly stood out on stalks—the rule about not riding pegasi apparently *had* filtered comprehensively through the entire population.

Just lift the kid up there and stop fussing, he'd said the first time. *Only the tiniest, mind. Nobody big enough to break a feather if they get too thrilled and start kicking, that's the rule.*

After that their invitations came even more often. The most pressing, Sylvi noticed, seemed to be from towns where the mayors and sheriffs and head councillors—and fête organisers—had children or grandchildren old enough to sit up but too young to kick very hard.

But then something else happened. The older children—and far too many adults, who should have been old enough to know better—began to ask her to ask Ebon questions. Maybe it was the petting and the pony rides. The first time it happened Sylvi was so nonplussed she simply did—the question was so harmless ("What is your favourite colour?"), and the young woman who asked it was obviously trying to make some kind of friendly contact with the pegasus who had been kind to her children—twins, about a year old, and they'd each had a pony ride. And the woman looked so tired—too tired to remember explicit royal prohibitions—and so grateful. And perhaps Ebon's answer ("The colour of the sky at dawn over the mountain called Cuandoia when we're in the lower meadows. It's best in autumn when we're harvesting the *llyri* grass for the winter") sounded a little too mystical, "mystical" not being a word anyone who knew him would apply to Ebon. But the king's ban against questions, Sylvi and her attendants bemusedly realised, had been translated into "no political questions": no questions about kings and treaties and government. And magicians. But the people had decided that Ebon was some kind of oracle.

The king, when this was reported to him, himself looked nonplussed and bemused, and then started to laugh. "Why should I have thought it was a simple, straightforward proscription? No questions. How can that be misinterpreted? Very well. I am willing to leave this to your judgement, Sylvi. Keep Ahathin close to you; he'll intercede if you need him to—if you're the least bit uncertain, let him do so. And come tell me about it afterwards."

"And—Sylvi—try to remember not to wander around with your fingers curled in Ebon's mane, will you? I realise that the—er—pony rides have confused the issue, but I did say something about behaving no differently than any other bound pair. The tradition of no physical contact is as old as the Alliance, and the casualness of your behaviour is disrespectful."

If he were really cross he would call her Sylviianel, but he was right and she knew it. It was mostly comfort, having her hand in Ebon's mane, especially on fête days when everyone was looking at them—and it was so easy to put it back there after she'd lifted a little rider down. But there was showing off in it too. "Yes, my sir," she said.

"Good," he said.

The pegasi weren't that uncommon, even outside the palace—even outside the Wall. It was true that they mostly stayed in their own lands, but—Sylvi knew this from her father, but Ebon had told her the same thing—they felt humans needed to see them, and so they made a point of flying over all parts of the country, even the ones farthest from either the palace or their own territory, and stopping to graze and drink at meadows and streams near towns and villages. They never quite grasped human land ownership, and on at least one memorable occasion during Corone IV's mother's reign, a small group of pegasi had settled down for a mouthful and a nap on a piece of ground so hotly disputed that no human had set foot on it for a decade. But they knew to stay out of standing crops, because they raised crops themselves.

Any fête or festival big or important enough to host a member of the royal or any baronial family would expect the bound pegasus to attend also; as the presence of the pegasi at the palace was known to promote the welfare of the country, the presence of a pegasus or two at a fête was believed to contribute to the success of the occasion, especially if it were an occasion like a spring or a harvest festival. And there were the open court days at the palace, and occasional parades, all of which would feature pegasi. But ordinary people seemed as stirred at the idea of being able really to talk to a pegasus as Sylvi herself was—which she could understand. Perhaps it was this that had transformed itself into a hope that the pegasi could answer private questions the interlocutors couldn't answer themselves merely because such questions weren't about kings and treaties and governments.

Some of the questions weren't difficult. *The little girl with the grey-and-black zurcat in her arms wants to know if it will have any spotted kittens.*

Spotted zurcats always had spotted kittens. *If it's pregnant it will*, replied Ebon with perfect logic.

Sometimes she was surprised at the things the pegasi knew, and wondered why humans hadn't worked harder to learn some of them. Ebon was very good on weather, for example, and certain aspects of farming. *No, he doesn't want to put veer in this year, it's going to be a hard winter, it'll be too cold to grow. Djee would be better—you humans use djee, don't you?—it thinks a good snow layer is warm and comfy.* Maybe the Speakers' Guild wasn't very interested in farming.

She'd learnt early on not to ask him the truly oracular ones. *The big good-looking girl wearing the red scarf wants to know whether she should marry the blacksmith or the baker.*

Tell her she should run away to sea and become a pirate.

The tall man with the scar on his cheek wants to know if the gods live on the moon.

I'll look around the next time I'm there.

He'll think you can fly to the moon!

He already thinks we can.

Which was probably true. But what did you *do* with questions like that? She'd come storming—or rather, she'd walked perfectly calmly, but inside she was storming—from a council meeting where Senator Barnum had wished to discuss her *comportment*—hers and Ebon's—at their public appearances, and how they needed to appear sensible and mature. "Mature!" she'd burst out later to Ebon. *Mature! And Dad and Ahathin just say that that fat tick Barnum is a citizen too and he's not the only—the only pompous pudding-head we need to remember will be doing his best to find fault!*

Ebon had unfolded and refolded a wing—*whoosh snap*—and shook his head violently two or three times, which was the nearest a pegasus ever came to angry: *Yes. I've already had the pitch from Dad, and Gaaloo. I promise not to trample any small children or to sneeze in anyone's food. If they think we're so dangerous to concord and prosperity, why do they want us to go?*

After a little silence Sylvi said, *You know why.* Ebon made a half whuffle, half hum, that she knew from the rituals; it meant "our fate is our fate." But he added, *That's always been a dumb line. It just means shut up and don't make trouble. Sometimes you have to make trouble.* He paused. *But this isn't one of those times. Okay.* He sighed a vast gusty sigh—the *vast* gusty sigh that only a pegasus can sigh—and Sylvi rubbed his mane. And he tried to repress himself—not always successfully— and Sylvi tried to be careful what she repeated back to their human audience.

They saw magicians in the crowds sometimes—never among the people immediately around them wanting answers to their questions— but rather more often at the outskirts of those people than seemed to Sylvi at all reasonable. These were not the village witches, the little wizards, whom they often saw, and who could be expected to come to their local fêtes, but the big magicians, the members of the guilds, who didn't come to little country fêtes. Except that they did. Sylvi tried to tell herself that before Ebon she hadn't gone to many country fêtes herself, and maybe guild magicians came to more of them than she realised. But she didn't believe it.

She rarely recognised any of them, but the magicians' robes were easy to spot—and the way ordinary people tended to leave space around them. What were they watching for? What were they seeing?

What were they reporting back to Fthoom?

She thought of asking Ahathin about the number of guild magicians she saw, about why there were so many ... but couldn't think how to do so without betraying the intensity of her dislike and distrust of magic and magicians. What had still been half a joke on her twelfth birthday was, since the morning after her twelfth birthday, no joke at all. She often thought, bleakly, that all the things she most wanted to ask Ahathin because he was a magician, she could not, because he was a magician.

Ahathin himself she was glad to have beside her. Ahathin's presence—and, she had to admit, Glarfin's or Colm's or Lucretia's—made her feel braver; as her Speaker, Ahathin could whisper in her ear, even when he was saying things like "you need not answer that question" or "tell him that is a question for a judge." And most of the questions were innocuous enough—she also learnt to wait, fractionally, for any stir or startle from her entourage. She asked the questions about the pegasi themselves, like how many of them there were (*Yikes. I haven't a clue. Lots. Not as many as you humans, though*), or where they lived (*See the mountains that start behind the far Wall of the king's palace? If you fly—er—if you walked, uh, up and down, over those mountains, Rhiandomeer begins on the other side*) and if their king lived in a huge grand beautiful palace too (*Yuck! No way. Who wants to be trapped in the same old stiff up-and-down walled-in thing all the time, where the sun can only come through the same holes?*).

Sylvi had some trouble translating that one. *Okay, it's not trampling children,* she'd said crossly to Ebon, *but can't you think of a little nicer way of putting it? Your shfeeahs stay in the same place, don't they?*

Sort of, said Ebon. *But most of the walls come off or roll up or something. They're not made of stones as big as our bodies.*

And he answered all the weather-and-crops questions. He was not good about livestock questions: *If I knew what would make your wethers grow faster, I wouldn't tell you. Their lives are short enough before they go to the—the what-you-call-'em—the killer. Let them have their few months in peace.* He also knew some odd herbal remedies for things that she

135

didn't dare pass on because neither of them had any idea whether they'd work for humans or not—although she told her mother, whose best friend was a healer ("the best friend a soldier can have," said the queen). The queen shook her head. "We'll have to ask your father."

"Careful," said the king.

"Cory—" began the queen. "*Dad!*" said Sylvi at the same time.

"Sylvi first, I think," said the king. "Persuade me this is a worthwhile exception—*another* worthwhile exception—to the rule. You'll be sixteen soon enough, when everything will change, and you'll have more—"

"Of course it is!" interrupted Sylvi. "A good exception. A good exception *now*. This is the sort of thing that could make everyone *happy* that Ebon and I can talk to each other, if it turns out there's something we can use!"

"I agree," said the king. "And I have no intention of forbidding it. You still need to realise what you're doing."

He was looking at her in a way that reminded her of Ahathin waiting for her to answer her own question. She smiled involuntarily, quickly and mirthlessly. "And perhaps we'll be grateful for a few extra friends when I turn sixteen and the Speakers' Guild tries to block Ebon and me doing any Speaker work."

"Perhaps," said the king. "But the Speakers' Guild won't block you, if that's what you decide you—and Ebon—want to do."

She looked at her father, and remembered the hatred in Fthoom's glittering eyes.

But she had her permission, and one of the remedies got the queen's friend, whose name was Nirakla, very excited. She begged for the opportunity to speak to any of the healer-shamans who were willing to speak to her, and Minial translated.

"You've thrown a rock in a pond," said the king.

"It's a good rock," Sylvi answered. "Why hasn't anyone thrown it before now?"

"Good question," said the king. "But the shamans come here very little, and those who do come stay in their annex."

I wonder what Fthoom has heard about it, she thought, but she didn't say it aloud.

Sylvi couldn't help picking at the thought of Fthoom, scratching at it like a wound that won't heal, partly because you keep scratching at it.

"Darling," said the queen, "if you don't stop fretting, I'll ask your father to give you another project. You know Hester and Damha's binding went just as it was supposed to."

"*Did it?*"

"Do you mean we didn't tell you about the ultimatum we had from Fthoom about it? Darling, don't be silly."

Kachakon had been the Fifth Magician, and Sylvi had thought he looked uneasy, and the other magicians furtive. Hester and Damha couldn't talk to each other—but it had been a blow to Sylvi when she read relief in Hester's face after the ceremony. She might just have been relieved to have the ceremony over, but Sylvi didn't think so. She didn't think so even more when she and Ebon went up to give the new pair their congratulations, and Hester looked worried as soon as she saw Sylvi coming toward her. What, do you think it's catching? Sylvi thought irritably. But she said the correct words, and Hester said the correct words back, and then Sylvi and Ebon went away. *Did Damha say anything to you?* said Sylvi. *After you said congratulations, or whatever you say.*

Are you kidding? She was too busy being overcome. We're famous, you know.

What? Oh, leave me alone.

Ebon looked at her sidelong. *No, I don't like it either.*

But at that moment Lady Denovol came up to them and begged the favour of being allowed to present her son to them. The son was about Sylvi's age, and looked even more miserable at being faced with Sylvi and Ebon than Hester had, and his pegasus seemed to be trying to hide behind Lady Denovol's. The older pegasus stepped smartly aside and swung her head round in a gesture that needed no translation: *move it, you.* Sylvi used this as an excuse not to reply as she made her bow to the son and he bowed back. She didn't catch his name.

CHAPTER 8

The next day was a beautiful one, and she and Ebon were together.
Ebon was at the palace more than any other pegasi but Lrrianay and
Thowara, but he had to go home sometimes, and he'd been gone
nearly a fortnight before returning three days ago in time for Hester
and Damha's binding. They had had lessons to do in the morning,
but it was afternoon now. Sylvi half sat, half lay with her head on
Ebon's shoulder and the tip of his half-open wing negligently across
her lap. There was grass under them, and trees nearby if the sun grew
too warm, or more wing if Sylvi felt chilly, and the smell of flowers
drifted over them. This had used to be enough—especially after they
had been separated—especially when their next public appearance
wasn't till the day after tomorrow—especially when they'd gone flying
two nights in a row. This had used to be enough, before they'd been
to too many fêtes, and been asked too many questions that only a real
oracle could answer. Before their cousins had found them intimidating because they were famous. Before it was that much sooner till
Fthoom presented his findings.

But she and Ebon had had almost four years of flying together—
glorious, intoxicating flying. How they had remained undiscovered

Sylvi had no idea, only that it was one more thing she would not think about. Ebon could do almost anything with her lying along his back that he could without her, and while his family teased him about the muscles he had developed—his nickname was *Whyhrihriha*, which meant Stone-Carrier—and occasionally one of his brothers or his sister called him a cart-horse, so far as either he or Sylvi could tell, no one thought any more about it.

The sun was warm and she felt sleepy. She had often felt sleepy in the last four years. She and Ebon mostly managed to go flying at least one night a week when Ebon was at the palace; they made it more often when they could. But the demands on even the fourth children of kings can be considerable, and she and Ebon had become very popular. Two nights in a row was very unusual.

One week about six months after their binding, when she and Ebon had slipped off three times, and gone farther than they had before because Ebon's wings were suddenly growing stronger, she fell asleep so much that Ahathin, abetted by Lucretia, Guridon and Glarfin, decided not unreasonably that she must be ill. (Lucretia had said, "If you were a little older I'd say you were sneaking out at night to meet your lover." Sylvi held her breath: if they started keeping watch on her. . . . "But you don't have quite the dazzled, fatuous look of first love." Lucretia grinned. "And I haven't heard of any footpages—or any of the young stablefolk—falling asleep a lot either.") Sylvi only avoided the doctor's prescription of bed for a week by agreeing to take *the most ghastly, horrible, revolting tonic* as she described it to Ebon. *Nirakla made it! I thought she was my friend!*

She yawned. *They're going to start threatening me with that unspeakable tonic again*, she said. *I can see it in Mum's eye.*

Ebon rubbed her hair with his feather-hand: mane-rubbing among pegasi was considered comforting. *I'm sorry*, he said. *Day naps aren't so unusual with us, any more than night flying is. My problem is trying to explain where I go on all these dark expeditions. Pegasi did not sleep alone: Ebon's absence would be noted every time, and would need explanation every time.*

*It's a good thing our parents **don't** talk to each other,* said Sylvi, *or somebody would have noticed I'm sleepy the days after you've been flying at night.*

Eah, said Ebon. *Dad's pretty okay about it. But Gaaloo and Striaha and Dossaya and . . . well, several of the rest not only notice but have to talk about it.*

But you had that brilliant idea, she said, shifting her position so she could rub his mane.

It was brilliant, wasn't it? said Ebon, not quite smugly. *There started off what looked like a big commotion about it, did I tell you? Because we don't do human stuff in the Caves. But my master spoke up for my idea, saying that the land wasn't human, that we used to live on it ourselves a long time ago before the taralians came, and then Dad started wittering about how this could strengthen the Alliance and . . . well, the rest of 'em listened,* he finished. Sylvi wondered what he wasn't telling her, but she wouldn't ask; both of them knew that each protected the other from some of the fuss their friendship produced among the grown-ups. He hurried on: *And I'm making sketches, which is pretty unusual. You don't get to make your own sketches till you've been an apprentice forever.*

Sylvi tried not to be jealous. Ahathin and her father were pleased with Sylvi's work on rivers, dams and bridges, but it wasn't like it had been her own idea. Ebon wanted to be a sculptor more than anything—he'd never admitted it, but Sylvi was sure that the reason he'd tried to escape being bound was that he knew it would interfere with his chances at being accepted for apprenticeship. But Ebon had told his father after his—his and Sylvi's—third night flight that he wanted to work toward doing something about the landscape of the palace grounds at night. *My master did say I had to focus. But he didn't tell me what I had to focus on. The funny thing is that no one has done this before.*

Not so funny maybe, said Sylvi. *How many sculptors are bound to humans? And it's only you bound pegasi who ever come to the palace much. It's like Nirakla talking to your shamans. Funny. Not funny.*

Hmmmh. I think my master has only been here when your dad was crowned.

Well then. Sylvi wasn't sure what exactly Ebon wanted to do with the night landscape they flew over, only that, if he succeeded in becoming a sculptor, he would some day begin to carve some of it into a piece of wall somewhere in the Caves; and, later still, his apprentices would help him.

He'd shown her some of his drawings and she'd had to squint to see the tiny pale lines. Pegasi drew with their feather-hands, which were only just strong enough to hold a light pen. Pegasi pens were noro reeds, which were too light and fragile for humans; one stab with a human hand and the tip broke off. She'd known not to comment on how faint the pen-strokes were, but Ebon mentioned it himself, bending one wing forward to lift her hands on its leading edge, and then stroking them with his other feather-hand. This tickled. *You've said so many times how much humans envy us flying,* he said. *We envy you the strength of your hands . . . more than I can tell you.*

But your drawings are so beautiful, she said, truthfully. *They shimmer.*

They may, he said sadly. *But I would give anything to be able to make big black marks. Like you do just writing your name.*

Ebon saw her making her big black marks because sometimes they studied together, she with her books and notebooks and diagrams of dams, he making a curious almost humming noise which was saying over his lessons. Sometimes he did apprentice work with his hands, which was usually accompanied by a different, fainter but more complex sort of humming. Ahathin presided over these occasions—it had been Ahathin's idea to allow them to work together: "I do not see that it is much different from Lrrianay attending court with your father, or Thowara accompanying Danacor on convoy or survey," he said. Ahathin did not tell them about his conversation with either king, but permission had been granted.

The pegasi had very little written language—*We've got some really old scrolls and some of the stuff in the Caves is more like letters than like pictures*—but a great deal of history, tale and song was passed on orally. Every pegasus child memorised the treaty, for example. *Old Gundam never used one word when three would do. Hunh.* They also had to memorise certain scenes in the Caves—*When they're doing stuff for record, everything means something. You can pretty much read what a sovereign's reign has been like by the plaits in their mane and what they've got round their neck and the way whoever's near them is standing. If there's a rearing shaman, uh-oh.*

And sometimes he brought a tiny piece of wood or stone that he spent hours polishing, which (he said) was a sculptor technique: *One of the nicknames for sculptor apprentices is Shiner. Or Polishhead.*

These tiny scraps of matter looked—and felt—like jewels by the time he was finished with them; even when she watched him using a variety of bits of cloth (both the cloths and the fragments he used them on he carried in a little bag around his neck), it had only looked like someone polishing something: a pegasus someone, lying down, balancing the shining atom between his folded-under knees, polishing away with a series of cloths in his feather-hands, his pinions trailing (carefully) through the grass or on the floor under his belly. Until he decided it was finished, and let her look at it.

She was lying wrong: whatever was in the little bag around Ebon's neck at present was digging into her back. She sat up to shift it.

Sorry, he said. *But—oh. I wanted to show you.* He bowed his head, and rubbed the ribbon that held the bag off over his head with his feather-hands, and then carefully spilled its contents on the ground. There were several of what Sylvi recognised as the polishing cloths—and one tiny gleaming stone. He picked this up. *This one turned out really well. It almost . . . um. It's pretty good for an apprentice. I wanted you to see it.*

He held it out to her and she accepted it on her palm. It was darkest red, almost black, and the pinprick of its centre seemed to glow like the heart of a fire. *This is some kind of—magic,* she said. It was a soft sort of magic though, she thought. Soft not itchy.

Ebon frowned—ears half back, head turned slightly to one side—*I don't think so. Well . . . there are words you say while you're doing it. Different words for different cloths.* He picked one up, and then another one, and handed them to her, and Sylvi could feel—faintly, subtly—that the two cloths had different textures. *It's a . . . it's a . . . I don't know how to explain it. It's a little like learning stories or histories. You kind of go to a different place in your head. You go to a different different place from the lesson-learning different place to say the words while you're polishing. And it was a shaman—several shamans—who made up the words originally, but that was thousands of years ago. Some of the words don't exist any more, except in these chants.*

Sylvi, fascinated, said, *Could you tell me one of the chants?*

Ebon looked surprised (drawing back of head, raising nose, slight rustle of feathers at the shoulders). *Probably. We'll have to stand up.*

Usually we do it like this, and he put his feather-hands to her temples. *This is the first one, the simplest one. These words are all normal.* And then he began to make one of the funny almost-humming noises again, and Sylvi heard the words he was saying in her mind, as she usually heard Ebon, but they sounded strangely far away and slightly echoing, as if she were listening to her father addressing an audience in the Outer Court and she was at the back, next to the Inner Great Court wall.

And as she thought that, another picture began to cohere as if it were being built by the clean shining words Ebon was saying, and she closed her eyes to see it better. It bloomed from the blackness as if she had been walking in a dark place and had now stepped into light. Candlelight, firelight, light flickering off the glossy black flank of the pegasus standing just in front of her, polishing, polishing, polishing some curve—some complex series of curves—on the wall in front of him; the flame-light made those curves flicker with movement, with life: a human woman stood, holding a sword. . . .

With the sky we make this thing
With the earth we make this thing
With the fire we make this thing
With the water we make this thing
Here is sky
Here is earth
Here is fire
Here is water
Here is our making
Here
Here
Here
Here

He stopped humming. He took his hands away from her temples, but patted her face as he did so. *Syl?*

Oh, she said. *Oh, I . . . oh . . .*

Golden summer sunrise and blue winter sunset, he said, *don't tell me you had a vision.*

Well . . . yes. I think so. Perhaps she had imagined it; she knew that this was to do with Ebon's desire to be a sculptor, and the pegasus Caves—it was an obvious thing for her to imagine. But the black pegasus was bigger even than Ebon—and a human woman with a sword? She suddenly and powerfully did not want to tell him what she had seen.

Golden, he said wonderingly. *Gold and blue. Well. That doesn't happen all that often. It happened to me. It's a good omen if you want to be a sculptor. Or a shaman. Never knew it ever happened to humans. . . . But then I don't suppose there've been a lot of humans who've tried. Maybe you should be a sculptor too.*

Or a shaman, she thought involuntarily. She noticed he didn't ask her what she'd seen, nor tell her what he had seen. *I'm hungry,* she said abruptly. *Let's go find something to eat.*

Yes, let's, said Ebon, who was always hungry. Usually they went to the pegasus annex because Sylvi liked to pretend that the palace's best fruit was always given to the pegasi—and because she'd discovered she loved the open feeling of the rooms with only three walls. The windbreak of trees kept the worst of the weather out, and in winter she tended to stay on the lee side of Ebon, pressed up against his side or tucked under a wing. Sylvi had also developed a taste for pegasus bread, which had a lighter, airier texture than dense human bread kneaded by strong human hands.

The first time he had offered to take her there, she had hesitated. *Won't they—the others—mind?*

You and your minds, said Ebon. *As long as you don't eat all the grapes or pull anyone's tail they won't mind.* Grapes were very popular; the pegasi could not grow them.

Ebon wrapped the little black-red stone up again, tucked it into its bag, flipped the ribbon over his nose with a feather hand and tossed his head in an obviously habitual gesture so the little bag settled round

his neck again. As they walked down the corridor Ebon said, apparently as eager to change the subject as she was, *We're going out again tonight, aren't we? You can stay awake tomorrow?* Even between themselves
they rarely said "flying." *The weather's going to change; this is our last
chance.*

Yes, said Sylvi. *There's that stupid banquet—you have to come too, don't
you?—for the Echon of Swarl, because Dad wants to use some of his soldiers.
They're good at climbing trees. Swarl is all forest. But we can go straight from
there and no one will notice. I'll wear my flying stuff under my dress.*

They did. But Sylvi, choosing in the dark, had not been lucky with
the tree she had left her banqueting clothes in, and she had green
smudges and bird slime to explain the next morning. But no one had
been very surprised that she had crept outdoors after the banquet.
Lucretia said, "Get one of the Echon's folk to show you how to climb
trees in daylight next time, okay?"

But she couldn't think about unimportant things like her court
clothes when she was focussed on flying. They had explored the countryside in every direction, up to almost half a night's flight away, and
there had been one or two terrifying near-dawn returns. Sylvi had
learnt the rota and schedule of the Wall guards at the very first, so that
they could fly over a bit whose sentries were at the other end of their
span; the same pegasus seen flying regularly over the Wall at night
would be taken note of, and Ebon was black, which was an unusual
colour in pegasi, and therefore would be recognised too easily as himself. That he was known to be flying at night for a project he was doing
as part of his apprenticeship was some help, but they wished to take
no more chances than they had to.

Spring and autumn were the best seasons for their expeditions,
when the nights were longer than they were in the summer, and
warmer than in winter. *Summer used to be my favourite season,* Sylvi had

said to Ebon as they snatched a quick midsummer's flight between late and early twilight, in the first year of their friendship. *I used to love the long days and short nights.*

Even Ebon could not fly very far carrying a passenger; they set down once, twice, maybe three times in a long night's flying, to let him rest and stretch his wings: Sylvi had learnt where to rub and dig in her thumbs along his shoulders, especially the thick heavy muscles that were the beginning of his wings. *Mmmmmmh,* Ebon would say. *Harder.*

They discovered which villages had nervous dogs that barked at everything, and which villages had easier-natured dogs who, once they'd met you and sniffed you thoroughly, never bothered you again, except perhaps for petting. (Sylvi began to seek out dogs at the fêtes they went to, as a form of pre-emptive security—and she watched any accompanying palace dogs for their reactions to those they met.) They discovered which meadows were nice and flat for landing and taking off, and which had nasty hollows and hummocks that didn't show up properly when there was only moonlight to steer by—and which, once or twice, had short-tempered bulls in them.

There were a few very alarming occasions when it had seemed that Ebon wasn't going to be able to get aloft again with Sylvi's weight on him. This had never quite happened, but the worst night was when he'd had to gallop down a road through a village. Not only did this make them conspicuous to any insomniac who might choose to look out a window at that moment or any light sleeper who might be awakened by an odd, not-quite-horse-sounding half thud, half patter of galloping hooves—and while Sylvi wore black clothing, she was still far too visible—and even with Ebon's wings spread, the pounding was very hard on his legs as well as making too much noise. It was, furthermore, a bad road, with the worst of the ruts carelessly half filled with rocks and rubble. Ebon took no harm of it, but he did admit to being a little stiff the next day. About six months later they were invited to a fair at that village and Sylvi arranged for it to be pointed out that the road in and out of their village was in sad repair which should be remedied.

What had made them both extremely stiff—although Sylvi more than Ebon—for much of the first six or eight months of their adventures was learning to *land*. Sylvi's mother had become seriously worried that her daughter had developed a strange bone or muscle disease which would explain why a twelve-year-old creaked out of bed some mornings like a little old lady. As an emergency measure Sylvi had considered deliberately falling off her pony, but in the first place, on top of the bruises she had already from (obligatory) falling off Ebon she could not face this with equanimity; also she guessed it might worry her mother more rather than less. She put up with being cross-examined by Nirakla nearly weekly, and prodded by a series of healers. . . . She balked at being prodded by magician-healers, but allowed Minial to touch her; Minial, like Nirakla, could find nothing wrong—beyond the bruises.

"Child, what are you *doing* to yourself?" said the queen. "If Lucretia—"

"It's *not* Lucretia! Diamon says I'm not ready for Lucretia yet!"

"Or Diamon—"

"Diamon's on *my* side! He's not going to get me in trouble with *you!*"

The queen laughed. "Very well. But what *is* happening?" She ran her finger lightly along Sylvi's purple forearm, and Sylvi bravely managed not to wince. Her bruises weren't usually so conspicuous, but there'd been a lamentably ill-placed rock two nights ago in one of those lumpy fields. At least there hadn't been a bull. "It's true that physical stoicism

149

is a very useful attribute in a soldier, but it's not something I recommend practising in advance. The world will take care of it. And you're not going to be a soldier anyway; you're going to be a negotiator like your dad."

There was a silence. Sylvi knew this silence; the queen wasn't going to go away till she got an answer she found acceptable. Sylvi should have been prepared for this moment, but she wasn't. Then she thought of something Ebon had said, the night of their binding. It wasn't a very good excuse, but it was better than blaming anyone at the practise yards—or telling the truth. And it would help provide an excuse for the concomitant sleepiness. "I—I've been sleepwalking," she said. "Since—since Fthoom."

The queen let out a long sigh. If she hadn't been a colonel of the Lightbearers, thought Sylvi, she'd've drooped. "Oh, my dear. Well—"

Sylvi said hastily, "I never go far. I bump into something and wake up. But sometimes I bump kind of hard. And sometimes it's hard to get back to sleep again."

The queen looked at her and Sylvi stared back, trying to look like the king staring down a miscreant. The queen began to look a little amused. "And you'll flatly refuse to agree to someone sleeping in your room with you, won't you?"

"Yes," said Sylvi in her kingliest manner.

"Well, I don't blame you," said the queen. "I'd refuse too. And there's always someone outside your door—you know that, yes? Your father said you weren't best pleased not to have been told. Very well. But if this goes on much longer we'll have to think again. I could ask Nirakla if she has anything for sleepwalking."

She didn't, but she gave me some liniment that your shaman-healer gave her the recipe of—she said it was better than the stuff she'd always used before— you don't have to rub so much. I thought that was pretty funny.

It's for flying bruises, said Ebon. *The first few years you're flying you go through the stuff by the lakeful. Maybe some of us more than others. I was maybe one of the mores.*

She and Ebon finally began getting this sorted out just before the queen made a real fuss, and the danger passed. The experience had a further interesting effect however. Sylvi had always had to fight for her time at the practise yards; everyone kept telling her to wait till she'd grown a little—even the queen, who had introduced her there in the first place. She was thirteen when she was finally allowed her first mounted lessons—and Diamon said that she fell off better than any student he'd ever had. "Anyone would think you'd been riding with the horse-dancers," he said.

Everything was an adventure, at night, when you were where you shouldn't be, even if it was somewhere you could go perfectly well in daylight, and it was then only ordinary. The scrumped apples (they only stole a few) tasted better than the ones from the bowl in your study; the wind in your ears sang secrets it never whispered under the sun; even the dogs that came out wagging their tails were an adventure at night, and it wasn't only because you were glad they weren't barking at you. Everything was an adventure, at least when you could stop yourself thinking that you were defying your father's ban.

Everything was an adventure at night, but not every adventure was a good one. There were the bulls, and the big snarling dogs, and once they saw a magician walking swiftly down a little side street and knocking on a door before he slipped inside. Sylvi had just time to wonder what a magician in his official robes was doing in a tiny country alley before panic swamped her thoughts and she and Ebon spun round and headed for the deepest dark they could find—which happened to be a barn, luckily dog-free; a few of the cows glanced at them, and returned to cud-chewing.

But the worst was the night that Ebon, gliding for a landing, suddenly changed his mind, lurched frantically in the air, nearly unseating Sylvi—**Don't** *fall off* she heard—and clawed his way upward again while Sylvi clung on, slithering with every wingbeat and miserably aware that if he failed to get aloft again it would be her fault—but he banked clumsily as soon as they were clear of the ground and flew away faster than they'd ever gone. He didn't stop till they were back over the Wall, and then he came down like a stone dropping, and when he fell on landing this time—neither of them had fallen on landing in months—it was a second or two before he got up again. Long enough for Sylvi to have taken a first running step toward him, shouting *Ebon!* in her mind and breathing his name aloud, as if mind-speech was not enough in this extremity.

But he was on his feet before she reached him. *Sorry,* he said, and that was all.

Ebon—?

After a long pause, he said, *Norindour. I smelled it.*

Norindour!

Norindour—so close to the palace. Just outside the Wall. Norindours didn't come this far from the wild lands. Taralians sometimes. Never norindours.

You're sure? I—I wouldn't know.

We're taught norindour, although they don't like our mountains—oh, you don't teach smells, do you? We're taught taralian, and ornbear, and norindour— well, and human—and, he went on desperately, *also stuff like if a drak bush is fruiting or not—it all goes on underground so you can't see it, you have to know what it smells like because they're poisonous if they're fruiting, and they can do it any season although sometimes they don't for years. . . .*

Sylvi could hear how frightened he was—frightened and exhausted—so she didn't say anything, but put her arms round his neck, and after he'd run through a little more pegasus botany he fell silent. At last he sighed and said again, *Sorry. I'm so tired I can't.* . . . *We'll have to walk the rest of the way.*

Sylvi had not had a chance to think about how close inside the Wall they had come down; it would be a long walk, and not without its own danger of discovery. But they did it, Sylvi guiding them, both because she knew the grounds better, but also because Ebon stumbled along with his head down, barely noticing anything. She took him right up to the pegasus annex of the palace—as close as she dared. There was a faint flicker of candlelight through the trees, and she thought she could see a smudge of pegasus silhouette. She stopped.

When she stopped Ebon stopped too, and raised his head and looked around. *Oh—Syl, go away. We can see better in the dark than you can.*

Yes, it was an honour to do you a service, she replied.

When he gave a little humming snort of laughter she felt better. *Thank you,* he said. *Thank you, beautiful human of the bright wings and the matchless sagacity—* He stopped abruptly. *I'll have to tell my dad, you know.*

Tell him anything you need to. Do you want me to say anything?

No. They know I go out flying at night. I just have to figure out what I was doing out there over . . . over . . .

Stonyvale, she said.

Oh, but—rain and hail—do I know it's Stonyvale?

She thought a moment. *Yes—we were there for a fête. The little girl with a spotted zurcat.*

Okay. Good. Thanks. But he didn't immediately move away, and she could feel the tension in him. She put one hand to his face and rubbed his mane with the other, and he touched her temples with his feather-hands, and they parted.

The next morning when she tried to get out of bed she made a little squeaking noise and fell back on her pillows.

"Lady?" said the attendant who had just set the tea tray beside Sylvi's bed.

Sylvi lay motionless and then said calmly, "It's only a bad dream. I'll get up in a moment." The attendant bowed and left. Gingerly Sylvi turned over and discovered that most of her left side was one long, angry, midnight-purple bruise. She hadn't noticed last night: she didn't even remember falling, only being afraid for Ebon.

Well, I'm not *going* to be caught out, she thought. She'd just have to be sure neither her mother nor her attendants saw her undressed for the next fortnight or so; she didn't think she could pass this off as the result of a sudden return of sleepwalking—or if she did her mother would insist on someone sleeping in her bedroom with her. If she didn't tie her to the bed.

Sylvi was (apparently) deep in her papers when the study door opened and Ahathin came softly in. She looked up, trying to smile as she always did. Trying to pretend that she didn't know why Ebon was late this morning; he sometimes was late. Ahathin stopped a little inside the door and looked back at her soberly. Suddenly it was too difficult to keep the corners of her mouth turned up, and her smile disappeared.

"Ebon has reported the scent of a norindour—possibly more than one—outside Stonyvale," said Ahathin.

It was easy to look shocked and horrified—she *was* shocked and horrified—but surprise was harder. Maybe shock and horror would do. "Oh," she said faintly.

"He was flying last night," Ahathin went on, his eyes never moving from her face. "He flies somewhat regularly at night, I believe, but—I believe—it was something of a revelation that he flies beyond the Wall."

She could think of nothing to say.

"Our king has already sent a company to investigate," said Ahathin, and paused. Sylvi felt as if her bruises were glowing—that Ahathin would be able to see them too, even under two shirts and a tunic. They began to itch furiously, and she had to twist her hands together not to scratch.

Ahathin took two steps forward and leaned over her study table. He put his hands over her knotted fists—his hands were barely bigger than hers—and said suddenly, urgently, "Child—both you children—*be careful*. No, don't say anything. I don't want to hear it. Because I stand at your elbow so often I think you, both of you, forget why else I am there, why else beyond that I am the princess' tutor, because you do not need me."

"Ahathin," she said, distressed, "we—"

Ahathin shook his head. "That does not matter in the slightest, and I do not think it is rudeness. But it is carelessness. I *am* a Speaker, and perhaps I hear more than you guess. And if I hear anything at all, then it is possible that others may hear something too."

She wanted to shout at him, Would it be so terrible if we were found out? If it was known we went flying together? But she remained silent because she knew the answer: Yes, because it was forbidden. Yes because if they tried to claim that they had not been expressly forbidden to go flying together it would mean they were irresponsible children. And yes because everything about the unprecedented strangeness of their relationship was risky, because some people were frightened by strangeness. Because some people listened to Fthoom.

There was a knock on the door. Ahathin stepped back from the table and became his normal self again, small, faintly rumpled, mild, ordinary, nearly invisible, except for the fact that he was tutor and Speaker to the princess. "Come," she said, and one of her mother's women entered, bowed first to Ahathin, and then a much deeper bow to Sylvi: "A change of schedule, princess, because of this news your pegasus brought. . . ."

CHAPTER 9

They still flew after that, but less often, and it was increasingly difficult. More than once they saw a party, torch-lit, riding or walking
swiftly with the unmistakable purposefulness of someone bringing
news to the king, or going on the king's urgent orders. Ebon had been
forbidden to fly beyond the Wall—*I nearly got grounded completely*, Ebon
said. *I said it would spoil my project, and Gaaloo said I should have enough
sketches—unless I was being negligent, I shouldn't need to fly around at night
any more.*

Oh no! This had been what she'd been afraid of.

*Oh yes. But I pointed out that it was a little unkind to ground me when I'd
brought them useful news.*

Once when she was younger—before Ebon—Sylvi had found a
silver penknife that her father had lost, found it somewhere she was
expressly forbidden to be. She had stood with the beautiful, treacher-
ous thing in her hands, not deciding what to do—she already knew
she would take it to him and tell him the truth—but nerving herself
to do it.

When she had done so he too had stood looking at his penknife with an expression, she imagined, very like the one she had worn when she found it: delighted, dismayed, baffled, unhappy.

"What were you doing in the Hall of Magicians?" he said at last.

Again she answered honestly; her father did not try to make you say things that would make it worse for you. He wanted to know.

"Someone"—Garren, but she didn't need to say that—"told me that the Hall of Magicians smelled of magic, and if I went there some time by myself when no one else was around, I would learn what magic smells like, and then I would always know." He had also told her that on a sunny day you could see faint reflective ribbons of the enormous power used to maintain the protective magic of the Wall, dancing in the sunlight like dust motes.

"And did you learn what magic smells like?"

She hesitated. She knew, now, that her brother had set her up. She should have known immediately, because that was, in her experience, what brothers did; but she had badly wanted to know what magic smelled like—or some other way to recognise when magic was being used around you so you knew why you felt so queer. So she had ignored her common sense, and gone to the Hall. Where she'd realised she'd been played for a fool—she couldn't see that the dust motes in the sunbeams were any different from any other dust motes either—and found the king's little knife.

"It doesn't have a smell, does it?" she said. "Just when they use incense and things, it smells of incense. But . . . but it does *something*, doesn't it? Because you do feel it, when you're all alone in the Hall."

"That may merely have been the apprehension of approaching trouble for being where you oughtn't," said her father drily, and sighed. "I don't know what it's like to be an ordinary person bound by ordinary rules—you can perhaps ask your mother—I was born the ruling monarch's eldest child. And as a person who may rule absolutely over other people you must absolutely obey the rules. I will ask Ahathin to set you new work: in a month's time you will bring me a paper on village magic, on what the local wise woman or wise man can be expected to do, and how likely it is to be successful. You will, as I say, bring me a paper in a month, and another paper in another month, and thus, until I tell you you may stop."

There was a little silence, during which Sylvi considered that she would have less time to ride her pony, and go out with the huntsfolk and the falconers. But she also recognised that this wasn't punishment like a slap with a riding-whip was, or nothing but plain porridge for a week. This was much worse. But it was also much better.

"And yes . . . magic does . . . something: makes its mere presence felt somehow. I don't think it's a smell either. I don't know what it is. I would like to know. You may consider that this is the purpose behind your research; I think you are more likely to discover the answer investigating straightforward, practical village magic than what the guilds send to the palace. And no one pays much attention to hedge wizards; I have thought before that I would like someone to pay attention and tell me what they see."

She had brought her father monthly papers for three years. He had let her off a year ago, but by then she was interested—and the network she had set up for people to bring her stories (people who were first carefully vetted by Ahathin or, lately, one of her guards) was working too well for her to be willing to close it down. She had brought her father three more papers in the last year, and they were all long ones.

She continued to carry them to him herself, and with the third one this year she finally caught him smiling. "This was as much a set-up as Garren sending me to the Hall in the first place, wasn't it?" Her father had guessed that one of her brothers had been responsible, and Garren had admitted it—and been assigned three months' attendance on

Nirakla as punishment. She used no magic herself, and was happy to have an extra pair of hands for the summer to bundle and hang, chop and grind herbs for her. "She wanted to know if I wanted to *apprentice* to her," Garren had said at a private family supper at the end of his term with her, trying to sound outraged. "She said I *chopped* really well."

Sylvi said again to her father, smiling over her latest paper on hedge magic, "*Wasn't* it?"

"No. Yes," said her father, and laughed. He didn't laugh often enough. "One has various things in the back of one's mind. Occasionally an opportunity presents itself to bring one forward. Most of these opportunities come to nothing. Once in a very great while one—or two—do come to something."

Garren had not apprenticed to Nirakla—his father could not spare him so far. But Nirakla had agreed to a half apprenticeship, and the king had allowed his youngest son a certain latitude in terms of creating unnecessary work for his new tutor by knocking people down who were inclined to tease him about his new assignment.

The thing that had stuck in Sylvi's mind during her long atonement was that the Hall of Magicians was used when someone wanted the truth about something—the truth when it concerned magic or magicians. The guilds sometimes used it; the king, with or without the presence of the council or the senate, sometimes used it. She wondered—she couldn't help wondering—what effect the Hall itself had had on her experience and its outcome. She had found the possibility that its enigmatic half-sentience had been involved curiously cheering, as if it was an indication that magic was not quite as inimical as she'd thought. As if magic was more often like Ahathin than it was like Fthoom. Although writing her papers always took longer than she expected, because even the most trifling of village magic didn't like being pinned into paragraphs.

But a shadow had grown over this, as over so much in her life. After her twelfth birthday she had wondered if her little study was one reason Fthoom had been so ready to hate her—but surely a princess studying witch-charms for love philtres and fortune-telling and fly-strike in sheep was pitiable, not dangerous?

Do you have to do something else instead? she asked Ebon. *Since they didn't ground you.*

Mmmh, said Ebon. *Our dads are so alike, aren't they? I have to teach a class of littles flying safety.*

Sylvi laughed.

She and Ahathin were in the garden examining the botanical structures of loomberries when another king's messenger trotted past, looking grim and intent; he did not seem to notice them standing in the shrubbery with their notebooks. Without knowing she was going to say anything, Sylvi said: "Ebon says our dads are very alike."

After a pause Ahathin said, "Yes. They are."

Sylvi turned to look at him. He looked mild and rumpled, as he always looked. "Is that good or bad?"

"What do you think?"

"Oh, good, of course. But . . ."

"There are always 'buts.'"

"I heard Lord Kanf say that we should make an alliance with Swarl, which has a strong king and a large standing army who would know what to do with our taralians. And norindours. And whatever else keeps coming out of the wild lands."

"And your father said he didn't want someone else's large standing army underfoot."

"And Lord Kanf said, Better allies than taralians."

Ahathin said nothing.

"And then my father said, This is the taralians' country too," said Sylvi, "and Lord Kanf said, My lord and king, you are human, not pegasus."

But Sylvi could still put everything out of her mind when she and Ebon flew. She never grew weary of flying: after four years the sky-wind in her face delighted her as much as it had on the night of her twelfth birthday.

The baffling thing to Sylvi was the way the thought of the Caves grew on her—the Caves which, the first time she had asked Ebon about them, he had told her were not a human sort of thing. The Caves where Ebon would some day sculpt some sky view of the landscape around the palace, despite some of the pegasi protesting that the Caves were not for human things. The Caves where the pegasi *sssha-sssha* was held. The Caves where no human had ever set foot.

She could forget taralians and norindours and their night flights' newly restricted scope; she could forget how often her mother wasn't home, and the deepening shadow on her father's face. She could— sometimes—even forget Fthoom. But lying along Ebon's back with the great sweep of his wings framing her, peering through the lash of his mane, the one thought that could take her away from the present moment was the thought of the Caves. She longed to see them—she didn't know why. She guessed perhaps it had begun with listening to him humming his lessons, listening to his stories about the histories on the Cave walls. She thought it might also have to do with his feather-hands on her temples saying the polishing-chant, and the vision that had bloomed behind her eyelids: a curiosity—no, a longing—to try and comprehend *sshasssha*.

Ebon had described his favourite bits of the Caves to her till she felt she could almost see them herself—but only almost. She wanted to stretch out her own hand and stroke the silky surfaces which generations of tiny alula-hands and their light tools had smoothed to a perfection that rougher, stronger human hands could not emulate. But the Caves were far more than half a night's flight away; nor would it have been possible to enter the Caves without being discovered. There was always someone at the various entrances—

Oh! said Sylvi. *You have guards? Who would want to damage your Caves? They are far inside your country, are they not? Where no one goes but you? And you've said taralians and norindours don't like the mountains—*

Ebon stared at her. *Damage? There's a rite-fire kept burning at the three main entrances, and anyone who isn't familiar with the Caves needs a guide, even near the entrances. And unless you're a sculptor, you have to go with a shaman.*

No guards. Sylvi thought—briefly—of a life, of a location, without guards. It made her longing for the Caves even greater.

At certain seasons, for certain ceremonies, most of the pegasi come there, over a few days or weeks at a time, mostly, the main entrance has a monster hall just inside but it's still not big enough for all of us at once. But at any time of the day or year—there are always a few pegasi, sculptors and visitors. You can go for hours without seeing anybody, or sometimes there's someone in every room, round every corner, shaping every bump in every wall, Ebon said.

Sylvi dreamed about the Caves sometimes, and sometimes, on dark nights with no moon or stars, she imagined that they were flying through huge Caves. It was on those nights that the wind most seemed to whisper words in her ears, words she could almost understand.

* * *

Ebon had been gone for nearly a fortnight; the days were almost endless without him, despite all the work she found herself doing, and the hours in the practise yards. Lucretia was an excellent sparring partner, and didn't knock her down—or off her pony—nearly as often as she could: "Naah," she replied, when Sylvi said as much. "What's the point of that? Interrupts the flow of a good practise session." Lucretia had also, however, complimented her on her falling off. "You wouldn't like to try and teach me how you do that, would you?" she said.

Sylvi blinked at her and after a moment said, "I'd have to figure out how I do it."

"It'll be good practise for both of us," said Lucretia.

A group of pegasi had only just arrived at the palace that morning—including Lrrianay and Ebon. A messenger had come to her study to report this fact, and afterward she'd had trouble keeping her mind on her work. Finally she gave it up as a bad job and fled outdoors, knowing that Ebon would come looking for her as soon as he could, knowing where he'd look first. She was sitting under a tree, trying to pretend that she wasn't facing the way she was facing because that was the direction Ebon was likeliest to be coming from. It was too cold to be sitting down outdoors doing nothing, so she stood up and paced, looking over her shoulder. . . . There he was: dazzling black, graceful as a bard's song, her pegasus, her best friend.

I've got a birthday present for you, Ebon said gleefully—it was months before the day. *I have **got** a birthday present for **you**.*

Well, don't tell me now, Sylvi said, surprised at his eagerness. *It's not till forever.*

The pegasi didn't celebrate birthdays the way humans did, but they did attend human birthday parties with their usual aplomb—and brought gifts. Last year she and Ebon had gone to Orthumber for her birthday, with the queen and Hirishy, and Sylvi had had the pleasure of showing Ebon where her mother had grown up and the excuse to ask her all sorts of impertinent questions because she was asking for Ebon too, who didn't know about human childhoods. The queen had been laughing and relaxed all week—but that was before the ladon in Riss, before Ebon had smelled the norindour in Stonyvale.

She had just been thinking about her birthday, for no good reason—thinking about the party that she would give at the palace this year. Sixteen was an important birthday: you became legally a grown-up at sixteen. The first thing she was going to do as a grown-up was give a birthday party that would have as many pegasi as humans attending—exactly as many. So for every unbound human she wanted to come there would have to be an unbound pegasus. She was going to ask Ebon if it would be impertinent to invite a shaman, and if not which one, or (better) more than one. Maybe those who'd spoken to Nirakla? She didn't quite have the nerve to ask him if she could invite his master.

It's not like that, Ebon said. *My dad's talking to your dad about it right now. I'm pretty sure it's going to be all right. . . .* Ebon was giving off waves of excitement so strong it was like trying to stand up in the middle of the Anuluin in spring flood. *There,* said Ebon, as a pegasus appeared on the steps of the palace. Ebon and Sylvi were loitering under the cherry tree near the little garden door that Sylvi usually used—it was the one closest to her rooms. This wasn't anywhere you would expect to see a pegasus, unless it was Ebon looking for her, or someone looking for Ebon. *Come on,* said Ebon, and surged forward, trotting a few steps before he stopped and turned back to her, repeating, *Come on—* and reaching out his nearer wing to scoop her toward him. Usually in public they did try to remember the ban on physical contact—but this wasn't really public, was it? she thought guiltily, and twined her fingers into the mane at the base of his neck, over his withers, and let his momentum pull her along.

This is Drahmahna, said Ebon, nearly running the pegasus at the door down. Sylvi, with her fingers still caught in Ebon's mane, managed to make the *Honoured to meet you* sign as they swept past. They were obviously going to the king's private office—how did Ebon know? What was Lrrianay—

The two footmen flung open the doors without waiting for them to make the formal request: they were expected. The footmen were also wearing hai. What—?

Her father was smiling, but it was a strange smile, sad and elated and worried all at once. The only people present were the human king and the pegasus king: Fazuur was not there; nor were any of Corone's privy council or Lrrianay's court. Whatever conversation had been had, whatever decisions had been made, they had been made between the two kings alone.

Lrrianay said something to Ebon. Ebon, she thought, asked something in return—she caught a sense of a rippling phrase, a pegasus question, although she could not hear what it said. Sylvi looked inquiringly at her father, but he said, "This is for Ebon to tell you."

Ebon shouted or neighed something, suddenly, briefly, an astonishing, startling sound, especially indoors, in the king's small office, surrounded by human furniture. The sound her ears heard was accompanied by a sensation like a kick *inside* her head—cautiously she put her hands up as if checking that her head was still securely fastened—and Ebon did a prance and bounce where he stood. There was a behave-yourself snort from his father—parental disapproval was easily recognisable across the language barrier—and Ebon said, *I can't help it. This is the best, the **best**. Syl, you can come home with me—I mean,* *will you please come home with me? To where I live. I mean, I'm inviting you. This is my birthday present to you. That you come to Rhiandomeer—to my country. To the pegasus country. Like we went home with your mum last year. Will you come? Please. Please say yes. You wouldn't believe what I've been through for this. Syl, I can even take you to the Caves! Please say you'll come! Please!*

To—? said Sylvi. *To—?* She could feel the disbelief on her face, hard and stiff as a mask. She looked at her father. He was still smiling, but it was now a sympathetic smile, an encouraging smile. He nodded. She put her hands up again, touching her own face, pulling the mask away.

Home with you! Of course I'll come! Of course! Oh, Ebon, really? And the **Caves***?* She threw her arms around his neck and was promptly blinded when he swept his wings forward, around her: she could feel his feather-hands dancing like butterflies in her hair.

Now that the heroic deed was accomplished, Ebon poured out the tale of the doing of it: *I started with Dad, of course. I'd figured if I got Dad on my side that was all I needed—I guessed there would be a lot of dust and shouting on the human side so I started—oh, months ago—but I thought our side would be pretty simple, other than, oh, you know, Gaaloo and a few like him. Dad was expecting it. He told me later he was sure I'd ask for your sixteenth birthday. I kind of knew it would have to be a public thing—like going to your fêtes here—but I wasn't expecting it to be as big as it was. And I also thought, you know, Dad'll take care of it. But he didn't. He said he'd back me but I was the one who was going to have to do the talking. Gods and clouds, I didn't know we* **had** *that many shamans! And they all wanted to know why I thought bringing a human home was a good idea. Never mind the Caves!*

Humans rarely ventured into the pegasus lands—they didn't even have a proper name in any human language: the original treaty with King Balsin only specified them as the Lands of the Pegasi, and drew some lines on a map. A few human wanderers had penetrated into the edges of the pegasi country, the sort of folk who travelled because travelling was in their blood and they couldn't help themselves. But they never went farther than a day's journey in from the boundary and never stayed longer than a few days—which was especially surprising in light of the fact that all foot ways into the pegasus country were long and difficult. All that effort and you turn around? Sylvi thought. But there had never been even one official expedition, and there'd apparently never been any discussion about making an easier way in—not so much as a track a laden pack animal could follow easily.

It was curious, Sylvi thought, that all her fellow humans had been so uninterested—how could they be uninterested?—for so many years. She thought of the second commander's journal: ". . . They are like nothing I have ever seen, except perhaps by some great artist's creative power. . . . Several of my folk came to their knees, as if we were in the presence of gods; and while I did tell them to stand steadfast, I did tell them gently, for I understood their awe" . . . or maybe that *was* why. Nearly a thousand years of familiarity hadn't really changed that sense of awe.

She had nonetheless said something about it to Ahathin, years ago, when she was first studying the Alliance.

"It is curious," Ahathin had replied. "I agree."

"Curious!" she said. "Is that all you can say? It's the *pegasi.*"

"Yes," said Ahathin, "which may be the answer."

She put her head in her hands. She knew that if she said "What do you mean?" he wouldn't respond. She thought about the crowned pegasus on the royal standard; why did the relationship between pegasi and humans seem to have borders around it as absolute as the bound edges of a banner? "Because we don't know why having the pegasi here means our crops grow and—and nobody is struck by lightning?" Nar II had several nicknames; one of them was the Lightning King. Old Glunch was another; he was also famously grumpy. He didn't like the pegasi because he didn't like anyone, and while there had been no wars—and no roc sightings—during his reign, it had been remarkably accident-prone, including an unusual number of lightning strikes.

Ahathin nodded. "What do you remember of Nar's pegasus?"

She didn't quite groan. *Teachers.* "Um. Oh. Queen Sufhwaahf. She—she came here anyway, bringing a few courtiers who could put up with Nar's temper. Some historians say she's why nothing worse happened." Which only contributed to the bound-edges feeling, she thought.

There was a little silence, and Ahathin said, "The usual reason given, if the subject comes up at all, is that we've always found enough to do in the lowlands. Balsin, I believe, was the first to make that excuse."

We're afraid, Sylvi thought with a shock. We're afraid of what we might find, beyond the sleek pretty paper and the little embroidered bags, if we went exploring. She thought of her mother saying, *You know where you are with a taralian.* We're *afraid* of the pegasi, thought Sylvi, but she didn't say it aloud. If she did, Ahathin, by his silence, would make her say more, and she didn't want to say any more. She was wrong. She had to be wrong.

After she had Ebon to talk to she said to him, *You don't mean to keep us out, do you? Out of your country,* and Ebon looked surprised. *No. You lot just don't want to come.*

Why? said Sylvi. *Ahathin says it's because we've always found enough to do in the lowlands. But there must be more to it than that.*

I don't know, said Ebon. *I'll ask.*

But the answer he brought back to her was even less of an answer than what he had told her about why the pegasus shamans had not been party to the writing of the treaty. *They don't come,* was the only response.

Why? Ebon had said.

Because they do not.

Sylvi snorted with laughter—she'd noticed that her laugh had become much snortier since she'd had Ebon to spend time with, who himself had a very snorty out-loud laugh. *That's not an answer,* she said.

That's what I told them!

And then what did they say?

That they began to understand why you and I could understand each other, said Ebon. And they both laughed.

That was as much as she'd ever brought up the subject of humans in pegasus country to Ebon. She'd never asked, nor even hinted, for an invitation, although she thought of it often. The tactical problems were severe enough—how long would it take a party of humans to clamber up and across the Starcloud Mountains? Longer than her father would let her be away from the palace, she thought, let alone the size of the troop he would feel it necessary to send with her; they might be safe from taralians and so on once they arrived, but they wouldn't be on the journey. And she was careful—or she tried to be careful—not to say, Oh, I would love to see that! when Ebon told her about his home. (She had expressed a wish to taste *fwhfwhfwha* and Ebon had said dubiously that he'd bring her some some time, but he thought it probably wouldn't like being bounced around in transport.) She had also asked her father why no human ever visited the pegasi: "I know it's a long way! But it's not as far as to Swarl or Chaugh, where the traders go every year. But nobody goes to the pegasi—not even us! Not even us who are bound to them!"

Her father smiled. "There are roads to Swarl and Chaugh, and inns and way stations. There are none over the Starcloud Mountains. I said exactly the same thing to my mother—oh, about forty-five years ago. I think I remember her saying she'd said the same thing to her father. But it's perhaps not as simple as you think. Barring you and Ebon, no bound human has ever been quite sure what he—or she—says is heard by their pegasus the way they said it—however much faith they have in their Speaker. Ahathin has told you the failure rates among those who study as Speakers, yes? How sure are we that even those who succeed—do succeed? Why do we need magic just to talk to each other? And magic is a notoriously tricky servant, even when it's doing something straightforward like reinforcing the Wall or helping a tracker find a strayed lamb or a taralian.

"What does our connection with the pegasi consist of—besides the Alliance itself? Which appears to include the peculiarly unquantifiable fact that our prosperity is in some fashion dependent on the presence of pegasi? And our—problematical—bindings? The pegasi, so far as we can tell, don't use money, and there's apparently nothing they wish to barter. They have been bringing us a few handfuls of gems from their mountains now and again since they discovered Balsin liked them—to pay for the annex, to pay for their keep. And they bring us gifts. That's all. Although our gardeners say that their dung gives the palace the best fruit and flowers in the country. Before you had Ebon, what did you think about the pegasi?"

"Wings. Flying." She paused. "Weird. Scary. Beautiful. And—er— maybe a little vain."

"Yes. How could they not be vain, when they're so beautiful? I thought exactly the same. And after you're bound, you merely have a specific weird scary beautiful and possibly vain individual with wings to fail to communicate with, and how are you going to go about hinting to such a person that you'd like to intrude on his privacy? Especially given their deferential status here with us—and the importance of the Alliance?"

"But you're the king."

"Yes. So is he. And, to the extent that I know Lrrianay, 'vain' is approximately the last word I'd apply to him. Which makes me wonder what other human attitudes we're assuming the pegasi share because it doesn't occur to us they're assumptions."

Sylvi thought of the many times she'd said—assumed—the wrong thing with Ebon. But . . . there were barely any *stories* of humans in the pegasi country. It seemed to be almost as comprehensive a ban as on stories of friendship between pegasi and humans. There were a few folk-tales and ballads where you didn't know which were the made-up bits or the stories themselves made it plain the travellers in question were not to be relied on. In spite of what her father had said, it seemed to her astonishing that no bound human had ever tried to visit their pegasus at home. And yet Ebon said that the pegasi said that the humans didn't come. The pegasi made assumptions too.

She didn't bring it up again to her father or to Ahathin—she had nearly managed to forget her disturbing conversation with Ahathin. And she was vigilant in not bringing it up again to Ebon. But she went on thinking about it. As it turned out, so had Ebon.

There were many more pegasi than usual present for the official announcement of the human princess' impending visit to her pegasus' homeland, more than Sylvi could remember since Danny's ritual of acceptance as the king's heir. They had begun streaming in the day after Ebon and Lrrianay had returned to the palace, and Ebon had made his astonishing invitation. Even the pegasus queen was here: Sylvi had only barely met the queen; she rarely visited.

"Oh, help," said Sylvi's mother, when she'd heard that news. "I don't think we have a prayer of getting Lori here for it, do we?" Lorival was bound to the pegasus queen—to Lorival's dismay. Lrrianay had made his unexpected marriage to Aliaalia over two years before Corone had married Eliona—"I spent those two years staying as far away from Cory as I could," Lorival had said once in Sylvi's hearing, and laughed. Lorival lived in the port city of Told, where she and her husband, Lord Prelling, were cloth merchants; neither of them came to the palace any oftener than they could help, although one of their daughters had recently married a courtier.

"She won't thank us for trying," said the king. "I've sent a messenger with strict orders not to hurry. She can come to the dinner. I think Prel's pegasus will be here too."

Sylvi was wondering if Lorival would arrive in time while she and Ebon waited for their official summons: lucky Lorival, who could be late. They were again loitering under the cherry tree, but they were standing stiffly, and couldn't lounge, against the tree or each other. Sylvi was in her court dress, and Ebon was brushed and plaited, with a twinkly little bag around his neck on a wide scarlet ribbon, and neither of them wanted to appear before kings and queens wearing little bits of grass and twigs.

Ah, said Ebon.

Sylvi looked up from examining the silver half-moons on her court shoes. Glarfin was coming slowly—grandly—toward them. He did grand extremely well. He walked toward them like someone bearing an important message to a princess and a prince. She sighed.

And although there was no one else there to hear but the birds, Glarfin bowed deeply and said, "Lady, sir, the king of the humans, the king of the pegasi, the queen of the humans, the queen of the pegasi, thus your royal parents, request your presence."

Her father wanted the public announcement made as quickly as possible—before the rumours gained momentum. The crowd was waiting in the Great Court, but the first words would be said in the Little Court. Sylvi's heart was beating faster again, even though she knew what was coming. There were about fifty pegasi present in the Little Court, aside from the king and queen, and about twice as many humans, all of them senators, or blood, or councillors or courtiers: all people important to the palace and the king. The pegasi were all wearing flowers and *siragaa*, the decorated ribbons that they sometimes wore over their necks for special occasions; the little embroidered bags, the *nralaa*, that hung from them glittered with tiny jewels. The humans were all wearing their best clothes, grander than the pegasi if not as beautiful; Sylvi's father was wearing some of the sovereign's jewels, so that he sparkled as he moved.

It's just that no one has ever done this before, Sylvi thought, trying to swallow the lump in her throat, but she hadn't realised she'd thought aloud till Ebon said, *That's right. Think about how much easier we're making it for everyone who comes after us.* But she looked out at the human faces turned toward them and saw that many of them looked solemn and watchful. Uneasy. Uncertain. Uncomfortable. Fazuur, who hadn't been needed for the pegasus king to make his revolutionary invitation to the human king, looked haunted.

Most of the pegasi were on or near the dais with her and her family; she could not read the expressions of the few who stood with their humans among the audience, although she could see that their wings lay flat and smooth. Here, at the front, the pegasi outnumbered the humans.

Her father stepped forward, shining like a star, and *bowed*: bowed to her and Ebon. "Daughter and Daughter's Excellent Friend, Sylvi-ianel and Ebon, welcome. We are here to make known to both our peoples the great adventure that the two of you are about to embark upon. Lrrianay and his queen, Aliaalia, on behalf of their son, Ebon, do invite you, my daughter and daughter of my queen, Eliona, to visit them in their high land *Rhiandomeer*, beyond the Starcloud Mountains."

There was a rustle of movement and a whisper of suddenly-exhaled breath at the sound of the name Rhiandomeer.

Sylvi stood frozen. She knew she had to say something—but everyone was looking at her—looking at her with those doubtful, sceptical eyes. The great adventure that no one had ever done before: she had had no ritual lines of response to learn because there were no ritual lines of response. When her father had told her there would be an official public declaration of the invitation she had known she would be expected to say something—and sitting surrounded by diagrams of the stress patterns of bridges she had written a few words for this moment, and stared at them till she knew them. But sitting at her desk with no one else present but Ebon and Ahathin and no sound but birdsong and the faintest *hush* of Ebon's polishing cloth had not made her words strong enough to withstand this moment, and all those wary eyes. . . .

There was a delicate pinch on the back of her neck, and the tickly feeling of Ebon's feather-fingers. *Say yes, babe, or I'll spill you off over the Wall next time—got it?*

Sylvi sucked in a great lungful of air and said, "I thank you, my father, my mother, and I especially thank you, King Lrrianay and Queen Aliaalia, who are father and mother of my—my Excellent Friend, Ebon, for this most gracious of invitations. I shall try my best to be—be worthy of your generosity and—and—and a—an acceptable ambassador for my people." She'd had an awful time with that "acceptable." What could she say about herself that she might be able to live up to, that didn't make it sound as if she shouldn't go—as if she knew she shouldn't go?

She tried to find a friendly face to look at as she spoke, a friendly face among all those mistrustful eyes. There had been a minor flurry at the back of the room as her father spoke, and she looked to see who had entered late: Lorival and Prelling. They were both smiling, and Lorival must have seen Sylvi looking toward her, because she held up her hand in one of the most basic sign-gestures, which meant "excellent" or "well done" or even sometimes "thank you" if you were at a loss—or had to be seen across an audience. Lorival didn't look to be at a loss; she looked pleased to be present at this historic occasion. Sylvi took another deep breath and said, directly to Lorival, "And I'm looking forward to it!"

This proved to be the right thing to say. Some of the watchful faces relaxed, and there was even a faint murmur of human laughter. She turned gratefully to the others on the platform with her, and she could see Lrrianay smiling—was he picking up what she'd said from Ebon, from her father, from the change in the tone of her voice, from hearing the human audience begin to relax and even laugh a little? Fazuur's hands were motionless, his face turned away from the pegasus king. Now Aliaalia was smiling too—was she smiling to be seen smiling (how many of the humans present could recognise a pegasus smile?) or because Lrrianay had told her what Sylvi said . . . or because a pegasus shaman had translated for her? She recognised Hissiope, whom she knew to be a shaman. Did they have an official translator? Or more than one? There were a dozen Speakers present, including Ahathin, Fazuur, and Minial.

It was all too complicated. For a moment her courage disappeared and she thought, louder than she meant to, *Oh, is this all a terrible mistake?*

No, said Ebon. *It's the best idea I've ever had. You've just never learnt to like being the centre of attention.*

But then her mother and father stepped forward to embrace her—and, despite the ban, to embrace Ebon too—and Lrrianay and Aliaalia followed, and did the beautiful pegasus bows, and both of them lightly touched her cheek with a feather-hand. Then Sylvi's father said to her quietly, "Stay a little while longer, and let everyone congratulate you—including the ones who clearly don't want to: in fact, especially the ones who clearly don't want to. You don't have to say anything but 'thank you'—or 'you'll have to ask the king.' And then you can go. I'll face the mob in the Great Court. But I'm afraid you'll have to come to a few of the discussions about ways and means: breaking tradition always comes with a noise like mountains falling."

CHAPTER TEN

Sylvi was afraid of what great company she would perforce be assigned to, or they to her; if she and Ebon couldn't go to a country fair without a dozen minders, what would a visit to Rhiandomeer require? And had they figured out how long it would take to climb the Starcloud Mountains on slow human feet? She kept thinking about how the Starcloud Mountains had come by their name: this too was from Viktur's journal.

> Thee land where their Caves do lie, which are thee spirit and thee heart of their people, repose beyond thee mountains to thee north and east. When they do come to visit us, and watch our toil upon thee lowlands to create thee great city-palace Balsin sees so clearly in his mind's eye, we most of us pause in any work of our hands to watch their approach; and I will not comminate ourselves by declaring us lazy thereby. It is thee sheer sight of thee pegasi that we do not habituate to— cannot so do. I wait in expectation of what our children

may make of thee pegasi, for they will have grown up accustomed to looking upon them; perhaps it may be different for them; or perhaps it is a *human* thing, to look upon such beauty and fail to encompass it, either when walking upon thee ground as they do, as lightly as a bird one might hold in thee hollow of one's hand, or as great winged beings above our heads.

It was one evening at twilight, with thee last of thee lowering sunne's rays upon them, brightening their great wings much as they had been illumined on thee first day we had ever seen them, 'tis years ago now, and yet we do still catch our breaths when we look upon them so. There were many of them this evening; thirty or more, for Balsin had called a great Feast for thee laying of thee cornerstones of thee central Palace which was now accomplished, and they did come to honour him and us and thee thing we did create.

Thee border mountains behind them were dark against a blue damask sky; and thee beating of their wings did glister and coruscate. My Sinsi, who was working beside me though her belly now did make it difficult for her to bend far, stared at them and said, "They do look like a cloud of stars." This was taken up, till all have begun to call thee border mountains Starcloud.

Sylvi's party would only be able to ride as far as the foothills of the Starclouds. It was all very well that Ebon had permission to take her to the Caves, but how *far* were the Caves? Was she going to be another pathetic human who only got a day or two inside the pegasus border—and then had to turn around and go home again, because they had already been gone too long?

And could you *walk* over something called the Starclouds?

She did, as her father predicted, and upon his request, attend a number of meetings on the subject of her journey. These seemed mostly to be a series of prosy old bores standing up in turn and being prosy and boring, and so it was difficult to pay attention and even more difficult to understand any details they might be trying to put forward, although some of them spoke with considerable vehemence. What she did learn was that about a third of the senators, a quarter of the blood and a delegation from the magicians' guild thought she should not go—and that if there had been so much as one sighting of a taralian or a norindour or a ladon anywhere near the Starclouds, that would have been the end of the matter, and she would have gone nowhere. But there wasn't, and there hadn't been for decades. (This didn't stop her from a small anxious startle every time she saw another travel-stained messenger coming to see one of her parents. It *wouldn't* be . . . fate *couldn't* be so cruel.) She heard her father once say to Lord Cral that he was tempted to suggest that he was sending his daughter away for her safety; at present there were far too many sightings of taralians and norindours and ladons in the human lowlands.

But she did go.

And only *she* went—she and her father. They would not have even one minder, one attendant, one courtier—one guard. And her father was staying only one night, while she was given three weeks.

The reason for the lack of a grand procession was that they *flew*.

They flew.

Not as Sylvi and Ebon flew; she and the king were to sit or lie in something like hammocks. The king's had eight ropes and Sylvi's had six, and the ropes ended in great loops that hung round pegasi necks, and a spider-work of straps to hold the loops in place—plus a little crucial shamanic magic to make the system work. The pegasi had spent some time inventing them before they'd extended the official offer of transport.

Actually they didn't have to invent anything, but they did have to find the old plans. I mean, we carry all kinds of stuff in draia—slings—hammocks—when we have to carry anything. You've seen us fly in or out with them, haven't you? But we don't carry humans. Gohrocoh said we didn't need plans, that a drai was always a drai, and draia are not a problem, but Dad got all kingly and said that we weren't in the habit of carrying humans in our draia and this was going to be a historical event, doodah doodah, and he wanted you to be comfortable as well as safe. Which also meant the shamans had to check out the ooffhaloah . . . the . . . the magic web that makes the whole show possible. Ropes and wings are not a best combination to begin with. And if we drop a load of apples or siragaa it's not a big deal.

What old plans? said Sylvi.

Well, a long time ago I guess we thought about carrying you around—maybe about bringing you home. I've never heard that we ever did—

There aren't any stories about it on our side, Sylvi put in. *Even Ahathin hasn't heard of any. Just a few stupid ballads that you know are made up.*

Eah. But we still have the designs for the draia. Dad's usually right about stuff but I was afraid it would be winter before they found the devil-blasted plans and then I suppose I'd've had to wait till your next birthday.

A pegasus delegation brought one of the human hammocks for inspection and approval. You'd think weaving was weaving, Sylvi had thought, the first time she'd seen a pegasus hammock—a *drai*—up close, when an envoy had come with chains of silk flowers and banners for some state occasion, shortly after she'd been bound to Ebon. Most things delivered to the human court were brought in the variety of small bags that usually hung round the pegasi's necks or possibly in a larger bag slung between two pegasi, and they bowed or knelt and pulled a cord, and the bag collapsed, and whatever it was lay revealed or rolled out. It was, to the little Sylvi, only one more strange, unhuman thing the pegasi did, and she had never thought about it, till Ebon.

The next time she had the opportunity she touched—stroked—not only the flowers themselves but the sling the flowers had been carried in, and the lengths of gauzy fabric they'd been wrapped in. Pegasus fabrics remained rare and exotic in Balsinland. They used several plant fibres in their weaving as well as their paper-making, which produced glossy, drapey fabrics human weavers could not emulate; their silk was finer than any made by humans; they furthermore had perfected the use of *whhayahaay*, cobweb or spider-silk. Their silk was not merely finer but stronger than human-made; Sylvi discovered that a pegasi phrase for "well done" was "tight as silk."

The human sovereign had several robes of pegasi weaving, and several human-adapted *siragaa*, and many who saw them would have been happy to buy similar for themselves; but there was no regular trade between the two peoples, and any attempt at discussion on this topic foundered on the pegasi's blank incomprehension. The pegasi seemed to want nothing, and perhaps it was the empathy of the bindings that prevented any of the sovereign humans from demanding something the pegasi apparently did not wish to offer; and any bound human or family which had been so fortunate as to receive a gift of weaving from the pegasi treated it as an heirloom of their house.

You'd know, Sylvi thought, that there was something strange about this weaving even if you didn't know anything about the pegasi. The fibres themselves were unfamiliar; the weaving was so delicate you couldn't see how it fit together; and it had a curious shimmer—a shimmer you seemed to see with your fingertips as well as your eyes. The gauze was as soft as chick down; the sling was stiff and strong, and as sleek as Ebon's shoulder.

The human *draia* were less glamorous, but they still shimmered in the golden afternoon sun as if with their own light. Sylvi knelt by hers; it had some kind of padding woven into it to make it comfortable for the passenger. It was like pressing your fingers into a thin, well-stuffed mattress: if you pressed hard enough you could feel the rope supports crisscrossing at the back. Sylvi would have been happy to leave at once—not least because it meant she *would* go.

She looked up from the mattress-hammock and caught her father's eye. The *drai* was making it all real. She was going to go—senators or no senators, blood or no blood . . . Fthoom or no Fthoom, since every-one knew who was behind the delegation of magicians. "It's *perfect*," she said firmly, as if in answer to any unspoken doubts. "I shall want to ride in it *forever*."

Her gaze shifted to her mother, who was looking worried with that old-general-measuring-up-inexperienced-troops gaze. Hirishy—the least likely soldier's pegasus—was standing at the queen's side. As Sylvi glanced at her, she cocked an ear, which usually meant yes, except when it meant no. And then she unfolded one wing just enough for her feather-hand to brush the queen's cheek. The queen glanced down: Hirishy cocked the other ear and then the first again, a gesture that meant "Well?" or "There, there." The queen's face softened, and she stroked a quick, furtive hand down Hirishy's cheek.

But the discussions among the humans about the princess' journey still went on and on. After one particularly harrowing one, when Lord Bullen and Senator Gathshem, who had never agreed on anything before in their long lives at court, had been on their feet at the same time, positively shouting that the princess should not be allowed past the Wall, in the present unsettled state of the country, let alone be sent off—*flown* off—like a parcel or a diplomatic gift into the utter unknown, and the Holder of Concord had had to shout louder to regain control of the meeting, Sylvi said to her father, "They can't stop me going, can they?"

When he didn't answer at once she said in a voice a good deal higher and sharper than she meant, "*You* won't stop me going, will you?"

The king sighed. "No, my darling, I am determined you should go."

After another pause she said in a very small voice: "Fthoom. . . ."

"Fthoom," said her father grimly, "is one of the reasons you must go."

There was a petition gathering signatures around the senate and the court—asking that Fthoom be reinstated to his old place in the king's council. Sylvi only knew about it because of Lucretia: "I'm forbidden to tell you, and I don't know what they'll do if you let on it was me—cancel my appointment as your lady, I guess. And Glarfin will personally beat me to splinters. But I remember how much you minded that no one told you about your guards—and I'd've felt the same. I'd feel the same way now." Lucretia looked at her, troubled, and tried to smile. "Us short women have to look out for each other."

"Thank you," Sylvi had said. "I would *much* rather know." She looked at her father now and thought, This is not the moment to remind him he was going to tell me, next time.

The next several weeks were an eon at least. Sylvi wasn't the slightest bit interested in anything but *going*; the details threatened to drive her mad. She couldn't have cared less about what clothing to take with her—that it had to be lightweight, warm and not merely tidy and relatively hole-free which, Sylvi always felt when dressing for a formal occasion was quite enough to ask, but it had to look like, well, like she was a princess. She was going to have to try to look like a princess for three weeks, and it was going to kill her. She did understand about being respectful and so on: "But the pegasi won't *care* what I'm wearing!" she wailed to her father.

"Sylvi—" he began.

She put her hands over her ears. "I don't want to hear it! You're going to tell me that *I'll* know it! That after you leave I'll be the sole representative of the entire human race and it's a huge responsibility and I have to act like I know it and it means something even if I'm the only one knows that's what I'm doing!"

"I have frequently had the suspicion that Ahathin gets more over to you than we think he does," said her father, smiling.

"It's not Ahathin," she said sadly. "Or it's not only Ahathin. It's you and Mum and Danacor and . . . I'd rather wear clothes with holes in so they *didn't* take me seriously but . . ." She stopped and then added, "Doesn't it occur to you that if I *did* think about being the sole representative of the entire human race I'd just, you know, crumble?"

Still smiling, her father said, "No." And then a runner was announced, with news of another taralian found and dispatched, and Sylvi had to leave, feeling a rather sick-making mixture of pride and dismay.

Even worse was writing her speech. There was going to be a banquet, of course, for her father. And for her, she supposed, since she was there too. She knew about banquets; she'd sat through a lot of banquet speeches. She was going to have to *give* one? That was worse than having to look like a princess for three weeks.

"It doesn't have to be long," said her father. "Just a few polite sentences. Oh, and—" He paused.

Sylvi's heart sank. Every regular at the king's court learnt to dread the king's "Oh, and—" with the pause. If the rest of the sentence followed immediately, it would be okay. When there was a pause, there was trouble.

"I'd like you to give it in as much of the pegasus language as you can. You can use sign too, if you wish, but I want you to say at least a few words in our hosts' own language. In what we think we know of our hosts' own language." Briskly he added, "You can ask Ebon to help you with your pronunciation."

Sylvi's heart continued sinking. It would reach the centre of the earth soon. What the humans understood and could use of the oral and kinetic pegasus language was of the grand and the courtly but mostly meaningless variety—the sort of language that appeared in the treaty. Every court meeting where pegasi were present began with a welcome that included *hraasa ho uurha*, "esteemed allies," and if you met one at a banquet and felt the need to say something, one of your choices was *niwhi goaraio whanwaidio*, which meant something like "I hope you will enjoy your food." She'd been meaning to ask Ebon for a translation check, but it was one of those things she never thought of when she was with him.

"Are you going to speak in pegasi?" she asked mutinously; but she already knew the answer. Even though she had Ebon and he did not, he wouldn't ask her to do anything he wouldn't do.

"I'm going to try," he said ruefully. "My speech will be longer than yours, and about half of it will be in something resembling pegasi, I hope. Remember we won't have any Speakers with us—"

"We don't *need* them," Sylvi interrupted. "We'll have the shamans, and you and Lrrianay nearly—and away from the palace Ebon and I—"

"It's not the same thing," said the king.

"Like wearing nice clothes," said Sylvi, and sighed.

She did ask Ebon to help her. *Your ears are going to twist themselves off if you spin them any harder,* she said crossly. He stopped grinning, flattened his ears sideways and then, after a second or two, let out a guffaw they could probably hear on the other side of the Wall.

*You sound like a **donkey,*** she said.

This is going to be fun, he said.

But he did help her. She'd never given a proper speech at a banquet before, even a short one—even in her own language—but she'd become accustomed to saying a few sentences at opening or closing ceremonies at fairs and name days and occasions when she was ranking royalty.

First there was the confusing business of stopping their silent-speech for the words spoken aloud so she could concentrate on the sounds of the oral language; and then there was the decision to dispense with trying to learn any of the pegasi kinetics—there were a lot of what Sylvi thought of as adjectives that the pegasi did in body language. *But there isn't a good way to, uh, translate the, uh, difference in body parts,* said Ebon.

Yes, said Sylvi. *Or that I've got ears but can't wiggle them. The sign-language is dire enough—and anyway I **don't** want to be saying "it's a pretty day but I think it will rain tomorrow."*

But the meanings of even the usual court-speech words seemed to keep slipping away from her, even with Ebon helping. They ran away like mice, or a handful of sand through your fingers.

It's weird, isn't it? said Ebon.

Yes, she said grimly. *Very weird.*

It's like the binding, said Ebon. *When it felt like they were separating us, rather than tying us together.*

They had never said this to each other before.

Yes, said Sylvi.

There was an awful little silence, and then Ebon said, *Well, it didn't work. We got bound anyway.*

And then there was her pronunciation. *You haven't got a tadpole's chance at a heron party of saying that so anyone will understand you,* Ebon declared in response to her first try, so they had to find other words that she could get her mouth around—could remember long enough to learn. Sometimes by the time they'd found a compromise, the original meaning of what she'd wanted to say had got lost on the way. *It's not like you're such a—such an elocutionist in human,* Sylvi said crossly, after Ebon had had to roll over on the ground and kick his legs in the air in reaction to her attempts to say *honoured,* which was *gwyyfvva* in pegasi.

"Hhhhh, eeeee?" said Ebon: *Who, me? If the world depended on me giving a speech in human, the world would just have to end, okay? How about* "respected"? *That's only* "fffwha," *which you might manage.*

"Fuwa," said Sylvi. *I've heard your dad speak human pretty well,* she added.

"Fffwha," said Ebon. *Yes, and he's impossible to live with for weeks before he does it too. Don't go there. How's your dad doing?*

"Fuuuwa," said Sylvi. *You could say he's impossible to live with. Although in my dad's case, impossible to live with means because you never see him.* Ebon raised his head from where he was still sprawled on the ground and looked at her and she looked back. Her father sometimes used a speech-writer for an ordinary human speech. Not this one.

Fthoom? said Ebon.

Sylvi shrugged. *He's behind the magicians who want me not to go. But . . .* She didn't want to talk about it. She didn't want to talk to Ebon about all the humans—all the courtiers and councillors and ordinary people—who didn't want her to go. About the petition to bring back Fthoom. Who had wanted to turn her into a newt.

You—you are still coming? He sounded as uncertain as she'd ever heard him.

If they try and stop me I'll flap my arms and fly over the Starclouds.

I'll meet you right outside the Wall, said Ebon, recovering his spirits. *Flying is hard work when you're not used to it.*

I believe you, said Sylvi. *Now listen. "Fwee henny awwhaha blaiahaa-nuushor anawha: na, fa, zinanah. Fffwha nor, daboorau." I bow my best bow to you, to each of you I bow once, twice, three times. Respected friends, my thanks and gratitude.*

You sound like you have a bad head cold and a mouthful of mouldy reeds. But . . . not bad. And that's two whole sentences.

Now tell me the one about foes and stuff.

"Liananana oria nolaa, auroneewhala, dom. Norwhee da norwheerela."

"Li . . . dom. Noriwee. Um. Norewela."

Needs work.

*But we started there! Remember? We started there. "Foes press round us, as they did at the beginning. But we stand friends." We've done it over and over and over and **over**. I still can't remember the foes sentence at all and it's like it spills over into the friends sentence, which I can almost half remember, sort of.*

"Inskawhaksha," said Ebon. *Say it. It's really short. Never mind your pronunciation. Just say it.*

I can't remember, said Sylvi in frustration. *Say it again.*

"Inskawhaksha," said Ebon.

"Is—in —" *I can't remember!*

It means "my darkest enemy." And you can't remember it.

If it's a spell, said Sylvi slowly, *then it's wearing off on the friendly words first.*

+ + +

189

Sylvi was grateful for her daily practise under the master-at-arms with sword, staff and bow—glad for the excuse to go *bash* at something, and sweat and grunt. Aside from any other considerations, she had fought *for* this much too hard not to keep to her practise strictly—and now, under the pressure of bearing with the uproar about her coming journey to Rhiandomeer she had the dubious pleasure of being told that, pound for pound, she was the toughest fighter of her family. Diamon himself was not a large man—and Lucretia was a small woman, though not as small as Sylvi. Between the two of them they knew the sorts of things that someone small and quick and accurate can do to upset the advantage of a bigger, stronger adversary; and Sylvi found that a practise sword in an opponent's hand (especially Lucretia's) focussed her mind and her reflexes wonderfully.

It didn't seem to her respectful not to know how to use *a* sword, having sworn fealty to her king on *the* Sword. Her mother, a noted swordswoman herself, had been fully on her side about this, although the royal family tradition was that the nonreigning women were archers. Her father had looked at her thoughtfully when she suggested, shortly after her twelfth birthday, that she wanted to train properly with Diamon, to a plan and a schedule, but he had let himself be persuaded. "Your mother wouldn't let me make any other decision, of course," he said, "but she says this was your idea."

"I would have asked you years ago, only I'm so *short*," Sylvi said. That on the night of her twelfth birthday she had discovered one enormous advantage to being small had not eased frustration with her situation elsewhere; and her twelfth birthday was also when she had been obliged to begin going to council meetings, which produced a different form of frustration. "All my brothers started when they were *seven*. I think Danny was taller than I am now when he was seven."

"My disgraceful heritage, I fear," said her father. "There is one more hurdle for you: you must ask your unnecessarily tall eldest brother's permission as well as mine. He will be your king and commander some day and it is his choice where he would have you to command."

Sylvi opened her mouth and shut it. Opened it again. "He'll tell me I'm *too short.*"

The king sighed. "He may. In which case refer him to me, and you will be a lesson for him in allowing his people to make their own decisions, for they will work much harder doing what they feel they themselves have chosen to do."

Tall Danacor visibly had his mouth open to say "you're too short" when Sylvi added, "And Dad says that if you tell me I'm too short you're to talk to him and I'm going to be a *lesson* in letting your *subjects* make their own decisions." Whereupon Danacor stopped looking like a pompous prig and more like a young man who still sometimes found being the king's heir rather a strain.

"Okay." He smiled a little. "Diamon is pretty short himself. I think he likes short people best. First time you knock him down I'll—I'll give you a sword."

She had still not attained such a height of glory, although on a good day she could make him take a step backward he hadn't meant to take. Four years ago it had been a matter of principle that she wanted lessons in combat, and Sylvi, as she crossed swords or staves with Lucretia or Diamon or any of the others, or as she released her arrow or fired her crossbow bolt or rode at the large straw bolster (on wheels, to make hitting it more interesting), told herself it was still only a matter of principle that she should learn the arts of war. There had been skirmishes many times before, since Viktur and Balsin had come through the Dravalu Pass; with humans beyond the borders of her father's realm, and with taralians and norindours, ladons and wyverns within it. Some of those skirmishes had been fierce enough and lasted long enough to be called wars.

"There is a theory," Ahathin had once told her, "that we are here in a kind of—nexus, a crossroads, a meeting place of force and power. That there is a reason why we are so plagued not merely by taralians and norindours, but that ladons and wyverns, which should not be natural to our climate and geography, are drawn back here. That it is this convergence that attracts rocs. And . . ."

"And pegasi," interrupted Sylvi, not wanting to think about rocs or magical convergences. "The only pegasi there are are here, are ours."

"Yes," said Ahathin. "So far as we know, the pegasi that are a part of our lives are the only pegasi anywhere."

"Then we had better keep them alive, hadn't we?" said Sylvi.

"Yes. Yes, we had indeed."

That's what it is like at a crossroads, Sylvi said to herself. They were only having a bad season, an unsettled year—or two years, or three. Nothing to do with a princess and her pegasus, or with Fthoom. The Alliance did live, visibly, in the bond between her and Ebon. Let them exploit that. . . .

Especially if it included seeing the Caves, she told herself honestly, the night before they were due to leave. Her head was still ringing with the good wishes (and the good advice) of all of those who had come to the medium-sized dinner in her and Ebon's honour that evening— ringing as well, she felt, with all the things that had *not* been said, mostly by those who had continued to oppose her going, but whom her father had thought it was politic to invite to the dinner to send her off.

She was not going to be able to sleep. If her ears were ringing with other people's words, her mind was ringing with her own. She paced her bedroom restlessly; she had packed and repacked and re-re-re-packed what she was taking with her; changed her mind dozens if not hundreds of times about the individual gifts she was bringing. She had had the various choices laid out on a shelf in her wardrobe, where she could be indecisive without troubling any of her attendants. Would the pegasus queen like the gold chain, or the silver and gold one better? Was the little mother-of-pearl bowl—light enough for pegasus hands—really grand enough for Lrrianay, even with the sparkle of tiny diamonds in a ring below its rim? Grand—oh, *grand* was another of those cumbersome, confusing human things, like choosing the clothes to take with her to make her look like a princess. What did you give people who didn't want anything?

Since she was at that end of the room, she opened her wardrobe and stared at the things she wasn't taking. I am *not* changing my mind again, she thought, as she stared at the embroidered ribbons she wasn't taking for Ebon's little sister. They were extremely pretty, but Sylvi thought bringing human embroidery to a pegasus was probably like giving farm boots to a dancer. She thought of her farmer uncle Rulf telling her how his eldest son, who had never cried about anything, cried the first time he saw pegasi, flying with the sunset gilding their wings. Sylvi couldn't remember the first time she'd seen pegasi; for her at the palace they'd always been there. But she was going to be alone with them for almost three weeks; alone with creatures so beautiful and strange that they made a little boy cry for their beauty and strangeness.

Her eyes drifted to a glint from farther inside the wardrobe. Until a few weeks ago her practise gear had all hung on a peg in the armoury, but a few days after Diamon had told her that pound for pound she was tougher than her brothers, he had come up behind her at the end of their session together, as she was shrugging out of her extremely beat-up leather breastplate. Her sword was already rubbed clean of dust and dirt and hanging up, but he lifted it down again and once she was free of her armour, handed it to her. Puzzled, she grasped the familiar hilt and accepted the scabbard with the other hand. She'd graduated to a real sword a few months ago, even if it wouldn't have been much more than a dagger in Danacor's hand; Diamon said that he'd known the young woman who'd last carried it, and that it had been responsible for the deaths of at least two taralians. Lucretia liked to tease her that it was the sword that young Razolon had run his first Speaker through with; it was probably almost old enough, although very plain for a sovereign's heir, even a twelve-year-old one.

"Take it back to the palace with you," said Diamon. "Time you started learning to live with it. The sword is your weapon, clearly, just like it's your mum's, and a soldier or a princess should be ready. You don't want to have to come pelting out to the armoury when the battalion of rocs is sighted." He smiled, but his eyes were serious.

No sword practise for three weeks, she thought. No thumping and being thumped, and getting dust up your nose and in your eyes; her pony would be baffled but pleased by an unexpected three weeks' holiday; her father's dogs would be less pleased that she didn't appear to take them for walks. . . . At least no *council meetings*, she thought. She would miss Nanthir's next report from the Kishes—but she'd also miss the Chaugh ambassador's daughter's birthday. She was going to be all alone. . . .

I'm going to see the Caves, she thought, before her courage failed her. The Linwhialinwhia Caves. The Caves that I've been longing to see for years—that I've known—*known*—that I never would see. I'll probably even get to taste *fwhfwhfwha*.

Eventually she climbed into her bed and lay stiffly down. Last night in a bed for three weeks, she thought. Last night indoors. I hope it doesn't rain all the time.

There would be hundreds of people to watch them set out tomorrow—far more than at any mere village festival. There was no centuries'-old traditional script for this occasion either. "Be your father's daughter," her mother had said, smiling. "And try not to worry too much."

Sylvi gave a little gulp of laughter. "Well, *that's* not being my father's daughter!"

CHAPTER 11

It was a fine clear day for flying, the sky blue and very far away in that come-chase-me way that always made Sylvi especially yearn for wings—and almost no wind, at least not on the ground. She had learnt, by flying with Ebon, that what was going on a few spans straight up might be quite a bit different from what was happening standing on the ground, but the few wisps of cloud she could see didn't seem to be moving very fast. There were three *draia*—one for luggage, including gifts—and twenty-two pegasi to carry them, plus a dozen more who would fly with them.

They collected themselves in the Inner Court, those who were going, where the private good-byes and good wishes would be said: the pegasi, her father and mother, Hirishy, Danacor and Farley, and Thowara and Oyry—Garren and Poih were on patrol, and Lrrianay would meet them on arrival—and half a dozen human attendants, including Fazuur, Minial and Ahathin. But there were more pegasi than humans. It felt very strange to be outnumbered . . . and she was soon to be *alone* with . . . She looked at Ebon, who was looking at her. Ebon had never given any sign of minding being far more outnumbered than she was now when they went to a festival, but she wondered what he might think about it that he had never told her. And he had never been *alone* with . . . Again she stopped her thoughts.

She glanced around; a good half of these pegasi she didn't recognise. Several of them were noticeably broader and sturdier than the average, although none was bigger than Ebon. They all seemed bigger to her today than they usually did. Once her father left, and she was . . . She silenced her thoughts yet again. The Caves! Think about seeing the Caves with Ebon.

All of these pegasi, when they caught her eye, nodded, and said, "*Fwif*," which was an honorific like "lord" or "lady." She nodded back and said, carefully, "*Wheehuf*," which was a polite greeting like "good day, sir" or "good day, madam." The pegasi rarely used gender specifics, which was one thing she didn't have to try to learn; *wheehuf* would do for everyone. And it was one of her better pegasi words; not only was it one of the harmless ones that everyone knew and could remember from one day to the next, she could say it without Ebon making faces. She had said this to him a few days before and he'd wheeled his ears mockingly and replied, *Choose the mountain you have to fly over, as they say. I don't want to wear myself out.*

The crowd was waiting in the Outer Great Court—no, the crowd *began* in the Outer Great Court. A Silversword major had informed the king that much of the huge space inside the Wall was full of humans wanting a glimpse of the historic event, many of whom had travelled a long way for the opportunity. As a result the human king had asked and the pegasi agreed to fly one complete circuit inside the Wall before heading northeast toward the Starclouds. Sylvi discovered that she was trembling. She walked out through the high wide arch on her father's arm, with the queen and the heir behind them. The crowd roared, and the sound was bewildering. She didn't understand; what were they roaring about?

Her father had stopped in the gateway, so perhaps he hadn't noticed her involuntary recoil. Old stories came into her mind and she thought, They sound as if they're seeing off a war party. She gave a convulsive shiver and her father squeezed her arm against his side and murmured, "Courage, young one; be glad of their enthusiasm. Be glad of all those village fêtes you went to, and all the pony rides Ebon gave the littles, because they're part of the reason you're going today—because all these noisy people thought you should." He lifted his other hand and waved and, after a moment, so did she. The crowd was divided into two parts, and between was a long clear straight path stretching as far as she could see: for the pegasi to gallop down, carrying the *draia*.

The pegasi came through the arch behind them. Human servants were carrying the already-loaded luggage *drai*, and they set it down, spreading out and then lifting the loops of rope that went round the pegasi's necks; but the pegasi themselves, with their tiny feather-hands, fastened and checked what on horses would be cruppers and belly bands: there were two shamans per *drai*, to ensure that the *ooffhaloah* worked as it should. The *draia* for herself and her father lay over the pegasi's backs; the pegasi slipped them off, where they lay in unrecognisable little huddles on the ground. Even knowing what Ebon had told her about the *ooffhaloah*, even knowing that the pegasi had to be able to use their wings and their legs freely in flight and therefore the passengers needed to hang below their carriers' feet—Sylvi had perhaps been betrayed by her forbidden knowledge of flying because she said at once, shocked, when she'd first heard of the prototype human-carrying *drai*, "But what about *landing?*"

Even after almost four years' practise, she and Ebon didn't always get it right, and she was lying free on his back with no ropes to complicate the issue. She realised what she'd said and blushed so violently she thought she could feel her hair frizzle in the heat, but several of the humans also present laughed and her father said mildly, "Well spotted, Sylvi."

Pegasi did carry other things this way, and when they glided down toward landing they leaned against the ropes—their harnesses were asymmetrical to take this odd strain—till they were horizontally taut, to lift the baggage, whatever it was, above ground level, and the carriers said their words to hold it there. It still took a good deal of practise for a team of pegasi to learn to do this reliably and accurately. Their very best teams were carrying the king and his daughter—and there were the six shamans flying with them to strengthen the holding words.

Ebon was one of the six pegasi carrying the princess. *How did you manage that?* Sylvi had said, very impressed, the evening the names of the carriers—the *doorathbaa*—were read out.

Ebon, unusually for him, took a few seconds to reply. *Well,* he said *at last, I pleaded and pleaded and pleaded and pleaded and begged and begged and nagged and whined and whinged and so on like that. I really didn't think I was going to make it. And then I thought I can't **not** make it, so I went on begging and being a pain in the neck and the rear and all four legs and forty wings. They won't take you unless you're grown, you see, although I'm bigger than Traa or Maoona. Dad, who never gets cross, said to me once that I could mess up the whole trip if I kept on about it and I thought about that, and about telling you you couldn't come after all because I'm a . . . a . . . hafwuffab. What do you call someone who is really irritating and stupid?*

Fool, dolt, nitwit?

Eah. All of those. But I thought about it some more and I couldn't not do it. I think even Dad got it finally. That I wasn't just being . . . I don't know. But what happened is that Guaffa—he's the one who—who takes care of the doorathbaa—there's another word, clafwha, which is being the head of something when you're not the head of something. You humans don't seem to do it—your heads head. But Guaffa is the clafwha of the carriers, the doorathbaa. Guaffa cracked, thank wing. I'd been pestering him as much as Dad. He told my dad that if it was okay with him and I could do it he'd have me. And Broraakwha kind of wanted not to do it because his hrmmhr is about to pop with their first baby and he was sure it would happen while he was gone.

So Guaffa took me out with a rope around my neck and his and a beastly great boulder in the drai—I swear it was half a mountain, heavier than you'll ever be unless you bring some of those stone heads you walk down your wall on in your pockets—but I wasn't going to fail so I didn't. I think we flew to the end of the world and back. I was never so tired in my life but I wasn't going to tell him that. All Guaffa said was "I can see why they call you Stone-Carrier" but he took me. Then I had to learn all this team stuff—and I had to learn it fast. Once they'd taken me, though, there was no more question and they just drilled and drilled me. It's all tricky but landing's the worst. Well, landing's always the worst. I was kind of hoping I'd get some ideas about our landing problems but I didn't, and I don't think any of the holding words would do anything, they might make it harder to roll if you fall. I haven't had any special training for ooffhaloah either. Never mind. I'm third rope on your drai and that's what matters.

Ebon was kneeling by his rope-loop now. A single pair of human hands could pick up even a thick rope easily, but the pegasi's alula-hands were too weak. It took two pegasi to lift a rope loop, and the pegasus whose neck the loop was to lie round would kneel as well, to make the effort less. Once the rope was settled, the pegasus would stand while the rest of the harness was fastened and fiddled with till the fit was perfect. They did it so gracefully there seemed no anxiety or hurry to it—no forced allowance for weakness—and they did it quickly. It seemed almost a dance, perhaps a cotillion, or a sort of high-level musical chairs, because all the pegasi who weren't being or hadn't yet been fastened into the harness helped with the harnessing, pair and pair, till the last six were harnessed by the six pair who were not carriers.

Although Ebon was the only black, the pegasi were variously coloured, from white to cream to gold to copper-red to dark, fresh-ploughed-loam brown and deep shadow or silver grey, and the three groups that made the three circles, six or eight spokes around each central boss, seemed to be creating some pattern with some meaning beyond the simple fact of preparation for the flight to come. Some . . . Sylvi shook her head; I'm just a little dizzy, she thought. Too many people watching us. Too many people watching the princess who is going to the pegasus country—and the pegasus Caves. How many of them know about the Caves?

Ebon caught her eye. *Don't worry*, he said. *We've got this netted. Tight as silk.*

It comes with the breathing, she said. *Worrying.*

When every particle of harness was secure exactly where it should be, the accompanying pegasi moved away from the carriers. For a moment—as if the purpose of the pattern they had created was about to be revealed—all twenty-two carriers stood motionless, perfectly arranged in their three circles, tails and necks arched, wings only a little roused—and more beautiful than moonlight or summer dawn or the face of your true love. The mutter of excitement and curiosity among the human crowd died away to silence.

And then Guaffa, who was, in the absence of Lrrianay, leader of the pegasi, bowed his neck, stamped one foot, and lashed his tail twice, left, right, and murmured a few words: and Sylvi, without thinking about it, only grateful to understand something, and having spent the last several weeks cramming herself with the pegasus language including everything Ebon told her about the *doorathbaa*, immediately moved forward to settle herself in her *drai*, because she knew that was the signal. There was a quick rustling whisper through the crowd, but she didn't think about that either.

Fazuur bowed calmly to his sovereign as if Sylvi was supposed to go first, and the king then settled himself in his *drai* too—and Sylvi realised what she had done. When I blurted out Ebon's name at our binding, I didn't notice, she thought. This time it's only that I've been doing my lessons. But I'm sure someone will tell Fthoom anyway. . . .

Two pegasi tucked a blanket over her, leaving her gloved hands free, and one of them, one of those she didn't know, quickly and neatly threaded and tied a light rope over her, in a zigzag through the rope-loops that edged the *drai*, and stepped back. Sylvi thought she felt just the lightest brush of a feather-hand against her cheek, and looked up: there was a faint smile-wrinkle across the pegasus' nose. She smiled back, and felt a little better.

Guaffa threw up his head and lashed his tail right, left—Sylvi heard *awwhinnaw*, which means "listen"; but she got a bit lost after that, and he'd be mostly speaking in silent-speech. *He's just reminding us that this baggage will get a sore bum if we mess up the lift-off*, said Ebon, but Fazuur was translating it as "We thank you for the extraordinary honour and privilege . . ." Blah blah blah, thought Sylvi, and stopped listening.

Then, more precisely than a company of the King's Own Silver-swords, the pegasi moved, back and forward and sideways, till the *draia* were clear of the ground. Inside wings were arched to allow for the presence of ropes, and Sylvi felt the tingle of magic, felt it slipping down over her like another sort of slender pegasus cord, strong and soft as pegasus silk. Then she heard the *Now!* through Guaffa's nostrils, and the pegasi burst forward in a canter that became a gallop almost at once, and then a run, the flat-out run of a sighthound after a hare, thrilling and terrifying, and before she believed it could be possible they had leaped into the air. Sylvi's stomach gave a lurch, indicating its desire to stay behind, and she felt sick in a way she never had flying with Ebon—not only, she thought, because he was a little more gradual about their take-offs, not least to avoid spilling her off. She wound her hands through the pair of loops thoughtfully made large for this purpose and stared down at the sea of dark and pale faces staring up at her.

The pegasi banked right, for the flight round the inside of the Wall. She glanced over at her father, who was also holding on, but with only one hand, and waving with the other. She looked at her own straining fists and thought, Be a princess. Be your father's daughter. And he's never even flown before. She untwisted her right hand, and waved.

Once they'd flown over the Wall and were headed toward the mountains Sylvi began to enjoy herself—although she didn't dare look down. She'd never flown in *daylight* before. She could look ahead toward the rise of the Starclouds' green foothills—her view constantly interrupted by the beating wings—and up into a blue sky that seemed both close enough to touch and farther away than it ever seemed from the ground. There was more wind up here, as she'd guessed, and as they drew nearer the mountains it began to be gusty, and the pegasi side-slipped like birds to take advantage, or to keep their course, the *draia* swaying beneath them—and Sylvi's stomach, having decided to make the best of it after they'd left the Wall behind, began to object to the mode of transport again.

It was not a very great distance between the two realms—ordinarily the pegasi flew it easily in less than a day—but carrying heavy burdens slowed them down and wearied them sooner. They stopped three times, in each case setting down in mountain meadows surrounded by pathless trees. Sylvi knew there were no land-routes to Rhiandomeer but there was something a bit daunting about the unbroken circle of trees, despite the size of the meadows and the bright friendly scatter of wildflowers. She thought, *Yes, you would think so, you poor wingless human.* She would have liked to ask her father if he felt the same way, but it didn't seem polite to suggest that the pegasi were doing anything that might make their human guests uncomfortable (aside from failing to persuade the wind not to gust), even if they couldn't understand what she was saying. And where were they supposed to stop, in a country with no roads?

Ebon may have guessed. *What do you think?* he said on their first halt. She'd been washing her hands and face and having a drink at the stream, and was now staring at the whispering trees on the far bank. The rustle of their leaves sounded like counterpoint to the noise of the water cascading over its bed: beautiful but lonely. *It's very—quiet, isn't it?* she said finally.

This wasn't what she meant. It wasn't quiet; there was the wind among the trees, and birdsong, and the melody of the water, and scuffling in the undergrowth, and a few hums and whiffles from the pegasi—and the occasional word from her father. She was trying to think what else to say that was nearer to what she did mean, before Ebon started teasing her for being hopelessly urban and too accustomed to the bustle of the palace, and how noisy humans were, when he said, *It is a bit, isn't it? It's nicer at home. You'll see.*

They had set out as early as there was good daylight, and it was still nearing twilight when a huge double spiral of torches began to light up below them. There was a wide space at the centre of the spiral, and Sylvi knew they were going to land there when the pegasi tightened the ropes of her *drai* again—and this time, although she had not heard anything earlier, she heard all six of them say the holding-words, one right after another, a singing sort of noise on a falling scale, almost like a very short round in six parts: and then once, twice, more, as the shamans flanking them spoke. She saw the air shimmer with the *ooffhaloah*—or perhaps that was just her eyes, tired after a long windy day, staring at torchlight through the fast-dropping twilight—felt it settle around her, felt both the *drai* and the ropes stiffen with it—and her *drai* bobbed up till she was riding even with the straining necks of Ebon and Sorlalea on her either side, their inner wings brushing the edge of her *drai*.

They had set down and flown out again from their three rest stops with the great heave they'd made in the Outer Court—and counter-heave on landing, with the vast wings arched and scooping the air like bells to slow them as quickly as possible—and each time she found herself worrying about fragile pegasus legs . . . this final time, audibly enough, apparently, for Ebon to hear her, because he said, *Stop it, you baggage, we know what we're doing.* She was distracted by the slight breathlessness of his remark, since they didn't have to breathe for their sort of talking. And then they were down.

They set down with astonishing gentleness—the more astonishing for how exhausted they must all be. But her six bearers were galloping before she knew they had landed—she could see her father's bearers galloping ahead of her and only then realised that she was hearing the faint soft tap of pegasus hoofs to either side of her as well; her *drai* glided as smoothly as a boat on a still lake. They galloped on through the path made by the spiral, emerging as the last torches were lit: It's another dance, she thought, like the dance of the harnessing.

Lrrianay came forward first to greet her father—the back pair of his *doorathbaa* were still holding the ropes tightly while the front ropes had been gently let slacken so that he stepped, standing, out of his *drai*—and he put his hands on either side of the pegasus king's eyes as the pegasus king put his feather-hands on the human king's temples. His wings met behind Corone's back, like an embrace.

Sylvi had belatedly stripped her gloves off and was fumbling for the ends of the lacing that held her in her *drai*.

Hey. Move before I strangle.

She wanted to say something appropriately rude—the harnesses were made so beautifully they didn't move a finger's breadth, or a feather-hand finger's breadth, as the *draia* swung up or down—but she was too occupied. And then she realised they had stopped, and she was standing too. She let the last lace-end drop, and stepped forward, and her pegasi all moved lightly toward her, so the last ropes fell slack and her *drai* fell to the ground. She half heard a kind of exhale—not the pegasi—no, as if the magic were sighing in relief—and there was a faint twinkle on the ground, as if the magic had coalesced, and fallen, as a kind of shining sand.

Oh, thank you, she said. *Thank you, thank you.*

Lady, your closed-wing servant, said Ebon drily.

Remembering her manners she said aloud, "*Genfwa, esshfwa,*" which was the best all-purpose thank you she knew—the pegasi had rather an abundance of different thank yous for different occasions. There was probably a better one for now, but Sylvi's memory refused to provide one. She turned where she stood, and all six of her bearers nodded, and five of them smiled—she couldn't see whether black Ebon did or not, in the torch-flickering dark. But by then she was facing forward again, and the knots were let loose and rope-loops lifted off her bearers, and here was the pegasus queen herself to welcome her. Sylvi took a deep breath and bowed.

"Welhum, fwooth shile off humaa hing an swaah bohn-bluah uff ouu deeahss Ebon," Aliaalia said, or almost sang: Welcome, fourth child of the human king and sworn bond-blood of our dearest Ebon.

Ebon sounded like a verse in the song: *Ehhboohn*, and she swept her wings out and back in a gesture so grand and beautiful and effortless it brought a prickle of tears to Sylvi's eyes. The queen's golden wings caught the torchlight and for a moment there was no sky and no land, just two vast burning wings. And then she folded them and was the queen of the pegasi again, greeting the strange human child—briefly she half roused her wings to stretch her tiny feather-hands toward Sylvi, and softly brushed her temples.

Sylvi thought, even their speech is a dance, and, shyly, because her own voice seemed rough and flat, with none of the singing echoes of the pegasi's voices, replied, "*Genfwa, ihhu, Ebon sa sshira* **sshira** *fra, dooafwa swhee*," and she held her hands out, one toward the queen and one toward Ebon: the important person she was speaking to and the important person she was speaking about. It was a much grander gesture when you had wings: her arms felt very thin and naked. She hoped she'd said, Thank you, crown-wearer, Ebon is my very best friend—and was feeling a little bit pleased with herself, because it wasn't a sentence she'd memorised, as she'd memorised her speech, and the words had come to her as if she were speaking a language she knew.

It was only then that she noticed another pegasus standing near the queen, and without knowing anything about him except that he was important enough to be standing alone by the queen she knew immediately that he was much more than that—that he was terribly important—perhaps more important than the queen, possibly as important as the king himself. The queen dropped her hands and stepped back and Sylvi was left to face this alarming pegasus by herself. She wasn't accustomed to pegasi being alarming.

No, not quite by herself; five of her six bearers had left her, but Ebon had stepped forward and was standing by her right shoulder.

Even without his silence warning her, she knew not to speak to him in front of this pegasus.

She had no idea what to do. The queen's gesture had been both generous and flattering; putting your hands on someone's temples in greeting was both a great honour and a great intimacy. She had no trouble resisting any temptation to reach out to this pegasus; she felt that trying to touch him might be like putting your hand in a fire—while the queen's burning wings had seemed like a blessing. She shook herself out of her paralysis, folded her hands over her breast and bowed.

When she stood up again and looked at him, he was still looking expressionlessly back at her. Pegasi were rarely expressionless, even if you couldn't read what the expression was, and after four years with Ebon she read most pegasi very well. After a silence that could have been no more than a few heartbeats but felt like a century he said, "And so you have come to us, Sylviianel, bond-sister to Ebon."

She blinked. He'd spoken the words aloud—managing the individual words very clearly. The oral pegasus language all ran together; there were breaks between phrases, not between words—and the phrases tended to be long (pegasus lung capacity had something to do with this). On the rare occasions Sylvi had heard a pegasus try to speak human—usually Lrrianay—they sounded as the queen did, a kind of singing blur with no sharp consonants. She'd never heard a pegasus speak as this one just had—but he had also, she thought, half said them in her mind. In her *mind*? Like Ebon? In this case—if she weren't imagining it—it was an uncomfortable and off-balancing mode of communication, almost scratchy, as if she were sitting on a burr. No, she thought, don't be silly, it's just strange. And it's too strange after the day I've had, she thought, hopefully or sternly, not wanting to be frightened if she didn't have to be, when she'd only just arrived, when her father was leaving her here *alone* the day after tomorrow.... Her father was standing statue-still on the far side of a row of torches. She knew that stillness: he was stopping himself interfering. He was *leaving* the day after tomorrow.... But the queen hadn't frightened her.

"Sir," she said, "*fffffwifwif.*" Great sir. There were several more *ff*'s than she needed, because she was stuttering with nerves, but that made his greatness greater, which was perhaps a good idea. She did not try to speak silently—she didn't want to speak silently to this pegasus, even if she was able to. She tried not to shrink toward Ebon, although out of the corner of her eye she saw that his feathers were ruffling up, which indicated he was upset too.

The queen said, "Thiiss iss Hibeehea, ouu gheaaesss shamaaahn."

"And Speaker," said Hibeehea. "A service you appear not to require."

"Oh, sir!" she blurted out, too miserable at the revelation that she'd gone wrong already to try to think what she ought to say, or whether she could say any of it in pegasi. "I only wished to show that I am *trying!*" Awkwardly she added, "*Ffffwhifwif. Sangharaharah. Tisianhaa!*" Sir. Beg much pardon. Am trying!

Mysteriously, this was the right thing to say. Some of the stiffness went out of Hibeehea, and the queen laughed aloud, raising her head and letting a long, light, singing *heeeee* slip out between her lips.

"It is partly my fault," said her father from where he stood next to his bond-brother, and Sylvi noticed that he was not speaking slowly, as he did when, in the human palace, he hoped Lrrianay might understand. "I have told her to study your oral language and to ask Ebon to help her. I'm afraid I have led her to believe that the unusualness of the bond between her and her bond-brother puts a greater responsibility on her, in this and in other things."

"As it does, king," said Hibeehea. "As it does. And it is not to be expected that children should understand all the ways of speech and courtesy, especially in a stranger's home. Nor perhaps should it be expected that an old shaman, long accustomed to the undisturbed ways of his people, should at once perceive what is happening under his nose—especially in a strange child of a people whom my people have believed for a thousand years cannot learn to speak to us as we speak to each other. Welcome, small one, you have studied well."

Now what? Do I say thank you or *genfwa?* she thought. Oh, wasn't there a thank you just for shamans? What ... *mlaaralalaam* perhaps? Should she risk it? So she said all three, getting into a muddle about the *aa*'s, and added some extra *ff*'s again to *ffffwifwif*. To her surprise he unfolded one wing and touched the centre of her forehead with the tips of his primaries. And then he walked away.

Whew, said Ebon. *That was worse than flying over the mountains with Guaffa and a boulder.*

What just happened? Can he hear us?

Not now. I mean, yes, me anyway, but he won't be listening. Shamans don't listen unless they give you fair warning. But don't talk to me if he's talking to you!

But what happened?

I don't know exactly. But he hasn't been happy with you and your dad coming here. You particularly. Your dad didn't get a Speaker here because he and my dad are bond-blood. If you can talk to the reigning monarch you don't have to be able to talk to anyone else—that's something out of one of the oldest chronicles, from before your first king, before the Alliance—I don't know who else we're supposed to be able to do silent-speech with, but it's a really long time ago. And then you humans happened and you couldn't talk to our sovereign but we were still allies, and this bonding thing was invented. Although before you and me they'd decided being able to talk to the sovereign was symbolic—but humans never come here so the rule never got used with you anyway. Some of the older ones, especially the shamans, who—who hold us together, you know? The shamans hold all of us together like those words they taught us hold the draia— they got really worried about the old rule with you coming here and they decided that our dads were going to count as being able to talk to each other, but what about you?

*So it's this big good thing that your dad doesn't get a Speaker and then it's this big uneasy thing that you're going to have to have one because you can't talk to the king even though the **reason** you're here is that you can talk to the king's fourth son. So to make the uneasiness go away you have the huge honour of Hibeehea as your Speaker. He's scary but he's not a bad old bird really and having decided to support your coming he said he'd be your Speaker. And it may be an even huger honour to you as a mere fourth child to have Hibeehea Srrrwa as your Speaker as it was for your dad not to have one, are you following me? And then you act like he's superfluous. I didn't teach you anything to say to my mum! You see?*

I see.

She turned and looked for Hibeehea. She didn't see him at once, and shouldn't have been able to pick him out from the crowd of pegasi; in the torchlight, and tired as she was, the silky gleaming backs of the pegasi swirled together and began to look like some exquisite and impossible kind of marble. But perhaps he felt her looking for him, because there was suddenly a little space around him, and he turned and looked back at her. She crossed her hands over her breast again and gave him her deepest bow, even deeper than she'd offered the queen: the sort of bow that, when you're tired and worried, you could easily not be able to get back out of, or you might even fall over, the sort of bow you shouldn't risk making when it was important. She told herself that this was the best bow she had ever made, and felt herself come gracefully back to upright again in a way that even when she wasn't tired and worried and a little frightened was rarely possible for her. But she was surrounded by pegasi, who were perhaps the most graceful creatures in the world, and she wanted, very badly, to make a good impression on one of them.

He couldn't have known what a bow like that cost her, the graceless human princess. But in spite of the distance between them, and the uncertain light, she saw his ears briefly quirk, and the black shadow lines when he smiled at her, and while his return bow was only a lowering of the head, he held it down the length of time it took to take a long, slow breath. And then he nodded at her, and turned away.

There was food after that, but she was by then so tired she could barely eat, except to recognise that she *didn't* recognise about half of what was offered to her. It all tasted good however—and she realised with the first bite that she was tremendously hungry, and was even willing to put off sleep a little longer to eat—and she ate and ate. She sat next to her father, but he spent more time looking around than he did eating, and when she looked at him he seemed so baffled and disoriented that she felt even more lost and far away from home. . . .

And he was *leaving her here alone.* . . .

The banquet in her father's honour was tomorrow, and the morning after that one human passenger in one *drai* would fly back to the palace. She looked at him again, and he caught her eye and smiled, and with the smile he was her father again, king of his country, visiting his friend, king of the pegasi.

But the day after tomorrow she would still be here, alone.

They had brought certain things from the human lands: grapes and melons from the king's glasshouses, tender crumbly white rolls from the king's kitchens, which the king and his daughter knew the pegasi liked. There was a whispery murmur of speech, which Sylvi was too tired to try to translate; she was too tired also to try and read the

pegasi's kinetic language; she did respond to the sign-language gestures of *welcome* and *welcome, friend,* that some of the pegasi had learnt
to greet them.

Please feed me and go away, she thought. She hadn't realised she'd
thought it aloud till there was a tickly sensation across her ear, which
was Ebon's mane as he shook his head and laughed at her.

All you did was sit there, he said. *Why are you so tired?*

I sat very diligently, she said.

CHAPTER 12

When she woke the next morning she couldn't imagine where she was. She was lying on a mattress on the ground, which should have been cold and uncomfortable, but was not. It was a feather mattress, and as she slept, it had shaped itself under and curled itself around her like a friendly animal, or animals; she thought of the way her father's dogs lay together in sinuous heaps. There was another, lighter feather mattress or feather-stuffed quilt over her, and pillows beneath her head, and sunlight dappling her face through leaves. She didn't want this mysterious idyll to end, but as she turned her head she saw a bright rufous pegasus walk past, in the clear daylight beyond the tree shadows, and it all came back to her in a rush.

She sat up with a sigh, and thrust her feet out from under the coverlet. She'd somehow managed to get herself into her nightgown—she didn't remember this at all—but she knew she needed a bath. She stood up, waveringly.

A pegasus she didn't remember meeting before appeared almost as if by magic, briefly touched her cheek with a feather-hand, nodded and turned away from her, looking back over her shoulder to see if she would follow. She did, bemusedly stroking her cheek where the pegasus had touched her. The pegasus led her toward a sound of running water and then Ebon emerged from the darker tree-shadows.

Clear morning and clear sky to you all day, he said. *And it looks like we might get them. You humans like privacy for bathing, don't you? Straight through there, then, there's a pool, and it's yours while you're here. Someone even thought of, uh, towels. When you're done rattle the bushes and I'll come for you.*

I'll need some clothes, she said.

Right away? Surely it's warm enough in this sun even without any hair? Never mind. I'll get your dad to show me what to bring, and I'll leave it here.

She had a glorious bath, made only slightly less glorious by an ignoble fear that some pegasus or other would forget that humans like privacy while they bathe and interrupt her; there was nothing (she decided) like being entirely surrounded by pegasi to make a human feel stringy and pathetic, naked as a rat's tail. She wondered what the towels were for when there weren't any humans to use them as towels—since there never were any humans to use them as towels, and they felt soft with some kind of use. Perhaps the pegasi had other things that needed drying. Maybe baby pegasi had baths; perhaps they dried the dishes after a banquet. She looked at the towel she wrapped herself up in: it had the same kind of soft, close, near-invisible weaving that all the pegasus fabric she'd ever seen did, but it was thick and heavy, like fine wool, but smoother than any wool she knew.

Her bag of clothes was hanging on a branch as promised and, assuming she'd be warned in advance of any formal occasions, she dressed in tunic and trousers, and then took hold of the bush and rattled. She could smell food, and she was hungry again.

That first day was all about her father, which suited Sylvi very well. Her father did all those royal and gracious and diplomatic things better than she did, the catching on to unknown customs and unusual situations—he, like Danacor was doing now, had travelled a great deal when he was the sovereign's heir, both round his own country and outside it. Sylvi was more than happy to stay in his shadow and let him take the brunt of the attention—and perhaps pick up what she could. *He was leaving her here. . . .*

They went for a long walk for most of that day, the two humans, Lrrianay and Ebon and a dozen more pegasi of those the visitors had met the evening before; they stopped often, and there were cushions for the humans, and food and drink were offered. Sylvi found the strangeness much more tiring than the walking. But she was glad to see that they walked on well-worn paths. *I told you,* said Ebon. *We walk a lot.*

Everywhere they went there were more groups of pegasi, who came as if from nowhere to see them—but they always appeared from round corners of rock, or up steep paths or through trees, never flying overhead. The pegasi would walk up to them, slowly, heads and tails raised and wings a little arched in what Sylvi thought of as their best-foot-forward pose; often they had ribbons or flowers in their manes, and intricately embroidered *siragaa* and *nralaa* around their necks. They would bow their heads and lift one curled foreleg and then the other, setting each down very precisely; a few had ribbons around their ankles. Most of them said "welcome"; a few said a sentence or two. Sylvi noticed that they hummed through the breaks between words: *welhummmmfrennnnhuuumaannnnnnn.*

Very occasionally Lrrianay would make a quick open-and-shut gesture with a feather-hand, and a few murmured words, and a pegasus might then touch the face of one or both the humans as he or she also said a few words. There was for Sylvi a funny hazy quality to the entire experience of meeting so many new pegasi, and it grew hazier yet when a pegasus touched her, as if the attempt at communication was turning into a cloud, like water turns into steam when heated.

The visitors' party paused the longest in a *shfeeah* at the edge of a wood; Sylvi had no warning that this glint of sunlight through the trees was going to be anything other than another meadow. But instead there was a series of small fields, tucked together as cleverly as the pieces of a sky hold to take advantage of the land's contours, with the early spring crops showing in neat rows of green, and a few small low buildings together in a cluster which had, Sylvi saw at once, not nearly enough walls.

That evening's banquet was very grand indeed. There were long tables with what looked like banners laid over them—longer, wider and more elaborate versions of the *siragaa*. Each was a different colour, or more than one colour swirled together, and many had cut or scalloped edges, and most were embroidered, with birds and leaves and flowers, as well as many other symbols Sylvi did not recognise. There were candlesticks of wood and stone, and a scattering of small sculpted shapes, mostly of creatures—deer, foxes, bears, badgers, hedgehogs, squirrels, erenooms, fornols, pegasi—curled up sleeping. The tables looked magnificent even before the bowls of food—mostly wooden and beautifully carved, and some copper or copper-bound, and a few silver platters she recognised as human gifts—were put on them. There were more banners threaded through the branches of the trees at the edge of the meadow where the tables were set. The spiral of torches had been taken away, although there were poles with fresh torches set round the edges of the meadow. She noticed this evening, as she had not the evening before, that the torch-poles were also sculpted, with long curling lines not unlike the flow of a pegasus tail.

Sylvi had watched a little of the setting-up process—it was already well begun when they came back from their day's walk. The tables were stored in a kind of pavilion similar to the *shfeeah* buildings and near the stream, but they were brought out to stand in the meadow the human king's party had flown into the evening before. The tables were moved by pairs of pegasi again wearing harness. Poles were laid on the floor of the pavilion and run between the legs of the tables. The harnessed pegasi again knelt, so that the little hands of other pegasi had only to lift the poles high enough to thread them through the harness, sometimes assisted by a boost from a strong pegasus foreleg. Then the kneeling pegasi stood up, and the poles took the weight of the table. Even the bowls of food had to be filled gradually, in deference to the weakness of pegasi hands, or moved by a carrying frame. There was a flagstone path to the edge of the stream and low knapped-stone platforms there for food preparation, but the exquisite little flint knives, wooden chopping boards and other tools (including baskets to carry the rubbish to the mulch-and-compost area) were kept in the pavilion. But everything the pegasi did they did as if they were dancing, as if they would do it this way even if their hands were as strong as humans'.

There were even two chairs, one very tall one at the narrow head of one of the tables, and a not very much shorter one at the head of the table next to it, and you climbed up two steps to sit in them, so you were no shorter than the standing pegasi.

For the banquet the pegasi all wore ribbons or flowers plaited into their manes and tails, or feathers some other colour than their own wings tucked into the plaits, and a few had ribbons around their ears and ankles as well. The royal pegasi wore flowers but also wide silky *siragaa* spangled with tiny shining gems; Hibeehea was wearing two *nralaa* on two damask ribbons.

Sylvi wore the one formal dress she had brought with her, an almost-pegasus russet, long and very full and flowing, with a pegasus-

chestnut red-brown garnet on a pegasus-gold chain around her neck. She twisted her hair onto the top of her head and held it there by a pin whose head, no bigger than her littlest fingernail, was pegasus-made, glinting with silver netting and splinters of gems so small you only knew they were there by their sparkle: Ebon had given it to her on her fifteenth birthday.

*Can't I give you **anything?*** she'd said, as she said to him every year on her birthday.

Just make sure there are always grapes when I come visiting, he'd replied.

You couldn't look regal when you were this short, Sylvi thought, but she felt she looked as nice as possible, in spite of having only two legs and no wings. The swing of her skirt was almost a dance—and yesterday she had managed her bow to Hibeehea. She was embarrassed by her relief that he had not come on the walk with them today; she had known it was too much to hope for that she would not see him tonight either, but her heart still sank when she caught sight of him.

The pegasi wandered around, plucking up a bit of this or that from any bowl they chose as they moved, sometimes using their feather-hands, sometimes delicately using their lips. Sylvi noticed that if it was a long reach they used their necks; there was far too much wing to fold out of the way if they had to reach with their hands. They talked among themselves in gesture and aloud, and as they moved, they were careful also to pass the two chairs and greet the human king and his daughter, and to exchange some communication too, if they could. The human king and his daughter had bowls in their laps, which pairs of pegasi had brought them initially; these were full of delicacies, but many of the pegasi who paused to speak to them dropped further morsels into them. Everything Sylvi sampled tasted superb—including the *fwhfwhfwha*, which was indeed infinitely nicer than watered wine—

but she began to feel trapped, sitting in her chair, weighed down by her bowl. Even Ebon went wandering, although he always came back.

Sylvi had met several more of the pegasus shamans by now, and was careful to let any one of them translate for her, if one were near her—and one usually was, like sentries on duty, Sylvi thought. Ebon, when he was beside her, remained silent, and let the shamans speak. But this evening, with the clear daylight gone, and the stippling, unreliable torchlight again seeming to manifest the essential, the absolute mystery of this place she found herself in, the haziness apparently caused by having her face touched by the pegasi's feather-hands earlier that day seemed strangely now to focus any attempt at communication . . . perhaps it was only she felt that she was understanding more, since most of what was said to her was something about welcome: welcome, welcome human, welcome human child, welcome princess, welcome to our country, welcome, welcome; but she seemed to hear *What a pretty dress!* when the shaman said to her gravely, "She wishes to praise your garment"—although this shaman did not have Hibeehea's clear diction, and it sounded more like, *Sheewhishesstoopwwaisssyooah-gahhmen.* But Sylvi was preoccupied with having understood "dress," which was more nearly "long encircling human *siraga.*" It is not really so surprising, she thought; it's always been the little dumb superficial stuff that us humans can understand.

After a while Sylvi picked up her bowl in her two strong human hands, and set it down on the nearest edge of the nearest table, and went wandering too—letting the swish of her long encircling human *siraga* and the marvelousness of the pegasi teach her how to walk lightly. It was too peculiarly formal to sit still when everyone else was moving, like endlessly sitting out at a ball. She couldn't stop thinking of the pegasi as dancing, and while her own real dancing was middling at best—at those formal occasions at home when a dancing princess was required—she felt, here, that her best, lightest, swingiest walk was more accepting-of-the-welcome-offered than sitting still. Although she kept a wary eye out for Hibeehea or any other sign that she was getting it wrong again.

You would tell me if I were totally messing up again, wouldn't you? she said to Ebon. *Like yesterday, with Hibeehea.*

Ebon made a small noise she recognised as ironic. *I would tell you if I knew soon enough. You went over the edge really fast yesterday.*

Has anyone—said anything about it?

Said anything? Why would they? You apologised and Hibeehea accepted your apology. Hey, that was a formal thing. When you leave the formal thing, you leave it.

Well, this is another formal thing, isn't it?

It's a different formal thing. If you mess up here it'll be a new mess.

Oh, thanks. Thanks a lot.

Her father only smiled at her—and stayed sitting down. He didn't stand up till it was time to give his speech—which he did beautifully, and she knew he did it beautifully, and she knew that the pegasi accepted it as having been done beautifully. But it was all wrong, she thought in distress. It wasn't a dance.

The pegasi had stopped wandering while her father spoke, so it was easy for her to stop too. She stood with her arm along Ebon's neck, her hand holding on to a plait; he arched the wing behind her just enough to give her something to lean against. There were pegasi all around her, standing quietly but for the occasional flick of an ear, swish of a tail, rustle of a wing. And yet the torchlight was still dancing, and as it danced across pegasus backs, the pegasi danced too, as did the trees and the long grass at the edge of the meadow: all these danced with the torchlight and with the shadows the torchlight cast. All but her father, who remained a standing human with light and shadow dancing over him. Sylvi held out her free hand and looked down at it: I suppose I'm just a standing human in dancing shadows too, she thought.

There was her cue: "And I am glad to introduce my daughter to you. . . ." Her father's speeches were never long—"no one listens to a long speech" was one of his precepts—but he had teased her that the real reason he wanted her to give a speech on this occasion was so that his could be shorter yet. "I can't get my mouth around all those pegasi vowels," he said.

"The *ffff*'s are even worse," Sylvi had replied: but her father was saying *aooarhwaia mwaarai*—beloved daughter—as if he'd never had any problem. She sighed, and Ebon said, *Three wings*, which was pegasi for "good luck." The pegasi parted before her—there was no looking around; they seemed to know where she was—and she walked, trying to feel that she was dancing, along what was now a path among them. They moved, gently, gracefully, so that their heads were toward her as she passed them: cream and gold, brown and copper. A few of them pulled out flowers or decorative feathers from their wings and manes and tossed them down before her. She went slowly, skirt swinging, and stood beside her father, who bowed to her and then moved away, to sit down again in his chair.

She folded her hands in front of her as if she were reciting a lesson for Ahathin, but also to keep her hands from trembling—her arms from trembling, her whole body from trembling. The long skirt hid her trembling knees. "I am beyond honoured to be here," she began: "*Waarooawhha niira hee.*" And then she couldn't go on.

It wasn't that she had forgotten the words. She knew what came next: *It has been my great wish since I have known Ebon that I should see his home. I knew I would not, because humans do not come here. That I am here is a gift beyond my imagining. I bow my best bow to you, to each of you I bow once, twice, three times. Respected friends, my thanks and gratitude. Thank you.* But the words would not come out. They were trapped, trapped between her folded hands, between her arms and her body, between her pressed-together knees.

She took a deep breath and dropped her hands. She took a step forward. She bent down and picked up one of the flowers the pegasi had thrown in her path. She looked at it for a moment and then tucked it into the collar of her dress. She opened her mouth.

"*Genfwa*," she said, thank you. That wasn't what came next; that was supposed to come at the end. "I knew Ebon's country would be very beautiful"—she stumbled over "very beautiful," *fffooonangirii*—"but it is beautiful in a way that speaks to my . . ."

Spirit, she wanted to say. She could feel her mind slipping away, her memory disintegrating; *spirit* was the sort of word a human could not say in pegasi, nor a pegasus in human: you could say *beautiful*, you could even say *friend;* but you could not say *heart* or *spirit*, and you could not say *anger* or *love*. Spirit, she thought. She looked out into her audience; she was speaking slowly, so no one knew yet that she could not say her next word.

Pegasus eyes are mostly dark; some are copper; a few are pale honey. Ebon's were as black as his hair. Sylvi looked at the pegasi looking at her, and her eyes met the queen's eyes, which were a gold a few shades darker than her coat. The queen smiled at her, holding her gaze. Spirit, thought Sylvi.

". . . *Swaasooria*."

She thought she heard a few pegasi sigh; it was the first sound any of them had made since they parted to let her through. She held up her hands, palms together, and then spread them out, embracing her audience.

"I am not only honoured to be here," she went on, "I am glad and grateful." *Waaee shaar daeal.* "Thank you, thank you."

She remembered something Ebon had told her: *It's not just ffff for emphasis, although that's the usual. You ever really want to knock someone out, say "vraai." You can stick it in pretty much anywhere, but you have to mean it. You don't use "vraai" for* . . . Ebon had paused and looked suddenly uncertain, and then distressed. *Maybe you can't use it. You wouldn't use it for any of the stuff humans can talk to us about.*

"*Vraai,*" she said. "*Genfwa, esshfwa, vraai.* " Heart, she thought, *gafweehaa.* Love, *oranooiaka.* Thank you from the love in my heart. "*Esshfffwa gafweehaa oranooiaka gloh.*" And she walked up to the queen, and unfastened the garnet from around her own neck, and lifted it up to tuck it round a lock of the queen's mane.

Again she woke the next morning not able to remember how the night before had ended. There had been dancing, she remembered—human dancing too. She had danced with her father, who had asked her when she had rewritten her speech. "I didn't, " she said. "Those were the words that wanted to come out."

He had looked at her, smiling, but the smile was a little sad. "Well, I'm sure they were all excellent words—congratulations."

But she couldn't remember much more after that. She remembered feeling very sleepy, as if the pegasus feet and wings were writing a sleep spell. . . . Even before she opened her eyes she could feel herself smiling; the last thing she could remember was watching the pegasi all seem to flow together in the rhythm of their dance—was it that that made her smile?

There had been a dream—presumably after she'd fallen asleep, although perhaps it was still a result of the spell of the dancing—a dream of flying. She was flying with Ebon, but she was herself flying—she could almost feel the weight of wings now, pulling on the ordinary human bones of her shoulders as she lay on her side with her face on a pillow and the gentle hummocks of the mattress all around her. The friendly feather mattress would no doubt curl itself under and around wings as it did the rest of her. She didn't want to open her eyes, or to move . . . to have her wings go away. . . .

She woke again, knowing that it must be late—*her father was leaving today!* No, he wouldn't have left without saying good-bye, but— She shot out from under the coverlet this time without thinking of either the comfort she was abandoning or the wings she had briefly possessed (for she had had them, brought momentarily out of her dream) and looked around. She heard voices, one of them human, and turned that way.

"Good morning, young one," said her father.

"I'm sorry—"

"No, I overslept too. Something very hypnotic about the dancing, wasn't there? If you want to call it dancing. Dancing seems too frivolous a word somehow."

Slowly she said, "It's as if they were making—creating something. It was like . . . another sort of weaving." Or another sort of spell, she thought, remembering the rainbow veil and the smoke of binding. But it had been everyone, last night, all the pegasi, not just the shamans—and even, a little, herself and her father—who were the makers.

"Torchlight and shadow weaving," said her father.

No, thought Sylvi. That's just turning it into human words.

"And being pegasi," said her father. "But what were they making? A rope, a basket, a *drai*, one of those amazing collars—"

"*Siragaa,*" murmured Sylvi.

"A tablecloth?" her father continued. "I've tried to ask Lrrianay, but I don't understand his answer. Or maybe he doesn't understand my question." He looked a little downcast. "Mostly it's been a little easier here—the air and my head are clearer." He tried to smile. "I don't suppose you've noticed any difference? But you and Ebon never have any trouble talking to each other, do you?"

She thought of telling him about the haziness, about the disorienting sense of standing in a huge space listening to a noise like echoes, except that what made the echoes and what they reverberated against were unknown to her—and decided not to. "No." She looked at him and smiled. "Don't worry."

"I—" He hesitated. "Your pegasi has improved just since you've been here—two days. I didn't understand all of your speech last night, but I could pick up that Lrrianay did."

"I'm not sure it has improved," said Sylvi honestly. "I was inspired, I think. Somehow. Something about last night."

"The torchlight and shadows," said her father. "They were weaving a . . ."

He stopped, but she could hear what he wasn't saying as clearly as she heard Ebon's words in her mind: ". . . a net to pull you away from us."

"Dad," she said, "I'm human. I'm a human among pegasi. I've only got two legs and I can't fly. None of that's going to change." To her horror, her voice wavered. Almost three weeks. Here. Alone. One human among all the pegasi. . . .

"If there is *any* doubt in your mind—come back with me. We've already made history, coming here. You don't have to make any more if you don't want . . . if you can't . . . if it's too hard. Many times in the last weeks—since you had Ebon's invitation—I've thought, what are we *doing*, sending a fifteen-year-old child where none of us has ever been?"

"Fifteen isn't a child," said Sylvi. "And I'm nearly sixteen. I'm just visiting my friend at home—and you and Mum like my friend *and* his parents. They'll take good care of me. And I'm going to enjoy it. I won't make any of the kind of history anybody will have to learn later. I promise."

"You'll do it beautifully," said her father. "If you find out what the dancing makes, you can tell me when you get back. But Sylviianel . . . be careful of your promises. I'm not going to hold you to this one," and for a moment he wasn't her father, but the king.

She stared at him, then looked quickly past him, not wanting to know what was in his face. She looked anxiously at the sky, wrapping her arms around herself in her nightdress, telling herself she was shivering only because she was cold, and maybe just a little because her father was going away and leaving her . . . but the weather was warm, and Ebon was here. "It's already later than when we left the palace," she said. "That was barely dawn."

"The prevailing wind is in our favour going back, I'm told," he replied. "Also they won't have to spend any time or energy making any circuits so the earthbound can point and wave at one of their own flying with the pegasi. But we do need to go now—I was going to come and wake you in another minute. You'll come and see me off?" He took her by the shoulders and stared into her face as if memorising her. "It's not going to be easy to fly away and leave you behind."

She smiled, but her face felt stiff. "You promised. *We* promised."

"Yes. We promised. King and king's daughter." He stooped and kissed her, and turned away.

So she was still wearing her nightdress as she followed him to the big meadow where twenty-two pegasi had landed in a candlelit spiral a day and a half ago, and where the banquet had been held last night. The meadow was clear this morning, of both banqueting tables and spirals. She lingered briefly at the edge of the trees; it didn't seem respectful to be in her nightdress, barefoot, her hair standing on end and her face unwashed. She rubbed her face with her hands and smoothed her hair back; but then in an odd way—a way that seemed to align itself with the haziness, which this morning seemed to be standing close to her, almost like a human or a pegasus whom she could turn to and ask questions of, like, *Who are you? What are you? Why are you standing near me?*—it almost seemed more respectful to be barefoot and in her shift than in the gown she had worn last night, and with her hair put up like a grown woman's for a ball. She stepped forward, out of the trees, and the pegasi who were already there silently made room for her.

She didn't notice when Ebon joined her; only noticed that he had. He and she and many other pegasi watched as the draia were laid out and the ropes stretched away from them. The luggage drai this time was very small, and a mere two pegasi would carry it: much of what Corone and his daughter had brought had been gifts; most of what was going back now was gifts from the pegasi.

The pegasi made everything ready just as they had done in the Outer Court of the palace; this was the way they did it, and it had nothing to do with who was or wasn't watching. Even the way the pegasi who were not immediately concerned with the harnessing were standing seemed to be creating some kind of shape or sign; Sylvi thought it might have been an extension of the wheel-and-spokes of the draia and their ropes, only made of standing pegasi. A charm for a safe flight? They're just naturally polite and elegant, she thought, half despairingly, holding the edge of her nightgown down against a little eddy of wind.

My father is leaving me here alone—

And then there was a violent blow to her shoulder and she staggered away, narrowly missing running into the pegasus standing on her other side.

Oops, said Ebon. *Sorry.*

You're as clumsy as a human, said Sylvi.

Never, he replied. *Say that again and I'll stand on your foot.*

She looked up at him and realised he was worrying about her. This seemed so implausible she laughed, and—because she read Ebon very well now—she saw him relax. *You did that deliberately.*

Hmmph, said Ebon. *Would I do that?*

This morning, because there were fewer harnesses to put on, and perhaps because her father was leaving, it seemed to Sylvi that it took no time at all before she had to say good-bye. The pegasi rearranged themselves into another shape, which made her and her father the centre of it, but they bowed their heads or turned aside as the king held out his arms to his daughter and she rushed forward into them.

"You'll have an amazing journey," he said. "I envy you the Caves."

"You could have stayed longer," she said into his shirtfront. There was a pause, and she looked up into his face. He was wearing an expression she had never seen before, quizzical and a little uncertain.

"Only you were invited to see the Caves," he said. "I'm only here at all because I wouldn't send you all alone to this place where almost no human has ever been—and certainly no one specifically bound by the Alliance has ever set foot. Lrrianay understood that I could not let you come alone, and so agreed to bring me too—for a day, two days, before your real visit begins, I imagine. And I agreed to that because I trust Lrrianay even more than I trust my own right hand."

She stared up at him. "You didn't tell me that," she said.

229

He raised his shoulders. "I wasn't planning on telling you at all," he said. "There is something about the air of this place. Or maybe it's just the pegasi."

She looked around. Even in their turning-away the pegasi had made a pattern; the smaller smooth arches of their bent necks and bodies provided counter-curves like a scalloped hem, around the edge of the circle she and her father stood in. "I think it's the pegasi."

"So do I," said her father, and bent and kissed her again. "I won't tell you to be good, because I know you'll do your best, and your best is very, very good, young one, and don't let being my daughter blight that fact. Your mother says that I can worry that I'm not worrying well enough, and I suspect you've inherited that talent. I won't tell you to take care of yourself, because I know the pegasi will take the best care of you that anyone could—better than the mere human care you mostly have to put up with. Perhaps I'll just tell you to have fun. And that I love you and will miss you. How very unkingly of me."

Sylvi meant to say something—good-bye, I love you—but her mouth wouldn't work.

He turned away as if it hurt him, and walked to his drai. Two pegasi fastened the safety-ropes around him, and then stood away. The eight pegasi moved sideways, taking up the slack till the human king swung clear of the ground. Sylvi caught her breath: she heard Guaffa say the necessary word, heard it echoed by the others—heard echoes she was sure had nothing to do with her ears—heard the chord the shamans sang. Almost she saw the magic-weave that held the king's drai twinkle into being, but perhaps that was just something about her eyes this morning, watching her father *leave her*—and then, in perfect unison, the pegasi broke into a canter, and almost immediately into a gallop, racing away from her. Six pegasi accompanied them; three of them she knew were shamans. The two luggage-bearers followed last, a little to one side, as if aware of the princess' eyes on her father's drai. It was interesting, thought Sylvi distantly, her immediate attention floundering in what her father had just told her, in her awareness that she had chosen to stay, and that he *was leaving right now*—it was interesting seeing what was happening from the ground, seeing what it looked like. It was just another pegasus dance.

The pegasi leaped into the air. Her father raised his arm over his head. She started to raise hers in response and realised he couldn't see her. It seemed barely a breath or even a heartbeat before he was little more than a black dot above the trees on the horizon.

Her eyes burned. She kept them stretched wide open, watching the dot disappear. Ebon had joined her, and tucked the top of an open wing around her as she stood where her father had left her. She stood like that for a long moment more, still and cold as stone, but then she began to notice the warmth of Ebon's feathers and the gentle movement of his side as he breathed. The dot had disappeared; she was staring with her dry, burning eyes at empty sky.

"I'll have my bath now, please," she said aloud, as if she were talking to a human.

"Baff," said Ebon. "Fwaayomee." *Follow me.*

Those were almost the last words she said aloud for the rest of that day. As soon as her father was gone there seemed very little reason to speak out loud; there was Ebon, of course, but more mysteriously she seemed not to want to speak aloud to the pegasi. Their own oral language was liquid and musical, but it was only "spoken" with the kinetic language which the human body could not emulate, and it seemed to her, listening and watching, that the unspoken word breaks were instead created by gesture; the sound alone was a kind of murmur, like wind or water. All those pegasi vowels, she thought. This was something else she could not imitate; she had to breathe too often, and her breaths were shallow.

Ebon had tried to tell her, when he'd helped her with her speech: *Stop making those great thumping human pauses. Someone could fall into one and disappear forever. Just speak it, don't—I don't know, don't* **march** *it, like Fthoom coming down a corridor, thud thud thud.*

She hadn't known what he meant. She thought possibly she did now.

That morning Ebon was rattling the bushes at her before she had climbed out of her pond-bath. *If you don't want me to come in there after you,* he said, *hurry up. It's late, and we have a long way to go.*

She emerged from her little private glen still damp, crossly, rubbing her wet hair but already aware that the pegasi themselves were speaking aloud less since her father had left. This, presumably, was the usual pegasus way; they had spoken aloud more for her father's sake, since humans were accustomed to mouth-language. Now that it was only herself, the human who could silent-speak to one of their own . . .

All alone. Her father had left her all *alone*—

She had washed out her clothes from the day before because she didn't want to be dirty. She hadn't seen a pegasus bathe, or swim, or even seen one wet, but they all *gleamed*, while she was almost hairless and faintly wrinkly—even the wrinkles across her knuckles, the folds in the bends of her elbows, looked ridiculous to her, surrounded by pegasi—and couldn't gleam. But that meant she now had wet clothing to do something with—what long way did they have to go?

Here. Eat. There was a thin wooden bowl of something hot and soft that tasted a little like oatmeal with the bran still in, and another bowl of cold liquid that was almost but not quite water. Her face was the wrong shape to eat the oatmeal out of the bowl, so she dipped it up stickily and inefficiently with her fingers. It wasn't too hot for her mouth, but it was for her fingers. She sucked them, and eyed the bushes, wondering if she could use a twig. . . .

Oh, wet textiles, you humans, ugh, you're obsessed with putting things in water.

She didn't know what he did with them; he bore them off distastefully, tossing them round over his neck with his teeth and shuddering dramatically when they smacked down across his back, while she tried to eat without burning her fingers or getting oatmeal on her forehead. At this rate she'd need another bath.

But out on the meadow her drai was being laid out. She wouldn't say the pegasi were hurrying, but the dance was quicker. The bowls were gently taken away from her, one at a time, by a pegasus whose name was something like Feeaha, and, putting her tentative new understanding into practise she said, "Thank you, lady," trying to make it all one word, *Genfwaalloofwif,* and making what she hoped was a recognisable word-sign with one hand, since she didn't have a tail and neither her nose nor her ears were mobile enough.

Feeaha looked at her what she feared was blankly for a moment—she'd probably said something like "may all your children have seven legs"—and then answered *"Gwahayiiaya,"* which Sylvi heard as distinctly as if her father had wished her good morning. It meant, more or less, "your thanks are unnecessary but thanks for thanking me," which did at least mean Feeaha knew what she'd tried to say. It wasn't really peculiar that it might be easier to talk to the pegasi here, in their own country; it wasn't that the air was clearer and sweeter and the sounds were only things like birdsong and wind. It wasn't that there were no other humans here . . . that there were no magicians here. It was only that the pegasi were concentrating on her, and she on them.

The pegasi harnessed to her drai lifted it into the air as she sat down; as the ropes took the strain she heard the web-magic words breathed into the air, and then she was swaying gently slightly higher than she was tall when standing on her own feet. As the feather-hands tucked a blanket over her and tied the safety ropes around her, she felt something being attached to the back of the drai, but she thought it would probably be rude (and impossible) to crane round far enough to see what it was. Perhaps it was only that she was expecting it this time, but she felt much less apprehensive this morning as the pegasi surged into a gallop almost instantly, and they were airborne before she'd had a chance to remember that she still didn't know where they were going.

Where are we going?

To the Caves, of course!

CHAPTER 13

They flew for about four hours. Lrrianay flew with them, and Aliaa-lia; Sylvi did not see Hibeehea. Of the *doorathbaa*, the only one Sylvi had known before this journey was Ebon, and of the dozen or so peg-asi who now flew free with their king and queen, she still knew only two, Hissiope and Aary, from the palace; they sometimes came with Lrrianay. Aary was unbound; Hissiope was a shaman, and shamans were never bound. Feeaha was also with them this morning, and Dri-ibaa, who was the rufous pegasus she'd seen when she woke on her first morning in Rhiandomeer. It was colder today than it had been when she and her father had flown together, and she was glad of the drai's padding and the blanket; the pegasi's wings were brighter than banners in the sunlight.

Do you ever get cold? You're probably working too hard.

If it's that cold we don't fly. Something weird happens to the air, or maybe our wings, when it gets that cold. It doesn't very often—well, in the farthest northernmost mountains, but nobody goes there much. The Caves extend that far, I think, but I've never been half that way, so I don't know what it's like there. Flying in snow is fun, except it's kind of easy to get lost.

The mountains that marked the edge of the pegasi's land rose up abruptly out of the plain on the human side of the boundary, but wandered and rambled on the pegasus side for a long way, losing very little height, or losing it for a while and gaining it again. With the exception of three peaks Sylvi could see a great distance away, they were not tremendously tall, but there were a lot of them, steep and ragged, and she was glad she wasn't toiling up and down the crests and ridges and long crooked passes on foot. The plateaus that lay between were surprisingly level if irregularly shaped; some seemed only wild meadow but some of them were clearly cultivated. Occasionally she also saw small wooden roofs, like the pavilion at the edge of the first meadow which had held the banqueting tables—and the bedding—and the cooking utensils. But the shfeeah were all small; there were no towns and no houses, and she saw no pegasi other than those around her in the air.

Already her father seemed very far away—farther away than a few hours' flying—and the palace, and her mother and brothers, Ahathin, Glarfin, Lucretia . . . everything about her life was half a dream. Either what was happening now was imaginary, or her previous life was; the two must be incompatible. But she was here now, suspended over nothing, flying with the pegasi, the sharp wind stinging her face. What was she going to believe?

When they banked, steadied and then pulled the ropes taut again over another meadow, her heart began to beat faster. The landing itself was, of course, perfect, but she found that she was stiff with cold, which made her stagger a little, although that wasn't why her heart was beating in her throat. She looked around, half in anticipation, half in foreboding, for a dark cave mouth, but she didn't see anything but the meadow itself, spangled with spring flowers, and another pavilion at

236

one edge. She looked again at the flowers: lavender, violet, yellow, blue—they were also new and strange to her. Even the flowers were different in Rhiandomeer.

Most of the pegasi who had attended the banquet had left before Sylvi's little band had taken to the air, and since then Sylvi had seen only those she flew with. But now pegasi began to appear from among the trees, as if they had been waiting there for their arrival—as they had on her first day here with her father. She looked round at them—she recognised several from the last two days—and unthinkingly looked round for her father too. When she stopped herself looking, the stopping was an almost-physical pain.

For a moment she wished she'd gone home with him—that she'd never come, that Ebon hadn't moved the many heavens and the one earth, as only Ebon could, to invite her, to enable her invitation to be made—that she'd never seen this country, with its strange flowers and leagues of silent empty landscape, and its ability to make her doubt everything she had known about herself up till two days ago. For a brief, awful moment she couldn't move; she was a statue in an alien landscape, its unknown flowers clustering round her feet, another of the bizarre, useless gifts humans had pressed upon the pegasi, which t he pegasi were too polite to refuse.

Feeaha and Driibaa unfastened the safety ropes, and the drai dropped away. She made herself move: one step, two steps. This was what it was like being human: this was how you moved, your queerly tubular and attenuated body swaying upright above a mere two legs, your long awkward arms and big outlandish hands pointlessly hanging. . . .

Sylvi pulled the blanket around her, to wear as a shawl, although the two pegasi who had carried the two small bundles of her baggage individually round their necks came to her and bowed to the ground, rubbing the ropes off over their ears with their own hands, and she could have found something of her own. But the pegasus blanket was marvellously soft and comforting, and she didn't want to give it up. One pegasus was detaching something from the back of her drai—she suddenly remembered her curiosity when she'd felt it being fastened there, when she could not see what it was. The pegasus came toward her—with her no-longer-wet clothing draped over his neck.

Sylvi laughed. She didn't mean to; it burst out of her; it was about the strangeness and aloneness as well as about finding out that the answer to the mysterious question of what had been hung on the back of her drai was the mundane one of her clean laundry. When she laughed, several of the pegasi moved themselves as if into a new pattern—the pattern of looking at a human making an baffling and incongruous noise. She could feel her face heating up in one of her hair-frizzing blushes, but Lrrianay raised his head and called out—the resonant clarion sound that pegasi could make, except they rarely did so.

And one of the pegasi who had come shyly out of the trees and paused—paused so *intently* that Sylvi had noticed her at once among the others—now came dancing toward her. No, prancing, like a young pony or a long-legged puppy. She pranced directly up to Sylvi, lifting her knees very high and shaking her long glossy mane—and put her soft nose to Sylvi's cheek.

Sylvi blinked; surely this was very brash for a pegasus one hadn't been introduced to. She then said—something; it was very long, and had no audible breaks in it, and no consonants either, so far as Sylvi could hear, except she thought she might have heard Ebon's name tucked in there somewhere. And there was a queer background hum or buzz, like a bee caught in her hair—no, caught in her skull.

"No," said Sylvi in sign. "Slower."

"Yooooo—*mmwyyhuma*—Ebohnwaanno—Iha—onnyno." Her

ears and tail were going all the time, teasing and flicking; she nodded and shook her head, and rippled the skin over her shoulders, rustled her feathers. Sylvi thought, those aren't just word breaks, those are all the interesting adjectives too, and I don't know any of them.

"You're Ebon's little sister," said Sylvi. "Ebon. *Shaarraia*," she said, which she hoped meant "sibling."

The pegasus reared up and clapped her wings together. Sylvi had never seen a pegasus do this before. This was not a gesture Sylvi could match in any way at all; she felt very small and boring and wrong as she anxiously said one of the first things Ebon had taught her, when they first knew that she would be coming to visit him here: "*swahavi-haahwhahodh*," and involuntarily made the old human gesture of apology and placation too, holding her hands spread and palm out.

The pegasus promptly dropped back to four legs again and put her nose into one of Sylvi's hands, and without any thought or intention Sylvi brought her hands together, so they were cradling the pegasus' muzzle—which was probably even more brash than the pegasus' behaviour, but she seemed to like it, and leaned toward Sylvi till her nose was resting against Sylvi's breast, and Sylvi's hands ran up her chin, and stroked her face.

The pegasus sighed. "*Ebonfffffwahoowhooftha*," she said. Ebon is lucky. All the *ffff*'s meant very lucky.

"*Sahaliliyo*," said Sylvi, which was one of the other thank yous she knew; she hoped it was the right one. This one was supposed to be for nonmaterial compliments when you wanted to be modest.

She was aware that the adult pegasi watching the two of them were watching very closely indeed; she had been constantly aware of their watching her since her father left—how could they not be watching her? But she somehow felt that this, now, meeting Ebon's little sister, was more than that, more than meeting another member of her bond-

239

mate and host's family; more than that she was about to be the first human to visit the pegasus Caves since the pegasi's chronicles began several thousand years ago. Wasn't that enough? She knew the pegasi wanted something from her, or from the visit, but—wasn't the visit itself enough? But there was something else. . . .

As she stroked Ebon's little sister's cheek she suddenly thought, I didn't know there was a something else. A something besides, a something further. I didn't know till right now. But I can feel it.

She looked up.

Lrrianay was standing at an angle in front of Ebon—a blocking sort of angle, she thought, as if Ebon was going to interfere and Lrrianay was saying "no, don't." But as she looked at Ebon he ducked round his father and trotted the few steps to where Sylvi and his sister stood—and bit his sister briskly over the withers. The young pegasus jerked her head up out of Sylvi's hands and Sylvi didn't need any help translating her open-mouthed snort as "ow."

Hey, bird-face, you don't rear at humans. They're all smaller even than you are! Don't you have any manners?

Sylvi thought, How very odd. I can hear him, and he's not talking to me.

Of course I have manners, you big ugly thug! I'm very small and I know what it feels like when everyone tiptoes around you just because you're small!

It was like—what was it like? It wasn't like anything. It was like flying when you have no wings; it was like galloping on four legs when you have only two; it was like hearing the colour red; it was like being someone else. And, being someone else, you no longer know how to be you. Sylvi wobbled on her suddenly-too-few-for-balance legs, and—fell down.

Ebon was on his knees beside her almost before she finished falling. *Syl?*

She heard me! said the young pegasus. *I know she did! I heard her hearing me!*

Slowly Sylvi said, *I don't know your name.*

The young pegasus spoke both aloud and silently, *Niahi!*

Sylvi said—still sitting down, but one hand gripping Ebon's mane—*Ebon, your name isn't precisely Ebon either, is it? It's—*

Ebon is close enough, said Ebon, sounding worried. *Are you all right?*

There were murmurs all round her, in her ears, in her head—in her *eyes*, she thought, I am *seeing* murmurs. *Tell me your real name!*

"Eeehboohhn," said Ebon, and it was one of those ripply, pegasus noises in her ears, and a seen murmur, as well as the familiar nonsound in her mind. *Who cares? Ebon for short. Like Syl.*

I care, said Syl. *Everything's different.*

Nothing's different, said Ebon, rather desperately. *I'm still me. You're still you. And we're still bound to each other. The only difference is that we're here rather than there.*

Sylvi was still listening to the difference. It's only the difference between being alone with someone and being in a crowd, she told herself. It's only . . . but it's not. It's not *only.* There's nothing *only* about it. It's . . . maybe it's a little like the difference between hearing one person singing and a choir. Maybe, if you were used to listening to someone singing by themselves, a choir—a sudden choir—all those different voices singing slightly different things, would make you dizzy. It might make you so dizzy, perhaps, that you'd fall down. She'd said to her father, "I'm human. I'm a human among pegasi. I've only got two legs and I can't fly. None of that's going to change." It was easier if she could only talk to Ebon. It was *easier* to have only two legs and no wings, to be carried around like a parcel or someone's washing—it was easier to be *different*, if she could only talk to Ebon. She wanted to cry. She did *not* want to cry. She bit down on her lip. She should try to stand up. She didn't think she could.

And then someone else knelt beside her: Lrrianay. *Oh, no!* Sylvi said, and struggled to sit up, climbing Ebon's mane like ladder rungs.

Syl— began Ebon.

Don't struggle. Rest a little. Let yourself find yourself again. This is a tremendous change—a tremendous thing that has happened. Please, said Lrrianay. And then Sylvi cowered back against Ebon, and put her hands over her face, because she heard Lrrianay too. We are *born* knowing we can't talk to the pegasi, she said to herself; it's as much a certainty as anything written on the treaty—as *not* having wings.

How can I bear to talk to them when I cannot fly?

Did you bring me here hoping this would happen? Is this what this is about? Is this why I could say spirit and heart and l-love in my speech at the banquet— say them out loud? Why don't humans ever come here? It's one of the first things we ever talked about. You come to us. We don't come here. Ebon, she said, stumbling over using his name because for the first time she needed to specify who she was talking to—*I just wanted to see where you lived. It was too strange that I didn't know what your home looked like, even if it didn't have four walls, and—and bedrooms. It was even stranger that I didn't know where you lived than that we could talk to each other—*

Lrrianay interrupted. *Child, believe me, you would not have been a disappointment to us if this had not happened!*

And she heard the colour red; she listened to the choir. She believed him.

She sat on the ground among the little unknown wildflowers, clinging to Ebon's mane and the saving familiarity of their friendship, and the breeze in her nostrils smelled sweetly of green spring and of pegasi. The pegasi accepted what came. Ebon had been telling her that for four years. Here, in his country, talking to his father and his sister in the pegasi's silent-speech, she finally believed him. *I don't know the wildflowers yet*, she thought, *but I know I'm sitting on* llyri *grass.*

But it was—worth the thinking of, Lrrianay went on, tentatively, watching her, watching her closely, earnestly, kindly, gauging her reaction to what he wanted to tell her—reminding her, suddenly, powerfully, in that gentle but implacable watchfulness, of her own father. *That your father and I can half talk to each other is much more than most bondmates have. True talking is so unimaginable that we barely tell stories about it—we pegasi do not, nor humans either, I believe. Your magicians translate, as our shamans may also; what real need have we to talk? It is the way things are. But we—your father and I—hoped that what we had might repeat itself. We have thought of it since before Danacor and Thowara were born. But it seemed less likely after each of your brothers was bound, and none of them can talk to their bondmates even so much as your father and I can. I was not thinking of it at all when Ebon said you should have Niahi, and not him. There are precedents for such discontinuous bindings.*

Ebon put his nose in Sylvi's hair and said, "Phoooooey."

We did think of it: the youngest child of the king and the only sister after several brothers. But the shamans advised against it, and so it was done the usual way.

But it was Niahi just now— began Sylvi.

Yes, said Lrrianay. *It was. It may only have been that you were another day distant from your own land—a day distant from your father's departure—a day farther into our land. Perhaps also that Niahi was very—er—eager to meet you. We did not allow her to come to your banquet, much to her dismay, hoping that these other things might help produce a new connection with the sister of your bondmate, the sister you might have been bound to, when you finally met her. It was nothing we did that put those words in your mind last night—but you are right that we took note that you used—could use—them.*

I'm afraid, he went on, *I'm afraid this has been in our minds since the beginning—since the extraordinary binding between you and Ebon. Since Niahi is a king's daughter and your father has no more children, and because she is small for her age and until this year would have found the journey to your palace difficult, we have been able to avoid binding her. Because we have been wondering . . .*

Sylvi said sadly, *None of us has wondered anything. To us—to us humans—Ebon and I are just freaks. The magicians translate; that is the system. There is nothing to—to talk about.* She looked at Lrrianay, and he looked back, from his dark, deep, inscrutable pegasus eyes. *What are you still not telling me?* she said. There was a pause. She took a deep breath, finished letting it out and said, *It's about our magicians, isn't it?*

There was another, longer pause. The other pegasi had now retreated a little farther—beyond eavesdropping distance, Sylvi assumed; she'd heard Niahi being herded away by her mother, protesting every step.

You have held to the treaty, Lrrianay said at last, *and that great promise has given us our lives, by your strength to hold. And your commitment to our bonding ritual tells us that we are a part of your lives and not merely ink marks on an old page.*

Ebon interrupted. *What Dad will take the next day and a half to say in king talk is yes, the problem is your magicians, or anyway the magic they do, or the way they do it—it's all wands and smoke and—and—**stuff**. Have you ever wondered why none of our shamans seems to stay long when they visit your palace? And you don't see the same one very often? Is there any shaman you knew by name but Hissiope? At first—eight hundred years ago—they thought it was just* that we were so strange to one another. Later they decided that the magic your magicians made was keeping it that way.

Lrrianay said gravely, There has never been any such decision—

Oh, Dad, that's king talk again! Can we please go the short way? We already know Fthoom is a bad guy! Syl and I have known it since our binding—or anyway I knew it then and I guess Syl has known since she first met the brute. It stands out around him like that weird robe he likes to wear. Syl?

It was a long journey, Sylvi thought, going Ebon's short way. I've always been afraid of Fthoom, which isn't the same thing. It wasn't till the binding . . . I knew something was wrong. And . . . not all our magicians are bad. Ebon, you know Ahathin.

Yes, said Ebon. He's another freak.

I take my son's point about—er—king talk, said Lrrianay, but it's not as simple as that human magicians are the villains in our story. There is a great deal of strength in humankind that we do not have. It is a good strength when it stops the taralians and norindours from killing all of us, but it is not a good strength when one of your villages goes to war with their neighbours over the ownership of a field. We think there is something of the same about your magicians' powers. It was a good power when it forged our Alliance, much quicker, and possibly more securely, than our shamans would have been able to do it. But it was . . . perhaps not the best alliance that could have been made.

We feel that perhaps the misfit of our Alliance is coming to a time of crisis. It is interesting that you—the link that you and Ebon have—should come at the same time as the magician Fthoom. It is that sense of crisis, I believe, that made your father force through an acceptance of you coming to us. He had to . . . displease some people it would have been better not to displease.

Lord Kanf, Sylvi thought. Senator Barnum. "The king is the most tightly tied by his freedom to rule," was one of Ahathin's favourite maxims, and she tried not to believe it because she knew it was so— and because she was the king's daughter.

Only about ten days before she had been due to depart, and when she knew that the senate had still not officially ratified her going, one of the oldest of the king's council members had sought her out at one of those state dinners she was now obliged to attend. She knew that Senator Orflung was one of those who were against her journey. She braced herself, and tried not to let it show that she was bracing herself.

"My lady, my apologies for my presumption"—which was a phrase she was accustomed to hearing in her father's court but she'd never heard it addressed to herself before—"but would you be good enough to tell me if you—you yourself, with no one whispering in your ear—if you *want* to visit the pegasi's land?"

She looked at him blankly for a moment, as if he were a strange pegasus speaking pegasi. She had given a short, formal speech to the combined senate when her father had first introduced the news of her impending journey, in which she had said that she did want to go, very much. But she had also been saying it to two hundred senators, lords, ladies, barons and granddames, and she had been concentrating on getting through it, not on being convincing. She noticed now—having not studied his face close up before—that there were deep smile lines round Senator Orflung's eyes and his mouth, and the frowning look he wore at present was more worried than angry or bullying. She relaxed a little. "Yes, my sir, I do wish to visit it. The—the full senate is very intimidating, you know."

The frown disappeared and he smiled. "Yes, my lady, I do know. After forty years I still have to take a deep breath before I climb to my feet to address it." The smile disappeared. "I am, of course, aware of the prohibition against querying you about the pegasi. But I would ask you to indulge me so far as to tell me . . . you feel you and *Hrrr* Ebon to be true friends, is that correct? As—as you might be friends with my daughter."

His youngest daughter was eight years older and a foot taller than Sylvi, and almost as daunting as her father. "Ebon and I are friends, yes," she said carefully. "And I can speak to him as I could speak to your daughter." She realised that this might sound too similar to what she had said to the senate, and cast around for something she could add that would sound genuine, that would not sound as if she were hiding some important truth. "We can laugh together. He—he teases me. He tells terrible jokes."

The smile crept back into his eyes again. "The pegasi tell jokes? I am glad to know that. They are always so grand and solemn at court— and we rarely see any but those who are human bound. We never see the little ones, the children—I understand that it is too long a flight for them. Do they play, like human children? Do they scamper and jump and fall over? It is not only that we cannot speak to them clearly—how can you know anything about a people if you have never seen its children? But I am sure, if they tell jokes, that their children also play.

"And I will ask you one more question, and then excuse you from the burden of my company any further. My lady, forgive me, but I wish to recast the question I began with. Do you *want* to visit your friend at his home? Aside from any other question of who you are or who your friend is, or what your parents'—er—colleagues think of the matter, or whether anyone else with a friendship such as yours has done such a thing. Do you *want* to go—not just over the Starclouds to some-where no human has been, but to visit your friend, because you can laugh with him, and exchange terrible jokes?"

She thought, how odd that no one has asked me this but my mother and father, and Danacor, and Lucretia and Diamon—Ahathin didn't have to ask, and Glarfin would think it was none of his business. But it was easy to answer immediately: "Yes, my sir, I do wish to go. For just those reasons. Because he visits me at my home. I want to visit him at his."

He nodded, staring at her. "Thank you, my lady. I believe you."

The next day her father said to her, "I don't know what you said to old Orflung last night—I saw you talking to him—but Barnum tried to begin a last-minute rebellion this morning about your journey and Orflung essentially shouted him down. Said you were no longer a child but a young woman and you knew your own mind and wanted to go, and we should let you. *Finally*. Barnum wouldn't have won, if it had come to that—I'd've invoked king's fiat. But I have hoped I wouldn't have to—and everyone listens to Orflung. But why it never occurred to anyone before to ask *you*—I've even suggested it two or three times, to Orflung among others."

"It's because I'm so little," said Sylvi. "I'm just big enough to be a parcel to be wrapped up and sent somewhere. Or not."

The king snorted. "Helpless wrapped-up parcels don't knock their experienced sparring partners over—with tricks the sparring partners have taught them." Lucretia had been so delighted by her protégé's progress she'd brought the story to the king herself.

"You should have let me challenge Barnum to single combat. I'd've shown him what a parcel can do."

"I should have," said the king half ruefully.

Sometimes even being the king isn't the answer, she had thought then, and thought again now, sitting on the llyri grass, talking to the king of the pegasi. Sometimes one of your oldest councillors does the job better. Sometimes your daughter is the only one who can do it at all.

What do I do now? she said.

Lrrianay wrinkled his nose and did a very unkingly ear-whirl. *Eat dinner. Sleep. Wake and rise tomorrow morning and come with us to the Caves. That is all.*

And talk to you.

Lrrianay bowed his head solemnly, arching his neck so that his forehead nearly touched the ground, and his long mane fell over his face, so she could see only the stiff alertness of his ears. When he raised his head again all the mischief was gone and he looked every inch a king, even lying on the ground with his legs folded under him and his wings negligently crossed over his back. *Yes. If it is not too great a strain for you. I would like you to find out how many of us you can talk to, and how well.*

Sylvi let go of Ebon's mane to press her hands together and bow her own head. *It is my honour to do as you would wish me to do, great lord.* Then she put her hands carefully on the ground, and began to try to stand up. Ebon stood up first, with that quick forehand-first heave that should have been very like a horse's but was not—especially when he had one feather-hand still in her hair. *Climb up my leg, why don't you. Go on, borrow one of mine. Then we'll have three each.*

Sylvi laughed a small croaking laugh and cautiously stood up. She didn't quite climb Ebon's foreleg, but she certainly hung on to it—and once upright she transferred her grip to his mane again. Niahi, her head over her mother's back, half shouted and half whinnied a noise like cheering, and opened her wings and shut them again instantly, like a sort of applause.

They were all watching her, all the pegasi, beautiful, poised, attentive—several of them held their wings half roused—hopeful. One of the things she'd learnt just in the last two days was that there was a hopeful half-rousing as well as a wary one. She would have liked knowing this more if it didn't make her aware that she'd only ever seen the wary one at the human king's court.

The hopeful gesture was more open. Hopeful of what she might do for them, for all of them—her people, Sylvi's people too. But the faces looking at her now were all pegasi. Niahi's tail was lashing back and forth in what Sylvi was reasonably sure was excitement; Sylvi didn't have a tail to lash. As she stared at them, their motionlessness—barring Niahi's tail—made them, in her still rudimentary understanding of them and in the newness of this moment, almost expressionless—as if by gaining speech she had lost the fragile beginnings of her kinetic understanding. She looked again at the half-roused, hopeful wings: but there was no individuality that she could read. They were an artist's representation of pegasi, beautiful and enigmatic.

She was conscious of Ebon's skin beneath her hand: the warmth, the silkiness of his black hair, the feel of his breathing as his shoulder rose and fell—the ordinary, the habitual feeling of these things. She held out her free hand, caught Niahi's eye—which was not difficult— and waved her hand back and forth in a swishy sort of gesture, like a switching tail. Niahi made a noise very like a giggle, ducked her head and whipped her tail twice as fast. Sylvi grinned—and saw the smile-wrinkles appear on Aliaalia's nose.

Hey, aren't you hungry? said Ebon. *Thinking always makes me really hungry.*

Yes, said Sylvi. *Yes, I'm very hungry.* It was only then that her stomach roared like six taralians and she realised she'd been smelling for some little while not only the faint sharp whiff of wood smoke but also the mild grainy scent of the porridgy stuff that the pegasi often made for her since she had this queer predilection for hot food. And she further realised that the pegasus porridge, which she'd never had before she'd come to visit Ebon at his home, was no longer strange to her. It was just food. Good food.

She ate, and listened to a rustle of silent voices, like wind through slender trees. But the only pegasi who had addressed her directly were Ebon and Lrrianay and Niahi; and while she ate, only Ebon stayed near her, eating from a bowl that had been brought with her porridge. It looked like chopped-up grasses speckled with seeds, but it smelled both spicy and flowery. His bowl was refilled three times while she ate her porridge, but he never left her, while the other pegasi wandered, as they usually did.

But when she laid her bowl down and licked her fingers, she saw a shadow pass very near her and looked up quickly: the queen, Aliaalia. She was still wearing Sylvi's garnet, but now it hung on the gold chain that had been Sylvi's official gift to her. Ebon put his nose to Sylvi's hair, gave a brief, gentle tug, came gracefully to his feet, bowed to his mother, and left them. Sylvi scrambled to her own feet, stopping herself from looking after him apprehensively. The queen paused, almost hesitantly, Sylvi thought, taken aback, as if she was not quite sure of her welcome.

Queen, said Sylvi, and bowed. *Great Lady.*

It's true, then, said the queen. *I knew it was—Niahi told me—Niahi has told everyone—*and she laughed, both silently and aloud: *wheeeee. But we, like you, grow up knowing we cannot talk to each other. This—today—is a story come to life, a story as amazing as any that our bards tell us. How hard this must all be for you, my dear. A little exciting too, I hope, but hard. How much we all hope from you—how much we cannot help but hope, while we try not to. Do not let us crowd you too closely!*

But I hope too, said Sylvi. *And my father does, and my mother, or they would not have let me come, I think—it was very hard to let me come, you know. We cannot help hoping either. And if—if you crowd me very closely, you will hold me up, and I will be grateful because I—I am oddly wavery, since—since Niahi spoke to me.*

You poor child, said the queen. *Is there anything I can do for you?*

Talk to me, said Sylvi. *So it doesn't seem so . . . strange. So that it's just talking. What are the stories your bards tell you?*

The queen raised her head and looked away from Sylvi. Sylvi followed her gaze—as dark dappled Hibeehea seemed to materialise from the shadows. She had not seen him since the first evening. He bowed to them—to her and the queen, and the queen bowed back—Sylvi hastily following suit. Hibeehea, she thought. Oh dear. The queen then looked back at her, and her voice in Sylvi's mind sounded grave and sad and proud. *Our favourite stories are that we have hands,* she said. *Hands like yours: strong to grasp and hold, and wrists that turn back and forth.*

Sylvi spent most of the next day asleep. She woke once, early, and lay quietly, watching the sunrise, pink and gold and soft blue-green, thinking sleepily, wistfully, confusedly, that it was the sort of sunrise that ought to happen in the pegasi's land, beautiful but somehow enigmatic and unattainable; and then she thought, But why should either a sunrise or a pegasus be attainable, that its not being attainable should make me feel all doleful and spooky? And she turned over and wriggled farther into her friendly feather mattress, and went back to sleep.

She woke again and found a bowl of fruit by her pillow: two apples and three pears and a handful of plooraia, which the pegasi grew instead of grapes, because grape-vines here (Ebon had told her) only grew leaves and hard, sour, inedible black pebbles. And it was raining gently, but the pegasi had thrown something like a tent roof over her, tied to tree branches above her head; she could hear the rain as it fell, and smell the wet earth, but she was dry, curled up in her feather-bed. She ate a pear, thinking, It must be late, I must get up, and only managed to finish it before she fell asleep again.

The third time she woke, it had stopped raining, and Ebon was lying near her. There was a little bag with a long loop of ribbon—long enough to hang round his neck—lying on the ground beside him, and he was holding a small wooden bead with one alula-hand, and buffing it with a cloth he held in the other. She pulled herself onto one elbow to see better. She had seen him do this back at the palace, when they had their lessons together, but she had never had the excuse to watch from only a handsbreadth away before—to watch when she wasn't supposed to be doing her own lessons. And there was something almost miraculous about this bead; it shone like a tiny moon.

I think that if you sleep any more the Night Shaman will take you away and make you a star, but Dad says yesterday was a hard day and we won't go anywhere today and if you want to sleep through it that's fine. And I say that I don't want to sleep through it and there's stuff to show you and you don't have to talk. And you should get up because what if the Night Shaman isn't just a fairy tale?

Night Shaman?

Eah. He gets you both ways—if you don't go to sleep when you're supposed to and if you don't wake up when you're supposed to. Then you're a star awake in the sky forever and ever, showing pegasi where to fly. When you're little you think that if you fly high enough you'll be able to see the stars even in daylight. I used to think there was some kind of mountain ridge up there where all the star-pegasi stood, shining and being awake all the time. And you should be able to visit them for a while when you don't feel like sleeping and then come back again. Dad recommends against telling the story like that when I have kids, though, because I'm likely to have kids like I was a kid.

You tried to fly up to the ridge, right?

Of course.

A star sounds like a nice thing to be.

Not if you're supposed to be a pegasus. The story really scared me for a long time—that's why I wanted it to be somewhere you could go and come back from, because I never went to sleep or woke up when I should. He riffled his feathers and looked up through the trees, as if the memory still made him restless. *Because I couldn't. And the Night Shaman always needs more stars. What do human grown-ups tell you is going to happen to you if you don't behave?*

Oh, that the bogeyman will come and carry you away, and grind your bones for his bread.

Ebon, who had begun polishing again, stopped. *The bogeyman? The hrundagia, with all the teeth, and the long tail it can throw after you and catch you when you think you've run away? You say that to a little kid? You humans really are savages.*

Sylvi sat up and laughed. *That's what my mother said when she found out one of my minders was telling me that. I didn't see that minder again. I've never heard of the hrundagia.*

You don't want to. They're bigger, meaner, and smarter than taralians. And if they're real, they live **here***.*

You're right. I don't want to. What are you doing?

Ebon held it up so the sunlight glinted off it. *It's good, isn't it? It's the best one I've done. It's coetotl wood. First you polish it and then you oil it and then you polish it and then you oil it and you go on doing that. There are some words you say over it too—like the ones I taught you, but there are more of them, and they make everything dark and light around you while you say them.*

And then at the end you hang it around your neck when you go to the Caves because it glows in the dark. This one's for you. It doesn't really need any more polishing but I begged some sihria oil off my master, and maybe it'll glow a little more. The Caves have candles and torches and lamps everywhere but . . . well, you'll see. You want to glow in the dark yourself when you're in the Caves.

Sylvi pulled her knees up under her chin and hugged them. *We really are going?*

Ebon gave her a look even more disbelieving than when she'd mentioned the bogeyman. *To the Caves? That's what you're here for. Never mind the talking. You can't have forgotten.*

She hugged her knees harder. *It's just . . . the Caves. And . . . ssshasssha,* she added, stumbling over all the *sss*'s.

I know, said Ebon. *But after yesterday . . . if you said you wanted to be empress they'd say, Oh, okay, what do you want your crown to look like? And even if you'd hated everything you saw here and stopped talking to me too and kept saying you wanted to go home . . . we'd still haul you to the Caves and shove you in, because we promised. I'm glad you're not, you know, but we'd still take you. We told your dad we were going to take you to the Caves so we have to.*

Why?

Why the Caves? Which part of the story do you want? I wanted you to see the Caves. And it was the best way to tell your dad how serious we were. I was already serious, and I wanted you to see the Caves. I knew Dad and Mum had been thinking about bringing Niahi to you, as soon as she was big enough to fly that far easily—she'd've had a hard time if she'd had to come for your twelfth birthday—but she could do it now. I hadn't realised they were already thinking about how they might bring you to us. But . . . I think my dad and your dad get stuff over to each other even when they can't talk about it. I think your dad was waiting for my dad to say something.

You wouldn't really drag me to your precious Caves if I'd been whining and horrible, would you?

He looked surprised. *Of course we would. We promised.*

Things change, she said, thinking of old Orflung asking her if she wanted to come here, thinking of what had happened last night. *Things change.*

Not giving your word, said Ebon firmly. *Giving your word doesn't change. Ever.*

She looked at him and for a moment the chasm that had lain between every human and every pegasus since Viktur had first followed the path through the mountains lay between her and Ebon, and it was so wide she knew they could never bridge it.

And then Ebon leaned over and shoved her hard with his nose. *Aren't you ever going to get up? It's really pretty here and there's a hill that has the best sunsets, and it's a day for a good sunset. And there's a shfeeah with a paper maker on the way, and an orchard. But you have to walk to it and I suppose you're going to insist on having one of your baths first? I'll make your breakfast—hrrifinig—*pegasi usually had two or three more quick meals in a day than humans did, including *hrrifinig* between breakfast and lunch—*lunch. Late lunch. Hurry up.*

She could see that it was a day that should have a glorious sunset. But what was even more glorious to Sylvi was that she finally met some pegasus children: little ones, with long knobby legs and little ribby bodies—and barely fledged wings. There were several of them, and they hid behind their parents and their bigger siblings and peeped out at her. How can you know anything about a people if you have never seen its children?

She didn't know how to make friends with them—she didn't know what would look like a friendly gesture to a pegasus baby—and somehow she didn't want to ask. If she had to ask it would be no good.

But children are always curious. She sat down on the ground to eat her porridge, thinking about what she could do to attract them that wouldn't look totally foolish when it didn't work. After she'd finished eating she put her bowl on the ground and crouched over it (it was shallow enough that she could, and did, lick it out first), staring into it as if it was the most interesting thing she'd ever seen. This was not difficult to do: the bowl had the same gentle luminescence that every pegasus-made object she had seen did: the soft glow of the endless tiny rubbing of feather hands that produced it. And the wood it was made of was strange to her, and the colour of the tree-rings as they faded one into the next was very beautiful. She remained staring—very conscious of a baby who had come right out from behind its mother to stare at *her*—hoping that Ebon wouldn't come along and laugh at her too soon.

The almost-inaudible tap of tiny light hoofs. She didn't dare look; the baby's mother must be aware of what was happening.

With one of her little cousins she'd have needed a better toy than a bowl. But wasn't she herself the new toy? Very slowly she put out one of her hands, very slowly uncurled one finger and very slowly touched the bottom of the bowl with her pointing finger.

The baby was a small but definite presence a little to her right; she could see out of the corner of her eye the slender shadows of its legs move as it took another step toward her. And now she could hear as it breathed in and out sharply, as if surprised at the smell of human. Sylvi hoped it wasn't an unpleasant smell. She continued to stare at the bowl, and at her own finger.

Around her silence was falling: the silent voices were falling silent; the slight rustling of pegasi going about their business stilled.

The baby gave a prance. No, Sylvi thought, I'm not going to look at you; you have to come to me.

And it pranced up to her, and stopped, and put its face down, and touched her hand with its nose. Her nose: this fine little nose had to belong to a girl. Sylvi looked up then and smiled—smiled involuntarily, showing her teeth, the way humans do; humans bare their teeth when they're pleased. But the baby didn't skitter away, but wrinkled her muzzle in a pegasus smile as if she understood. *Hroooo* drifted through Sylvi's mind, as soft and faint as the tap of baby hooves.

Hrooo to you too, Sylvi said, trying to say it quietly, how do you silent-speak quietly? she thought in despair, and the baby positively giggled: Hreee hreee hreee hreee, kicked up her heels, spread her infinitesimal wings and galloped around Sylvi three times before dashing off to stand behind her mother again. She poked her head out long enough to give one last cheeky "Hreee."

Sylvi laughed, and stood up, and realised she felt better—lighter, freer—than she had since her father left—certainly since the night before, when she'd crawled into her nest of feathers feeling that she might never be able to stand up straight again from the weight she'd felt laid across her shoulders that evening.

That, said Ebon, *is Hililin, and she's a brat. It **would** be Hili who had a go at you first.*

She's a very cute brat, said Sylvi.

The walkers set off almost at once, Ebon and Sylvi, Niahi, Feeaha, Aary, Dorheemiha, and Flanoohr; and the queen, Aliaalia.

There was a minor hubbub behind them—followed by the sound of tiny galloping hooves and an exasperated out-loud call. Even shouting, thought Sylvi, they have that musical resonance.

Why did I know this was going to happen? said Ebon. Hili bolted to Sylvi, hid behind her and poked her nose out to look at her mother, who was trotting toward them with her wings half roused. Sylvi could feel Hili panting as she leaned against Sylvi's legs. "There's not much of me to hide behind, is there?" she said out loud.

Lady, said Hili's mum uncertainly.

Lady, Sylvi replied."*Fwif.* "

Viawahah, said Ebon. *Hilililin's mum.*

I— began Viawahah, and then stopped, obviously at a loss, dropping her wings and her head in a gesture, Sylvi thought, like spreading your hands and shrugging. It's hard for them too, she thought. Of course it is.

Hilililin is a darling, she said.

"Hrooo," came a little voice behind her knees.

Viawahah's head came up and her wings flattened and then folded neatly across her back: her upper lip just wrinkled and then smoothed again. *She is a broliglag.*

Monster, translated Ebon. *It's a small monster that gets into things. Like rats.*

I am **not** *a rat!* put in Hili.

No, said Ebon. *Your tail is too hairy.*

I am not a broliglag!

Yes, you are, said Viawahah, *and you're too little to walk to the Golinghagah Hill. Come along.*

I am **not** *too little!*

And furthermore, you weren't invited, said Ebon.

At that, Hilililin drooped. She touched her nose to Sylvi's hand like a good-bye, and went and stood by her mother.

The next time I come, said Sylvi, *you'll be bigger, and I'll invite you.*

Promise you won't jump off anything and say you're flying, and you can come now, said Ebon.

Hili's head snapped around, and her mother's wings began to rouse again. *But—*

I **promise!**

She can ride, said Ebon. He gave Sylvi a look through his eyelashes and added, *I have a nice, broad, flat back, good for carrying passengers. I won't let her fall off.* He knelt, and then lay down, legs curled under him, and drew his nearer wing back. *Climb up, small one, and mind where you put your hard little feet.* Hili dithered for a moment, and then rushed forward and threw herself up Ebon's side.

"*Ggh*," said Ebon.

I'll steady her while you get up, shall I? said Sylvi. She had already stepped forward and begun to put her hands out . . . and stopped. The pegasi had fallen silent again—that too-silent, too-still way they had. Sylvi curled her big strong human hands back against her body, trying to tuck them between her elbows and her rib cage where no one could see them, where she couldn't embarrass herself or the pegasi with them, with what she could do and they could not. Surely the pegasi carried their babies on their backs sometimes? How did they do it?

She hadn't meant to speak to be heard, but her inexperience betrayed her.

We have draia for many purposes, said the queen softly. *Yes, of course we carry our babies. In the old days, before the Alliance, we had always to be ready to fly for our lives; and our children do not fly till they are several years old, and cannot fly far for some years after that. But we rarely carry them on our backs. There must be at least two of us to hold the baby while the bearer stands up; and our shamans have found no supporting word for this. A baby as big as Hili is now would be very difficult—indeed dangerous to those holding or lifting her. Our hands, once broken, do not heal readily.*

I'm . . . sorry, said Sylvi, feeling wretched.

Yah, said Ebon from the ground. *Since we have her, let's use her. And she just said she'd come back, so we can use her some more. Come on, Syl, the sunset is soon. Grab the broliglag and let's get on with it.*

So Sylvi unfolded her hands again, feeling them like great ugly shovels suspended—sternly, unforgivingly—out in front of her. Hili quivered ever so slightly when Sylvi touched her—but at once put her nose to one of Sylvi's hands again, this time as if in apology. She seemed to Sylvi to weigh so little that she might have floated off Ebon's back if she moved incautiously.

Ebon stood up and Hili gave a little squeal of what was obviously pleasure. *Watch yourself, you,* said Ebon. *I said I wouldn't let you fall off—I didn't say I wouldn't make you **want** off.*

CHAPTER 14

The next day they flew again, and when they landed they had arrived at the entrance to the Caves.

Tomorrow morning they would go inside. Tomorrow morning she, Sylviianel, fourth child of the human King Corone IV, would enter the pegasi's mythical Caves, where no human had ever before set foot, the Caves which were the centre of their lives and their civilisation, and of *ssshasssha*, the pegasi history and recollection, which no human understood.

Ebon had told her which of the mountain peaks roofed the main entrance to the Caves: there was a double-crowned mountain and then a falling-away series of smaller ones that made a zigzag line against the sky much sharper than those surrounding it. They were their own little range, visibly of some other, less erodible material than the rest. Ebon had first pointed them out to her the day she had arrived with her father, but she hadn't taken it in; or rather, she had allowed herself to be distracted, because there were so many things to see, to make sense of, to try and understand.

Look at old Cuandoia, Ebon had said. *He's the big one in the middle, with the two peaks. He used to be a stag, you know, and the peaks were his antlers.*

One of our story-tellers can sing you the story. Can you see how he looks like he's leaning toward us? Our weather-seers will tell you it's something about clouds and temperature but it's still a good omen when you see him like that.

The days had passed, and those mountains had come closer, and Cuandoia seemed to watch them—watch and beckon. *Well, he's glad to see Lrrianay and Aliaalia,* Sylvi said to herself. But it was hard not to feel, if she were going to think in terms of a mountain watching them, then he must be seeing her too, strange conspicuous creature that she was, and that it was acceptable to him that she was included.

She was shivering when she climbed out of her drai that evening near the main entrance of the Caves, although it was no colder than it had been the evening before, and the close-woven pegasus blanket kept the wind out better than several of the sheep's-wool blankets she was accustomed to would have done. Cuandoia's double crown was lost in the twilight, but she still seemed to feel him watching—as if she could sense, even in the darkness, that there was an *awareness*, sharp as a beam of light, coming from the crowned mountain above the Caves—and not from anywhere else.

They were here.

If she had been among humans she might have been able to pass off her oppression of spirits as mere tiredness: but she was not among humans. The problem with silent-speech was how much else was available about you than only your words.

I was scared gutless the first time I was brought to the Caves, Ebon said without preamble.

I'm still scared, said Niahi. *They're so big and they're so full.*

They're nothing like full, said Ebon, in best big-brother-brushing-off-little-sister style. *They're hardly started.*

Oh, Ebon, don't be a strawhead! said Niahi, obviously flustered. Sylvi could hear herself in Niahi's silent voice, talking to one of her brothers.

Niahi went on defensively, *You know what I mean. There are leagues and leagues of them that are empty, but there are leagues of them that are full of **us,** of what we've been doing for the last thousands and thousands of years. And it's not just the stuff on the walls. It hangs in the air. It follows you. It stands up ahead of you and calls you in a voice you can't hear, but you know you're being called, and it knows your name.*

Like Cuandoia, thought Sylvi. She had a brief impulse to kneel and put her hand on the ground, like a salute, but it might be impertinent, as she had once been taught—it seemed ages and ages ago—that touching a pegasus was rude.

They're the most beautiful thing in the world, said Ebon. *And you want to go and make a spook story out of them. Fine, you can stay outside and watch for bears. Syl and I are going in with Dad.*

There are no bears here!

Then it should be easy to watch for them.

Ebon, I hate you!

Sylvi thought Niahi sounded near tears, if pegasi wept, and she also sounded like some of Sylvi's cousins, when they had all been younger, when Sylvi's brothers had been tormenting them. She went over to her, not knowing if it was the right gesture or not, and pushed the forelock away from Niahi's eyes as she might have pushed hair out of the eyes of one of her cousins, and swept a hand down her neck and shoulder as she might have patted her cousin. She wanted to tell Niahi that Ebon was her brother, she couldn't afford to let him wind her up this easily, but she could guess it was her, Sylvi's, presence that made it so easy. Niahi was the little sister who might have been Sylvi's pegasus, if their fathers had decided that the human king's daughter should be bound to a daughter of the pegasus king. And Niahi had been the second pegasus Sylvi had found she could talk to. Niahi had opened the door that their fathers had hoped would open—could be opened.

Tell him he has no imagination, she said to Niahi. *Tell him he's a thickie. That all he has is muscles.*

Hey! said Ebon.

I'm a little sister too, you know, she said. *And all my older brothers are big bullies. And I've only got three of them. I probably will be frightened of your beautiful Caves.*

Yes, you probably will. That was my point, said Ebon. *But they're—they're not—* He switched his tail in a sign of frustration that was one of the first pegasus gestures she'd learnt to read after she met Ebon— before Ebon it hadn't occurred to her that the pegasi would feel anything as ignoble as frustration—it was not dissimilar to the frustrated tail-switch of a horse. But a horse didn't follow up with the long almost-invisible-unless-you-were-watching-closely sinuous shiver which was the signal of transition from gesture to language. *They're not spooky. That's all wrong. There's a . . . there's an **immensity** to them, even in the smallest spaces. That's what Niahi means about hangs and follows and calls—and full. You'll see.*

Niahi put her velvet lips briefly to Sylvi's face. *You'll see,* she said. *And I don't mean the Caves aren't wonderful too. They are. They're too wonderful.*

They're too wonderful kept recurring to Sylvi's mind the next day.

She'd slept well—thanks to a sweet-smelling drink the queen had given her; she could feel it begin to work with her first sip and she went to her feather-bed smiling and relaxed. But she woke at dawn when the pegasi themselves were first stirring, and she was awake immediately and absolutely. She felt excited, but the wrong kind of excited, the way she might have felt on a test day for a test she hadn't practised or studied hard enough for and she knew it, and whoever would be testing her would know it too. *Ssshasssha*, she thought. How does a human practise for that? But I *wanted* to do this, she told herself fiercely. I *still* want to. And it's the most enormous compliment.

Which was the problem.

She missed her father—any other human—so badly it made her curiously achy, as if her humanity were a cramped or injured limb. A part of that discomfort was her relentless sense of herself as wrong, as alien—stiff and clumsy, a grotesque unnatural shape and freakishly unbalanced posture (how ridiculous to spend all your life rearing!). And bald. And wingless.... She felt her arms—her forelegs—flapping foolishly at her sides; how bizarre human shoulders were, pulling the forelegs apart and forcing them to dangle. She drew her arms forward, jerking her shoulders and letting the rest of her arms trail as if she'd forgotten how they worked. Slowly she bent her elbows and held her big spindly-fingered human hands out in front of her. She spread the long fingers, curled them up, spread them again, turned her wrists back and forth so she looked at the palms, and then the backs, and then the palms of her hands again. They were big hands only here in Rhiandomeer; at home, among humans, they were little, like everything about Sylvi was little. The sword Diamon had told her to take back to her rooms with her was still only three-quarter-sized because her hands weren't big enough to get a proper grip on the hilt of a full-sized one.

She let her hands droop at the ends of her wrists, and then folded her arms across her stomach and tucked her hands behind her elbows, holding on to her rib cage as if she were holding herself together. This was becoming the way she most often stood here, in the pegasi country, where she was bald and wingless and always rearing.

It was only going to be herself and Ebon and Lrrianay going into the Caves, and Ebon and Lrrianay were used to humans. To the funny way they looked, and the funny way they moved. There was no human equivalent of *ssshasssha*, which filled the Caves and called your name. It won't call mine, she thought, but this gave her no comfort.

That morning even Ebon was subdued. She asked him on her way to her bath if she should hurry. *No*, he said immediately, but then he hesitated. *Do you have—do you have a way of putting yourself in—*and then there was a word she didn't know. She stood there in her crumpled nightdress, clutching her towel and staring at her best friend— her best friend who was so hopelessly unlike herself—and saw the unbridgeable chasm lying between them again. *You know, in your head?*

I don't know that word, she said, and she said it as if she were pronouncing her own doom. It's only one word, she told herself. It's just one word.

Uh, said Ebon, and she thought she heard in his silent voice that it was an important word, and that he was seeing the same chasm she was. *Eah. Dad said you wouldn't. Dad said— Never mind. You humans, you only seem to see now. A kind of squared-off, pillar-at-each-corner now, and a few weighed-and-measured years before and after. All of us in bound families have to study some of your history, whether we're individually bound or not. I always thought it was something about the translation, about the fact that we can't talk to each other and even our shamans couldn't get it right, that it was all "he was king from the eighth day of the first month of spring in 892 to the eleventh day of the last month of winter 921," "her army contained ninety-six regiments and the colours on her banner were red and gold." Your history is only what someone remembers or has written down—and it's just history, it's not—*and he used the word again. *It's the way into ssshasssha—your magicians talk about our ssshasssha, don't they? You've asked me about it. But how do they describe it? It's easy to get stuck in now—are you hungry, what's the weather, what are you doing tomorrow? What words can you give these things so you can give them to someone else? From when we're really little we practise getting out* of now. I'm not very good at it. Niahi is hopeless, although Mum says she'll get better as she gets older, but she's worse than most kids, which is probably why she thinks the Caves are spooky.

Sylvi said, I'll be okay. I can stand spooky. I won't embarrass you. I'll—I'll try so hard and be so respectful you'll scarcely recognise me.

Ebon stamped, and lashed his tail so violently it was as if he were trying to shake it loose. That's not what I mean. He stepped forward and put out one of his feather-hands to her cheek again; the tiny breeze of his half-opening wing fanned her face. I want you to—to like the Caves! He stamped again. Oh, **like**! It's a stupid word. Liking the Caves would be like liking water or daylight. If you'd lived in the dark or never tasted water they'd be overwhelming. You wouldn't be able to think about liking.

Like flying when you haven't any wings, thought Sylvi.

But I don't care if this is a historic moment or not, bringing a human into the Caves. All that is grown-up stuff. I knew something was up when I asked Dad if I could bring you here and he didn't say no. I'd been thinking how to be a royal pain in the pinfeathers and then it didn't go like that at all. But then it was too late, I'd got used to it that I was going to be able to bring you here and I told myself the other stuff didn't matter, the grown-up stuff didn't matter to us—and Niahi, Niahi's okay, and it would be nice if you **could** talk to more of us than just me. But it does matter, the grown-up stuff. Why the grown-ups wanted to bring you.

You're not happy here. I never thought about that. I never thought . . . I **shouldn't** have brought you. I wanted you to see the Caves, and I didn't know how else to do it. They'd never have agreed to bringing a lot of you—you humans. I couldn't bear your palace—even with you—if it weren't that there are always at least twelve or a gazai of us around too. I was blind with what **I** wanted. I'm sorry. I'm so sorry. . . .

Stop, she said, and put her hand to his mouth, as if he were human, as if he were speaking aloud. He dropped his own hand and dipped his head, pressing his nose into her hand, till she was looking at the arched crest of his neck, and in that moment she thought that the way his glittering black mane fell down his shining black shoulders was the most beautiful thing she had ever seen. *Stop*, she said. *I knew before I came that it was really **all** about grown-up stuff, that that was the only reason they were letting me come. That you and I—the way we think of you and me—would be a little thing that happened accidentally too. Have you ever wondered what will happen when they lift the ban on letting us translate? If the guild lets them. . . . But I still wanted to come. I knew better than you did—I went to all those senate meetings. I thought . . . I didn't think. Just like you. I wanted to come. It is worth it—whatever it is—to come.* She couldn't resist running her hands up his long silky face and down the perfect arch of his neck, and burying her hands in his mane. *It's that I'm all wrong here. You must feel it at the palace, even though there are more of you.*

You're not all wrong to me, said Ebon, and turned his head to rest his nose on her shoulder.

They stood silently for a moment or two and Sylvi thought, if I could just stand here like this forever, I'd be happy.

And then she sighed, and stooped to pick up the towel she'd dropped. *I'd better get ready. Did you ever say when I should be there? Wherever. I don't know where it is yet either.*

It's not like that, going into the Caves. The right time is when we all get there—the right time only happens some time after we all get there. That's part of getting out of now, into— This time she almost heard the word as a distinct word, but she still had no translation for it: *ssshuuwuushuu.*

The way to *ssshasssha*, she thought. I wonder if Fthoom knows? I wonder how much our magicians know that they haven't told us?

Time—

We have time, said Ebon. *Time isn't a—a thing. And the Caves are the Caves; day and night aren't things either. And days—hours—are different.*

269

The Caves themselves help with going there, with ssshuuwuushuu. You're half there just by crossing the threshold. It's why if you can't go there yourself the Caves are harder—like the difference between jumping and being thrown. He paused. *Once you're there, it's—it's almost like dreaming, when you're in your dream as yourself instead of your dreaming self, when you're both nothing and everything in your dream.* **Everything** *matters when you're not in now.*

She gave a little grunt of surprised laughter. *I almost know what you mean.*

Ebon smiled. *Of course you do. How could you not at least almost know anything I know?*

It'll be all right, she said.

Eah. Yes, it will.

But her heart was beating rather too quickly when she and Ebon arrived at the clearing near the entrance to the Caves. Sylvi had one hand wrapped around the little wooden bead Ebon had just dropped round her neck; he was wearing one too. Its creamy glow was startling against his blackness.

Lrrianay was there ahead of them; he too wore a bead. From a distance it seemed as if Lrrianay himself shone with a soft brilliance. If Viktur's soldiers had first seen a pegasus like this, Sylvi thought, they would have been sure he was a god, or at least the numen of the land— the sweet green land. There was another pegasus with him, wearing a little bag around his neck which did not glow. It took her a moment to recognise him: Hibeehea.

She didn't mean to—she meant to be poised and perfectly behaved—but she stopped dead. Ebon stopped too, and looked at her inquiringly.

Hibeehea, she said, and felt that even her silent voice shook.

We have to have a shaman with us to go into the Caves, said Ebon.

He had told her that. She had forgotten. *Hibeehea?* she said. *No—wait—you're going to tell me what a great honour it is again.*

Well, it is, he said. *I didn't know it was going to be Hibeehea either.*

She made her feet start moving again. Poised, she thought. Perfectly behaved. Lrrianay and Hibeehea turned to look at her and Ebon, but they showed no impatience—would I know what impatience looks like in a pegasus? thought Sylvi. I've never seen one impatient. Maybe I just don't know what it looks like. But maybe they're never impatient. She glanced at Ebon. *He* gets impatient, she thought.

Some of this slid inadvertently into her speaking range. Not knowing where the border was was a good deal more worrisome now that she was talking to more pegasi than just Ebon, and *Hibeehea. . . .*

Ebon glanced back at her. *Impatient? No, I don't feel impatient. I . . .* There was a brief pause. *Come to think about it, I feel kind of scared. That's good, right? We can be scared together.*

She tried to laugh and almost succeeded. She thought, He's afraid I'll make a mess of it. She was sure she had been careful to think that on the safe, private side of the silent border, but Ebon turned on her and said, *Don't **ever** think that. About anything. You're my heart's sister, even if you are a funny shape and walk on your hind legs all the time and rattle away out loud like a donkey or a bird. I'm frightened because you're frightened, and because it's hard—it can be hard—the first time going into the Caves, and you're old for it—you can't do ssshuuwuushuu and the ssshasssha will be like . . . being thrown in a cold dark lake when you can't swim and you've never seen water before.*

Unbidden, something Ahathin had said to her years ago came back to her, something he had said to her shortly before her binding, about apprentice magicians learning the language of the pegasi: Imagine learning to swim by being thrown into a lake in perfect darkness, never having seen water before.

I need to think about this, she thought suddenly. I need—

We start 'em young, and you only go in for a mouthful of moments your first time, and . . . His silent-voice trailed away.

And I'm a funny shape, and I talk out loud, she said.

He looked at her and there was another pause; but all he said, un-Ebon-like, was, *Yes.*

Then she was making her bows and greetings to Lrrianay and Hibeehea, and Hibeehea was standing very close to her—so close she had to stop herself stepping backward—to distract herself she looked up, and saw that there were many pegasi standing at the edge of the clearing, among the trees; she had not noticed them before. Niahi nodded her head and—*waved,* stretching one wing out and forward, and flicking it up and down. Hesitantly Sylvi raised a thin bare arm and waved back. The queen, standing beside Niahi, stepped forward, and at once Sylvi turned toward her: she was less scary than either Hibeehea or Lrrianay. Sylvi's eyes fell to her garnet, still round the queen's neck, lying where the bright beads lay round Lrrianay's or Ebon's. As the queen moved into the sunlight, the little garnet flared briefly, red as a torch.

Aliaalia said, *As you are a girl, it is your mother who should take you into the Caves for the first time. But the leader of your kinsfolk may choose to do it instead. Ebon is your kin here, and Lrrianay wishes to take you. But I want you to know, little Sylvi, that I would have been happy and proud to bring you into our Caves myself. Go well, daughter, and may you see all you will see.* She brushed her velvet cheek across Sylvi's cheek, and walked back to the edge of the trees where Niahi waited for her.

See all I will see? thought Sylvi.

Lrrianay nodded and led the way. Hibeehea followed, and Ebon dropped half a step behind Sylvi and (she felt) chivvied her forward. She thought she was probably glad for a little chivvying. She let go of her bead as they passed the threshold, into the twilight of the Caves.

Her first impression of the Caves was merely the sound of her first footstep, when she crossed from turf to packed earth. Her second impression was of darkness, in spite of candlelight and her bead, as she stepped from daylight into the cave mouth.

There was a pegasus she had not seen before just inside, who bowed to them all; there was a little round space like an antechamber with a cluster of tall candles at its centre, and Lrrianay paused. Sylvi involuntarily looked back, toward the daylight and the trees and the open air. She was looking past Ebon, blacker than ever against the light, with the tiny dazzle of his bead against his chest. He seemed taller than a carriage-horse, bigger and broader than a war-horse, standing between her and the sun. She didn't even know how long they would be in the Caves, how long before she would see daylight again: *It depends*, Ebon had said. *It's not—not a useful question, "how long?" We'll stop when we get tired or hungry.*

"Stop"? thought Sylvi. Don't you mean come back outdoors? But she hadn't asked.

Lrrianay glanced at her. Yes, I'm here, she thought—to herself, she hoped. With my two legs and my preposterous hands. I wish I could *stop* thinking, so I could stop worrying about anyone overhearing me. But . . . She thought of Niahi: spooky, she'd said. Full. Very cautiously Sylvi tried to feel her way into the little anteroom of the Cave she stood in—"felt" in the way she "listened" to Ebon.

Spooky. No. Yes. No. Full—?

It was nothing like a velvet nose against her face or a friendly feather mattress curling around her as she slept, or even the shockwave of the

273

ting as her father dropped a magician's spiral on the floor of his receiving room. But there was something there—here—something besides pegasi and rock and candles. Something not unlike what had made her fall down, only three nights ago, when she'd heard Niahi speak for the first time.

That was three days ago, she thought. *That is a long time. And time doesn't matter in the Caves.*

There were dark tunnel openings all round them, and Lrrianay chose one and led them into it.

It was a gentle downslope, but there were also small fat candles in niches along the walls, so it was easy enough to see your way. At first Sylvi kept her eyes on her feet, and then on Hibeehea's long smoke-coloured tail, with occasional sidelong glances at the candles, as if checking that there was enough wax left that they would keep burning and not plunge them suddenly into darkness.... Her hand crept up again to the bead on its string round her neck. She kept wanting to hold it like a talisman, blotting out its light; she touched it and let her hand drop again. It was not only the darkness, the awareness of it barely held off by a few small candles and smaller beads; it was the awareness of the inconceivable weight of all the rock and earth of the mountain above them, as they went farther and farther down and in.... There was no record in the thousands of years the pegasi had been using their Caves of any ceiling or tunnel collapse; Ebon had told her this. *Occasionally someone gets lost,* he'd added cheerfully. *But never for very long. We've always found 'em before they got very hungry.*

Sylvi wanted to ask Ebon if he knew where they were going, if he recognised the tunnel his father had chosen, but she didn't want to be overheard. She tried to concentrate on Hibeehea's tail and wingtips, on the consciousness of Ebon just behind her, on Lrrianay leading them calmly and surely ... where?

It's just the dark, she told herself. It's just the dark and the ... the *caveness*, the mountain overhead. The rest is just ... like the story of the prince who ran away; there wasn't anything chasing him but fear. I am *not* going to be the princess who ran away....

It wasn't sounds, exactly. There were sounds, of course: the soft tap of hoofs and the lighter, slappier tap of her own feet, the sound of Ebon's breathing, the faint rustly noise of trickling water. But there was something else. She'd felt it in the anteroom. It had come with her. No, it was all around her.

Almost involuntarily her hand reached out and touched a smooth knob of wall. It was curious, she wasn't used to caves, so why shouldn't the walls here look strangely sheeny and almost fluid? She could hear the sound of water, but the wall she touched was dry. But these were the Caves; the pegasi had chosen them thousands of years ago because they were exceptional, because they were extraordinary. Because they were unique.

She knew, as soon as she touched the wall—knew—what did she know? That the wall was not like a human-built wall, not like even the oldest wall of the eight-hundred-year-old palace. She knew, of course, that the pegasus sculptors were greatly honoured; if the pegasi created hierarchies the way humans did, the sculptors would be behind only the shamans and the monarch: what the sculptors did created *ssshas-ssha*, which humans feebly translated as "recollection."

She knew that the Caves contained hundreds of amazing chambers of thousands of years of sculptors' work. She hadn't realised that mere passageways had also been carved and shaped—she thought again of Niahi saying, *They're so full.* As almost involuntarily as she had first put her hand on the wall, she stopped and put her other hand next to the first. The wall seemed almost to quiver, like a horse's skin dislodging a fly. She lightened her touch and then thought despairingly, Oh, I'm human! *Ebon, may I not touch the walls?*—and she heard the pleading in her silent voice.

Ebon's nearer wing unfolded, and his feather-hand lay lightly over hers, pressing it delicately—so delicately—against the wall. She could never quite adjust to the fineness, the fragility of pegasus hands, especially Ebon's—Ebon who was nearly as big as a small horse, and could fly even carrying her on his back. Suddenly she was trembling, trembling as she imagined the wall was trembling—surely it could not really tremble, rock and earth and mountain that it was?—in the overwhelming knowledge of the thousands upon thousands of tiny pegasus sculptor hands that had made even an ordinary passage wall beautiful. It was perhaps as astonishing as the touch of a human hand was to the Caves, accustomed to thousands of years of the pegasi.

They're so full, Niahi had said. If the corridor walls were overwhelming, what would the chambers be like?

She would not be the princess who ran away.

With Ebon's hand over hers she dared keep hers against the wall a little longer. She rested only her fingertips and the heel of her hands against the wall, as lightly as she could, as lightly as Ebon's hand touched hers; the tenuousness of contact seemed to sharpen her senses, so her fingers seemed to identify each individual grain of the stone, each tenderly-sculpted brush-stroke. She was still shaking as if with shock; but then it was as if the wall *bloomed* under her fingers. It was no longer stone, but silken-warm like a pegasus' side. What she'd thought was trembling was the rise and fall of its breath. . . .

For a moment she thought nothing at all. She was not Sylviianel, daughter of Corone, who was king of his land; she was not the first human to set foot in the pegasus Caves in thousands of years; she was not standing in those Caves with her hands on a corridor wall and her bound pegasus standing next to her with his hand over one of hers.

She was nothing; she was Cave; she was pegasus; she was everything . . .
ssshuuwuushuu.

It was over in a heartbeat, and she was Sylvi again, standing in a
dark tunnel with a mountain over her head and candlelight flickering
across the wall and making it look as if it was moving. Lrrianay and
Hibeehea had stopped as soon as she did, as soon as she had spoken
to Ebon. She dropped her hands and turned away from the wall, toward them, and toward the way they had been going. She felt Ebon's
feather-hand just touch her hair and then withdraw. She was still shivering somewhere deep inside herself, but much of the light-headed,
off-balance, *wrong* feeling she'd had for the last three days, since she'd
heard Niahi speak and had rediscovered herself as awkward and bizarre, had faded away. Walking on her hind legs seemed normal again,
acceptable. She was human. She took a deep breath, aware of how
shallow her lungs were in comparison to a pegasus', but aware that
that was as it should be. She was small, and human.

Child, are you all right? said Lrrianay.

She did not know how to answer him; she knew that she heard
"all right" because her human mind, her use of language did not contain what he asked her: was she at peace with herself was perhaps
closer. She could not think how to put her answer—her question—in
pegasi terms. *Have I just passed another test?* she said, knowing the pegasi
did not set tests any more than they created hierarchies.

There was a pause as Lrrianay thought this over. *What we show you
depends on what you see, yes,* he said. *And we hoped you would see the walls
here, yes.*

She thought, His "see" is not quite what it means anywhere but here.
It was the "see" that the queen had used: *May you see all that you will see.*

*What you would see if we told you to look, and where to look, would be
different,* said Lrrianay.

Less, she said, but she was thinking, *that is another human concept, less.*

There was another pause and this time Hibeehea answered: *Not less, different. But we would have you as much like us as possible, yes. To see these walls, as you evidently do see them, is like us.*

But they are strange to me. Strange. She could not think of the right word, a word that would reverberate not only through her bones, but through Hibeehea's, and Lrrianay's, and the bones of this mountain.

We can turn around now, child, if you wish, said Hibeehea, and there was only kindness in his silent voice. *We have our answer, and you have visited the Caves.*

Oh, no! she said before she thought. *I have only seen one corridor! A little of one corridor! I mean—whatever you say, great lord, srrrwa! But—I—please—sir!*

Lrrianay wrinkled his nose and flicked his ears. *I see again why you and Ebon are so close*, he said. *I wonder how much that closeness has to do with how much you were alike before you met? Very well. We will go on.* And then he turned away from her and led them on the way they had been going.

She thought of the sky and the trees and the daylight. But she was not sorry she had answered as she had; she did not now want to turn around, even if the ceiling did seem to lean down toward her—as if it would stretch down a stony hand and smack her forehead. The pegasi's heads on their long upright necks were higher than hers, and they did not stoop. She squared her shoulders—such a *human* gesture—and followed.

The corridor walls around her opened, and she was walking on grass under the sky with many pegasi all around her—white and cream-coloured, all the shades of golden from flaxen to dark honey, amber-red to russet-red, coppery and tawny and dark loam brown;

silver to twilight-grey; and occasionally black. They were cantering past her, their wings half spread, the occasional pale feather in a dark wing catching her eye. Where were they all going? They streamed past her, hundreds upon hundreds of them; occasionally one would turn its head and nod at her, although she recognised none of them. They seemed to be going somewhere, and they seemed to be drawing her along with them: where her slow walking feet were taking her was ultimately where all their quick cantering feet were taking them.

Then the landscape, or her dream, changed, and there was a small round valley in the hill before them, and this was their destination. Or, no—this was her destination, for most of the pegasi ran on, parting around the way into the little valley and disappearing behind the shoulders of the hill. A few pegasi slowed to a walk and accompanied her.

But the moment she entered the little circle of the valley she wanted to go no farther; her feet slowed, dragged, and finally stopped. The pegasi with her quietly stopped too.

The valley, now that she was in it, was bigger than it had looked from outside. A group of perhaps twenty pegasi stood in the flat centre of the valley, and with them stood a group of perhaps thirty humans. Sylvi saw the humans with a shock like a blow: how graceless they were, both squat and elongated—how ungrounded and unbalanced—with their strange thin pawing arms and huge clutching hands—and she forgot again that she had remembered how to be human, and she grieved that she was one of them.

A few of the pegasi standing with the humans turned their heads and acknowledged the newcomers, but most did not. None of the humans looked at them. And now, with another shock, Sylvi recognised that the humans were wearing armour, worn, stained armour, and they wore it as if they were used to wearing it and had been wearing it for a long time. They had swords slung round their hips or over their shoulders, and two or three had bows and quivers, and she saw one with a short dagger and halberd; all their faces were tired and grim.

As she noticed these things it was as if the scene were building itself around her. She knew, suddenly, that there was an army camp on the far side of the hill; now that she knew it was there she could hear it, smell the smoke of its cook- and watchfires; there was even a sentinel standing on the brow of the little hill to her right. He could not have been there before—she could not have missed him? Surely she could not have missed him?

She glanced back over her shoulder. The land was empty and silent. All the galloping pegasi were gone, all but the few who stood with her, and the grass they had galloped across was a smooth unruffled sea. Pegasi ordinarily left little mark of where they had been, but there had been hundreds of them, and even if they had contrived to bend not a single grass-stem, her plodding human feet should have broken a path—and there was no sign of her passage either.

She turned forward again. There was a small table, now, at the centre of the valley, around which the humans and the pegasi stood—or rather, on either side of which they stood, the humans on one side and the pegasi on the other. This distressed her; she wanted to walk forward and join the pegasi, or seize two of those ugly human arms with her own ungainly hands and draw them toward the pegasus side of the table. It was not good that they should stay so divided from each other. Was that not why she was here? To help end—to help soften—that division, between human and pegasus?

But where was she? She was walking in the Caves, the pegasus Caves, where no human had ever walked before. She was with Ebon and Lrrianay and Hibeehea. . . .

Where was she?

The armour the humans wore was unfamiliar to her. Old-fashioned perhaps—some of the poorer barons were still using armour their grandparents' troops had worn, and some of the bits and pieces still in use in the practise yards at the palace were older still—but this seemed to her more than merely that. These men and women did not carry themselves like soldiers in a held-together-with-string unit—nor would one of the poorer barons have twenty pegasi as members of his company.

She knew a little about armour; lessons with Diamon included learning about your equipment and its history. This armour was like nothing she had seen before, mostly leather and very little chain, and the chain curiously linked; they wore no chausses or greaves, and their gauntlets and gorgets were peculiarly cut, as were the panels of their leather cuirasses. When one turned and spoke low-voiced to another, she could half hear the words, which seemed to be at least half known to her but strangely pronounced, and the rhythm of the sentences was odd and outlandish.

The one who had spoken glanced up. There was something odd about him; something about him marked him out from the others . . . no, the man standing next to him was another like him. . . . But what was the oddness? Did they stand differently, move differently, was their skin a different colour, their armour a different kind? They were both wearing slightly shabby once-grand gowns over their armour, but so were several of the others. Nothing she could put her finger on but she was certain. . . .

One of the two drew a short baton from under his surcoat, held it flat across his palms and offered it to the other one.

She'd seen that gesture at hundreds of rituals. They were magicians. And in the rituals she knew, that particular gesture heralded some confirmation, validation, agreement—although the baton was usually brought by a third, more subordinate magician. She looked round again. But the rituals she knew took place at the palace, or at carefully planned and organised festivals elsewhere. This was not a battlefield, but the battlefield was obviously nearby.

Two humans unrolled a large, long sheet of what, by its pliancy, must be pegasus-made paper. The humans, perhaps disconcerted by something so unlike stiff, crackly parchment, handled it uneasily and laid it—cautiously, warily, protectively, attentively—on the table. Everyone was staring at it. The two humans holding it touched it as if they weren't sure what sort of beast it was: was it an ally, was it hostile?

A battlefield alliance . . .

The strange armour, the language whose words were familiar but whose rhythms were not . . .

One of the magicians looked tired and worried and grim, like all the other humans.

The other one turned and looked at her . . .

. . . and for a moment he was Fthoom.

And she was walking in the Caves again, except that she wasn't walking. She was standing still, and her three companions were standing with her. Lrrianay and Hibeehea were gravely watching her, and Ebon had his nose on her shoulder.

You okay?

She nodded. And then, startled, looked around. They were no longer in the long corridor, but a huge room, the ceiling lost in shadows overhead. There were other pegasi here—three that she could immediately see—one of them was lighting a candle in a niche in the wall. There were candles all around the walls at irregular intervals, and as the niches were various sizes, so were the candles. In the centre of the room, a low table stood, a dozen tall lamps on it, blazing with light.

In the light she could see the walls. ... Millennia of tiny, frail feather-hands, smoothing and scooping, carving and scoring the natural walls of the cave. ...

There were portraits of pegasi everywhere on the walls, walking and flying, standing, running, lying, bowing, pawing, dancing, rearing, and doing other things she had no names for, as when two stood face to face and clasped their feather-hands together; or when, again face to face, four stood in a four-pointed star, knelt and bowed their heads, and wrapped their wings over each other. The curves of one pegasus, the billow of one tail or the fall of one mane, became a curve or a billow or a fall of the next; and in the flicker of the light, the rounds and hollows of all seemed to move as if with life.

Among the stone pegasi there were other things: trees and flowers and climbing vines, leaves and branches and blooms, saplings and bushes and forests—rabbits, deer, foxes, fornols, badgers, bears, birds—many, many birds, from the tiniest wrens to great raptors with wingspans nearly as great as the pegasi's own—spiders and beetles and butterflies and bees. There was a stone stream near where Sylvi stood with several pegasi prancing in it: every drop of water was clearly and lovingly detailed.

And humans. Sylvi had been turning slowly round as if looking for something—and yet she did not want to see humans—see them here, surrounded by pegasi, to be forced to look again at the coarseness and gracelessness of what she was herself. She wrapped her gawky arms around her clumsy body and hunched her shoulders.

Ebon saw where she was looking and said, *Hey, don't worry. They're only stone.*

We're so ugly, said Sylvi miserably.

Ugly? There was a pause, as if Ebon were considering the matter; he was certainly looking first at the carved humans and then at Sylvi, and then back. *I don't think so. I like the way it's all up and down with you, and no sideways. It's very—direct. Like you humans are. Although you're better-looking than that lot.* He looked hard at Sylvi, seemed to make up his mind about something, and went on: *When Dad first told me I was going to have to be your pegasus, I used to come here and stare at these guys. I'd only seen live humans a few times, when a crowd of us went to your palace for some big rite or festival or other, after I was big enough to fly that far. And then us kids were always kept well back and never went to the banquets.*

I never saw you, said Sylvi. *I'd remember, black is so unusual. I can hardly remember seeing any young pegasi, unless it was one of you being bound to one of us.*

Yes—well—you do have to be nearly grown to fly that far. Ebon was silent a moment, and then went on: *You—you humans—saved our lives—and you go on saving our lives. The taralians and their friends would be all over us in a few generations if you left. And we'd just sit here and let them, because we wouldn't leave the Caves, and without the llyri grass we'd stop flying within a generation or two. We'd stop flying but our legs still wouldn't be tough enough to run like deer and horses run. Our shamans say the grass grows out of the stone that the Caves are made of, that's what makes our wings strong enough to carry us. Two thousand years ago the taralians found us—that's what the stories say—we could have run away, but we couldn't've either, right?*

Taralians and norindours and ladons don't like our mountains much and don't like our Caves at all, but we couldn't stay here all the time. Did you know that we used to raise llyri grass where your palace now sits? That field of it your gardeners keep for us has been growing there for probably four thousand years. Even the barn where you keep it after harvest is where our old winter pavilion used to be. A roc knocked it down a century or two before you came. . . . That's pretty much when we pulled out of the lowlands.

Our shamans told us we'd get rescued at the last minute. And we did—you came. But something went wrong. . . .

Sylvi turned and walked toward the wall where the carved stone humans stood. It took her a moment to realise why the scene looked familiar. It was where she had just been, what she had just seen, although she was seeing it now from a different angle, as if the army camp was behind her, and the way she had come with the hundreds of pegasi in front of her. The humans were now on her left and the pegasi on her right. Even now that she could not hear them speak, the strangeness of the humans' armour drew her attention; even now that they were inanimate images on a wall she could see the tension of them, the set concentration of their faces.

And she could still pick out the two magicians although the baton was not visible. One of them looked as the other humans looked, fixed on the matter at hand but worried about its outcome. The other was the one who reminded her of Fthoom.

She knew he was not Fthoom; this man did not even look like him. But that sense of power, of power held for hidden purposes, held in a way meant to be intimidating so that the wielder of it can better judge the strength of any opposition—that was Fthoom. That inward look, the look of a miser always preoccupied with his private treasure, of the greatness of what was his and his alone, and of how to make it greater yet—that was Fthoom. She found herself thinking that this man even moved like Fthoom—except that she was looking at a sculptured wall. Perhaps the candlelight slid over him differently than it glinted over the others.

I don't like this one, she said.

I don't like him either. He's ugly, if you like.

Ugly, she said. *Why did you come here? When you knew you had to be my pegasus.*

The skin over Ebon's shoulders shivered and he nodded his head once quickly, a sign of embarrassment. *Well. These are the only humans in the Caves. If I wanted to look at humans, these were it. That was a long time ago, okay? I was a lot younger, and I hadn't met you.*

These are the only humans in the Caves? I'm surprised there are any, she thought. *Why these?*

Ebon looked at her in surprise—tall neck drawn up even straighter (how regal he looks, she thought), ears stiffly pricked, just one wrinkle across his nose. *That's the signing of the treaty*, he said. *I thought you'd recognised it. That's your king Balsin, and our Fralialal. And that's Dorogin, the ugly one, and Gandam.*

The signing of the treaty.

Ssshasssha. History and . . . recollection.

The motionless stone picture was taking place just after she had watched the living scene: the two humans were still holding the treaty paper flat against the table, but a pegasus—it would be the pegasus king—was holding one wing, with the first three primaries curiously spread, just above its surface. These were astonishingly artfully done, for the shadows fell in such a way as to show, now that she was looking for this, the inked tips of those feathers. As the candlelight flickered she felt she saw him draw his feather-tips across the surface of the paper in the quick, graceful, triple stroke she had seen replicated on so many documents, so many commemorative plaques and paintings at the palace. She thought of the mural in the Great Hall where, when she was younger, she had thought she could hear Fralialal stepping down from the wall onto the floor. That Fralialal was bigger, grander— more human. This one, here, on the wall of the Caves, this one was a true pegasus: smaller, finer, graceful as candlelight . . . exotic. Inexplicable. Unknowable.

The signing of the treaty.

She had just been standing on eight-hundred-year-old grass, smelling the smoke of the eight-hundred-year-old war that had given her people and Ebon's their Alliance. She had seen the treaty itself unrolled, when it was only a new piece of fine paper with some writing on it—she had seen it before it was signed, before it was the treaty, before it hung on the wall of the Great Hall, before Balsin's signature on it had become the reigning monarch's mark.

She had met Dorogin's eyes.

And Dorogin looked like Fthoom. In the mural at the palace, none of the human faces stood out: they were just humans. Only the pegasus king and the treaty itself had any reality.

No—she would not think of it any more. She would not think of the fact that she had been there, the fact that something about the Caves had made her imagine that she had been there. She would not think of it. But she could—she would—she must think about Dorogin and Fthoom.

So it began . . . at the beginning, she said slowly, *what went wrong.*

She held her hands out—her human hands—and looked down through them at her single pair of human feet. *It's a good thing I didn't . . . know all this. Or I'd've been too frightened to come.*

Eah. I'd be the same.

You would not, she thought.

I'd be the same, but I'd do it anyway, just like you would.

Well, I'm here, she said slowly, staring at the wall—at Dorogin's stony eyes watching her. *What am I going to tell my father?* She wasn't sure if she'd said that so Ebon could hear it, and she moved nearer to him, and twisted her fingers in a handful of his long mane as it spilled down his shoulder. He turned his head, and his nose rested for a moment on the back of her hand. The glow from the bead that hung round his neck haloed him.

They turned together, and found Lrrianay and Hibeehea standing at a little distance, watching them—*letting us talk together privately,*

Sylvi thought in surprise. Before she lost her nerve, she let go of Ebon's mane and stepped forward quickly, ahead of him. *What can I tell my father?* she said.

What have you seen, child? said Hibeehea. *What do you want to tell your father?*

You know what I saw, she said. *Didn't you send me? This is more of what I'm here for, isn't it? Ssshasssha, that humans don't understand? Is there any more you haven't told me? That you're going to throw me into without telling me? Well, I have heard—and spoken—and seen, and perhaps I understand— a little. But even if my father believes me, he will say, What can we tell our people? Our people, who think the pegasus ssshasssha is a bard's fantastic tale? How is a picture carved on a wall anything but a picture carved on a wall?*

And how will you answer him?

She took a deep breath. *I will say, because I was there, and I saw them. Why did you bring me to the Caves and not him? He is the king. He is the one you have to convince. And he loves you—you pegasi. He would listen to you. He envies me coming to the Caves. But he let me come—alone—because that is what you wanted. And this is why you brought me, isn't it? I'm already half in your—your world, because of my friendship with Ebon—because I can talk to Ebon. Because—and now I can talk to all of you, all you pegasi. I went there—* she gestured at the stony Alliance—*I **went** there. I walked into that scene. I saw them breathing. I smelled horses and campfires and human food cooking and human sweat. Did you send me because you could not send him?*

There was a little pause, but Sylvi was too angry and shaken to think about how she was addressing the king and his shaman.

We cannot send you or anyone—we cannot send ourselves, or each other, said Hibeehea. *But we can recognise those who may be able to go themselves. It is an unusual talent. Most of those who have it become shamans. I am one of them. We don't know what that talent would look like in a human—we have never seen a human who has made us wonder if they might carry that talent.*

But we have wondered about you a great deal since Lrrianay came back from your binding to say that you and Ebon could speak to each other.

And then Ebon came to us with his mad idea of bringing you here as what he called a birthday present, said Lrrianay, smiling, but he held his head low and worried.

What is it you humans say? That we backed into their hands? said Ebon.

Played into their hands, said Sylvi, and curled her fingers into fists. She turned around quickly and looked again at the signing: and she was sure—except that she knew it was nonsense—that Dorogin's eyes moved to meet hers and his mouth turned up in a gloating sneer, a sneer that said, *There's nothing you can do.*

I don't know what I can do, she said, because silent-speech had become her ordinary way of speech; and then she added aloud, as if for Dorogin's benefit, "But I will do something." The vibration of her larynx felt strange to her, and she uncurled one of her fists, and put her long nimble fingers on her throat.

CHAPTER 15

Usually there were other pegasi with them, or nearby; in all the big chambers they entered there were sculptors working, with their tiny knives and brushes and picks and whisks and rubbing cloths, and they were in some of the smaller rooms and alcoves too, and occasionally in the corridors. She was told she might watch them, if she wished, so long as she did not speak to them or touch them or their tools or otherwise disturb them. But once one spoke to her.

Welcome, small human child, daughter of the bond-friend of our king, and bond-friend of our king's son.

Oh—I'm sorry—I'm not supposed to—

You did not disturb me, said the pegasus. *I disturbed myself, that I might speak to you. So it is true—you can speak to us,* and he laid his brush down and turned fully round to look at her. She had to stop herself from blinking or fidgeting under that steady regard, but there was nothing hostile in his look or his posture. His neck was gently arched, his body relaxed, tail lying flat, and when he laid his brush down, he folded his wings only loosely. He nodded his head in an acknowledgement not unlike the similar human one and then held it down longer in an almost-bow and said, *I am honoured to meet you, little girl, king's daughter.*

She didn't mean to, but thoughts and silent-speech still got confused, and she said so that he could hear her, *I am **not** little.*

His laugh started with the nose-wrinkle smile and ran in ripples all the way to his hindquarters. He was a dappled brown, and his dapples twinkled as he laughed. He was smaller than Ebon or Lrrianay, but not so small as Hibeehea. *I beg pardon,* he said. *When I was younger, I went several times to your palace, and I have seen a few humans, and they were great clumsy creatures. You are not. You are smaller than I was expecting. Smaller and neater.*

For an awful, heart-stopping moment she thought—*He's guessed about Ebon and me, he knows about the flying!*—and she clutched that thought to her as she might clutch an escaping puppy, all legs and wriggle, that the sculptor should not hear it too. *I am sorry,* she said. *I have always been . . . among humans I am too small.* She thought—and pushed that thought forward, toward the dangerous speech boundary—of the years she had spent sitting on cushions so she could eat supper with her family, and the fact that she still used a child's sword in the practise yard.

You are not too small here, he replied. *Here you are just right.*

She couldn't help smiling. *Thank you,* she said, but her eyes drifted to the wall, where the pegasus had been working. Sometimes the walls were sculpted only, but here there were colours too: yellows, browns, umbers, dark reds and blues and greens. She thought she saw tree shapes, and if they were tree shapes, she thought she saw bird shapes among their branches.

It is the Forest of Areeanhaaee in autumn, said the pegasus. *Where we hold our main harvest festival, and the birds sing so loudly you cannot hear the sound of hundreds of us running the great rune-sign that is laid out as a path among the trees.*

There is so much I—we—humans don't know, she said sadly. *I do not know the Forest of Areeanhaaee, although Ebon has told me something of your festivals.*

You know more now, said the pegasus. *And you will take it home with you, and tell other humans, and you will tell it well, because you have been to the Caves and spoken to its sculptors. You will find the Forest and the festival on many other walls here, till it is more familiar to you than if you had been there—because that is what happens in the Caves.* He looked at her thoughtfully for a moment, and then unfolded one wing, and tapped the bead that hung round her neck with a tiny feathery finger. *That is nicely done,* he said.

Ebon made it for me, she said proudly, and looked round for him. He was standing with his father, but as if he felt her gaze on him he immediately looked toward her. He made a tiny, curiously stiff bow of acknowledgement to the sculptor she stood with, and looked away again. Surprised, she looked at the sculptor, who was smiling.

He works hard, said the pegasus. *The extra burdens on him must make him weaker or stronger, and they have made him stronger. We are all bound by what fate chooses for us. I am proud of him. I am proud of you too, not-little Sylvi.* And he turned away from her, and picked up his brush again.

They walked farther and farther into the labyrinth of the Caves, and while Lrrianay went always in the lead Sylvi was glad of the presence of the shaman, even when that shaman was Hibeehea—although she could not have said why she was glad, nor why she knew that Lrrianay depended on him too. Sylvi also knew by the third time they stopped to rest and eat that they would not leave at nightfall, that they would sleep in the Caves. But her fears of the morning seemed long ago, almost as long ago as the last time she had seen her father. By that third stop—leaning against a wall with a candle in a niche just over her head, a piece of bread in one hand and a handful of dried plooraia in the other—she had already watched the signing of the treaty and spoken to the sculptor; nor had her sense of *sshuuwuushuu* left her. She was still aware of the weight of the mountain over her head—and it was by this that she knew that they were going farther in—but she also sensed Cuandoia looking out over his domain, and felt no apprehension.

They slept in special chambers that the pegasi had hollowed out or closed off from the surrounding Caves for this use. These were small and plain, but Ebon taught her to recognise them by the small low doorways and the scatter of single flowers carved round the openings—and in each there was a strong draught of fresh air, like opening a window before you went to bed in your bedroom. (There were equally mysteriously well-ventilated little water-closets at irregular but frequent intervals along the corridors, awkward but not impossible for a small human to use, and with sweet-smelling rushes scattered on the bare floors; there seemed always to be one close to a bedchamber.)

At their first evening halt she was missing the prospect of hot food very badly—if it was evening, and if it was the first and not the fifth: the breadth and balance of *sshuuwuushuu* or no, Sylvi was so exhausted that she was occasionally putting a hand against a corridor wall to push herself upright. Some weary longing for sky and grass and trees had also crept into her consciousness, and she was cold and stiff and feeling her most homesick and alien, but she was careful to say (and think) nothing about it, and tried not to let her drooping spirits be too visible to her companions.

But she was tired enough that the moment they walked into one of the little rooms and there were a few of the familiar bags and panniers of her journey with the pegasi waiting for them, she sat down at once, as if her knees had given way. Ebon dropped down to lie beside her, and put a wing round her, and she felt more relaxed and a good deal warmer immediately. She leant back against his shoulder and sighed. *You should stuff mattresses when you moult,* she said. *You'd make a fortune selling them to us.*

What would we do with a fortune? said Ebon. *Our old feathers go with the rest to fertilise our fields. But I'll save you some if you like. They'll keep you a lot warmer and softer than dumb old duck or goose.*

Lrrianay and Hibeehea were still standing, and she tipped her head back to look up at them. Pegasi didn't stand up as much as horses did, but they didn't immediately sit or lie down when they were tired the way humans did either. She still had to listen carefully to understand pegasus speech, and it generally had to be addressed to her for her to understand it; two of them speaking quickly and emphatically to each other made a musical, if in this case somewhat edgy, noise in her head, but was entirely untranslatable. The one thing she thought she could pick out was that Lrrianay and Hibeehea's body language declared they were not happy with each other.

She felt the ripples running along Ebon's skin and realised he was laughing. *What?* she said.

It's about how we're going to sleep, Ebon said. *You're such a little bit of a thing anyway—*

I wish everyone would stop calling me little, she muttered.

Little bit of a thing, repeated Ebon firmly, *and you haven't even got any hair to speak of, let alone feathers, and bony—*

I am not bony! she said.

And the ground here is rock where it isn't dirt, hard-trodden dirt, and you're going to have kind of a rough night. Nights, because after your—after what's happened today we'll be here as long as we can.

I am not pathetic, she said, trying to sound not pathetic, trying to remember how she had spoken to Lrrianay and Hibeehea after she had watched the treaty being signed—remembering the sculptor saying, *I am proud of you too*. Trying not to quail at the prospect of more days without daylight. She said, *I know there are two blankets because I rolled them up myself. They're in that pannier right there. I'll be fine.*

So the obvious thing is that you sleep with me, continued Ebon as if she had not spoken. *But Hibeehea is getting his tail in a bramble because it's not proper.*

We travel, you know? We don't have houses and beds. When you're little you sleep with your parents and when you're a little bigger you sleep with each other. About the time you're old enough and big enough not to need someone else's back or wing to keep you warm all the time, if you do sleep with someone else it had better be an elderly relative or someone of your own gender. We don't make love lying down the way you do—I don't think we can—but it's the same idea. Mwrrrala—um, pairing off, what do you say, wedding?—sometimes happens really young, and if you're both the same gender it doesn't matter, but we're really strict that mixed gender hrmmmhr pairs don't produce babies too young, and sleeping together is seen as encouraging, uh, intimacy. So people our age . . . Dad is saying you and I are not the same species and the rule doesn't apply. Hibeehea is quoting a lot of dusty old chronicles at him about incorrect behaviour leading to moral ruin. None of which apply to bond-humans in the Caves, but that's not stopping him. Shamans get like this—the chronicles are more real to them than we are. Sculptors can get like that too about what's on the walls here. . . .

Sylvi could feel herself blushing, but she sank down a little farther till Ebon's wing was covering her face as well. And she was so worn out she fell asleep—even without her blankets to pad the hard ground—and didn't move till the smell of hot food woke her. *Hot food*: they had made her soup. There were carrots and *djee* and dumplings floating in it. *Oh—thank you*, she said, again trying not to sound pathetic. Ebon stood up and shook himself before moving over to the great heap of *llyri* grass that Lrrianay and Hibeehea had already begun on. *Little*, he said. *And bony.*

But she was too busy eating to reply. The soup smelled of daylight—as did the grass—and suddenly a few more days in the Caves was wonderful—was nothing like enough.

Some time during the second day the Caves became ... she didn't know what to call it. *Normal* was the best she could do, but that wasn't it; but *common* or *ordinary* was worse—was all wrong. It was reassuring and frightening all at once, the normality. It was a little like the evening she had met Niahi and had begun to hear the other pegasi speaking; it was an enormous thing, a glorious and sublime thing—but she feared it too, feared it drawing her away from her life, from her humanity—to where? She remembered her father's unspoken words: They were weaving a net to pull you away from us. She looked at her hands often, in the company of the pegasi; but she looked at their wings more often.

But some time during the second day she found herself walking with a longer stride, breathing more deeply, looking around more freely. She saw the Forest of Areeanhaaee several times, and once she heard the birds singing, and once she heard the faint, ghostly thunder—because pegasi never thunder—of hundreds of galloping pegasi. She saw the first meeting of Doaor and Marwhiah, when the two tribes of pegasi met, who would decide to unite; she saw how the pegasi learnt to sow crops and to build pavilions and *shfeeah*, to knap flint and press fibre into paper—and many times she saw the finding of the Caves. She saw the *greearha*—the crowning—of many kings and queens, and their families and shamans and *carrfwhee*, their court. But most of all she saw trees, flowers, running water and quiet lakes; birds and deer and nahneeha, frogs and toads and newts, butterflies and fish and iorabaha.

She was in the pegasi's Caves, and she had been invited; she was welcome. She did not think of where Lrrianay and Hibeehea took her; she followed, and she looked. The Caves themselves seemed to beckon to her, even to summon her, and everywhere she looked her eye was drawn farther: every leaf on a tree, every feather on a bird, every hair on a nahneeha, had a clear individuality.

Sculptors don't sculpt, you know, Ebon said. *They set things free.*

As a welcome guest, she wanted to take in as much as she could; she found herself murmuring to the vivid walls, as if they had begun a conversation. When a sculptor bowed to her she bowed in return, gladly—perhaps almost as gracefully as a pegasus herself. And her second, third and fourth nights in the Caves she dreamt of flying, but they were joyous dreams, and when she woke again, wingless and human, curled up against Ebon's side and warm beneath his feathers, the joy remained.

And on the fifth day, as they climbed the last gradual but steady incline to the door to the outside world, her feet dragged, and she was clumsy again, who had not tripped over a hummock in the floor for three days. It was difficult for her to take that final step across the threshold, even knowing that she would stand under the sky again, and hear the wind in the trees, and walk on grass. It was difficult, because she loved the Caves—and because the Caves too held sky and wind and trees and grass—and she did not know when she would see them again.

And after she left the Caves, although she still had several days remaining in the pegasi's country, it was all about leaving, about saying good-bye.

The first person she saw as she came out of the Caves was Niahi.

There were other pegasi present, but as she took that last step across that threshold, with her arm lying along Ebon's crest and her hand buried in his mane, Niahi took a hesitant step forward, and Sylvi's eyes focussed on her. *Oh, Niahi,* said Sylvi, *you're right about the Caves. They're amazing and wonderful—and scary—and very, very full.* And then the tears came—she hadn't known she was going to cry—but once she started she couldn't stop. *Oh, why am I crying? I don't want to cry!*

Niahi trotted forward from what Sylvi dimly realised must be an official welcoming party. The queen followed her daughter, and the two of them stood near Sylvi as if protecting her from a cold wind, or even an attack from an enemy. Lrrianay joined them, and Sylvi was the hub of a little wheel of pegasi. She dug both her hands into Ebon's mane and tried to stop crying, tried to stop her legs from trembling and her back—where no wings grew—from aching, aching, as if when she left the Caves she had again taken up a burden too heavy for her—or as if she were leaving her wings behind.

Hibeehea appeared between Lrrianay and Ebon, who made room for him, but Sylvi stumbled as Ebon moved, trying to press herself away from the pegasus shaman, whom she was suddenly afraid of as she had been at the beginning, poor human thing that she was, wailing like a baby, her nose running and her tears dripping off her chin.

No, child, youngling, you have nothing to fear of me.

And she couldn't even keep her thoughts to herself.

With something she recognised as amusement, Hibeehea continued, *Speech is a skill like any other. Do not your babies shout when they learn new words? Fall down when they are learning to walk? I believe human and pegasus children have these things in common. And our children often weep when they visit the Caves for the first time.*

But I'm falling to pieces, she thought, but she knew he heard her.

You are not. Five days is a long time to be in the Caves for anyone but a sculptor or a shaman; **no** *one is expected to remain in the Caves five days on their first visit. But we did not have time to be gradual. We wanted you to see. . . . Child, may I touch you?*

She had entirely forgotten the human ban on touching pegasi; the silk of Ebon's mane and the velvet of his shoulder were as familiar to her as his words in her head, and since she had been here in their country, especially since she had first heard Niahi, she had fallen in with the pegasus habit of touching each other as they spoke—of touching as part of communication.

Except the shamans. She learnt, without realising she had learnt it, to recognise the shamans partly by the fact that no one touched them, except formally, and with permission first formally granted. She had been presented to several other shamans after her dramatic first meeting with Hibeehea, but she had known, before she had been told, that they were shamans; she had thought it was the slightly aloof, rather regal austerity they all seemed to bear that gave them away; it took her a little while to realise that an important clue was that no one touched them. And they did not touch you. She thought now that she could still feel the spot where Hibeehea had touched her—so lightly and briefly—with the tips of his pinions, at the end of that first meeting, so long ago. She hadn't thought about it at the time; only that she'd needed to prevent herself from flinching.

Ye-es, she said now, hiccupping through her tears even in her mind-speech. *I—I would be honoured.*

He unfolded his wings with a tiny, curiously silvery noise like the faintest distant sound of ringing bells, and reached his feather-hands toward her, and touched her temples. It was not a quick brush of blessing, this time. He touched her, and left his fingers pressing gently against her skin.

It was like . . . the warmth of summer with the endless skies of a cold winter day; the bursting greens of spring and the rich russet-gold of autumn. It brought her back into *time*, into her body; her feet were on the earth, her hands were tangled in Ebon's mane, and Hibeehea's feather-hands were touching her temples. Some *thing*, some energy, passed between them, real as his hands on her face, something . . . slow, liquid, viscous . . . something tawny or golden, like barley syrup or honey. Without meaning to, she let go of Ebon's mane with one hand and held it out, cupped, as if the syrup-honey were a real liquid being poured. . . . She looked down, and something translucent pale gold was pooling in the palm of her hand. She raised her hand to lick it off . . . and saw a woman standing smiling at her, holding a small ewer whose lip glinted with the amber yellow that also lay in Sylvi's hand.

As Sylvi's tongue touched the little shining puddle, the woman said, "We're not all bad. Don't make that mistake."

Sylvi said wonderingly, "You're a magician." The taste in her mouth was a little like barley syrup, a little like honey . . . but most like something else. Something sublime.

"I am." The woman laughed. Her hair was grey and her hands gnarled, but she laughed like a young woman. "Your amazement is not flattering. Minial is a magician. Ahathin is a magician."

"Yes. I—I sort of keep forgetting. Minial mostly knits. And she talks to you like you're just another person. Ahathin does too. Athathin doesn't—he doesn't act like a magician."

"How should a magician behave? Ahathin is a very good magician."

"Is he? Who are—oh"—because at that moment she realised that some of the dark dappled shadows in the trees behind the woman was a pegasus, coming to join them. He was a dark iron grey—not quite so dark as Ebon's blackness—and as he stepped out of the trees and the sunlight struck him, he briefly glinted silver, and she found herself bemusedly thinking of the Sword: so too did it flash suddenly, as if it were alive, like a pegasus or a human was alive. She looked at him wonderingly. Pegasi were nothing like swords.

I am Redfora, said the woman. *This is Oraan.*

She knew at once and without thinking answered silently, as the woman had spoken: *You're bound.*

We are, said the pegasus.

But—magicians aren't bound.

Occasionally they are. I too am the daughter of a king. And Oraan is the son of another.

But—Sylvi had only just realised they were using mind-speech— *And you can speak to each other!*

Yes.

*Why have I—why don't we know about you? Who is your father? Are you queen after him? I **need** to know about you—Fthoom—Ebon and I—*

But they were gone, and she was standing outside the Caves with Hibeehea's hands on her temples, and she had stopped crying. Hibeehea was looking into her face as she blinked and looked back at him.

He said, *Are you with us again here, little one?*

Redfora and Oraan, she thought. *Yes. A woman gave me—* She looked down; she was still holding her hand out, elbow bent and palm up, but there was nothing in it now. Hibeehea dropped his hands and stepped back.

I am further in your debt, she said, and bowed.

We are more in yours, said Hibeehea. *Who is the woman you saw?*

Do you know a human king's daughter named Redfora, bound to a pegasus named Oraan, son of his king?

There was a pause, and gestures she didn't recognise flickered over both Hibeehea and Lrrianay. If they were human, she thought, they would look at each other. She thought there was a quick burst of silent-speech between them. She couldn't hear any words, but she felt Ebon, as she was still leaning against him, startle.

It was Lrrianay who answered her. *They are a tale out of legend. She was great-granddaughter to Balsin, your first king—so the story goes. She was the eldest child of her father, but while that should have made her queen, her brother said she was not fit, because she had trained as a magician.* Lrrianay paused. *And because she could speak to her pegasus. That is almost as much of the story as there is. No one knows what the people thought, nor what the king thought, nor if the brother was honest—nor why she trained as a magician, for your monarch's family does not take such apprenticeship, I believe.*

The only other part of the story is that the question was never put to trial, because while her father was still king, she—and Oraan—disappeared.

Lrrianay stopped. After a moment Sylvi said, *Disappeared?*

That is all the story says. That, and that either her father or her brother declared that her name should be erased from all records of the realm.

Sylvi found herself wrapped fiercely in a large black wing as Ebon said, *Well, **we** aren't going to disappear.*

Let go, said Sylvi. *I'm going to break feathers just by breathing, you're holding me so tight. Of course we're not going to disappear. And I'm not a magician. I'm not the oldest, either, and Danacor is very honest—and there's Farley and Garren after him too.* She thought of the sharp silver flash as Oraan stepped into the sunlight. *I wonder if anyone asked the Sword what it thought about Redfora?*

I hope they ran away, said Niahi. *I hope they ran away because everyone was being so stupid. I hope they ran away to somewhere really nice.*

So do I, said Hibeehea. *So do I.*

◆　◆　◆

They flew with the rising sun almost at their backs, now, back toward the border with the human land, but they did not hurry, and it took them four more days. Sylvi noticed that on the second day they flew more north than west and toward evening there was a silver dazzle in her eyes as well as the red-gold sun-dazzle.

Dreaming Sea, said Ebon.

But that's—that's a legend, said Sylvi. *Like—Redfora and Oraan.*

I think everybody has a Dreaming Sea, said Ebon. *You may have a different one. This is ours. And it's a legend too. The water's still wet, though.*

Hibeehea stood as if waiting for them as Sylvi's troupe landed, galloped, halted and let her gently down. She wiggled out of her ropes and blanket, looking at him looking at her. She waited till Ebon had been helped out of his harness, so she didn't have to approach Hibeehea alone.

It is at my request we are here, Hibeehea said, and turned, in obvious expectation that they would follow, and led the way through the long grass and the last ragged row of trees. The water whispered against the shingle, and Sylvi stared out across it till the water met the horizon, and imagined the folk standing on the opposite shore somewhere, staring back toward them. Were they human or pegasi or something else? She had been to the rocky seacoast of her own country only rarely, but she remembered the astonishing expanse of water, the sense of standing on the edge of another world, a water world; this was different yet. At home she knew the names of the other ports, the countries on the far side of the ocean; this was a Dreaming Sea. . . .

Watching the silky, late-afternoon-sunlit ripples moving toward them, listening to the tiny gasping noises they made as they broke on the shore, she said, *Our stories about the Dreaming Sea say that if you sail on it, you can sail for ever and ever and will never get out of sight of the shore you set out from, and never catch sight of any other shore. But I don't know where it is. I don't think it can be this one; Viktur mentions it in his journal as something they left behind. And he quotes Balsin saying as a kind of joke that he'd decided to climb the mountains that lead to the wild lands and see what was beyond them because he was afraid Argen would order him to take ship and cross the Dreaming Sea, to be rid of him.* It was the most she'd ever said in Hibeehea's hearing, and she thought, I never heard that the Dreaming Sea makes you brave.

It is called the Dreaming Sea because it is said that if you sleep beside it you will dream true, said Hibeehea.

Eah, said Ebon. *If you're desperate enough, you swim in it first and then lie down on the shore sopping wet, and near enough that the water touches you. Not recommended during the winter. And I'd've thought your dreams would still only be about how uncomfortable you are.*

I wanted you to see it, said Hibeehea, ignoring Ebon, *because whether you have trained as a human magician or not, you are half a shaman with no training whatsoever—that you saw the signing of the treaty in the Caves, and that it was Redfora who brought you back when I called you proves this. Part of our shamanic training involves drinking the water of the Dreaming Sea—and we sleep beside it, but contrary to Ebon's folklore, we choose a comfortable spot. I do not suggest you drink from it, Sylviianel, for the dreams it brings can be very powerful, and you have seen and done enough this three weeks. But I do suggest that you take a little of it away with you. I think the day may come when you have great need of a true dream.*

Hibeehea was wearing another little pouch around his neck on a string, and he dropped his head and rubbed the string over his ears with a foreleg, then knelt by the water. He loosened the mouth of the pouch with his teeth, laid it down, nudged it over with his nose, and a small stoppered bottle rolled out.

After over a fortnight in their country Sylvi was still not accustomed to the way the pegasi did things—the way they had to do things—because their hands had no gripping strength. At the palace the pegasi were rarely seen doing anything but being splendidly elegant—and, she thought now, that was partly because they were rarely seen to *do* anything except stand at the shoulder of their bound human or a little behind the bound pegasus they attended, as Lrrianay's courtiers did. It was some of why they seemed so enigmatic—and some of why the humans seemed so much in command. But she wondered now if some of that tradition came from some human, long ago, perhaps even Balsin himself, wishing to preserve his allies' dignity against human foolishness. It would be easy, in human terms, to think less of a shaman seen kneeling, using his teeth and his nose. . . . She had to stop herself, as she had often had to stop herself these last three weeks, from trying to help, which she knew instinctively would be utterly and grotesquely rude. She had forgotten, that once with Ebon and Hili—but that was because it had been Ebon. To offer aid to a shaman, to the king's shaman . . .

Hibeehea stood up, graceful as ever; she hadn't noticed till now that his long forelock had been twisted back round his ear and plaited into the mane at his poll, and tied there with ribbons. He was standing quite close to her, and she could see that the plait was made up of many tiny plaits; had his son or daughter done it? His—what was the word—*hrmmmhr*? Did shamans wed or have children? Or perhaps an acolyte did such things for a master? She couldn't imagine him doing it himself.

There is still so much I don't know about just ordinary things, she thought. Who plaits you if you're plaited?

The little bottle lay where he had left it. *Take the bottle*, said Hibeehea, *and choose your water.*

Choose your water? Sylvi thought—only to herself, she hoped—what an odd way to put it. But she bent and picked up the bottle (grasping it only with the tips of her fingers as if to minimize the length of her fingers, the strength of her hand), and knew at once what he meant; this was not where she should fill her bottle. She took a hesitant step along the shoreline, away from the rest of the pegasi.

Yes, said Hibeehea. *Go where you are taken. Ebon, you may go with her.* And Hibeehea turned and left them.

It was not so very far after all. They came to a place where the trees grew to the edge of the water and one bent old fellow bowed so low that his leaves trailed across the water.

He looks like a pegasus with a very long mane come to drink, said Sylvi.

Eh? said Ebon. *He probably has a name. You could ask Hibeehea. This is where your water is, is it?* as she knelt and flicked the stopper out of the bottle, wondering how a pegasus would do it, and not wanting to ask. *It's a little like something that happens when you're accepted as an apprentice to a sculptor,* Ebon said. Idly he pawed at the pebbles at the waterline. *The sculptor who has said he'll sponsor you—or she—takes you to one of the big chambers with several other sculptors who've agreed to be part of your choosing. There are a lot of small stones lying around—that have been scattered around. You have to choose one. Which one you choose decides what happens next. There's an old mwhumhum, a, er, scare-story that everyone who is trying to be accepted hears, that if you choose the wrong stone you don't get apprenticed after all, but I've never heard of it happening. What does happen sometimes is that you aren't apprenticed to your sponsor after all.*

Were you?

No. Silence.

What went wrong? she asked bluntly, standing up.

Ebon raised his head, but he looked away from her.

Ebon?

I don't know why I'm telling you this, he said, *except that mostly I tell you everything, and the Dreaming Sea does this kind of thing to you, like makes you tell stuff you weren't planning on telling.* He stopped.

My dad said that about just being here—I mean in your country.

Ebon cocked an ear and moved one foreleg back: thoughtfulness. *Did he? Maybe we can bring him here some day. . . . Maybe, now, they'll let us bring—* He stopped again.

Mum, thought Sylvi. *Not just Dad. Danny. Ahathin. I'd like to bring Ahathin here. Maybe he could figure out what went wrong. Maybe he could bend our magicians' magic so that ... Redfora ... I don't suppose I can ask her to help us.*

Sylvi rubbed his mane, and said, *Tell me.*

Ebon sighed. *There was some question about me being apprenticed at all, because of our binding. The sovereign's family doesn't usually get apprenticeships to shamans or sculptors because we have to spend too much time at your palace. Apprentices to shamans or sculptors may disappear for years while they learn their trade. I'm two years older than you, you know, and Niahi is a half year younger. I never even thought about it, when I was little, as soon as I found out about binding: Niahi was going to be your pegasus, and I was going to be a sculptor. They could find a third cousin who never came to the palace to bind me to. Then I found out I was going to have to be your pegasus after all—but I was still going to be a sculptor!* He gave one of the musical half-humming, half-snorting *huffhuffhuffing* noises that was his out-loud laughter. *I was going to be a sculptor like later on I was going to bring you here for your birthday. It was just going to happen.*

I did one or two things pretty well—that you have to demonstrate to be considered for apprenticeship—unexpectedly well for a king's to-be-bound son. Gedhee agreed to be my sponsor, saying that it still depended on the choosing. If I chose one of his stones, he'd accept me—he has a cousin who's bound to one of your cousins, and she's still a sculptor.

Deerian. I can't remember her pegasus' name.

Fwanfwah. Yes. But Deerian doesn't require her pegasus' presence much. She almost never comes to the palace.

Eah. And I'd be bound to the princess. So there was this question about whether I **could** be apprenticed to a sculptor. I wondered if the story about choosing the wrong stone and not being apprenticed after all was about a bound pegasus, but nobody knew, and Dad told me I'd chosen my path so walk it and shut up. Well, you know what I mean. Then there were almost no sculptors willing to come to my choosing. Gedhee said, Never mind, I'll take you, we'll work it out. What if I choose the wrong stone? I said. Well, you'd better not, Gedhee said.

On the day there were three. . . . Usually there are at least five sculptors, sometimes more. You're allowed to bring one person with you, who, uh, stands for you. Like declaring you're serious—as if there were any possibility you weren't, but you know how rituals are. So there was Dad and me and only three sculptors. Gedhee and Brax. And Shoorininuin. Ebon paused again. Shoor doesn't take apprentices. . . . So there's only three of 'em and one of 'em is Shoorininuin and I . . . it doesn't really work like this with the stones, it's not one stone for one sculptor, or at least I don't think it is—there's magic to it, of course. But I was completely blown by seeing Shoor there and I looked at all the stones, because there were **lots** of them—nobody had told me there were going to be so many that I was going to break either my feet or my knees just trying to walk across them. And I thought, if I pick up the wrong stone it'll be Shoor and he'll say forget it. What was Shoorininuin doing there, for rain and hail's sake?

And I blundered across the floor, stumbling over the wretched stones. I don't feel magic much, but I could feel it that day. Most of it seemed to be saying, No, no, no, not me, mate, don't pick me up. It was like walking into a cloud of ssillwha with all of them buzzing at you, Go away! Go away! And I thought, Oh, great, it's not that I'm going to pick up the wrong stone, it's that the right stone isn't going to let me pick it up. Maybe there **is** no right stone. And then there was one that at least wasn't telling me no, so I staggered over to it and picked it up before it changed its mind.

And then the other two sculptors sighed and Shoorininuin—**Shoor**—said, Well, Ebon, you're mine. I accept you. Welcome.

Ebon fell silent, still looking out over the Dreaming Sea. Sylvi was thinking of Ebon walking into one of the huge chambers of the Caves, he and his father, hundreds—thousands—of pebbles and small stones strewn over the floor—and three sculptors watching. She couldn't imagine Ebon stumbling.

She thought of a conversation they'd had long ago. So that's why they listened when your master spoke up for your idea about sculpting a bit of the palace grounds somewhere in the Caves.

He stirred, bowing his head as if his neck were stiff, rousing his feathers and laying them flat again. Yes. Yes.

I— She stopped, and tried again. I can't even imagine what you're going to do.

He extended one wing, stretching the tiny alula-hand as if he were grasping a brush or a knife and about to start work on a wall standing in front of him. Can't you? I can.

He looked at her at last. Syl . . . what are we?

She could think of nothing to say.

Ebon put his nose in her hair and tugged gently. Life is funny, isn't it?

I'm—sorry, said Sylvi helplessly.

Sorry? said Ebon. Oh, don't be so—human.

Well, I **am** human. I—this is probably human too—I wish I'd met him. Shoorininuin.

You did, said Ebon. The sculptor who spoke to you. That was Shoor. He wanted to meet you.

Sylvi caught her breath. She had envied Ebon his certainty, his focus on becoming a sculptor, while she muddled along being her father's fourth child, having projects assigned to her, village witchcraft, bridge-building, because she had no ideas of her own. She was still muddling, she felt; it was nothing she had done, nothing she had chosen, that had enabled her to talk to Ebon, and hear him when he spoke to her. She had not chosen to hear Niahi the other night; she had not chosen to walk eight hundred years back in time to watch the signing of the treaty that allied her people to the pegasi. It was perhaps not surprising that Ebon's master had wished to speak to her; she was what she was, however helpless she felt within that which had chosen her. *We are all bound by what fate chooses for us,* the sculptor had said. But he had also said, *I am proud of him. I am proud of you too.*

There was another little pause. *We'd better go back,* Ebon said finally, *before someone comes after us 'cause they think we've decided to try and swim across the Sea. We could start our own country there, where pegasi and humans just **talk** to each other.*

How big is your Sea, do you know? said Sylvi, grateful for a change of subject. *Has anyone ever crossed it?*

If they have, they haven't told us about it, said Ebon. *The legend is that it's another world wide. That if you managed to cross it, you'd be somewhere else than this world. That the only way from our world to get to the far shore of the Sea is to cross the Sea—and you can't do that either. Although there's another legend that says the Caves extend under the Sea and come out on the other side. And that you could walk it—if you lived long enough.* He paused. *There's another legend still that says that before your King Thingummy showed up with his troops—*

Balsin.

And started killing taralians, our King Fralialal was thinking of taking who remained of us and trying to cross the Sea—underneath, by the Caves.

CHAPTER 16

On her last night there was another enormous feast, in the same meadow as the feast held for her father, near the border between Rhiandomeer and Balsinland. She stood on the edge of that meadow as the pegasi set up the tables, chewing on a stem of llyri grass, naming the wildflowers to herself, because she knew them now; knew the names of the birds she could hear singing in the trees—recognised the fornol moving not quite silently through the undergrowth. The llyri grass was sweet and succulent, the first shoots of the new season, but she doubted it would give her wings.

This time the tall chair was for her. When the pegasi brought it out from the shelter, rocking on its poles, she said, *But that's my father's chair.* For a wild moment she thought, Perhaps he's come back for the last night, and felt a rush of emotion so confused it made her dizzy. Those first nights in the pegasus country seemed a century ago; she was almost used—almost—to being a queer upright wingless biped—with hands—among the graceful pegasi. She stood quietly, watching the pegasi setting the chair down and releasing it from its transport poles. Two of them carried it, but another four released the cords and slid the poles free. Aloud she repeated, "That's my father's chair."

"Tonight it's for you," said Hibeehea.

Sylvi turned toward him; she had not heard him approach. *You speak human as well as a human. Why—why—*

Why don't I? said Hibeehea. *Why don't I come to your country and become a translator and make everything right between your people and mine? Because I feel ill and faint in your country, so ill and so faint that I can no longer speak your language, and after a day or two I cannot understand it either. This is true of all our shamans—the healers may remain a little longer than the rest of us—Hissiope is unusual in that he can bear up to a fortnight at the palace, but, he says, he pays for this strength by being less strong at home. It seems to us that this is true generally: the stronger our magic here, the weaker we are as soon as we cross the human border. . . . The last time I came to the palace I could barely fly home again; we had to keep stopping for me to rest.*

Then it is true, Sylvi said. *It is not just a way of—of speaking. It's like—it's like flying or not flying—having wings or not having wings. Our magic and yours is—somehow—antipathetic.*

The traditional pegasi nod of agreement was a quick shaking of the head, more like the human gesture of no. Hibeehea first gave a quick pegasi shake and then a slower, human nod. *Yes. It is—to us—as clear as—as clear as wings or no wings. Your magic is, perhaps, more like rock, while ours is more like water. And your magicians are very strong. We . . . we seep.* Hibeehea smiled, but Sylvi, who had been immersed in pegasi for the last three weeks, could see the strain in him.

A few of us shamans go with Lrrianay when there is some important occasion upon us; I was there for his binding to your father, and for your father's marriage to your mother, and for Danacor's name-day, his binding to Thowara and his acceptance as heir. There is always at least one healer present at the palace, but that may be all. We do not stay long, and we do not—talk.

You've never—

Admitted it? There is little to admit, in the palace of the human king. I am considered slightly mad for having pursued the learning of your language as diligently as I have done when there is no use for it. In every generation of shamans since the signing of the treaty there are a few who learn to speak aloud as you speak; I found I had a talent for it, and so I went on with it—on and on— hoping that I would find at last some border to cross, some gate to pass through, that, once I had done so, I would have your language as I have my own. This has not happened. I come often to your country—

Sylvi involuntarily shook her head, in human negation and disbelief. *Oh,* she said, *srrrwa, fwif, forgive me, it is only that I have never seen you and I—I have thought I am—am aware of the pegasi who visit us.*

You offer no discourtesy, Hibeehea replied. *Another of my talents is that of being overlooked when I choose.*

With great self-restraint Sylvi managed not to shake her head again, but a faint smile briefly appeared on Hibeehea's face, and faded at once. *I often travel alone,* he continued, *and I rarely remain at the palace—and I will myself to be disregarded. Mostly I wander through your towns and your countryside, listening to humans talk. It is easier for me outside the Wall.*

There are fewer magicians outside the Wall, said Sylvi. *The guilds' offices are by the southeast gate; the Hall of Magicians is at the centre of the palace.*

Yes, said Hibeehea.

The Hall of Magicians is at the *very* centre of the palace, Sylvi thought slowly, and ordinary humans aren't allowed in it unless there's some great ritual thing going on.

Every shaman as a part of training and acceptance must go once to your palace, Hibeehea continued. *We are still hoping that one day there will be a shaman who can speak to you in your own country.*

Then . . . that is why humans don't come here. It's the other way around too, somehow. To herself again she thought, *I wonder if any magician has ever tried to cross the border? If they are rock while the shamans are water . . . I guess they cannot.*

We believe so. It is nothing there is any record of. It is certainly why I was extremely reluctant to agree to your visit. For both your sake and ours. We did not know if you as king's daughter might bring some unknown, protective human magic with you that would disrupt ours; and we were—I was—very afraid of having to send you home early, weak and ill and confused, and the reaction such an outcome would provoke among your people. I am not unaware of the difficulty your father had in persuading his council and his senate to permit you to go.

Boldly Sylvi said, *Then why did you agree?*

He didn't answer for a moment, and she was afraid he would not— and that she had gone too far. He said, *I drank water from the Dreaming Sea, and Redfora told me to let you come.*

She could not meet his eyes. The pegasi had brought the long table out and fitted the three sections together and set the tall chair at its head. By the time Sylvi had thought of something more to say to Hibeehea, when she turned back to him, he had gone.

At the banquet she found that she stood and wandered, the way the pegasi did. It had been like this at the first banquet, but then it had seemed odd, slightly embarrassing—perhaps slightly rude, as if, as a human, she was behaving inappropriately. This second time it merely was the thing to do: Why would anyone want to sit down for an entire banquet? She wished she could introduce wandering to her father's state dinners. . . . At first she thought she was avoiding sitting down because she did not want to sit in her father's chair; or perhaps that she did not want to be marked out among the pegasi any more than she inevitably was. But she realised she was standing and wandering because she wanted to—because she was more comfortable that way. And her banquet dress, far less crushed by its three weeks rolled up in the bottom of a pannier than she had expected—perhaps some fragment of pegasus fabric magic had worked its way into her clothing bag—made a nice swishing noise as she walked. She remembered that, three weeks ago, the swish and swirl had given her courage.

The pegasi, represented by Feeaha and Driibaa, had given her a siraga, embroidered with ribbons and feathers and small sparkly stones, and specially cut to lie smoothly over human shoulders.

She also realised with an odd little twinge that her strong human hands were useful for a wandering banquet: she could easily carry with her what she was eating or drinking, which the pegasi could not. She had been to many court gatherings where all the humans had goblets or bowls or plates in their hands, and she had thought nothing of it; she thought of it now.

And there were no speeches. Ebon had taught her to say "it's wonderful," *ifffawafi*, which was another kind of all-purpose pegasus thank you, when more formal, precise gradations of thanks were not necessary. *The idea is that you're both what's wonderful, that it's wonderful because it's something between the two of you. We don't throw it all on the other person the way you humans do.*

Sylvi laughed. *But if you give me a really nice present, it's you, it's not me. I'm just standing there with—with an armful of flowers or a necklace or something, saying thank you.*

Ebon said, *Don't be daft. Don't you think what you've done with my present—with coming here—is at least as important as my having brought you—so that it* **could** *happen? With a lot of help from Dad. Our dads.*

315

Sylvi said, *Hibeehea said that Redfora told him to let me come.*

Ebon looked at her. *Did she really?* There was a long pause. *Did she really. I wish we knew what had happened to them. . . .*

Yes, she said. *So do I.* They looked at each other, and both knew what they were thinking: Fthoom would not have discovered any story about Redfora and Oraan.

So Sylvi wound and spiralled her upright, two-legged way among the pegasi, saying *ifffawafi.* They said *ifffawafi* back to her, but some of them smiled, and she knew that she was saying it too much; but she couldn't help herself.

You don't have to wear it out, said Ebon.

But it's been wonderful, she said. Scary, she thought. Scary and wonderful. *It's been . . . I don't know what it's been. It's only been eighteen days since my father left. Twenty since we left the palace. It feels like years.* She added recklessly, *I feel ten years older—twenty.*

Well, stop it, said Ebon. *I don't, and I don't want you older than me.* He thought about it. *Maybe five years.* He rested his nose on her shoulder in a gesture that had become habitual in the last eighteen days. She remembered again with astonishment that she was not supposed to touch any pegasus; she had just had her arm around the queen before Ebon reclaimed her. *But it was my idea before the grown-ups stole it and made a big grown-up thing about it. I'm so glad you came. Glad— hiyahaimhia—glad isn't really good enough. I'm "hiyahaimhia, hya hyama," I'm glad you came. That you saw the Caves.*

Me too, said Sylvi, and raised her hand to put it against his cheek. *Me too. I don't care about the grown-ups.*

She was crying again when she had to say good-bye to everyone but the pegasi who would be carrying her back to the human world. She cried over Niahi, she cried over Aliaalia, she cried over Feeaha and Driibaa—she even cried over Hibeehea. Hibeehea's nose was showing one or two wrinkles as he said, *You're bound to us now, child. You're bound to the pegasi, not just to Ebon. You have changed the world, you know, little human child. And you'll be back, if you're crying for the Caves too.*

He sounded so like his shaman self—*You have changed the world, little human child*—that she stopped crying. But he was still smiling, so she said tentatively, *Well, I'm mostly crying for—for the pegasi. For all my— friends.*

Ah, then that is easy, he said. *For we will come to visit you—yes, I too. I wish to discover how much of the world you have changed. I wish to discover if perhaps . . . Child, listen to me a moment,* and he had stopped smiling. *Lrrianay may say something like this too, but he is king, and bound to your father, and he sees these things from closer in—almost like a human sometimes.* He looked almost grim, she thought, low-headed, his feet braced. *We will come to visit your palace now not only for the sake of the Alliance, but because of you. Because you were here, and because you spoke to us. This is a great thing—but it is also a greatly dangerous thing. It is possible that to have sent you home early, weak and confused, would have been more welcome than what has happened. If I may give you my advice, king's daughter, the advice of an old pegasus shaman, you will tell no one but your father the entire truth about your experience here. And,* and he moved his head till his eyes were looking directly and levelly into hers, *you may find you cannot tell even him everything.*

Eighteen days and twenty years ago she would have turned away hastily, or covered a spurt of anger with court politeness. But it was not eighteen days and twenty years ago, and she said, *Yes. I have already taken your advice.*

You are a wise child, he said, and to her astonishment he unfurled his wings and swept them forward, and his feather-hands reached out toward her, and the tiny feathery pegasus fingers pressed for a long slow moment against her temples. *Good-bye,* said Redfora's voice.

The flight back was unremarkable if—Sylvi thought—you could ever describe flying as unremarkable. There were clouds on the distant horizon but where she flew with the pegasi the sky was blue and bright and the wind was blowing over the mountains toward the palace strongly enough that occasional gusts threw the pegasi's manes and tails forward, and bounced her in her drai. A month ago she might have felt alarmed; she did not now. Wisps of cloud streamed past like the tails of invisible pegasi—she had a brief daydream of catching one in her hand as it flicked by and a long shining hair remaining in her hand. She stretched her arm out. Niahi had given her a bracelet she had plaited of hairs from her mane, and Ebon's, Lrrianay's and Aliaalia's, and several of the others'. *There are even three of Hibeehea's!* she said. *I told him what I was doing and asked if I could have one of his! I was very brave! And then he gave me* **three!** Niahi had finished the weaving round Sylvi's wrist, Sylvi watching, fascinated, at the little alula-hands working so quickly she could not follow what the tiny down-covered fingers did. *Your wrists are perfect,* Niahi said. *We make them for ears and ankles and necks. But I've decided human wrists are the best.*

Sylvi knew that the feather-fingers lay invisibly against the wing when not in use, pointing forward from the inflexible wrist, like a cap folded down over the leading edge of the primaries, or as if the wing itself were a cape the hand might hold open. But she had never had a chance to stare at a pair of pegasus hands—and Niahi's were creamy pale, unlike Ebon's shadowy darkness—working as close to her as her own wrist. The little hands were astonishingly quick and deft. *I am not surprised pegasus weaving and embroidery are better than anything we can do,* she said as Niahi finished, with a soft feathery pat to Sylvi's hand. *Your fingers are so clever.*

Niahi stretched out both hands and spread the fingers. Even like this her hands were barely as large as Sylvi's small human palms; Niahi's fingers were less than half the length and width of Sylvi's, the palm was a dot, and the littlest finger was barely there at all. She had five fingers on each hand—four and a thumb—which seemed to be the most common; Ebon, Lrrianay, Hibeehea and Aliaalia all had ten fingers, although Feeaha and Oyry had only eight, and Hissiope twelve.

Your hands are so beautiful, said Niahi, and stroked Sylvi's with both of hers. *It is not just that they are big and strong; they are—the way they fit together—the proportions are perfect. Ours are so little the joints make them knobbly, and the last joint doesn't have room to bend very much. And yours are not all covered in hair or feathers, so you can admire them properly, the long finger bones and the fan of bones across the backs of your hands, the long arc of the web between the thumb and first finger, and the littler webbing between the other fingers. And you have wrists that turn and turn—turn in all directions.*

Sylvi said, embarrassed, *I don't think we admire our hands much.*

You should, said Niahi. *If I were a sculptor, I'd want to sculpt human hands. Maybe Ebon will. The—yelloni—what do you say, when it's around your wrist? Bracelet—will last a long time if you don't cut it off. Oh—I should have asked—I'm sorry!—you may not want to wear it forever. Here, I can—* and she began to tease some of the hair-ends free.

Sylvi snatched her hand away from the little hands, noticing as she did so that there was no strength of resistance from Niahi: it was like drawing her hand through ribbons. *I will wear it till it falls off,* she said. Niahi gave a little *hrooo* of audible laughter. *That will be a long time!*

The flight went on and on as Sylvi thought about seeing her family again—and yet it seemed longer still when she thought of saying good-bye to the pegasi—when she thought of how far away they already were, and how much farther still she was going. *For we will come to visit you,* she heard, over and over again, in her memory. She also heard Redfora's voice saying good-bye. She had barely met Redfora, she could not possibly miss her—no, but she missed asking her all the questions she would like to ask another human who spoke to pegasi. She already missed Niahi. She missed her lightness, her laughter, the silent melody of her voice. . . . The pegasi's silent voices were as individual as their faces, as noisy human voices. How both simple and cumbersome it would be to talk always with her mouth again; how familiar and crude. How easy and familiar it would be to be a human among other humans again; how awkward and ungainly. . . . She wasn't sure if it was the wind tearing water from her eyes. . . . And soon she would be saying good-bye to *all* the pegasi.

Even Ebon. Their fathers had demanded this as a condition to letting her visit go ahead, that both their peoples should see that their loyalties were to their own first. *It's not for the pegasi, though,* she'd said sadly. *I know. It's for us humans.*

There was a long pause and then Ebon had said, *Yes. But it won't be long. I'll be back almost as soon as it takes you to have one of your **baths**.*

But that's not right either. I should visit you as often as you visit me! Oftener! You're apprenticed to a sculptor! I'm just the king's surplus daughter!

You're not surplus to us, said Ebon. *And—dearheart—you're forgetting. The Alliance says we visit you.*

There was another long pause, and then she said—sadly, drearily— *And I can't fly. You have to fetch me.*

There was the Wall.

And there was the palace.

Home.

They circled once over Banesorrow Lake before they came down. They were returning when they had said they would return, so they were expected; but her father wouldn't be waiting for her, he'd be working, and she could imagine—she hoped she could imagine—the messenger bursting into his office and saying, "The pegasi! They're here!" or perhaps "The princess! She's back!" The queen, she thought, would be pacing up and down along the outer wall of the Great Court, dictating to a secretary trotting beside her and watching the sky—she'd be the one who sent the messenger.

Sylvi thought, And she'd see twelve pegasi, with their shining coats and great beating wings . . . and a hammock.

There was a stream—no, a river—of people pouring out of the Great Court gates and into the parkland where the pegasi would land. She could hear some conversation among the pegasi, although—as if it were the wind in her ears that was preventing her—she couldn't hear what they were saying. But she saw the pause in the human river, and then the bright red-and-gold of the footmen's formal livery, two pairs of them pacing slowly, and then half a dozen senators in their court dress—she thought she saw Orflung's broad bright orange sash—oh, *dear*. Had her father told her her return was to be a state occasion? He must have done, and she had forgotten. But she should have known. She should have known it would be. . . .

There was her father, wearing one of the long sparkly king robes— and even the Sword at his side!—hand in hand with her mother, who was wearing a sparkly queen robe; a step behind the queen was Hirishy. Two of her brothers were there, wearing gold chains round their necks and dress swords at their sides. Danacor was missing. She felt a brief flicker of fear—don't be silly, she thought, he's often gone—and then the pegasi were gliding down the last little way—they were cantering with barely a jolt to their passenger—trotting—walking. She pulled her laces free, ready to stand up as gracefully as she could.

One of the footmen had come quickly forward, and he was beside her almost as soon as the drai had fallen to the ground. It was Glarfin, and he was smiling and trying not to smile, because smiling wasn't grand enough. When he caught her eye, however, the smile broke out anyway, and he mouthed "Welcome home, lady" at her. She grinned and murmured, "Thank you, lieutenant." He had a robe over his arm and he unfolded it gravely, and then flung it round her shoulders in a highly practised court attendant's gesture. Court robes tended to have monumental armholes, so she managed to slip her arms through them without finding herself trying to make her elbow touch her ear, or scrabbling at it like a cat clawing curtains. Glarfin, pretending to do nothing, delicately held the collar till Sylvi had it settled across her shoulders.

The robe, she saw, was one of her mother's—the one that was Sylvi's favourite, stitched all over with golden topazes. It had been her mother's mother's, and her mother's mother's aunt's, and the aunt's mother's, who had also been married to the king. It'll be too long, she thought anxiously, but it wasn't; it had been taken up for her. Surreptitiously she wiggled her fingers; the sleeves had been shortened as well. She put her foot out and the hem poured topazes over it; she crossed her arms with a flourish, watching the topazes sparkle and then threw her arms wide again as her mother put her arms around her and whispered, "Welcome *home*, and happy birthday, darling." Then her father hugged her too, and for a moment she forgot about both topazes and pegasi, as she felt her parents' arms around her for the first time in three weeks. Her brothers saluted her formally, Oyry and Poih at their shoulders, but Garren caught her eye long enough to give a quick flick and twist with his left hand, which had meant "let's run away" to generations of royal children: it was a slight revision of the formal sign of hospitality made to pegasi attending any official gathering.

She saw that Lrrianay, who had flown back to the palace with her drai-bearers, was standing just behind her father's shoulder, and she was suddenly angry that Lrrianay should always stand behind her father. They were bondmates, and Lrrianay was also king of his people, and no subject to anyone. She swept into exactly the same bow to Lrrianay that she would give to her father, the bow of a princess to a king. Lrrianay gravely returned her bow, and the flowers (somewhat wind-blown) that Niahi had plaited into his mane that morning twinkled at her.

Next the senators wished to be presented to her. She was surrounded by *humans*—swaying on their queer feet as they walked, their extraordinary quantities of clothing flapping and fluttering both with and counter to their bizarre motion. There were no brown-and-grey-and-gold-and-white horizontal backs to look over, no silky banners of mane and tail for the sun to shine through. And humans were all so *tall*. Involuntarily she took another step backward—and bumped into Glarfin.

He moved out of her way so quickly no one but the two of them knew it had happened. "My lady?" he said, very quietly.

"*Senators*," she hissed. "And everyone is so *tall*." The senators were forming a queue; the first would be bowing to her in only a moment.

"I am standing behind you," said Glarfin. "And I am taller than any of them."

She suppressed a little hiccup of laughter, but it meant that she was smiling when the first senator was presented. Last of all was Senator

Orflung—wearing an orange sash. To him she dared say, "Thank you for asking me if I wanted to go."

"It was a—valuable experience, think you?" he replied.

"Yes, my sir, I believe it was valuable."

She had guessed she would be expected to make a few sentences' worth of speech, and so had spent some of the morning's flight slowly putting words together while the wind hummed in her ears and the landscape flashed away beneath her—but she was only thinking of having to do it, of being prepared. Yet she hadn't been prepared: she hadn't expected footmen and a topaz-sewn robe—and the senators. She hadn't expected so many swaying, flapping, confusing, chattering humans to greet her return. She hadn't expected to find humanity so confusing.

Nor had she thought of how strange it would be to be back at the palace again. Most years she visited one or another set of her cousins for several weeks—but then her aunts' and her uncles' families were human—like her. Now it was very strange, standing on the Great Court dais to say her few little words, looking out at all the human faces, hearing the human sounds (she had forgotten how noisy humans are; she had forgotten how much noise always speaking out loud makes) and smelling the human smells. She had to concentrate on the words she was saying. ("It was a clear blue day when I left three weeks ago and it is another clear blue day for me to come home on: give me leave, please, to see this as a reflection of everything that has happened. . . . The pegasus country is beautiful and the pegasi have been nothing but kind and generous to me.") She had to wrench her mind away from how odd this business of saying a few almost meaningless words to a crowd was—and how she hadn't done it the night before, her last night in Rhiandomeer. And she had to stop herself, as soon as she had finished speaking ("Thank you all for your welcome; I have missed you all very much"), from looking round for a group of pegasi she could, with Ebon, go and stand with.

Except they were in her father's palace, and here the pegasi rarely stood in a group; they stood individually, each with the human to whom they were bound. The other five of the six pegasi who had carried her drai, she eventually realised, had not come into the Great Court with her, but had gone at once to the wing of the palace that was the pegasi's own. The only pegasi here now were bound: Lrrianay, Hirishy, Ebon, Poih, Oyry; four of the senators had pegasi; several of the blood courtiers present did also.

And all these pegasi had stayed well back as the humans greeted the returning human princess; they had, when necessary, bowed, letting their long forelocks sweep forward and not meeting her eyes. She did not try to speak to any of them—she did not think about choosing not to try to speak to them. . . .

She did not dare reach out to Ebon, standing almost beside her, only a little behind her, which is what she wanted to do. But when her father came up to stand beside her again, she reached out for his hand and squeezed it almost desperately. The clouds she had seen in the distance during the flight home seemed to be racing toward her, grey and cold.

When Ebon left the next morning she could hardly bear it.

She knew it was coming; they had said their real good-byes the night before, but she and her father and a few of the courtiers went out in the cool wet dawn to watch the pegasi spread their wings and leap into the air. Usually there was no formal leave-taking, but this time, her father said, was special, and so the humans would see the pegasi off; but he looked at his daughter with worry in his eyes.

It's only a week, said Ebon. *I'll be back.* He sounded subdued, not at all like his usual self.

I know, she said. *It's only a week.*

He said, *At least you get to sleep in one of your great human **beds** again.*

She'd missed being outdoors under the sky the night before. Her bedroom had felt small and cramped, although the ceiling was better than twice her height above her. She'd leaned on the balustrade that had in a way started it all, the balustrade Ebon had flown in over and landed, skittering, on her bedroom floor, the night of her twelfth birthday, four years and several centuries ago.

She had leaned out as far as she could over it, till the rain ran down her face and made her sneeze, trying to breathe air that wasn't in a room, thinking that the palace was so huge that even the air around it felt like house air, wondering if she could take a blanket out and sleep in one of the pavilions, knowing that she couldn't, for the same reasons that Ebon was going home tomorrow. She had to appear completely normal, completely untouched by the last three weeks, completely as she had been when the king had allowed her to leave her human home and visit her bondmate at his home in the pegasi lands. Bondmate, she'd thought. Bondmate or bondfriend—that's what the pegasi always call it. It's much better than the silly formal human Excellent Friend.

The Caves had never felt as stifling as the palace did now.

She wondered where Ebon was, if he was asleep. She knew that despite the openness of their annex the pegasi often wandered out into the parkland and on rainy nights might sleep in one of the pavilions. Which was why she could not. It would not matter if she chose an empty pavilion; the humans who had not liked her journey would not like her sleeping as the pegasi slept after she returned. I would not be sleeping as the pegasi sleep, she thought. I don't have wings to keep me warm; and my neck is too short to let my head be comfortable without a pillow.

She'd grow used to sleeping in a bedroom again—she thought, as the rain ran down her neck and wetted her nightgown—but some of the change in her was permanent, even if she did not know herself which part of it that was. Would she still be able to talk to other pegasi? Could she risk trying? What if what made the pegasus shamans ill now made her ill? Was there the tiniest, most minuscule, invisible *reason* for Fthoom's aversion to any closeness between human and pegasus? She remembered Dorogin's eyes. . . .

She did not want to remember Dorogin's eyes.

She thought of Redfora, and Oraan. For a moment she could taste Redfora's honey-syrup on her tongue. She had gone back to bed and curled round that taste, that memory, and fell asleep, her wet hair soaking into the pillow.

Now she wanted to ask Ebon which pavilion they'd slept in, the night before, but she didn't ask. She told herself, if I knew, I would go visit it, and he would not be there.

Yes, she said. *With lots of pillows.*

And hot water for all those baths, said Ebon. *You wouldn't like bathing in our ponds in winter.*

Her father came up beside her and put an arm around her. She touched Ebon's nose, briefly, barely long enough for her fingertips to register the velvet of it, and one of his feather-hands reached forward and swept over her cheek. Then she stepped back, closer into the circle of her father's arm, and Ebon turned away and joined the other pegasi—all but Lrrianay, who stood at Corone's shoulder, for he was staying at the palace. Only Guaffa was carrying anything; she recognised her drai, rolled up and lashed round his neck. The eleven pegasi who were leaving trotted, cantered . . . and flew. She knew it was only her eyes that made Ebon's leap into the air the most beautiful. The backdraught of their wings brought the scent of their land to her: she had not realised there was a characteristic smell—a grassy, flowery, earthy smell—she didn't remember noticing it on her arrival there. Perhaps that's the smell of spring, she thought. What does summer smell like, autumn, winter? I would rather know than have hot water for baths.

Sylvi found that her legs were shaking, and she put her own arm around her father's waist, to hold herself upright. They remained standing like that for a long minute, Lrrianay standing motionless behind them, till the pegasi had disappeared into the dawn twilight. Until Sylvi was sure her legs would hold her and she could let go, and speak lightly and aimlessly to the courtiers who gathered round the two of them; and she still kept one hand on the back of one her father's tall hounds, for balance, for the small consolation of warm fur.

She exchanged a look with Lrrianay, but neither of them spoke.

That night again she leaned on the railing of the window Ebon had flown through on the night of her twelfth birthday, leaned out till the air against her face felt cool and smelled of plants, not of wood smoke and laundry soap and furniture wax and potpourri. After a minute or two she sighed, went and fetched a chair, and sat on the railing with her feet on the chair. She was uncomfortably aware of her own body: the way it balanced upright and folded in the middle: the curious position it took to sit on a railing with its feet on a chair. And the usefulness of the strong hands and long bony fingers to clasp the railing. . . . I'm *back*, she thought. I'm *home*. They're *all* like me here. She let go with one hand and examined it, spreading the fingers, rotating the wrist to inspect both the palm and the back.

He'll be here again in seven days, she said to herself. Six and a half. And I'm human, and we're built like this. We can't help it.

There was a soft knock on the door. Sylvi dropped her hand hastily, as if she were doing something forbidden; but she seemed to have mislaid the power of human speech. She opened her mouth and no words came. She had spent all day talking and talking and talking. . . . The door opened gently, and her mother put her head through. "May I come in?"

"Of course," Sylvi said, surprised into remembering. She slid down off the railing as her mother closed the door behind her and looked thoughtfully at her daughter.

"Not 'of course,'" said the queen. "Not any more. Although I'm not sure when the change happened. Maybe only in the last three weeks."

Sylvi's eyes, to her horror, filled with tears. She stiffened against them, and blinked till her eyes burned. Her mother said nothing; she had made a gesture toward her daughter, but drew back again at the expression on Sylvi's face. At last Sylvi said, "How can everything change in three weeks? Three little weeks."

Her mother smiled. "Sometimes they change in a moment."

Sylvi thought of hearing Ebon's voice in her head for the first time: *I **know** that*, he had said. *Aren't you **excited**, or are you just a dull stupid human?* "Yes. Sometimes they do."

Her mother drifted across the room and sat on the foot of Sylvi's bed. "Can I do anything for you? Anything to—to help you come home again."

"Oh," said Sylvi. "Is it that obvious?"

"That you're wandering around like a lost soul?" said her mother. "Possibly only to your father and me. And maybe Ahathin; it's hard to guess what he knows. And Glarfin. He knows everything."

Ahathin is a magician, Sylvi thought. We are not all bad, Redfora had said: Don't make that mistake. I wonder, Sylvi thought, what would happen if Ahathin tried to cross the border into Rhiandomeer?

Real life began again tomorrow: real life, including lessons and projects. She wondered what sort of a report she would be expected to provide out of her trip to Rhiandomeer—she'd welcome a plain return to her work on dams and bridges, but she knew she wouldn't be let off so easily. Danacor would be home tomorrow; he'd been held up in Darkford by a report of ladons. She would be glad to see him; she loved all her brothers, but he was the most . . . she couldn't think of the word. He had that quality that their father did, that if he was present, then anything that needed to be fixed would be fixed.

Neither he nor her father could fix her—but how would she wish to be fixed? Not even a magician can turn you into a pegasus, so you can sleep in a pavilion and visit the Linwhialinwhia Caves for your feast days, discover if you have a gift for weaving, or sculpting, or paper-making, or story-telling . . . so you can *fly*. Not even a magician can give you wings. There were several little sky holds on shelves and tables in her bedroom; she kept picking them up and putting them down as if they were an answer to a question, but the wrong answer.

She had spoken only briefly to Ahathin: he had come up to her yesterday evening at the reception before the court dinner, made his magician's salutation and said, "Welcome home, princess."

"I am made glad by your greeting," she said formally, very conscious of Ebon at her shoulder—suddenly made conscious again of the fact that Ahathin almost never wore his Speaker sticks; he was not wearing them this evening.

"That is a very fine robe," he said. "The topazes are like tiny suns."

She could feel her heart lift and her face smile as she said, "It is very fine, isn't it?" But she looked at him as she said it, and even though he was smiling at her she thought, How did he know that was the perfect thing to say? Is it just what anyone would say? Or is it that he's a magician?

"It hasn't mattered, this first day or two," her mother continued. "You're allowed to be tired. Even your father—even Danny—comes home from a long journey tired. And you've done very well—that little speech when you arrived was just right—"

"The robe helped," said Sylvi hastily, feeling selfish and ungrateful. "It's the most gorgeous thing—and you know it's always been my favourite—"

"Yes, I know," said her mother. "And it's not worth losing Ebon even for a week, is it?"

Sylvi stared at her mother. "I—oh—well, maybe for a week," she said, trying to make a joke.

Her mother smiled, but it was an unhappy smile. "I hope we've done what's best," she said, "your father and I, about you and Ebon."

Sylvi said as calmly as she could, although her heart was beating frantically, "There's never been anything to do about Ebon and me, from the day of the binding."

"Yes," said her mother. "That's what we've always believed—your father in particular, because of his relationship with Lrrianay. You know I can't talk to Hirishy beyond 'I think the day will stay fair' and 'the flowers in your mane are very pretty,' although Minial learnt a pattern she uses for her knitting by asking Hirishy about plaiting ribbons into manes and tails. You can show things sometimes when you can't say them. But talking to a pegasus has always seemed to me a bit like talking to a tree or the palace—it's not surprising that we can't. Their minds and ours work so differently—of course we need Speakers. The surprise is the Alliance.

"But Cory feels passionately that there is something wrong about the fact that we cannot speak clearly to each other—and he believes Lrrianay feels the same. And that they both feel that the future of both our peoples may depend on our being able to talk to each other. . . ."

Sylvi held her breath, but her mother asked no leading questions. There was a fraught silence; the queen stared at her lap, and as the silence went on Sylvi could see her changing her mind about what she was going to say. You weren't made the youngest life colonel of the Lightbearers without knowing how to deal with awkward situations, even when they were caused by your daughter.

The queen found what she was looking for and smiled reminiscently. "You know the story about Lrrianay being Witness at our wedding?"

Sylvi did. The pegasi of a human couple to be married attend the wedding although they take no active part. Ordinarily the heir would have his sovereign as Witness, but, Corone had said, his mother blesses them twice, she doesn't have to be Witness too. Corone wanted to make Lrrianay his Witness; the Witness doesn't have to talk, the presence at the man or the woman's side *is* the witnessing. There was a spectacular uproar. The senators all said that it wasn't that the Witness *didn't* talk but that he *could* if the man's (or the woman's) honour was questioned. Corone said that if they were willing to accept an heir so shaky that his honour could be questioned successfully at his own wedding with his mother the queen looking on, they deserved what they got, but if they could find an instance anywhere of the future sovereign's right to marry and have children being disputed since his family took the crown over two hundred years ago, he would have the first senator as Witness.

Of course they couldn't find an example—he'd have checked first. The senators turned to the queen, who said that she thought he had a point, that Lrrianay would be an ornament to the proceedings and she wasn't going to interfere. That didn't end the matter, but Corone was young and fierce in those days, and Lrrianay was his Witness.

"The entire wedding felt like a battlefield—so I was perfectly at ease, of course," said the queen, "although I felt a little embarrassed that my Witness was the completely uncontroversial choice of my elder sister. But I'd rather dreaded the enormity of the heir's wedding. I told Cory I suspected him of inventing a skirmish to make his military bride comfortable, and he said it had been a consideration." The queen's smile grew, till Sylvi couldn't resist smiling back. "What is not generally known, I believe, is that your father and I were awake till dawn on our wedding night . . . discussing the pegasi. Discussing the pegasi isn't *all* we did, mind you, but we might have had some sleep if the pegasi and the Alliance hadn't come into it.

"Fifteen years—and three sons who can't talk to their pegasi—after we were married, you were born. And now here you are. You can talk to Ebon as easily as you can talk to me."

"Danacor can talk—has some sense of Thowara," said Sylvi. "Like Dad. Danny says it's like a thief breaks into his mind at night when he's asleep and steals the pegasus words he learnt that day, so when he goes to look for them, the next time he's with Thowara, knowing they should be there, they're gone."

The queen took a moment to answer. "I don't think Danny's connection with Thowara is as strong as your father's with Lrrianay, but that may only be they have not been together for as long. But Cory's link with Lrrianay is still nothing like yours with Ebon—your binding was like the opening of some great riverwork, and the water poured into the new channel. . . . And the only disadvantage is that you can't do without him."

Sylvi didn't try to deny it. "And that"—she didn't want to say one particular name aloud—"some people don't like it."

"All those people who tried to stop you going, yes," said her mother. "But you are thinking about Fthoom, aren't you? He is not the only one. But he is the worst. If we hadn't had Fthoom's creatures whispering in ears, I don't think the senate would have caused so much trouble." She hesitated. "I think you had better know: there is a petition collecting signatures in the senate and among the blood asking for Fthoom to be reinstated."

She had forgotten. Lucretia had told her this long ago, in her previous life, the life before she had been to Rhiandomeer. There were enough people who wanted Fthoom back—Fthoom, who was the most powerful magician of his generation—that there were signatures on a petition to try and force the king's hand. She wondered if anyone who signed the petition had been to a fête where she had gone with Ebon; if any of those signatures belonged to someone who had asked Ebon a question, or whose child or grandchild or niece or nephew Ebon had given a pony ride. She had forgotten the petition—she had wanted to forget the petition—but she could not forget the look on Fthoom's face the day after her twelfth birthday, after she'd climbed down from her chair and said *No*. "Has anyone ever been—unbound?" Sylvi said.

Her mother looked at her in surprise and distress. "I don't think so. There's a paragraph in the treaty somewhere about it, but I don't think it's ever been used."

But there's never been a bond like mine with Ebon, thought Sylvi. "Have you ever heard of Redfora and Oraan?"

"No-o," said her mother slowly. "Who are they?"

"They're a story the pegasi tell," Sylvi said, who had decided before-hand what she would say in answer to this question. "They're sup-posed to be bondmates who could talk to each other."

"I'd've heard if such a story had been unearthed," said the queen. "It hasn't. What a pity. It's just what we want, isn't it? It's interesting that the pegasi have such a story and we do not." She gave her daughter a long look. "Try not to worry. I'm not looking forward to what Fthoom has to say either, because there will probably be something in it we will have to take into account, but those of us who are bound now will stay as we were bound."

Sylvi's heart, which had begun to slow down to its normal pace, heard the tone of her mother's voice and speeded up again. "What about Fthoom?"

"He has asked for an appointment with the king."

"And you already know what he's going to say."

"We know your father's gamble hasn't worked, yes. Did any of us ever really think it would?" she added, almost as if speaking to herself. She sighed, and after a moment went on: "Which bears on what you and I need to talk about. Your birthday party is in nine days—two days after Ebon's return. And you must not only appear utterly, com-pletely normal for the next seven days—exactly as you were before you visited the peg—Rhiandomeer, you must not change by the flicker of an eyelash when you have Ebon with you again, and at your party. And I think perhaps you should not wear your inspiring new robe for all of that time."

Sylvi smiled at her mother's return joke. "You said 'appear,'" she said slowly.

"You've changed," said her mother. "You're not just lost in your own home, you're not just missing your best friend, you've changed. What we need to do is make it *appear* merely that you are growing up—which you are—and that it has nothing to do with three weeks spent alone with the pegasi. Listening to subversive tales of bondmates who could talk to each other."

Sylvi was silent.

"What were they like, the Caves?" said her mother hesitantly.

The question had not been asked before. There was—to Sylvi's ears—an unhappy little silence around it now. Sylvi had been home two days, and no one, not even her father and mother, had asked her anything about her journey. With Hibeehea's words still in the front of her mind, and dismayed and disoriented about her sense of strangeness in her own home, she had not tried to talk about it. When she came back from her cousins' she couldn't stop talking—although Powring and Orthumber and Nearenough and Shirrand, where her various aunts and uncles lived, were very well known to both her parents, and she could just talk, she didn't have to explain anything. Or avoid explaining anything.

Since she'd been back, this was the first time she'd been alone with either parent. She left her window-sill and sat on her bed next to her mother. She thought about how you weren't supposed to touch the pegasi, and yet the pegasi touch each other constantly—and her too, while she was with them. She reached out and took her mother's hand.

Her mother squeezed it and said, "I just said that sometimes you can show when you can't say the words. The one occasion I've ever felt that Hirishy and I were—were in contact somehow, was about the Caves. I'd had difficulty understanding how important they are, and your father was trying to tell me. This was long ago—Danny was a baby. Cory was explaining that the Caves are thousands of years of pegasus art and culture, and more than that: the heart of themselves as a people. I was wrestling with this, trying to imagine it, I suppose, as like our palace only a great deal more so. I looked up and Hirishy was looking at me. As if talk about their Caves—her Caves—was something she could hear and answer. For a moment—just a moment of a moment—I felt I saw the Caves, saw them as Hirishy had seen them, was seeing them in her memory at that moment and was trying to tell me."

"What did you see?" said Sylvi.

"Nothing I can tell you in a way that will make that sudden flash seem astonishing, which it was. It was so very . . . other. Alien. There are caves in the Greentops, you know, and some of the bigger, deeper ones have decorated walls. But this . . ." She threw out her free hand in a there-are-no-words gesture. The pegasi had a specific gesture for "there are no words," which included a single swift up-and-down tail-lash.

"Full?" suggested Sylvi.

"Full," said her mother thoughtfully. "Full of . . . full. Yes. And yet . . . it was only one enormous cave with—with knobbly walls, except I could see that the humps and valleys and ridges had been made. There was a pegasus standing on a low earthwork, with a tiny brush in its alula hand."

"*Chuur*," said Sylvi. "When you don't know someone's gender. *Chuur* and *chuua*. *Chuur* hand."

"I thought you heard Ebon in your head, like you hear someone speaking."

"I do. Mostly. But what happens when they use a word you don't know? Ebon had to explain *chuur* and *chuua* to me." And had found it strange and tactless that her language called a live, gendered being "it" for want of a better choice.

"*Chuur* alula hand, then. The wall in front of—of *chuua*—was beau-

337

tifully coloured in reds and golds. I couldn't see if any of the bumps and colours were a picture I might recognise; the flash didn't last long enough. But the feeling that went with it was extraordinary."

Sylvi smiled a little. "Yes. That sounds like the Caves." Good for Hirishy. "The whole last three weeks . . ." She paused. "It was all like that, a little. Like that feeling. That flash. That astonishment."

"Yes," said her mother softly. "That's what I'm afraid of."

CHAPTER 17

Sylvi got through the rest of the week without Ebon somehow. She spent as much time outdoors as she could. She polished the sword that might have belonged to Razolon till it gleamed like a bead round the neck of a pegasus. She took extra lessons with Diamon; she volunteered for extra bashing and crashing practise, as hand-to-hand was familiarly called out of Diamon's hearing, and was put up against a variety of opponents, from Lucretia to some of Diamon's smallest and youngest beginners, including one of her cousins, her uncle Rulf's youngest daughter, who had been sent to the palace for six weeks to find out what she needed to learn.

"Well done," said Diamon, after one long afternoon, as Sylvi was hanging up the rest of her practise gear, with her sword over her shoulder.

"I suppose I'm less threatening than someone bigger," she said. "Someone like Renny," her cousin, "is more likely to try what she knows against someone like me."

"I'm not putting you up against the littles for your size," said Diamon. "I'm putting you in because you use your strength well. Don't sell yourself as a three-legged donkey when you're a pegasus."

It was an old phrase, as old as "it will hearten us." She still had to stop herself from saying "I wish."

"Thank you," she said.

But she had to spend some time indoors. Ahathin said, "Have you given any thought to how you wish to present your report of your journey?"

"*No*," said Sylvi with loathing. There was a pile of blank paper in a corner of her table. She flicked the edge of the pile with her finger: it was beautiful, in its way, hard and crisp and shiny. The pegasi's softer, duller paper was meant chiefly to take paint, not ink. She had seen several shamans' sigils: Ebon said that how the paint bled into the paper told you how strong the charm would be, and also something about how it would do its work. *I can read a few of the easy ones, what they're for,* Ebon said. *But that's all. I can't tell you whether it's a good one or not. It's one of the things you learn if you're a shaman's apprentice. Like this one is for a good harvest. But it could be a good harvest that's full of weeds that we'll have to pick out. Sigils for rain are tricky, for example, because you want a nice steady medium rain, not like the rain-spirits overturning the sky-bowl so all the rain falls on you at once.*

"I recommend you do so," said Ahathin. "I wish to be able to tell your father before the festivities for your birthday when he can expect to see it."

Could she write about the shamans' sigils? She could at least write about watching them make their paper. Her outstretched arm revealed Niahi's bracelet below the end of her sleeve. She could write about meeting Ebon's little sister. She could write about how the pegasi made *yelloni* for each other, but for ears and ankles. She could not write that Niahi had decided that human wrists were best. She could not write that Niahi had said anything to her at all.

She had spoken to no pegasus since Ebon left. When she saw one in a corridor or in one of the gardens, they bowed to each other but did not stop. In human groups . . . the humans were always making so much mouth noise it was hard to think.

She looked at Ahathin and could think of nothing to say, no loud human words. But even the silence in the human world lay differently than silence with the pegasi.

"The king has faith in his daughter's intelligence and perception, and so do I," said Ahathin.

"You mean, be careful what I put in my report."

"Remember that your report may be read by anyone who goes to the library and asks to see it."

"Which might include Fthoom."

"Which will undoubtedly include Fthoom."

"Will you help me?" she said sadly.

"I will certainly help you, if you wish it."

"You mean you are a magician too."

"I am indeed a magician too. But my similarity to Fthoom ends there, as I would most humbly beg the lady Sylviianel to remember."

She thought of the Hall of Magicians, where he could go and she could not. She thought of Redfora; she thought of the fact that Ahathin was one of her oldest friends. She let her mind drift . . . and for a moment she was standing in the little valley with an army behind her, and the king of the pegasi was sweeping his wingtip across the bottom of a long piece of soft white paper: she could hear a faint rustling as some human hand shifted its grip. And the two magicians with the human king looked up. She remembered the one—the one whose smile, back in the Caves, said, *It is too late. It is done.*

But the second one looked at her now and in his eyes she read, *Try.*

"I believe you," she said aloud. "And I would be grateful for your help."

"It shall be my last official act as your tutor," said Ahathin. "I thank you for that."

At night—especially on the three quiet clear nights that would have been perfect for flying—she told herself that there had been many perfect flying nights they had not gone flying because Ebon wasn't there. There had been many weeks when Ebon had been at home among the pegasi, having lessons from his master, teasing his little sister, being bored by council meetings—not with her at the palace, among the humans. This had not seemed strange to her then. But that was then, she thought. That was before I visited their country, and their Caves.

She had after all told no one, not even her father, that she had spoken to other pegasi in Rhiandomeer—pegasi other than Ebon. It turned out that it was easy—miserably, painfully easy—not to tell anyone. It was not only that no one asked directly—who was going to say to her, "Did you find, in Rhiandomeer, that you could speak to the rest of the pegasi too? That for you almost a thousand years of the way things are were nothing at all?" She had not thought of this clearly; she had been too busy bracing herself to lie. She had been, before she was brought back to the human world, so *full* of her experience of the pegasi, it had seemed to her that anyone who met her might read the truth of it, somehow, off her face, her bearing, as visible as a siraga around her shoulders.

Instead there was a new, curious distance, an awkwardness, between her and—everyone. She had thought everyone would be longing to hear about her visit, the adventure that no one else had had before. And perhaps they were. But no one asked. Even Ahathin, helping her organise her thoughts and her notes into a presentation she could give to her father and the senate, asked her no questions except about what she had already volunteered, already written down. She wanted to ask him, Do you think the pegasi shamans' magic is antithetical to human magicians' magic? Would you go to Rhiandomeer if you had the chance? Do you think it would make you confused or sick or powerless? Have the magicians ever discussed this barrier between humans and pegasi? Do they know why so few shamans come here, and why they never stay long? Is there a special group within some magicians' guild that studies the situation, like Fthoom looking for stories of friendship between human and pegasus? Has it taken you over eight hundred years to reach no conclusions?

She wasn't even sure she could, here, in the human country, speak to pegasi, any more than Hibeehea could speak to humans, here. The air, like the silence, lay against you differently here, and she put her hand to her cheek as if to brush back a veil. The difference did not seem to make her ill, as it made the pegasus shamans, but it made her feel as if she had not come home after all—as if some of her had not come home, the part that understood sky views and sky holds, the part that found human noise and human sitting-down banquets normal.

She had dreaded what her father might ask her about speaking to the pegasi: she dreaded it because of the look in Dorogin's eyes, because of Hibeehea's advice, because she did not want to think about why she knew in her bones it was good advice. Lrrianay, on that first incredible night when she had begun speaking to the other pegasi, had told her what the two kings hoped, and her father had noticed that her speech at the banquet had already become more fluent after only a day among the pegasi in their own country. She dreaded almost anything he might now ask her about her journey, but he asked her nothing at all. The morning he and she had seen the *doorathbaa* pegasi who had brought her back leave to fly home to their country—the morning she had had to hold on to her father to keep herself standing as she watched Ebon vanish—he had said to her afterward, "I'm sorry, young one, that it's so hard. But I'm glad to have you back."

But he said nothing more, that day or the following days. And she never seemed to see him except in some councillor's company, or among a group of senators—or with Fazuur and Lrrianay. She could have asked to see him alone, but she didn't. She wondered if he thought she was avoiding him. She wondered if he was avoiding her. It was so easy to avoid someone, here at the palace, with all the bustling, clattering humans, all the comings and goings, all the meetings, all the discussions, all the messages, all the different groups of people concerned about different things and insisting on the greater importance of whatever their subject, their charge, their preoccupation was. . . . She had never realised before that it was too much. But it hadn't been too much, before. Before Rhiandomeer and its birdsong, rustling-tree silences, the hum of the pegasi; before the taste of her porridge, of *fwhfwhfwha*, of the llyri grass. Before the Caves. Before *ssshuuwuushuu*.

She didn't try to speak to any other pegasus, and none tried to speak to her. She felt that if she did try, she might fall down, as she had that evening she had first spoken to Niahi and then Lrrianay. She felt that despite the things that wouldn't change—the two legs, the big hands with the rotating wrists, the lack of wings—that she was less secure in her humanness than she had been before she visited Rhiandomeer, and that was exactly what she dared not risk revealing. She dared not risk trying to speak to a pegasus. And—changed as she was in other ways—she dared not risk the despair if she failed.

She wondered if Lrrianay had said anything about her to the other pegasi at the palace, about what had happened to her in Rhiandomeer—and if so what might he have said? Had he told them not to try to speak to her—she the wingless biped who had spent five days in the Caves, who, in Rhiandomeer, could speak to all the pegasi, and not only to Ebon? Had Lrrianay guessed about the despair? Or was it only that Lrrianay agreed with Hibeehea—although Lrrianay had, in the end, said nothing about what Hibeehea had told her. Lrrianay's last words to her had been on the morning of her flight home, merely: *Thank you for coming.* And she had replied, *Thank you for having me.* Her aunt or her uncle might have said just the same, and she responded the same, at the end of one of her visits to her cousins.

But her state of mind was not as important as the fact that any hint of communication between the princess returned from Rhiandomeer and any other pegasus than the one she was so strangely bound to would be reported directly and immediately to Fthoom. Fthoom, the powerful and power-mad, Fthoom, about whom a petition was gathering support and signatures, calling for him to be reinstated in his former place of authority and influence in the king's council; Fthoom, who hated her.

She thought Lrrianay was avoiding her—but she knew she was avoiding him. From the outside, she thought, the pegasi looked just as before—formal, aloof, polite, perhaps kind, but disinterested. That was a good thing, she reminded herself. She was supposed to pretend—to *appear*—that nothing had happened except that she had been gone for three weeks; except that she had made history. I won't make any of the kind of history anybody will have to learn later. I promise, she had said to her father. And he had replied, Be careful of your promises. I'm not going to hold you to this one.

The pegasi she met were careful to acknowledge her—but the pegasi were always careful to acknowledge any human bound to one of their own, and any pegasus in the palace grounds knew who the bound humans were. She wondered, as she punctiliously responded to peg-asus acknowledgements, just as punctiliously as she responded to human acknowledgements, how many of the pegasi disapproved of her visit to their country. Was it that she was human, and was accustomed to reading human gestures and expressions, that she so often knew im-mediately which humans disapproved of her journey, or was it that humans made their disapproval so obvious? She could not read the pegasi any more—was that because she had lost what she had learnt of them in Rhiandomeer, or was it that they held themselves differently—as she felt she held herself differently—here in Balsinland?

She could almost hear Ebon saying, *Disapprove? That's another of your human things. What's it for? Once something's been decided, that's it, isn't it?*

But what if someone—call it dislike rather than disapprove? Hibeehea didn't like me talking to the queen when I first arrived. Hibeehea didn't want me to come at all. . . .

But she couldn't hear his answer. Faintly she heard Redfora's voice, but she couldn't hear the words she said—and furthermore she knew she was making it up, to comfort herself.

She said aloud, "*Gonoarin, wheehuf*"—"the best of good days, noble sirs, noble madams"—making the correct human motions with her human hands. She could say the pegasi vowels, the *ff*'s, the *mrr*'s, better now than she had been able to a month ago. This much at least she could keep of her journey; a few clear superficial words, a slightly greater fluency with sign.

The pegasi bowed their heads to her so that their long manes swept forward like curtains of silk: beautiful, remote, unknowable.

Of course she never went near the pegasi annex. She had no rea-son to.

Once she met Hirishy alone, outside her mother's rooms. She

paused to make her bow and when she raised her head Hirishy was very close to her, reaching out one tiny feather-hand to stroke her cheek. Sylvi thought—she almost thought—she heard *Oh, poor sweetheart*—and in her mind she saw, briefly but so vividly she could not, *could* not, have imagined it, one of the cultivated hill-meadows of the pegasus land. There were pegasi hoeing between the little green rows, and a pavilion at one corner of the field: a simple, comforting, *homey* scene, nothing demanding or formidable, like the Caves, or the Dreaming Sea . . . or the palace where they stood.

And then Waina, who was one of the ladies-of-the-queen's-chamber on duty that week, opened the door. Hirishy moved unhurriedly away from Sylvi's side, nodded a slow human-style nod to Waina, and stood waiting for Sylvi to precede her through the door. The moment—whatever it had been—was over.

Sylvi had been rather hopelessly making notes toward the presentation she was going to have to give about her journey, writing down three things she thought she could talk about and then crossing two of them off again. It would be so much easier to have a pegasus to ask, she thought.

She sighed, and pushed herself away from the table, and went and sat on the window-sill. She had been given her own office when she began to work on dams and waterways, so she could receive reports and have a place to unroll the charts and diagrams that various people brought her. She had been offered rooms on the ground floor, where most of the rest of her family had their offices, but she had wanted something as high up as possible and was in fact in an attic. "I may try that," her father said. "Anyone who will climb four flights of stairs to consult me must really want my advice."

The attics had only slightly lower ceilings than the rest of the palace—and the wind that came through the windows tasted a little more like free air than house air, although when she had chosen the rooms almost four years ago she'd chiefly been interested in the view. She looked out over one of the palace's smaller courtyards, then the outthrust bulk of the Great Hall, with a curl of old trees softening its outline. Beyond it there was parkland, and beyond that she could see the faint haze over the practise yards—and very far away, the thick dark line that was the Wall.

She sighed again, and had just stood up to go back to her desk when there was a quick knock on the door—and the head that was put round it was Danacor's.

"Oh!" she said, and ran to throw her arms around him, her mood lightening immediately.

"How's my favourite sister?" he said, smiling, but when she looked up at him she thought he looked tired and worried. "I'm sorry I wasn't here for your arrival. How did it go? Or is that a bad question?" And he looked at her table. "When's your presentation?"

"Three days," she said glumly. "Three days before the party."

"Dad'll have scheduled it before you left. And written the list of questions. Which he wrote an addendum to after he got back, am I right?"

There was a list of questions, and there was an addendum, but her father had said, "These are only because I can't help myself. This is *your* report. Tell us what you choose to tell us." She had looked at him quickly and looked away. Lrrianay was standing just behind him; if she looked into her father's face she risked catching Lrrianay's eye. Fazuur sat at a table set end-on to Corone's desk. He looked up from the papers he was reading and smiled at her.

Danacor added, "I hope I'll be back in time to hear you."

"They're sending you away again immediately?" she said, dismayed.

He sighed. "We haven't got any quiet borders left at the moment—except the Starclouds. It's just a question of how far in, and how much effort to force them back. The wild lands are the worst, but we've got Ipinay and her Queen's Own holding the most hazardous stretch of that line. I'm off to look at Pantock—there are reports of sea monsters. Sea monsters are a new one."

Fthoom is from Ghorm, thought Sylvi, which is next to Pantock. Maybe it's his family come to visit.

"From some other messenger I'd be inclined to say, 'Mm hmm, send me another report in a month,' but the mayor of Pantock is pretty reliable. If he says sea monsters, there probably are sea monsters. But I'll be back for your party. So finish your presentation so you can enjoy it." He looked at her, smiling. "My little sister, all grown up. Well, maybe not *up*, exactly. . . ."

"Troll," she said equably. "Think of all the horse fodder bills I will save the realm by never getting tall enough to ride anything bigger than a pony."

"Of course. My future chancellor of the exchequer thanks you." He paused again. "You look so much like Dad. It's uncanny."

"And you look more and more like Mum."

He grimaced. "Yes. I'm the warrior, not the negotiator. You'll have to take over the negotiating when Dad retires. Farley wants to raise horses and Garren wants to find new plants for his herbalism."

"Not me," she said. "I'm going to—to—" But her usual declaration of her future—I'm going to become an engineer, and build dams and bridges all up and down the Kishes and the Greentops—wouldn't come. What came to her instead was, I'm going back to Rhiandomeer, if they'll have me, and then I'm going to find out if there's a little not very interesting Cave somewhere that someone would let a human try and sculpt. A human no one would miss much, being the king's fourth child. And I'd come back occasionally, and visit you humans.

But she couldn't say that, even to Danny.

Danacor said, "Mum warned me your journey had changed you. Maybe it's a little like after Mum said yes to Dad, or after the Sword accepted me. Everything does change. But nobody—no human—has ever been to Rhiandomeer before. You're the pegasus expert now. Everyone will want to know what you think about anything to do with the pegasi, now."

"No!" she said, horrified. "I am *not* the pegasi expert! I'm going to learn engineering, and build dams! They are—they are—oh!" She remembered her father sitting down through the long pegasus banquet; she remembered telling her mother about *chuur* and *chuua*. "Knowing more—oh—it's more like knowing less!"

Danny laughed. "Yes, I—er—know. But you're the expert to the rest of us. Dad would tell you he's not the expert on running a country, and I would certainly tell you I'm not the expert on making taralians and norindours—and sea monsters—go away and stop bothering us. But we're all we've got. You too. You'd better get used to it."

She stared at him. He was right, of course. But it hadn't occurred to her before. She was too busy thinking about herself—and missing Ebon—and worrying about her presentation. She wondered if this was why her father had not asked her any private questions about her journey—that he had guessed what she was feeling. The warrior had blurted it out when the negotiator had chosen to say nothing.

"But you'll give a brilliant presentation. Just like Dad would. It's written all over you, as well as on all those papers." He kissed the top of her head and was gone again.

◆　◆　◆

At the prospect of being the pegasus expert she had been even more careful what she had, and had not, said. Was it all right to describe the crops they cultivate? The fields of llyri grass so tall she could not see over their waving tassels, even in spring? The colonies of spiders they fed and tended, that they might harvest their silk? The spinning, dyeing and weaving, the paper-making? That they had no houses, but that each trade had its small cotes or cabins or cottages? Could she describe the pavilions, the furniture, the ingenious way they harnessed each other to carry loads? The last was done at the palace, but somehow humans rarely saw them doing it; nor would humans ever have seen them carrying their long tables on poles, and fitting the pieces together, and the tray-frames that let them carry full serving-bowls or anything else that must not be jostled, and the various pokers, prodders and hooks that let them shift the things they carried; and the deft way they used their knees, their chests and their teeth—everything based on, and arising from, their weak but clever hands. Why *did* humans see so little of this creative dexterity? On the rare occasions the pegasi hosted an event, they did it in one of the Courts, and there were human servants to do the fetching and carrying. Was this sense— there were human servants, why not make use of them—or was it the humans barging in where they were not needed because barging was what humans did?

Ahathin had come to see how she was getting on a little after Danacor had left her.

"I'm not," she said. "Getting on. Danacor was just here and . . ." But there was nothing she could ask Ahathin when she wasn't telling her own father the truth. She looked up from her increasing pages of notes. Ahathin was looking at her thoughtfully.

"If you had come back from a month at your cousins' and been asked to give a report, what would you have said?"

351

"I was asked," she said, half laughing and half impatient. "I was *always* asked. I hated it when I was younger, you know, I felt it spoilt the holiday. It was more interesting lately, when I could talk about rivers and bridges. But the pegasi don't need bridges."

"It is the role of teachers," Ahathin said tranquilly, "to spoil their students' pleasure. As I recall, when you were younger, you said a good deal about the food and the countryside."

"But that was just a holiday, like anyone might have," she said dubiously. "This was—"

"That you went is as much as anyone needs to know," he said. "The rest you may treat more or less as a holiday, as you choose."

The Caves? she thought. Can I treat the Caves as a holiday outing? I must say something about the Caves.

So she (again) praised the pegasi's hospitality, she described her feather-bed and her hot breakfasts—she described the pavilions, and the harnesses and frames, and the way almost everything the pegasi used came to bits small enough to be made and then fitted together by the tiny pegasi feather-hands. She described the paper and the weaving—and the spiders. She described the countryside, that it was like and unlike their human lands—she had mentioned the lack of bridges, and of dams, and the way the paths all connected within an area, but that there were no roads between discrete areas—and she described the fields of koy and fleiier for drying and weaving, of barley and oats and djee, of pumpkins, maize and zorra; the orchards of apples, pears and plooraia—and the fields and fields and fields of llyri grass.

Of the Caves she said only that she had seen but a fraction of a fraction of them—she allowed it to be implied that she had spent perhaps a single afternoon there—and that the corridors and individual chambers were often very large, and very beautifully decorated, some with great washes and swirls of muted colours, and some with representational scenes of landscapes, and of pegasi galloping or flying.

She did not mention that a shaman must accompany you into the Caves. She did not mention *ssshuuwuushuu*. She did not mention Redfora and Oraan; she did not mention the Dreaming Sea. To the best of her ability she made her journey sound like a kind of royal progression, as if she had been the king's ambassador to a barony a little farther away and a little less known than most, as if the strangeness could be contained in a description of the food and the clothing, and possibly a few local peculiarities about the raising of crops. She mentioned *ssshasssha* as a visitor to the palace might mention seeing the mural of the signing in the Great Hall, and the affecting historical token of the framed treaty.

Part of her training as king's daughter had included how to give a speech: speak slowly and distinctly, and don't keep your nose buried in your pages; look up as often as you can, and make eye contact with members of your audience. She had done these things, but the eyes she had met had stared back at her like painted porcelain. When she was done, she shook her pages together again, looked out over the faces looking up at her and smiled a trained princess' smile. She had been aware of them—senators, blood, courtiers and councillors, about a quarter of them with pegasi present who stood beside their bondmates' pegasus-tall chairs—listening closely to everything she said; no one had so much as sneezed while she spoke. But she had picked up nothing from them, any more than she had been able to read anything in the porcelain eyes. She permitted herself to glance to her right, where her father sat; he smiled encouragingly at her, and that made her feel a little better. But her eyes drifted to Lrrianay standing behind him, and to Fazuur's hands falling still as she fell silent—and she wished, again, for Ebon. She wished for Ebon as she wished every time she saw Lrrianay at her father's shoulder, or any pegasus at any bond-mate's shoulder, or any pegasus. Or any time she took a breath, she wished again for Ebon.

She turned back to her audience.

The first question she was asked was if there were any representations of humans in the Caves. She was ready for this, but she was a little shaken that it was the very first question: shouldn't her audience be more interested in the zorra and the djee? Or the flying? How could any human *not* want to hear more about the flying? But she smiled again, and looked levelly at Senator Chorro and said that she did not remember seeing any, no, but that even the little of the Caves she had seen had been rather overwhelming in its size and magnificence— "Imagine spending a day at the palace and then trying to report on what you'd seen." That, finally, gained her her first laugh of the afternoon, and the atmosphere in the Little Hall eased somewhat; Sylvi was grateful, not least because that should make them less likely to notice that she was lying.

She had originally planned to say that she had seen the signing of the treaty on one chamber wall—but when the time came she found she could not. It struck too near to what had really happened to her—admitting even so much felt dangerous, as if it were a crack in a dam wall, and the water might use that one tiny crack to bring the wall down, and the lake behind rush out.

There were murmurs in the hall now, neighbour speaking to neighbour, and one or two more questions, and Sylvi concentrated on appearing candid and at ease. She was wearing a long cream-coloured robe with the siraga the pegasi had given to her over her shoulders; she touched it once or twice in what she hoped was an appreciative but offhand manner. Young Vlodor stood up, smiling tentatively. He was tall enough that he could do this gracefully, despite the height of the Little Hall chairs, which was to allow for the presence of pegasi. Vlodor had only recently taken his father's place among the blood councillors; he had been introduced to her at the banquet welcoming her home. He was bound, and his pegasus' name was Nyyoah. The Holder of Concord recognised him, and he bowed to Sylvi and said, "I am sure this is a frivolous question and unworthy of our august company, but, princess, might you be kind enough to indulge us in a little more description of what *flying* is like?"

That produced another laugh, and Sylvi almost relaxed. In other circumstances she had thought, the other evening, that she might like Vlodor; she thought so again now. "I have both longed for and dreaded that question," she said lightly, jokingly, "because flying is most amazing—it is beyond amazing—I fear it is indescribable, and I wish it were not; I would like to tell you how amazing it is." She paused and glanced at her father and they exchanged reminiscent smiles. "You ride in a rope sling—but you are riding on *air*." She had to be careful not to be too enthusiastic; she had to remember that nothing had changed, except that she was now sixteen years old and had visited Rhiandomeer. She had to remember she did not miss Ebon with very breath she took—she had to remember that the only flying she had done was in a drai. She finished by saying, "It is a little embarrassing to discover that some of our most famous sky holds and sky views are inaccurate."

But it was Senator Orflung who asked the question that was, she was sure, in everyone's minds—she felt she could almost see it shimmering in the air, like she could almost see the magic that held the draia ropes taut—even more she felt she could see it flickering in Fazuur's eyes.

Senator Orflung got slowly to his feet and was recognised by the Holder of Concord. He then bowed to Sylvi and said, "My lady, we are glad to have you back. And I wonder if you can tell us now, my lady, now that you have turned sixteen, if you—if you and *Hrrr* Ebon—are prepared to begin some of the task of translation and mediation between our two peoples, as your father the king hinted four years ago might be permitted once you had attained your majority."

She was conscious of Fazuur and Sagda, Lord Cral's Speaker, standing behind her on the dais. Ebon was not there, so Ahathin was not there. She had wanted to ask him to come, for fear of exactly this question, but for fear of exactly this question she had decided it was better to face the senate alone.

"Yes," she said at once, and her voice rang out as clear and calm as her father's might have done. "Yes, my sir, and all my sirs and ladies, all my barons and granddames. I am ready to do anything I can for my people and my country—and for our peoples and our countries. Ebon and I have discussed this many times, and Ebon has assured me he feels the same." Almost—almost—she could hear Ebon saying, *Assured? Dearheart, I'll promise to do anything you like, but I don't* **assure**.

It's just king talk, she said back to him, knowing that she was making him up—and felt a pang of loneliness and loss every bit as severe as she had the evening she had met Niahi—just before she met Niahi—when her father's absence seemed too terrible to bear. "Tomorrow, my sir, you will be able to ask him yourself," and she was almost sure she kept the longing out of her voice.

But it was her father who came to stand beside her now on the dais, and Lrrianay briefly left her father's shoulder to stand at hers. "We have already begun the discussions about how best we may use our daughter and our son for this work," said Sylvi's father, Fazuur's hands flicking in counterpoint, "and if any of you wish to contribute to that discussion, you may wait upon us."

And Lrrianay said, "*Araawhaia*," which meant "I agree," and added the gesture for emphasis, which was to drop his right wing almost to floor level and give it a tiny, scooping sweep. But in her mind she heard him say—she was sure she heard him say—*well done*. And she unmistakably heard Fazuur murmur to her and her father both, "The king compliments the Lady Sylviianel on her poise and clear-headedness."

Ebon's return was the first time she had been a part of the formal ritual of welcome to the pegasus king. Lrrianay had flown home immediately after her presentation, to escort the pegasi coming to the human princess' birthday party, and there was to be the full ceremony of reception when the company arrived. She was still, that day, half in a daze from having given her report successfully the day before—that, and her answer to Senator Orflung's question had instantly begun a deluge of messages, papers and requests for appointments.

"We must ask your father for a secretary," said Ahathin.

Ahathin had appeared at his usual hour that morning, to ask her how her presentation had gone, and found her sorting through the first courier's delivery in increasing dismay.

"I don't know most of these words in my *own* language," she said, handing him a letter from a philosopher who seemed to want to discuss the pegasi's understanding of the nature of reality and epistemological truth. That had been six hours, two couriers and seven special messengers ago.

Sylvi pushed her chair back violently and went to stand by the window. It was raining again; with Ahathin present—and the likelihood

357

of the next courier arriving at any moment—she decided not to lean out in it, but she did put her hand through the open pane and let a few raindrops pool in her palm. She didn't want a secretary; she didn't want to be tied down by more fuss and commotion, more meetings, more quacking human voices demanding she do things, more piles of *paper*, till her desk resembled her father's. She rubbed the palmful of cool water over her face. "Yes," she said. "I suppose so." She turned round. "Can you—will you stay? Were you planning on writing the history of the world as soon as you were relieved of your duties as tutor? I don't know what to *do* with a secretary."

"I am still the princess' adviser as well as her somewhat superfluous Speaker," said Ahathin in his usual calm tone. "I will attend her as long as she wishes my assistance."

"The princess is extremely grateful," she said, and sighed.

She went back to her rooms for a quiet tea and to dress for the ceremonial meeting, thinking, Ebon will be here this evening. *Ebon.* And yet her best friend of the last four years seemed, for the moment, almost as unreal as her journey to his land seemed, after her cool dry recitation of pegasi food and furniture. The barrage of requests for their services as translators seemed only to push him even farther away.

Pansa had laid her topaz robe out ready for her when she brought her her tea. Sylvi went to lean against the window-sill again, holding a cup of tea, looking out—but her bedroom faced in the wrong direction to see the pegasi returning. Pansa brought her a plate with some of the food from the tray on it and said, "Lady, remember to *eat* something," and jiggled it under Sylvi's nose. Sylvi sighed and took it, went back to her chair and sat down. She looked at the robe lying across her bed: the orange-gold of the topazes, soft in lamplight, reminded her of the colours of the Caves. Pansa hovered, wanting to help her into it. Sylvi looked at the plate still in her hands, picked up something at random and put it in her mouth. And then there was a knock on the door, and a courtier saying that the pegasi were in sight.

Lrrianay was escorting not only his youngest son but also his wife, his daughter, and an assortment of other pegasi—including an unusually high number of shamans. "That's *Hibeehea*," Sylvi whispered to her father, as the two of them stood, waiting, while the pegasi landed, lightly as sparrows, shook their wings and folded them, and walked toward them. Behind the king and the princess were ranks of gorgeously dressed humans, including the queen and the king's heir; at their elbows were their Speakers, Fazuur and Ahathin, and Ahathin was wearing his Speaker sticks.

"Yes, it is," said her father. "For the birthday celebration of the only human who has ever visited the pegasus Caves."

She was silent, but the crowd around them meant she did not have to try and respond to this. Hibeehea had said he would come again to the palace—to visit *her*, the human who had walked into *ssshasssha* and seen the signing of the treaty of Alliance. *You have changed the world, little human child*, he had said to her when they parted, and she stood waiting to greet him now in her beautiful topaz robe, and felt ashamed. I have not changed the world, she thought. I am not a hero, and the world is too big.

She walked forward when her father did—trying not to think about anything, trying not to think about the fact that she was now the pegasus expert, and stood beside her father while the queen and the heir stood behind her. She tried especially not to think about the sight of Ebon walking toward her, a black hole in the twilight, next to his pale father. Lrrianay was wearing Balsin's opal, and her heart sank even further; he only wore it for very special occasions. No, she thought again. I have not changed the world. I am too small.

She did not run forward to throw her arms around Ebon's neck, as she wanted to, as she might have done if they were alone, as she had done with her brother. But here there were hundreds of people watching them, including some of those who wanted their interpretive skills, including some of those who had tried to block her visit to Rhiandomeer—and everyone present knew the prohibition on touching the pegasi.

The formal greeting ritual was hands held up, palms pressed together, then parted and held out; then you picked up a handful of flower petals, fresh or dried, according to the season, which a footman would be offering you from a bowl, and you scattered them on the ground between you. Lrrianay walked gravely forward and bowed to her father, the opal at his breast glowing like fire; Ebon, when it was his turn, did the same to her. He was wearing a black siraga, invisible against his blackness, so that the gems stitched to it looked as if they had been strewn over Ebon's naked shoulders. As neither of them had ever been a part of the sovereigns' ritual, they had never greeted each other this way before either. *Missed you*, was all he said.

And I you, she replied—her joy at seeing him muted and confused by the strangeness of their meeting; and there were Speakers listening. She even found she was relieved that she could still talk to him—of course I can still talk to him! she thought. That's where it all *began*!

Lrrianay and Ebon took their traditional places half a step behind the shoulders of their human bondmates and half a step to one side, to allow the Speakers room. Then the rest of the pegasi were presented to the two of them, the human king and his daughter, with their Speakers at their elbows, Fazuur and Ahathin bending slightly toward the king and the princess, murmuring names and greetings. Ebon did not interrupt. Sylvi bowed and repeated names and tried to think about nothing—and thought about her bond-friend's silence, while her mouth said the names that her Speaker gave her.

The pegasus queen, as she rose from her bow, reached forward with one wing, and brushed Sylvi's face with the tips of her feathers—there was the smell of Rhiandomeer again, the grassy, flowery, earthy smell. Sylvi's eyes filled with tears, and she blinked frantically. Niahi was presented with her mother, and while she did a faultless bow, she then took another step forward, close enough to put her nose to Sylvi's cheek. A tiny, whispering, almost inaudible voice in her mind said, *I'm not supposed to talk to you! Please come back soon! I miss you!* The last two sentences were almost obliterated by a very emphatic silent *sssssh* from Ebon, which made Sylvi smile as much as Niahi's words did—it was, for a few seconds, as if they were together and all was well.

Niahi took a hasty step backward again, and made a little bob of a second bow—and Sylvi held her hands out, stretching the one farther than the other, so the bracelet of pegasus hair showed clearly beneath her topaz-studded sleeve. She just saw the wrinkle form across Niahi's muzzle, and then she ducked her head and whisked after her mother.

Sylvi glanced at Ahathin, but if he had heard the exchange, he gave no sign.

None of the other pegasi spoke to her—but she had the answer to one of her questions with Niahi's words: it was not only Ebon any more, even in Balsinland. Although she almost doubted again when Hibeehea was presented to her: his mind-silence seemed absolute, as if the mere idea of that communication was inconceivable, and he looked as forbidding as he had the night she had met him, her first night in Rhiandomeer, when she began her historic visit by offending the greatest of the pegasus shamans.

After he made his bow, he said aloud, "I am proud and honoured to

be here," very clearly and distinctly, and there was a murmur of astonishment from the humans. But to Sylvi's ear he sounded strained, as if
the effort to speak even a few formal words was almost too great to be
made. And his limbs and wings and body were stiff; she could read
nothing in gesture.

When the presentations were over, the human queen stepped forward and took the human king's arm; Danacor stepped forward and
took Sylvi's—and squeezed it against his side. "Well done, princess,"
he said, but Sylvi was too conscious of their two pegasi, standing
behind them; as Danacor had come up to them, Ebon had dropped
back, and Thowara's forehead stayed near the nape of Danacor's
neck. "They're always behind us," murmured Sylvi. "They're always *behind* us."

They were slowly following the king and queen, who were flanked
by Lrrianay and Hirishy. Sylvi wasn't expecting an answer, but as they
passed under the Great Arch and turned toward the Great Hall where
the celebration for her birthday was being held, Danacor said, "If you
want to give up building bridges in the mountains and go back to
Rhiandomeer and negotiate a reciprocal visitation agreement, I'll engage now to stand behind Thowara when our time comes. But you *will*
have to build a road."

Then the first of the senators came up to them to say something
pleasant and flattering and meaningless, and they spoke no more about
it. Shortly after, they parted, and then it was just herself and Ebon—
and several hundred party-goers. And Ahathin. And Glarfin, neither
of whom let themselves be elbowed more than an arm's-length away,
however bad the crush. Sylvi kept wanting to drop back and put an
arm over Ebon's back, or twine her fingers in his mane—as she had
done so easily and so often for three weeks—and she had to keep stopping herself. But she spoke politely to everyone who spoke to her—

including a few pegasi, meticulously translated by Ahathin, while she half listened to the human words and did not try to hear the pegasi themselves. Niahi came and stood with them for much of the time, and Senator Grant and Lord Broughton, both of whom Sylvi knew had eleven-year-old daughters, asked as if idly if this was the king's daughter, and was it true that she was still unbound. And when Glarfin brought her food and a glass of wine—and two pages brought a great platter of grasses and fruit for her companions—they all ate and drank.

And while, with Ebon with her, she enjoyed her birthday party that evening far more than she had enjoyed anything about the previous week without him, there remained a strange formality between them, and her pleasure in his presence felt too much like missing him had felt during the last week. I'm still missing him when he's standing right next to me, Sylvi thought.

Her original plan that the party for her sixteenth birthday should have equal numbers of human and pegasus guests had been one of the casualties of her visit to Rhiandomeer. "Oh," she had said sadly, "oh," when one of her father's secretaries had presented her with the guest list, drawn up in her absence. It wasn't normal enough, she realised, to have as many pegasi as human guests at her party. She had flicked a look at Fazuur and back at the guest list.

"Is there anyone we've missed?" said her father. "That you'd like to include? The invitations have gone out of course, but it's not too late."

About a hundred more pegasi, she thought. I can give you some names. . . .

In fact nearly a third of those present at her party were pegasi, which was an unusually high percentage. That's also because of my visit to Rhiandomeer, she thought. It has to be more than the usual number of pegasi. But not too many. Half would be too many. She felt

363

restless, trapped, outmanoeuvred by the human gift for complication, for creating obstacles of words—and piles of paper.

They're watching us, said Ebon. *I mean, they've always watched us, but . . .*

Yes, said Sylvi. *It's different.* One more thing that was different. She didn't want to ask him what he had spent the last week doing. How could she *miss* Rhiandomeer? She didn't only miss Ebon; she missed his country, where she couldn't even cross a river dry-shod, because there were no bridges and no boats. She thought about what Danacor had said. Would it be worth it, to chop and slash a footway to the pegasus land, so that the human king could stand behind the pegasus king?

Not to the pegasi.

Well, it was still worth it, Ebon said. Their eyes met, lingered just a fraction too long and were hastily shifted away.

The birthday party went on and on, and it was very late by the time the princess and her parents—and their attendant pegasi—could leave. Ebon and Sylvi took a brief stroll around the gardens before they parted.

Here's the bad news, said Ebon. *I don't dare take you flying till some of these hrreefaar shamans leave. Shamans don't sleep like the rest of us. They also have some weird glaurau—uh—other-space sense of where we all are. It wouldn't be so bad if they just knew I was flying, but I'm not sure they wouldn't pick you up. I know being here messes them up, but I'm afraid it might not mess them up enough, you know?*

It's also a full moon and a lot of—movement. Scouts and things. Even at night. Danny leaves again tomorrow. . . .

He'd come back for her party, as he said he would, but he'd had three messages over the course of the evening—three that she saw happening. The only private words she'd had with him, since she'd been back, had been in her office, when he'd told her she was the peg-asus expert now.

She and Ebon stood silent for a few minutes longer; neither of them was ready to let the other out of sight—out of sound-of-breath, out of sense-of-other's-body-bulk-and-warmth, out of touch of human hand or velvet pegasus nose—after the long week apart. At least, out here, they could touch each other again.

CHAPTER 18

All sightings of taralians and norindours and their other old enemies were brought to the Balsinland king, even if the report was merely that the creature had already been dispatched by a baronial hunting party or a patrol of soldiers. Barring taralians, which were a more persistent problem, there were several reports every year, but—until recently— never more than several, not since Corone IV's great-great-grandfather's day. There were ballads about the Great Hunt that King Janek himself had led; the main fact about it was that it had been successful and had not been repeated.

Sylvi was with her father in his private office the morning the messenger from General Randarl came. It was three days after her birthday party. Ebon was with her, Lord Cral and his pegasus, Miaia, the two kings—and two Speakers.

They were again considering her travels in Rhiandomeer; she was tense and anxious, unsure what she could discuss and what she must not. She was afraid to say anything to Ebon that she wouldn't want a Speaker to overhear; whenever she asked him anything about what she'd seen or where she'd gone, there was an implication of *How much can I say?* and his answers were stilted and constrained. She wondered if his father was saying anything to him; if so, she did not hear it.

Both she and Ebon were oppressed by the knowledge of the suggestions that were still coming in from senate, council, individual bloods and courtiers, and from a surprising number of citizen groups, about how to use the ability of the princess and her pegasus to talk across the barrier between their two species: proposals and recommendations as well as specific requests for arbitration and intervention. The Speakers' Guild, however, advised caution and deferment, and requested the right to inspect any papers on the subject and to sit in on any meetings. On Ahathin's advice, Sylvi's new secretary, for the present, reported to her father.

"Welcome to my world," her father had said gently. "I'm sorry, my love, you and Ebon will have to make some decisions in a little while—after the senate decides what decisions you're allowed to make, and if the Speakers' Guild ever lets them decide. All your secretary can do meanwhile is sort into categories and write acknowledgements—and draw up summaries."

She said—it was the nearest she had ever come to telling her father the hidden truth about her journey, and she said it absent-mindedly—"Hibeehea told me, the last morning in Rhiandomeer, that I had changed the world. But this . . ." She was watching her new secretary pressing her emblem, the princess' seal, onto the back of a folded letter. The secretary, whose name was Iridin and who was not a magician, looked up and smiled, and put the letter on a pile of other letters.

"Sometimes it only takes a moment for everything to change," said her father, unknowingly echoing what the queen had said two days after her daughter's return from Rhiandomeer. "More commonly, however, it takes forever, and an astonishing amount of ink. This is only the fresh beginning of a new forever."

But her father and Lord Cral were both clearly and genuinely and openly absorbed by everything she could tell them, and they asked many questions based on what she'd described during her presentation—although Lord Cral asked more, and once or twice when she had felt herself floundering it had seemed to her that her father had deflected Cral's questions by talking about what he had seen during his brief visit. Lord Cral had said more than once, "Cory, we must look again at the possibility of building a human way through the Starclouds."

The second or third time he said this, her father caught her eye and smiled.

She thought, I *must* tell my father. I must tell him I can . . . I could . . . Niahi . . . She looked first at Ebon, standing at her shoulder—just behind her shoulder—in the correct way a bound pegasus in the human court—in the way that no longer seemed at all correct to her. Her eyes shifted to Lrrianay, who smiled at her also, but she could read nothing in his face or posture—she could read nothing of him, like any human failing to read any pegasus, like any human who had never spent three weeks in Rhiandomeer surrounded by pegasi. What if it was only Niahi, aside from Ebon? It could easily be only Niahi.

And at that moment the messenger was announced, a Lightbearer lieutenant. She came from the camp in the Greentops, and she came to report a norindour sighting.

But not of one norindour: of seven.

This was bad enough; there were too many sightings now, of all their old enemies, taralians and norindours, ladons and wyverns. We haven't got any quiet borders left, Danacor had said to his sister. But the sightings were still of ones and twos—unwelcome, especially as they kept coming, but nothing that the now-regular patrols could not deal with.

Not seven. Seven norindours presented a serious danger, even to a regiment. They were bigger than taralians, and they had wings. And norindours were normally solitary, barring breeding pairs. What would bring seven together?

But even that was not all of her news. The rest was much worse: there was a roc with them. A roc that made no attempt to hide itself, who saw them seeing it, and let them look. A roc who was—probably— the reason seven norindours were hunting together. Hunting—what? Even a greyear stag, some of which grew as big as horses, could not feed seven norindours.

"Y-yes, my king," said the messenger upon questioning. "Yes, I was there. It—the roc—is bigger than you—than I—can imagine. It stood there, watching us watch it—watching us fall back—watching us trying not to stumble over each other to get away from it—and then it spread its wings and flew. It . . . it wasn't just that its wings blotted out the sun, that there was darkness over us at midday. The darkness in the shadow of a roc's wings is like the end of the world. . . ."

Taralians are intelligent enough to be deadly enemies; norindours are cleverer than taralians. But rocs are at least as intelligent as humans or pegasi—and they had some powers of magic, possibly powers as strong as human magicians'. A confirmed roc sighting was the worst news the country had had in generations.

Everyone who lived in the king's palace, and everyone who had ever attended one of the high festival days when the king carried the Sword, had seen it flame up at the king's touch, but no one had ever seen it glare and dazzle as it did on this day. The news was already spreading, and people began to pour into the Great Hall to hear what the king would say—this too was reported, while the messenger still stood before the king.

"I—I came as fast as I could, my king," said the messenger. "As fast as I could without foundering my horse. But other people saw the roc, my king."

"Yes. A roc that wishes to be seen will certainly be seen," replied the king. "Go get yourself some food and rest." He put a hand on Sylvi's shoulder. "I'm afraid our previous discussion, infinitely to be preferred though it is, must now wait." He led the way toward the Great Hall, briskly, but not hurriedly. Sylvi, feeling superfluous and lagging a little behind, discovered Glarfin to have materialised at her other elbow. One did not lag with Glarfin at one's elbow. She caught up with her father and Lord Cral, all three pegasi dropping back to allow her more room. They are always behind us, she thought. And Lrrianay is king, and I am only king's daughter.

When the little group paused at the door, Sylvi's father said to her, "Walk with me, young one; we're all we've got at the moment. Danny should be around here somewhere, but everyone else is out on patrol."

The king went up to the burning Sword and laid his hand upon it; Sylvi thought that she would not have touched it if her life depended on it. There was a great shout, or clap of thunder, a sound that was more of a buffet than a noise, that no one afterwards was sure they had heard, and the Sword's light went out. Everyone found themselves gasping for breath; everyone except, perhaps, the king, who had turned to look at his eldest son, who had just appeared in the doorway next to the mural of King Fralialal and had paused, staring at the Sword. From where Sylvi stood at the king's side, her brother's face was in shadow, but she could see that his head was turned toward the Sword.

"I will ride west this afternoon," said Danacor. "The Skyclears are ready."

Danacor went with a party not only of his Skyclears, but also magicians and specialist trackers; he went to the mountain where General Randarl now watched, and where the roc had been seen. Danny had seen the roc—he had seen two rocs, although that was not generally known "—I hope," read the private letter that came with his official report. "We are doing our damnedest to make it only one roc; one roc is bad enough." The chief thing that he stressed and reiterated in all his reports—as well as why they had some prospect of preventing knowledge of the second roc—was that both rocs were still well to the far side of the boundary of the land King Corone called his, at the edge of the wild lands, where only the boldest hunters went, where there were known to be basilisks and chimeras as well as taralians and norindours and ladons and a wyvern or two. This territory had never been claimed by any human government because of the difficulty of administering it—although there were rumours of encampments of humans as wild as any of the beasts, and the occasional mad magician living there.

But if the rocs as yet came no nearer, neither did they go away. It had been two generations since anyone from Balsinland had seen a roc to be sure it was a roc—and more than one had not been seen, even in the wild lands, since the Great Hunt.

Farley took his own company of the Queen's Own to a different mountain, and Farley's company had also seen a roc. The messages he sent made it clear that Farley's roc was a third.

A little over a fortnight after Sylvi's birthday party there was a terrific row—between Thowara and Danacor. Thowara had Poih and

Oyry with him. Danacor had returned long enough to speak to his father in private, and was going out again at once. The pegasi were insisting on going with Danacor and Garren, who was accompanying his brother. Danacor was equally insisting that he did not want to risk them—as he put it. If they came, he said, they must not fly, on account of the norindours, on account of the *rocs*—in which case they should stay away altogether. They replied that this land—Balsinland—lay next to their own Rhiandomeer, and that they were the bound and sworn allies of the sons and daughters of Balsin, which meant that they were bound and sworn to protect Balsin's land, or hadn't Danacor read the treaty lately?

Eight Speakers were present to translate between the two humans and three pegasi—plus Lrrianay and Corone. Corone had sent a message to his daughter, requesting her presence, and so she had to go, however much she shrank from hearing—or not hearing—three humans and four pegasi talking to each other—arguing with each other.

At first she could hear nothing but the ordinary murmur of human voices—the ordinary murmur that was to her no longer ordinary— saying the sort of courtly-negotiation things that typically made her struggle to stay awake. Even in this case the orotund flow of the Speakers' voices—they spoke in a kind of overlapping chant, like a part-song—began to make her feel sleepy. Perhaps this relaxed her concentration till she began to pick out the three separate strands of the conversation: the humans, the Speakers—and the pegasi. She could not hear precisely what the pegasi said, but she felt she could not hear them as one might not be able to hear a lute if a huge drum was thundering away beside it. She *was* hearing the strange singing rhythm of the pegasi silent-speech, and she heard it because it was so different from the rhythms of human speech. She could hear what Danacor said because he was accustomed to addressing crowds, and because when the king's heir or his brother spoke, the other humans fell silent. When a pegasus spoke, a magician, or more than one, spoke at the same time, translating; sometimes a third or fourth magician broke in to add something. Sylvi began to wake up again, and listen hard. And she became uneasily certain that the magicians' translation was less than perfect. By accident or incapacity? Or by design?

I *must* tell my father, she thought. Her thought in his private office, with Lord Cral, before the news of the rocs had arrived, had been put away in the ensuing uproar; and she was half-relieved for the excuse. But she could not hide behind her uncertainty forever: she was looking at a forever about blood, not ink. Perhaps it was not forever, but it was as long as Balsinland had been in existence, and as long as it would remain Balsinland.

Everything was different since her trip to Rhiandomeer. Everything she had thought she understood was changed; how could she recognise or judge anything new? She could not forget being a tall, narrow, top-heavy human with flailing arms surrounded by pegasi; she could not forget the shock of returning to the palace after three weeks in Rhiandomeer. Perhaps I am not hearing the pegasi, she thought; perhaps it's just the strangeness I'm hearing, the strangeness of being here, of pretending to be the old Lady Sylviianel, fourth child of King Corone IV. . . . But the lute-singing in her ears now was only like pegasi silent-speech. She knew what she was hearing, in spite of the strangeness of everything, including the strangeness of hearing the pegasi in Balsinland, where the air seemed to swaddle you round, to both muffle and protect you.

She thought clearly and calmly, I must tell my father. . . . If the magicians would be quiet a moment I *could* hear. . . .

Eliona and Hirishy had joined the company on the low dais at the head of the king's receiving room; Hirishy promptly found a curtain to stand behind. The scattering of courtiers, barons and senators was growing as the word spread what was happening. Once or twice the discussion broke down while Danacor and Thowara merely shouted at each other. Sylvi had never heard a pegasus shout before; it wasn't something the pegasi did. Thowara made a noise like a combination of a horse's neigh and the king's Guild of Heralds on a feast-day: the only time she had heard anything like it was the day that her father had banished Fthoom, when Lrrianay had trumpeted. But today Thowara was not merely louder but angrier. The pegasi were never angry either. And Sylvi was increasingly sure that neither her brothers nor her brothers' pegasi were understanding more than one word in five of what the other was saying—despite the Speakers. What shamans were at the palace? Would it be worth asking—or was that one of the things she dared not do, because it meant that she favoured the pegasi? And perhaps the shamans would be as confused as she was. If Hibeehea were here, would he not be able to create some symmetry to this chaos? But he had left—he was back in Rhiandomeer—because human magic made him ill.

There was a brief pause in the proceedings—while, Sylvi thought, Danacor and Thowara got their breath back—and a rustle behind her, and a silky black head appeared over her shoulder.

I hope I've missed most of this, whatever it is, said Ebon.

I think so, said Sylvi. *I think Thowara's winning. He wants to go with Danacor—he and the others with their bondmates.*

Yes—I know about this. They've been rahmerarahmering about it a while.

374

Thowara's determined to go. He thinks he should take a—take a—what do you call it? Regiment. Of pegasi. With him. There're a lot of volunteers.

Rahmerarahmering was a good word for it. They were going at it again now. The magicians' voices rose as they tried to keep pace.

I . . . Sylvi hesitated. *I'm not sure the magicians are translating as well as . . . as well as we depend on them to.*

Danacor's Speaker was now translating Danacor back to Thowara, who was standing stiffly, head a little bit back so he could look Danacor, who was a tall man, in the eye. Thowara's wings were half roused, but held rigidly back, rather than curved out to the sides. Anger, thought Sylvus. *This is what pegasus anger looks like.*

Should we—no, we're not allowed, the senate and the council are still arguing about us, and Iridin—Why don't your shamans come? In frustration, knowing the answer, she cried out, *Hibeehea speaks human better than I do!*

They've all gone home—you know that. Nmmoor's the only one left, and she wasn't invited here, said Ebon. *Our shamans are never invited, except to parties. Not to the courts.*

*Who told **you**?* said Sylvi. *Who told you to come here?*

Glarfin. He said "Sylviianel" and then led me here. But I should be here. Even if neither one of us is doing any good, even if—

Even if they won't let us try. Should I tell my father—

But at this point Lrrianay stepped forward and slowly—that there could be no mistake—formally and quietly demanded his and his people's rights as set out in the treaty. There was a collective sigh from most of the humans present, because even without the Speakers' translation it was clear by the way Lrrianay stood—every shining hair on his body saying *king,* Sylvi thought—what he was declaring.

And so it was decided that Thowara and his two brothers would go with the human company; with Thowara, and under his command, would go five more, and another ten would follow, as soon as the message went back to Rhiandomeer that they were needed.

And Danacor would be carrying the Sword.

It had happened that way several times before, that the young heir rode out with the Sword while the elder ruler remained in the city, to govern and think and negotiate and plot. King Corone formally handed the Sword over to his eldest son—the Sword having agreed to be so handed—and the ceremony was a brief but very beautiful one. But what was a glorious tale in the history books was grim and awful when it was happening to you.

Dinner on Danacor's last evening was hushed and tense. The king and queen from long practise of difficult conversations did the best, chatting about ordinary things without ignoring the fact that Danacor was riding to war. Several times when runners or other messengers concerning the campaign came to whisper in the king's ear, the king responded as if the whispers were no more alarming than those on the night before a feast day, when the guild of flute-players was feuding with the guild of viol players and there was the dire threat that neither would appear. Danacor tried to take the lead from his father, but was only half successful. His left hand, as if involuntarily, kept touching his belt, where the Sword had hung this afternoon for the first time, and where it would hang tomorrow for . . . no one knew how long. Their pegasi had been present only briefly; Thowara and Oyry had preparations to make for the morrow—and even Ebon had said, *Best I go with my brothers now, dearheart.* Sylvi had nodded, feeling the difference between them again yawning like a void—or like the beak of a roc, which was big enough to catch and swallow a pegasus. Rhiandomeer seemed a million years ago.

Sylvi finally managed, at the end of the evening, to slip up to Danacor to say a private good-bye; and then she could find no words for it.

She looked up at him—she remembered when he was her age now, and she not much more than a toddler, and he had been so big and fine and grand, and she was so proud to have him as her big brother. She had been much more dazzled by the manifest splendour of her big brother than by the fact that her parents were king and queen of the country; being a king and queen seemed chiefly to mean talking to a lot of boring people about boring things (and being a princess seemed to be about being polite to people you didn't want to have to speak to at all, and learning boring indoor book-ink-and-paper lessons even on sunny days), while Danacor was spending his afternoons in the prac- tise yards with the horsemaster and the master-at-arms—and occa- sionally the queen, who didn't like boring indoor things very much either. Sylvi, when she could escape nursemaid and governess, would hang on the fence and watch.

Her mother told her years later that her governess had let her es- cape far oftener than a stricter or more traditionalist educator would have. The young woman gravely told the queen that fresh air was al- ways good for a growing child, and that since children will find people to idolise, it seemed to her a good thing to indulge the lady Sylviianel in idolising such a fine young man.

The queen told this story grinning at the memory: "Scai was such a *serious* young woman. Her mother had stood in your grandmother's army, and it makes me wonder what effect it had on her child- rearing."

Warfare. It had just been a proud glorious game, when Sylvi was four and six and eight and Danacor was sixteen and eighteen and twenty. Even when he had begun to take his turn on patrol, for they had since Balsin's day patrolled the border with the wild lands, she had felt no fear. No taralian had a hope of getting the best of her brother; any taralian with any sense would see him and run away. She looked up at him now, the night before he rode out with the Sword at his side, and remembered the tall boy in the practise yards. Danacor looked down at her and smiled, but he didn't seem to have anything to say either.

"I'll come watch you ride out," she said at last. "As I used to watch you in the practise yards, when you were learning. . . ." Her voice trailed away.

"Yes," he said, as if he knew exactly what she was thinking. He put his hand on her shoulder, and then looked at her again as if reconsidering something he had previously discarded. "You're growing!" he said, and this time his smile reached his eyes. "You *are* growing! Syl, you're growing at last. Soon you'll need a special *low* chair to sit at table with the rest of us," he said, teasing her, but she burst out—

"I'm not! I'm *not* growing!"

Danacor looked startled, and dropped his hand. "Well, you are, you know, but I thought you'd be pleased. I thought you always hated being small."

She couldn't tell him about Ebon and flying, so instead she muttered the first thing she could think of: "I'm sorry. It's just—everything is changing." Has already changed.

"Yes," he said again. His eyes strayed to the door. They'd had dinner in the Little Hall off the Great Hall where the Sword still hung for one more night. "Well, it does. Everything changes. But I'll be back, Sylvi, love. That won't change." He stooped and kissed her, and soon after that the melancholy party finished breaking up, everyone going to an early bed, for there would be much to do tomorrow for everyone.

Again that night Sylvi had difficulty sleeping, to the dismay of the hounds who had lately learnt to like sharing the princess' bed. She got up at last (to the hounds' relief), and put her dressing gown on, and went and sat on the window-sill. There was no moon, and the sky was low and dark with cloud; even the air was oppressive, and she could hear more voices and movements than she should be able to at such an hour—on any night that the heir was not riding out the next day carrying the Sword into battle. Restlessly she stood up again, and went to a little chest that stood on a shelf next to one of her sky holds, and opened it.

It had previously held hair ribbons, but with her sixteenth birthday she would use these rarely any more, and had moved them to the back of a shelf in her wardrobe, incongruously near the hook where her sword now hung. The little chest now contained small souvenirs of her journey to Rhiandomeer: a bright blue feather from an unknown bird, a yellow leaf from a seehar tree (seehars did not grow in Balsinland), a loop of badly plaited llyri grass—badly because she'd done it herself. The little vial of water from the Dreaming Sea. Her hand hesitated over this for a moment, picked it up and held it so that she was looking through it, toward the grey rectangle of the window. She breathed out slowly. *Ssshuuwuushuu.* . . .

The water in the little vial moved—expanded—no; her hand held the tiny bottle as before. But her vision sharpened, focussed. . . .

She saw the roc first: yellow-gold, tawny, huge, so huge that it was several moments before she saw that it moved in response to . . . a tiny human. A tiny pegasus. *One* tiny human. *One* tiny pegasus. No, that was not possible; she sucked her breath in in horror, because in the next moment she would see them killed. . . .

And with her gasp the vision was gone, and her hand holding the vial was shaking. She laid the vial back in the chest, unwillingly remembering what she had seen: the tawny roc, the bright red-gold pegasus, the human in battle leathers holding a short sword in one hand and a spear in the other—a spear shorter than one of the roc's toenails, a sword shorter than one of its pinfeathers. When the pegasus had spread its great wings—a blow from a pegasus' wing could break a taralian's back—they looked as tiny as the palms of Sylvi's hands. She stared unseeingly at the other contents of the chest for some minutes, till the remains of the vision left her.

Aliaalia had given her one of the pegasi's little embroidered bags as a farewell gift, and Sylvi had put Ebon's bead in it—the bead she'd worn round her neck during her six days in the Caves. She hadn't looked at it since she'd been home.

She tipped it slowly out into the palm of her hand. It lay there, dark, inert—dead. She closed her hand over it and felt as if something inside her were breaking. Her heart? Her will? She squeezed both her hand and her eyes shut. And then slowly opened them again.

As if it had taken a moment to wake up, sleepy after too long a nap, the bead was just beginning to glow, with a faint throb like a heart. At first she thought she was imagining it, but as she watched, the glow strengthened and steadied, till it was so bright she could not see her hand behind it.

For several weeks there was little news; Danacor sent terse descriptions, tied to the legs of carrier-pigeons, of quartering the lower slopes of the boundary mountains. Then a dusty, distressed pigeon missing a few primaries brought the news of the first skirmish; there were a few wounded—although neither Danacor nor his brothers, nor any pegasus—but no one killed. A human messenger on a tired horse brought more news, and, when he returned, he took a packhorse with him, loaded with small padded cages containing more carrier pigeons. About a week after that, a pegasus—no one Sylvi knew—came with more news, both what he could tell and a letter from Danacor hung round his neck in a little bag like a nrala: he was closeted with Corone, Lrrianay and Fazuur for several hours.

The day after he left, Garren rode in through the northwest gate of the Wall with Poih at his side.

Sylvi and Ebon went at once to the king's receiving room to hear Garren's report. The scouts, crossing the border and going deep in the wild lands, had discovered the mouths of caves leading—they suspected, as far as they dared explore, as much as the magicians with them could guess—to a great network of underground caves; and the passages they did explore were clearly used by taralians and norindours. Garren looked old and grim and determined. "This is not something Danny wanted to send a messenger with, even a messenger who had seen the caves himself. So I said we'd go, Poih and I. And we could bring more troops back.

"We had Doarday up to take a look, and he believes that there are many more of both taralians and norindours than we have any idea of—that they have been hiding and growing and increasing for a long time. Maybe generations. We should have been keeping better watch . . . but the truth is that we would still not have found the caves if we hadn't been searching that specific area—"

"Which means that the rocs wanted us to find them," said the king. "That this is something they have been planning. Neither taralians nor norindours plan far in advance; their great cleverness is on the immediate field of battle, when they can see openings and possibilities that slow humans cannot—and pegasi are too honourable to take such advantage. Nor do the two races live together. All this is, I fear, the doing of rocs."

Sylvi listened without understanding the details to the rest of the conversation; it ended when the king said, "I will write it down and send a messenger with it now. You need food and sleep, and a regiment cannot move as quickly as a single horse and rider, especially a quick horse and a clever rider."

"If it please you, sir," said Sylvi. "There is no one quicker or cleverer than Lucretia."

"Indeed," said the king. "If you can spare her, Sylviianel, please send for her."

Spare her, thought Sylvi. She's so edgy and impatient she's become the scourge of the practise yards. We'll be glad to see her go.

"We cannot know what the rocs' plan is," said Garren, "and Danny says that for now we must do the obvious thing—drive the creatures out of their burrows and destroy them—and watch our backs. How soon can the Second Horse Guards be ready to leave?"

"Tomorrow," said the king. "I don't guarantee before breakfast, but before noon. I will see if there is a company or two of someone else we can spare as well; because if the rocs are putting their plan, whatever it is, into action, then we must assume we need more eyes actively watching here too.

"That gives you time for food and sleep. And I would have you talk to the queen; she is out on patrol, but she will be here this evening. She hunted taralians in those mountains."

Garren nodded. "She kept telling us to look for caves—especially a network of caves. Ginab wasn't enthusiastic and even Doarday thought it unlikely."

"She'll be sorry she was right."

"Yes." Garren's smile had no humour in it. He paused long enough to hug Sylvi—without ever quite seeing her, she thought—and left.

Sylvi made to do the same herself. She had already sent a footman to look for Lucretia; it was as well she had someone to send, because her own limbs felt heavy, and her thinking stunned. Taralians and norindours living underground— many of them—ready to pour out upon the country—her country. She could not grasp it—she could not make herself understand that the king would be putting extra watchers on the Wall in response to Garren's report—that warehouses and under-used buildings inside the Wall would be readied for refugees, or wounded. What she could grasp was that Danacor and Farley, and Garren again soon, were in terrible danger. A terrible danger that, if they could not contain it, would indeed spread over the entire country . . . and at last come here, to the king's city within its Wall, to the palace, to her home.

She put out a hand blindly and encountered Ebon's shoulder. *Bad*, he said.

Very bad.

They turned to leave, but her father beckoned to them. There was a new look on his face. She could never remember a time when he did not seem tired and needing to think about too many things at once, most of which he would not or could not explain to his daughter. But always before he could set it aside occasionally, and play with her or tease her brothers or swing her mother around in an impromptu dance—he was an excellent dancer—or engage them all in a ballad-composing contest, which he would win unless all five of them united to outdo him. This new tiredness was of a sort that could not be set aside, till the end of some great matter was reached. She wished she could see it in his face that he believed that the end would be reached as he wished it to be. Lrrianay walked a few paces away from the human king, and Ebon followed him; Sylvi could hear a faint rustle of pegasus speech. She missed Niahi, and Niahi's gaiety and sparkle. Niahi had flown home with her mother two days after the party, with the shamans. But with this news even Niahi's brightness might go dull.

"I have seen Fthoom," her father said, and sighed. "I am sorry, child—sorry for all of us. But he demands to give his report. I hear in his voice that it is a report that pleases him, which means it will not please us. Those of his assistants who report to me say that he found something not long ago that pleased him tremendously, but they do not know what it is. I have said that we have other, mightier concerns on our hands, but Fthoom says that what he will tell us has great import upon those mightier concerns. You know of the petition to reinstate him—he has hinted all these four years that we need his strength; he says almost openly now that we will need it worse when we hear what he has to say.

"He says he brings proof of the tale that he will tell, and on my orders he spent yesterday in the Hall of Magicians, being grilled by his own. Andovan and Fahlraken have brought me the guilds' confirmation that what he says is true and that his proof is true proof, though they do not know what of any more than I do. I trust their word, and I trust the Hall."

It was one of the purposes of the Hall of Magicians that any magician standing in it had to tell the truth. It had been Gandam's idea that there should be somewhere in the palace of the monarch where not even the cleverest magician would be able to beguile and deceive. It did not work as well as Gandam had hoped, perhaps because his own powers had been failing when he laid its five cornerstones; but as Ahathin had explained, somewhat drily, to Sylvi some years before, it was at least a good deal harder to lie in the Hall of Magicians than out of it. A determined panel of questioners could get at the truth—or so it had been believed for eight hundred years. Andovan and Fahlraken were two of the oldest members of the magicians' guilds, and had been in the service of the monarch all that time—they were among the few magicians who were neither dazzled nor frightened by Fthoom. Neither of them had been present four years before, when the king had banished him.

"Sylviianel," said her father, calling her back to the present, "I have agreed to listen to him. I can do nothing else; I do not have the time to waste to keep putting him off—even more so now that we have heard Garren's news."

Sylvi thought, I do not want to depend on Fthoom's strength. I do not want to know that there are times when the king can do only what he wants not to do. I do not want to hear my father say to me, I can do nothing else. I wish that Danny and Garren and Farley and the folk with them were home safe—and that the Second Horse Guards were not going anywhere tomorrow. I wish those caves were empty. I wish that there were no caves. . . .

I wish I had never come home from Rhiandomeer.

I must tell Dad . . . tell him what? That I could talk to the other pegasi in their own country, but that I—I don't know how reliable it is now that I'm home again? That I am not reliable now that I am home again? That I see things in little bottles of water? That the air I breathe in Balsinland is heavy in a way the air in Rhiandomeer is not? That I agree with the pegasi that what is wrong between us is something about our magicians—our magic? That I think so because I met Dorogin in the pegasi Caves? Dorogin, who has been dead for seven hundred years?

That I am allying myself with the pegasi against my own people? Isn't that exactly what Fthoom would want, so he could exile *me*?

She put her hand to her throat, as if she could not breathe, as if she could not speak. I wish I might have had one more flight with Ebon. I wish we might have had one more afternoon lying on the grass in the sunlight, even knowing the end is coming. I wish. . . .

They had not gone flying since she had returned from Rhiandomeer. They had not been flying, therefore, just the two of them as they had once done whenever Ebon was at the palace, since before her journey to his homeland—a time that now seemed so long ago she could barely remember it.

Perhaps they had never been flying, just the two of them, with Ebon's mane tangling her own hair, and the world framed by his wings. Perhaps she had imagined it. Perhaps she had imagined that she could talk to the pegasi.

She wished she had imagined it.

She had said to her mother, How can everything change in three weeks? Three little weeks. Her mother had smiled and answered, Sometimes they change in a moment.

Her father continued, "I have given Fthoom a conference for the day after tomorrow. You and Ebon will attend, of course." He stood up. "I must talk to Lrrianay." As he looked around for his bondmate, Lrrianay turned his head as if he had heard his name spoken, and Fazuur materialised at the king's elbow. The king turned back to his daughter for a moment and put his hands on her shoulders and stared at her as if she held some answer to an important question.

"Dad—" she began, nerving herself to ask him for a moment of private speech, to tell him what she had to tell him, but as she said it her voice cracked, and he didn't hear her.

The same look she had seen in Danacor's eyes the last evening came into her father's. "You're growing!" he said.

She bit her lip. But she replied, "Yes. I know. I am."

CHAPTER 19

There were many more people present for Fthoom's report than there had been on the day, four years ago, when the king had plucked the magician's spiral from Fthoom's head and sent him away. Sylvi had been surprised when Glarfin had reported that the meeting would occur in the Little Hall—which was little only in comparison to the Great Hall—rather than the king's private receiving room. That meant that this was not only a semipublic occasion but that many people were expected to attend. Glarfin would be there again, as he had been four years ago; but this only made her remember his leaping in front of her, to protect her from Fthoom.

Ebon knew the business was serious, but he refused to admit that he took it as seriously as Sylvi had to. His response to Fthoom's prospective return from exile was, *Pity. Any day you see that great rolling barrel in the corridor is a blighted day.* And then, sadly, in a tone that sounded eerily like his father, *I don't understand why your magicians grow so—so—umblumbulum,* which was a pegasus word that meant, roughly, out of order. Pegasi did not use words like "belligerent" and "aggressive" about their friends and allies, and—she guessed—would hesitate to use such words about any human. Even "powerful" implied the misuse of that power, because why did you possess so much of it? Power existed to be given away. She had seen over and over again how his people approached Lrrianay, had seen how different it was from how his people approached her father—her father who was the kindest and quietest of men—far more like Lrrianay than Fthoom.

She thought again—as she often, involuntarily thought—of Dorogin's stony eyes in his stony face, staring out at her from the Cave wall, and his stony smile, all saying, *Too late.*

And Gandam's, saying, *Try.*

Sylvi said sadly, *I don't know either.* But magic was a power as her father's sovereignty was a power, which was why no magician was allowed to accept as a student any member of the nobility or of royalty—except on very rare occasions when the student renounced his or her family, or their family renounced them—nor was a magician allowed to marry a member of royalty or blood either, so that the available forms of power could not mount up dangerously in one individual or one rank.

Redfora could not have existed. She was just a story the pegasi told. A story that could seem to come to life when told by a wily old shaman like Hibeehea.

Sylvi wished she could gouge out the look in Dorogin's stony eyes, and change the course of history. She wished Fthoom had been eaten by a sea monster.

The thrum of suppressed excitement from the Little Hall was audible from a long way off. Well, these corridors do echo, she told herself, marching down the stairs from her attic office, where she had been pretending to read an historical survey of the reign of Queen Egelair III, during which nothing at all had happened except that the crops were excellent year after year and the children healthy and the people long-lived and happy—and the magicians calm and restrained—and

Sylvi stared at the paragraphs and wondered why the reign of King Corone IV could not have been similarly boring. Ahathin, who today had been sitting at the other end of the same table, kindly forbore to point out that she hadn't turned a page in half an hour. Perhaps he hadn't turned a page either. Ahathin would come with her today—she had asked him to—if what Fthoom had to say was so ill it stopped her thoughts, Ebon should still know what was said.

She had dreaded the occasion even more since she found out that she and Ebon would have to enter the Hall immediately behind, and at the same time as, the two kings, her father and Lrrianay. As mere fourth children they should have come in either earlier or later, with a minimum of fuss, and would ordinarily have been given places less prominent than the king's chief ministers and the highest-ranking senator and blood present. Or than whatever unfortunate person or group of people was the centre of attention.

But she and Ebon were the centre of attention. She and Ebon and Fthoom.

It was not the noise that struck at her the worst when she came through the door behind her father. It was the tension. It was like walking into glue; she had to stop herself from struggling to escape, wrenching herself backwards, wiping at her face with her hands as if something thick and sticky and clinging were smothering her. She thought Ebon had shivered very slightly when he'd come through the door at her shoulder. She wanted to say something to him— anything—just to hear him answer her, but even their silent speech felt unsafe.

That Ahathin and three footmen flanked them as they entered made it worse, not better: that Glarfin bowed her to her chair and another footman bowed Ebon to his place beside her made it worse, not better, even though she knew that her father was saying, *This is my daughter, this is the pegasus king's son bound to her, and you will do well to remember it* in king-language, a language of gesture as clear as any tail-lashing and wing-rousing.

Fthoom was there already. Sylvi had hoped that his bare head would diminish him as it had four years ago, but it did not. He was wearing a different cloak, and while it stood out around him as the old one had, the collar had been redesigned, and was heavily embroidered with the public symbols of the magician's art. It was worse—again it was worse, Sylvi thought, that he should look so potent and compelling without his magician's spiral. This was a collar to complement bareheadedness, to make a new fashion in magicianry. None of the other magicians present were wearing spirals; Gornchern and Topo always did, on any and all occasions. But they were bareheaded today. Fahlraken was wearing a single low coil, as he usually did; Andovan was always bareheaded; they stood near the back, together, looking grim.

Immediately in front of the dais stood a young magician she had not seen before, dressed in the long blue robe of a bearer, with the silver chain of truth witnessed round his neck. In his arms he carried a long thin object that might have been a scroll wrapped in a light fabric. He was standing near her chair, and she could see that the fabric was stamped and woven with protective sigils. These caught at her eyes like a hand grasping her arm. She found herself thinking of a great tawny roc, and a red pegasus, and a human with a spear and a sword.

She turned away from Fthoom, from the bearer, from everyone, glad of the excuse not only not to face any magicians for a moment, but to remind herself she could and, at this moment, as she entered the Little Hall and settled herself in her place, should. In formal Court, as this was, you did not turn your back on your betters. She was reminding herself and all the Court that she was a princess, and Fthoom was only a magician. With the roc of her vision still tugging at her attention she thought suddenly of the rocs and taralians and norindours, the ladons and the wyverns of Garren's report, and their leagues of dark tunnels and unknown exits—and hoped that Danny and Garren and Farley always had good eyes and good swords at their backs. For a moment her own eyes were dazzled blue, not the midnight blue of the bearer's robe, but as if Danacor stood in front of her, and unsheathed the Sword: but at least the blue flare banished the tawny roc.

She climbed the three steps to her chair, and then she had to turn round again and sit down, and face Fthoom. She was still taller than he, even sitting, on the king's dais, and her head was level with Ebon's, who was standing at her side. Ebon looked at her once—an unreadable, unfathomable, silent look—and then faced out, inscrutable as a black statue of a pegasus. She hoped her own face was as expressionless. Ahathin, with the faintest *tock* of Speaker sticks, took his place beside Ebon.

A herald announced that the Court was present on this day of six sixes after the vertex of spring at the request of the magician Fthoom and the sanction of the king; and herewith it begins.

Fthoom stepped forward, his cloak rustling. "My kings," he said, and knelt, in precisely his old unmindful gesture. Rising to his feet again he plunged into speech, eager as a child at a party. His eyes glittered—like jewels in sunlight, not like human eyes at all. "My kings," he said again. "I have done as my king bade me, and studied the records in the royal libraries for all mention of friendship between pegasus and human beyond the binding defined in the Treaty of Alliance. Years this work has taken me, as you know, for there have been many records to study and many reports to consider and weigh; and my work was the harder in that most of those chronicles which dealt specifically with such relationships did not tell plainly of their outcome. I had to use all my skill—all my skill and all my helpers' skill—to extrapolate what lay hidden: and still no clear picture emerged."

Which is to say that you found no support at all for your hateful theory and you were working away like anything to think of ways to discredit what you did find, thought Sylvi—and she thought this louder than she realised, for there was a silent hum of agreement from Ebon. But this gave her no comfort; Fthoom had not demanded an audience to declare defeat.

She felt a sense of dread as strong as if Fthoom were to announce a tawny roc waiting for them, now, this minute, in the Great Court.

"Until, but a few months ago, I had a dream. While I have also been suspended from my position in the Guild of Magicians, I have not lost my expertise."

Sylvi, listening hard, thought that for the first time his voice sounded a little too emphatic, and thought, something good may yet come of this, if his power in that guild has been shaken. She wanted to look at her father, but she didn't dare; and she also knew that he, of everyone in the Court that day, would never allow anything to be read on his face.

"I had a dream, and I knew at once that it was an important dream. In this dream I saw myself in a far corner of one of the libraries—the farthest oldest corner of our king's great library—a corner where such fragments of text as have little worth are stored. And in a corner of this corner I laid my hand upon a stone, and found that it was loose in the wall, and drew it out, and found a parchment roll in the dark hollow behind it, old and brown and fragile."

Sylvi wanted to shout, I don't believe you! I don't believe you! It's a trick! What you say you found—if you found anything—you put there for yourself to find!

The young bearer shifted his position and a breath of alien air fanned across Sylvi's face with a smell of hot metal and blood.

"My dream, as you will have guessed, spoke truly. I went to the corner of the library, and I found that stone—but it was not loose in the wall, and had I not spells to loosen it, it would remain there still, and its secret dark behind it; and had I not had the dream I would not have recognised the stone that I needed to loosen. This stone has the ancient symbol for lightning etched upon it, as guard and ward; but it itself had been warded, that no one might see there was something there defended, for whoever hid this thing badly wanted none to find it. And had I—I—not been so absorbed—consumed—by my desire to fulfil my obligation to my king that even my dreaming self did continue the search on planes of being and perception I cannot reach awake, I too might have passed it by. As it was I spoke certain subtle words of power, and I drew the lightning-blazed stone out, and there I found the parchment roll."

Fthoom paused, sure of his audience. "That parchment roll," he said, his voice now low, and slippery as oil on a plate, "tells a story of the reign of King Ascur II, who was also twelfth of his line."

Ascur II, thought Sylvi frantically. Ascur II—she could remember a little about him because he did not have a placid reign like Egelair III, and he made more interesting reading—what—there was a war, and the crown went to a cousin—it was a long time ago, long before the Great Hunt—some of the palace got knocked down—*the war had rocs in it*—

"In the days of Ascur II, there was a deadly invasion of taralians, norindours, ladons and wyverns, and led by rocs. The kingdom was hard-pressed by these creatures, and whether Ascur's forces or the opposing army would win at last was often in doubt. The war stretched on for years, with neither side able to claim a decisive victory.

"Ascur had three sons; the youngest was named Tilbad. He was bound, at the age of twelve, to the pegasi king's third child, a daughter, Erex."

Three children? But the crown went to a cousin. The Sword chose—I can't remember *anything*—

She heard the echo of a great—a vast—hoarse shriek, perhaps like the sound that a roc might make—she shook her head to clear it. No, she was imagining this, as she was imagining the tawny roc of her vision in the Great Court.

"The war broke out several years after this binding: four years, in fact, although the two events appeared to have nothing in common. When Tilbad reached the age of seventeen, he and Erex joined the army and they were, the records tell us, very valiant. But the army—including Tilbad and Erex—were now driven back till they were fighting within the palace Wall—the Wall which was still of some defense against taralians, but its magic was failing as the strength of Ascur's armies failed.

"The battle went ill for Ascur's army; so ill, at last, that the Wall was breached, and the palace fired. So much all our histories tell us. But this is where the lightning-guarded scroll takes up the story:

"The palace was torched and burning, and there were only scattered handfuls of defenders left. Everyone who could be sent away had been sent long ago; Ascur was now trying to gather what remained of his forces for a tactical retreat—even though he knew there was nowhere left to retreat to.

"His messages had gone out, and his soldiers gathered slowly round him. Those who came did not include Tilbad and Erex, although no one could say they had seen them fall; and as the beaten remnants of the army crept through what had once been the parkland surrounding the palace of the king, they saw Tilbad and Erex—fighting a roc. Alone.

"I assume you all know how large a roc is? Even the smallest of them can pick up a war-horse with one claw and its armoured rider with the other, and fly away with them. One man—and one pegasus—cannot possibly defeat a roc alone.

"And so Ascur watched in great anguish, waiting to see the death of his third son, for two of his sons had perished already, and he was himself sore wounded, and his horse killed, and he could not go to Tilbad's aid; nor were any of his soldiers in any better state, and Ascur feared any fumbling interference would only bring about the deaths of Tilbad and Erex the sooner. The only magician present lay half delirious on a rough pallet. His own pegasus—Erex's father, the pegasus king—stood trembling beside him, his broken wing tied awkwardly over his back. Time, for Ascur, slowed.

"And, because it slowed, and because of the great pain and distress of mind he was in, which sharpened his perceptions almost past bearing, he noticed something more clearly than he had ever done before: the curiously intense partnership of Tilbad and Erex. It was almost as if they could talk to each other—as if they could hear each other's thoughts. They moved around the roc as if each knew what the other was doing—even when they were out of sight of each other—what each was trying to do, and would do next. They covered for each other in ways no ordinary human soldiers, nor any ordinary pair of bound Excellent Friends, should have been able to do.

"It was at the moment Ascur was saying these things to himself that the truly impossible thing happened: Tilbad slew the roc. But in dancing out of the way of the roc's sword-sharp beak one last time—

for the death throes of a roc are also deadly to the smaller folk within its long reach—Erex stumbled with weariness. And a ladon which had been waiting its chance thudded down upon her, and broke her back, and she fell lifeless to the earth.

"Then the second miracle happened: for the roc, instead of seizing Tilbad as he threw himself heedlessly upon the body of his friend, seized the *ladon*—and squeezed the breath out of it, and tossed its body down to lic beside Erex.

"Everyone knows that a roc speaks truth as it dies, although rarely is the truth it speaks welcome. This roc opened its beak, and its dark blood dripped upon the ground. 'A curse upon that ladon, and a curse upon its children, and its children's children's children. For we have come within a breath of taking this land back from the inimical humans and the skulking pegasi which allied themselves with the invaders; and by the deed of one ladon we will lose all.

"'For that alliance is rotten at the heart of it; humans are set apart from the other creatures of the earth, and no other race may bind itself to them. You have been protected by the weakness of the binding between your two races, in that human and pegasus cannot speak each other's language and be understood. Have you not wondered why this should be so? That it takes your best magicians' best efforts to make any communication possible? The pegasus shamans gave it up generations ago; to save their miserable skins they forbore to tell you humans the truth. The truth is that your selves, your spirits, your *beings*, are absolutely opposed to each other: to draw you closer together is to press the sword point to your own hearts.'"

Ebon was hearing Fthoom through Sylvi—in her anguish the story poured through her; it was as if she were shouting at him. It would have been better if he had heard it from Ahathin, a story translated from another world, as if nothing to do with him. She wished she could hold it off, close that door, turn her face away from her best friend—no, she needed him to hear what she was hearing, and what use to protect him? She heard the faint creak of feathers as his wings flattened; she heard Fazuur, who was translating for Lrrianay, stumble over the soft pegasi syllables, and could imagine his nimble, speaking hands suddenly drop motionless to his sides; had his silent-speech also stuttered to a halt?

She had not noticed that the smell of blood and death had grown stronger; only that her sense of despair was growing as huge as the wingspread of a roc.

" 'Your son and your daughter, they who lie now at my feet, they could speak to each other. And by that speaking they have indeed bound your two races closer together; but that closeness is a wound, and the blood and breath of each is poisonous to the other, and the bodies of your two races are dying of it. When this war was first mooted, I was one of those who spoke against it: the humans are too strong, I said. And I have been amazed that it is not so. I have been amazed, till this last half hour.'

"The roc gasped, and the death rattle was in its breast. 'This ladon, this single, wretched creature, has ruined all that; for the partnership is broken too soon. Such a thing will not come again for generations— generations upon generations—and I—I—I will not be here to see it.' And the roc drew in one last, terrible, rasping breath, and died.

"Ascur, not knowing what else to do, went to his son, and attempted to lift him, but his own wounds prevented him; and he said, 'We must get away from here; there is nothing you can do for Erex.' Tilbad rose to his feet, but his gaze was turned inward, and it was as though he did not see that his own father stood before him sore injured. He said, 'I will die of this wound, Father,' though there was no mark on him.

"And so it was, for Tilbad died twenty-three months later, having lived long enough to be a part of the driving of the remaining rocs and their allies out of his father's kingdom, for as if upon the death of Erex, the human army rallied; it grew stronger and fiercer than anyone who had stood with Ascur that day and watched Tilbad kill a roc would have believed possible. Tilbad saw peace re-established, and the farmers growing a new year's crops untroubled in their old fields, and the stock fattening, and children playing in the meadows.

"It was said of Tilbad that from the moment of Erex's death he never smiled, nor spoke any word that was not absolutely necessary; and that he fought tirelessly, and took risks no sane man would take— and lived; which is as some men do, from a grief too great for them to bear. And when Tilbad had seen that his father's land—his own land—our sweet green land—was safe again, he disappeared. But when the news had come to the king that Tilbad could not be found, the king blanched, saying nothing, but rose from his chair and went at once to Erex's grave. Few pegasi are buried within the palace Wall, but Tilbad had begged this favour of both his father and Erex's, and so she had been buried in a little private glade some distance from the palace, in a place no one would notice or go, unless they wished to visit her grave. And there Tilbad's breathless body was found, curled up on its side, head resting near the head of the grave. And there was no mark on him."

Sylvi was paralysed. She could feel her mouth fallen a little open, feel her body bent a little forward and resting its weight on her two clenched hands on the chair-arms, her elbows bent up and behind her like rudimentary wings. In her mind a tiny voice said, And what wound was it Tilbad died of? The loss of his friend or the lie the roc told? Rocs speak the truth when they are dying, her conscience answered miserably; it is in the histories. They speak the truth when they are dying, and they live almost forever—if that roc hadn't been killed, it might be one of those facing us now; those we face might remember it, and remember its death. But the tiny wild voice replied, Who says they tell the truth? And what truth do they *not* tell?

Ebon still stood like a stone pegasus.

The bearer moved very slightly again, causing the faintest *hush* sound of his robe against the sigil-stamped fabric, or of the fabric against whatever it protected.

The smell of blood and death was overwhelming.

Since she had never heard such a thing before, Sylvi did not at first recognise the sound of her father shouting for silence over the tumult in the Little Hall. That there was tumult around her did not register with her at all, the tumult in her mind and heart was so much greater—the tumult inside her, and Ebon's silence. Why was he not saying what she wished to say—that Fthoom was a liar, that this story was a fabrication created of Fthoom's overwhelming greed for power, a power potentially threatened by her and Ebon, by the flood of eager suggestions Iridin was putting into order. Ebon's silence and still-ness was as if a part of her were missing; as if a leg or an arm, hitherto faithful, had simply ceased to answer her wishes. And with that she realised for the first time how much a part not just of her life but of *herself* he was.

And in that same moment she realised that she would lose him.

Again she heard the ghostly cry of a roc, but this time she knew it was a cry of triumph.

Her father was on his feet, shouting. The king never had to raise his voice to be heard; he was the king, and his subjects listened. But many people were shouting: Fthoom, and the magicians with him— and Fazuur was at the front of the dais, on his knees, shouting at them—and some of the courtiers, as well as the king. Most of the ministers, the senators and the blood looked dazed, but Senator Barnum was waving his arms and shouting too. . . . Sylvi found that she had also come to her feet as if the noise were a sea that threatened to drown her, and she was straining to hold her head above water. Someone's hands were holding her up, grasping her upper arms, and she knew without looking that the hands belonged to Glarfin, and she leaned into them as she struggled for some—any—clarity of mind.

She turned her head and that link at least was still there, for Ebon moved at last, and turned his head at the same moment as she turned hers, and they stared into each other's eyes, each reading shock and love and despair in the other's.

Sylvi—

Ebon—

We'll never forget—

They're wrong—wrong—

We are bound—

That is the true thing—

Never forget—you are my heart's—

And then a sound like the end of the world broke in even on their silent speech, for Lrrianay was standing on his hind legs and trumpeting a great belling cry: This was little like his shout four years ago, nor yet that of his son a few months ago. This was a war-cry, the sound of someone who goes into battle knowing already that the battle is lost, but knowing it must be fought, even if he dies of it. Sylvi said, *Oh, Lrrianay, you are also my father, and Aliaalia is my mother, and Niahi is my sister . . .* but she doubted he heard her.

No one had ever heard such a noise indoors before; pegasus bodies, with their hollow bones and vast airways are more resonant sounding-boards than most musical instruments, and Lrrianay was angry. He spread his great wings, and footmen and ministers scrambled out of the way, and the draft of just that first sweep open blew Sylvi's hair back. Again she smelt the Rhiandomeer smell of earth and flowers, and this time it smelled like good-bye.

Those who knew no word of the pegasi language could nonetheless hear what he was saying, with his ears flat back like an angry horse's but his eyes much brighter and fiercer and more intelligent than any horse: *Quiet! Quiet! There will be order in this place! I say so, Lrrianay, king of the pegasi!*

Sylvi, even in her desolation, saw Fthoom, who had come so far forward that he was leaning over the edge of the dais with the lustre of triumph rising off him like a stench, step back and fall silent.

Quiet fell quickly, and Lrrianay dropped back to four legs and drew his wings together again, though they would not settle, and his feather-hands were spread like fans. He might have knocked half the people off the dais, had he been even a little careless, but he had reared immediately behind his bondmate, and so briefly Corone had been haloed as if he too had wings. There was a little fox-fire glint on many pegasus wings, but it was very strong now on Lrrianay, and tiny kinked rainbows ran dizzyingly from his shoulders.

Fleetingly he put his nose to Corone's temple as if returning a mandate briefly borrowed—and Sylvi registered that Lrrianay actually touched him, as she felt Ebon's velvet nose briefly touching her own cheek. Corone's face was cold and angry, and Sylvi was so confused and unhappy that she wondered if perhaps he was angry at her and Ebon. If it were not for them, none of this would be happening . . . and perhaps . . . No, no, Fthoom was lying!

The room was now as unnaturally silent as it had been unnaturally noisy a moment before; the young bearer seemed to have stopped breathing. Corone spoke quietly, but everyone present heard every word. "This is a great matter that has been set before us, and the king must respond to it at once. The king's daughter and Lrrianay's son

402

shall be kept apart from this moment, until those who may understand such affairs have looked into this one with the care and caution vital in a situation which may bear upon the future of the entire country. If what Fthoom has revealed to us today is as simple as it appears, he has done us a very great service."

The king paused. Fthoom smiled, and again it seemed to Sylvi that his eyes glittered queerly. But to her now there was nothing human about him—he was a taralian, a norindour, a roc; how strange it was that he should stand upright and wear a human magician's robe. She shivered as if her father had struck her, but if Glarfin's hands had not still held her arms, she might have thrown herself at Fthoom and tried to draw his blood till his magic turned her into a pebble or a worm. Ebon stood with his feet slightly splayed, as if he too were holding himself back, and Sylvi half noticed that there was another, smaller pegasus standing half in front of him, her shoulder against his, although she was not big enough to hold him if he could not hold himself: Hirishy.

"However," the king continued, and he spoke very slowly and clearly, "Fthoom brings himself no honour in the means by which he chose to announce this discovery. He has produced disarray and disrespect in the king's Court, and this in itself is an offense against his monarch and his country. But I hold you responsible for a more grievous crime"—and there was a sharp general intake of breath at these words, for the king never spoke directly to a miscreant; this was very nearly declaring a personal vendetta—"that of causing unnecessary pain to my daughter, the king's child, and to the pegasus she is bound to, who is the son of the pegasi king who is himself bound to me. This news would be terrible to our two beloved children under any circumstances, and they need not have suffered it on public display."

Fthoom had stopped smiling.

"You will turn over your findings—*all* your findings—to such magicians as I shall appoint.

"And then I wish never to see your face again.

"This meeting is ended."

The well-trained housefolk leaped to open the doors, their muscles taking over while their confounded minds stood still, and the equally confounded audience began to pull itself together and file out. Little jerky bits of conversation began and broke off, and no one looked up at the faces of those on the dais; at most a few glanced sideways, at knees and feet and hoofs. Fthoom left with the rest, but Sylvi did not notice, for as soon as her father had stopped speaking, she pulled herself free of Glarfin's hands and ran to him, throwing her arms around his waist and burying her face in his chest, weeping and weeping and weeping as if she might die of it; and rather than setting her on her own feet kindly and firmly and reminding her that she was a princess, he wrapped his own arms around her and rocked her gently back and forth as if she had been a much younger child, saying, "Oh, my darling, I am so sorry. I am so sorry."

By the time Sylvi had cried herself out, she and her father were alone in the Little Hall, but for the footmen at the doors. Lrrianay and Ebon had gone.

"Perfectly shaped and
eloquently told . . .
A lavish and lasting treat."
—PUBLISHERS WEEKLY

CHALICE

BESTSELLING & AWARD–WINNING AUTHOR
ROBIN McKINLEY

FIREBIRD

Now in a handsome
trade paperback edition!

(PB) 978-0-14-241720-1 **$8.99 ($10.99 CAN)**